Ada Barumé graduated with a politics degree from Cambridge University before moving to London to become a journalist, specialising in African news. In her novels she draws on her own experiences of being a young, black woman looking for fun, love and adventure. When she's not working, you'll find her agonising over what outfit to wear or searching for the nearest dancefloor.

ADA BARUMÉ

Hooked on YOU

avon.

Published by AVON
A division of HarperCollins*Publishers* Ltd
1 London Bridge Street
London SE1 9GF

www.harpercollins.co.uk

HarperCollins*Publishers*
Macken House,
39/40 Mayor Street Upper,
Dublin 1
D01 C9W8
Ireland

A Paperback Original 2025
1
Copyright © Ada Barumé 2025

Ada Barumé asserts the moral right to
be identified as the author of this work.

A catalogue record for this book is available from the British Library.

ISBN: 978-0-00-872760-4

This novel is entirely a work of fiction.
The names, characters and incidents portrayed in it are
the work of the author's imagination. Any resemblance to
actual persons, living or dead, events or localities is
entirely coincidental.

Typeset in Birka by Palimpsest Book Production Ltd, Falkirk, Stirlingshire

Printed and bound in the UK using 100% Renewable Electricity
at CPI Group (UK) Ltd

MIX
Paper | Supporting
responsible forestry
FSC
www.fsc.org   FSC™ C007454

This book contains FSC™ certified paper and other controlled sources to ensure
responsible forest management.

For more information visit: www.harpercollins.co.uk/green

To the voice in your head that told you you weren't good enough: kindly, shut up.

Chapter 1

Ore

Nouméa, New Caledonia

Ore wasn't sure she was going to make it. Her footing was no less affected by the sway of the waves than her stomach was, and what had seemed a simple journey to the railings, now felt an impossible feat. She brought her hand to her mouth, and stumbled on.

As she vomited down the side of the boat, her mind cleared enough for her to register the footsteps approaching.

'What are you doing out here? Vicky is waiting for you inside, and you need to get into your uniform ASAP.' His voice was stern, low and gravelly; she'd lived in New York long enough now to detect a southern twang, though she couldn't narrow it down any further than that. She could tell he was black, as she usually could.

She armed herself with her brightest smile and turned around, ready to explain herself. She was painfully aware that she must look like shit. To make matters worse she found herself taken aback by how handsome the face looking back at her was. Still, he was the first to drop his gaze.

'I'm not . . .' she started, just as another wave hit her and she returned to her agonisingly inelegant position hunched over the railings.

'Just what we need,' she heard him mutter under his breath, which she felt was a little unfair. She threw up again, wondering what could possibly be left in her stomach.

When the retching subsided, she turned back, wiping her mouth and smiling apologetically.

The pretty man in the white uniform did not return it, and Ore wondered how bad she must look to have lost her touch. Most men could be relied upon to smile back at her.

'I'm sorry, I was just waiting for . . .' she started, but he held up his hand, to cut her off.

'There's no point spouting excuses. Let's get you to Vicky; she'll know what to do with you.'

Ore was taken aback, humbled even. The man turned on his heel and walked off briskly.

'Follow me,' he called over his shoulder, without slowing down. Ore scurried after him. 'I'm Captain Wilsons, but you'll be answering to the first stewardess.'

'I . . .' Ore tried to interject and explain, but she was trotting along to keep up and every time she opened her mouth, she faced the peril of something other than words spilling out.

Finally he stopped, so suddenly that Ore walked into him. They were standing outside a nondescript cream door, far too close to each other. He seemed to come to the realisation at the exact same movement, stepping away and looking down awkwardly.

'This is the mess,' he mumbled. 'You can meet the rest of the crew.'

'I'm not . . .' Ore felt as though the room was swaying. As

her vision blurred, she knew there was nothing she could do to stop what was about to happen.

It splashed across his highly polished shoes, onto the floor and a little up the walls. Ore was doubled over, and glad for it. She suspected she would never be able to look the man in his rather beautiful face, ever again.

Just then, the door swung open. Ore could only imagine what Vicky's first thought might be on finding the captain splattered with vomit and the errant reporter heaving onto the cream carpet. To her credit, Vicky seemed undaunted. She calmly ushered Ore through the door, leaving the captain out in the corridor.

'Drink this.' Vicky sat Ore down at a large table in the middle of the room and handed her a glass of cloudy-looking water. Ore eyed it suspiciously.

'It's just rehydration salts, dear. I'm not trying to poison you,' Vicky said dryly. She spoke with a slight accent, which Ore couldn't place. As she drank, Vicky got out a walkie-talkie.

'I have the journalist with me in the mess. She's . . .' Vicky unashamedly eyed Ore from head to toe '. . . looking a little worse for wear,' she finished diplomatically.

The response was so muffled, Ore could barely make it out: something something 'quarters', something something 'dinner'.

'Copy that,' Vicky said flatly, clipping the radio back onto her belt. Reading Ore's look of confusion, she explained: 'I'll take you to your room to get changed and cleaned up, and then Chuck will meet you for dinner at seven on the third deck.'

'Was that him on the radio?' Ore had regained enough of her senses to remember that she was here to ask questions.

Vicky chuckled wryly. 'No, that was *Agatha*.' Ore detected a hint of venom in the way she said the name. Ore already knew who Agatha was, but it was always best not to let on how much research you'd done. She remembered her favourite professor's advice: *play dumb; it's amazing what most people will tell you when they think you don't really understand what's going on.* Gail Fairweather had led the investigative course at Columbia.

'Who's Agatha?' Ore asked innocently.

Vicky gave her a hard look; maybe she wasn't as easily played as 'most people'.

'Mr Regas' assistant,' she said finally, clearly having decided that this information didn't qualify as 'classified'.

'Ah.' Ore smiled brightly. 'Thanks very much for that.' She gestured to the empty glass. 'I feel much better already.' Vicky nodded curtly. This had not been the plan. She had hoped to charm all the staff from the word go. They were the key to this story after all – a profile was just a puff piece if you didn't go hard on background.

Suddenly she remembered the captain in the corridor. 'I should apologise to Captain Wilsons,' she said, trying to stand. Immediately a wave of nausea washed over her, and she quickly sat back down.

'Oh don't worry about him; he's just a contractor. He'll hardly be able to tell you anything about Mr Regas, and that's why you're here right?' Ore felt very much that Vicky was the one calling the shots in this conversation. She had forfeited that privilege the moment she was found covered in her own sick.

'Noted.' Ore was keen to get to her room and get herself in

the zone before dinner with Chuck. She wasn't going to let this false start dampen her enthusiasm. 'I think I'll head to my room now if that's OK? I'm not sure where my bags are though . . .'

'Oscar will have taken them off the chopper to the room already.' Vicky was already at the door. Ore scrambled after her, noticing that the captain was nowhere to be seen as she was marched down the corridor, up some stairs, down some others, through a door and then down again. Ore realised she was going to have a hard time navigating this boat – literally *and* figuratively.

'Here we are.' The door in front of them was made of highly polished wood, not the flimsy beige laminate she had just seen in the crew quarters. Ore pushed it open and gasped.

The first thing that struck her was the light, streaming in through two floor-to-ceiling windows at the far end of the space. It was immense and momentarily blinding, somehow more so than being outside in its direct reach. Once her eyes adjusted from the gloomy corridor, the distinction between the midday expanse of sunlight sky, and the sparkle-dappled waves came into focus. They both stretched out into the infinite horizon. Wandering around the boat, she had begun to feel what she guessed was something like cabin fever. But the room in front of her was about as far from a 'cabin' as you could get.

The bed was huge, and half covered in an array of unnecessary cushions of various sizes. The carpet underfoot was plush and the ceiling surprisingly high.

'This is the bathroom.' Vicky pointed to another door, which stood opposite a huge built-in wardrobe. Ore was almost salivating over the shelf space, as she thought about the plastic crates stuffed full of clothes, crammed under her bed in her tiny room in Queens.

Ore turned the handle. She had high hopes for this bathroom, and she was not disappointed. For a moment her mind went on a tangent, trying to imagine how you go about getting a standalone marble bath onto a boat.

'Your bags are here.' Vicky, of course, was impervious, and seemed impatient to get on with other, more important things.

'Thank you very much – the room is absolutely lovely.' Ore couldn't help her childish glee.

Vicky smiled politely, though it never reached her eyes, then bowed her head slightly as she backed out of the room.

Ore was impatient to take stock of her home for the next two weeks. She would have to go exploring before dinner. It wasn't often that her freelance gigs involved staying on a six-hundred-million-dollar superyacht. Admittedly, that was only an estimate – it turned out the world of the international super-rich and the value of their assets were frustratingly opaque. She assumed that was the point. Maybe she would just ask Chuck directly. He had seemed surprisingly friendly, forthcoming even, when they had spoken on the phone.

Ore supposed that she was in a strange position in the hierarchy of the boat: not quite guest and not quite staff. A spy then, she thought mischievously.

It was hard to believe that this time two weeks ago she had been in despair, wondering if she even wanted to be a journalist anymore, and now here she was, in the thick of it and raring to go. Pulled back into the here and now, she knew that the very first thing to do was shower and change, and then let the adventure begin.

Chapter 2

Ore

Queens, New York
Two weeks earlier

Ore wasn't sure how much longer she could scrape by in New York. She had outstayed her welcome at Auntie Laurie's and after six months she still didn't have a regular paycheque to show for all her hustling. Freelance journalism was a tough gig. She'd known that, but she hadn't anticipated quite how hard it would be to watch all her Columbia friends waltz into prearranged internships and then straight into staff jobs, as she chased one late invoice after another. After one too many incidences of her card being declined, she started supplementing her meagre income with a side gig as an office temp.

She'd had dreams of working on the environmental beat but soon realised she'd have to significantly expand her repertoire if she wanted to get anything published. She'd written for entertainment columns, fashion segments, sports blogs, and even penned a story about the Harley Davidson convention for a niche motorsports magazine to pay the bills. Eventually she'd picked up more work doing profiles and had a semi-regular 'in' at the *New York Herald*. That is to say they would accept around one in every ten of her freelance pitches.

By the time she started looking into Pagonis, and their new expansion into 'sustainable' battery production, it didn't seem like such a stretch that she might also try her hand at tech reporting. Besides, what she was really interested in was Chuck Regas, its elusive CEO. She reckoned the *New York Herald* would have a hard time turning that away, if by some miracle she could get him to talk to her. She'd typed up a short explainer on why software companies like Pagonis were starting to expand into hardware.

That had been months ago and she'd almost forgotten having fired off that email to their press office, so rarely did she ever hear back from companies like that. It was standard stuff; what she needed was a brief quotable statement, but she had of course asked for an interview, as any good journalist would.

The article had sat unfinished on her desktop, all but forgotten. Then just as she was starting to consider the unthinkable – moving back to the UK and back in with her mum – a reply from Chuck's assistant, Agatha, pinged into her inbox:

Thank you for your interest in Pagonis. We would love to answer the questions you have submitted to us. Our CEO, Charles Regas, has informed me that he would be keen to speak in person, and he would like to arrange for you to fly out to meet him on *Lady Thalassa*, his yacht, which is currently cruising around the New Caledonian coast. We would of course pay for your transit and cover all other necessary expenses incurred.

She must have reread the email a dozen times. It was unbelievable that a company as impenetrable as Pagonis would even acknowledge a clarification request from a reporter, let alone agree to an interview, in person, with the CEO. For a moment she considered that this could be a hoax, some sort of elaborate prank. She double-clicked on the email address: a.horley@pag.o.nis. A quick Google search confirmed that Agatha Horley was indeed an 'executive secretary' at Pagonis, whatever that meant.

Ever the investigator, she found herself down a rabbit hole researching Agatha: Oxford grad, economics and computing. What was she doing working as a PA? She looked young. The image results showed her attending a coding competition, where she appeared to have won first prize. Even on the top plinth she only reached the shoulders of her male competitors. Her fine features were set in a stern expression, framed by a sharp ashy-blonde fringe. Ore wondered whether she might be on board and hoped she would be; the people that billionaires surrounded themselves with tended to say a lot more about them than they usually gave up willingly.

She read the email again, noting Agatha's use of 'we'. Ore deduced that that either meant she was a nepotistic hire, his niece perhaps, or that he was one of those employers that insisted 'we're a family here at Pagonis' to justify the unsociable hours and unpaid overtime he expected.

She was hooked, her brain fuzzing with adrenaline as she shot an email back.

Hi Agatha, thanks for getting back to me. I'm delighted to hear that. Tell me when and where and I'll be there. Very much looking forward to meeting Mr Regas.

And then she typed a message for Henry, the profiles editor at the *New York Herald*. The subject line read:

EXCLUSIVE: Chuck Regas speaks on the future of clean computing.

That would get his attention. In the email itself she simply wrote:

Regas has agreed to an in-person interview on his yacht in New Caledonia, exact dates TBC. Keep you posted – you interested?

It was ten o'clock at night but Henry's reply was almost immediate.

Impressive stuff, Ore. We'll take it.

And then thirty seconds later, another ping. It was from Henry again.

FYI, staff position coming up at the end of the month. If you can pull off this Regas story, it's yours.

Ore could hear her heart pounding in her ears as the words sunk in: 'staff position' for the *New York Herald*! She marvelled at how quickly her luck had turned. Over the course of one evening and a few emails, she gone from zero prospects to a luxury holiday on a multimillion-pound yacht, the scoop of a lifetime and the chance at bagging her dream job.

She squealed into her pillow, giddy with the sense that things were finally working out, and then researched flights to Sydney into the early hours of the morning.

Chapter 3

Ore

Ore was hoping that she might be able to sneak around the boat unnoticed, but almost immediately she spotted the one person she had most wished to avoid. He seemed as startled as her when they caught sight of each other across the deck. For a moment she thought she could see him deciding whether to turn around. In the end he strode towards her, arm outstretched.

'I don't think I introduced myself properly earlier,' he said briskly, shaking her hand firmly. 'My name is Daniel, Daniel Wilsons.'

'Ahh, so you're no longer "*Captain* Wilsons" then?' she asked playfully.

He looked down. Ore was enjoying his embarrassment; he was cute when he was disarmed.

'You must be Ore? Am I pronouncing that right?' He hadn't pronounced it right, splitting the word awkwardly into two distinct syllables: 'or-ray'. She was forgiving though. It was difficult to master in an American accent.

'Almost right,' she chirped. 'It's Ore, like "oar" actually but don't worry at all, it's totally fine – it happens all the time.' She was babbling, which she had a tendency to do when interacting with attractive people. Luckily for her, most of the time people found it endearing.

He was wearing all white, and had he not been as tall or broad, the captain's uniform might have looked costume-like. As it stood, with the dark skin of his face and forearms glistening in the bright sunshine, he looked almost regal.

'I should also apologise for earlier.' She giggled, and cringed a little at how girlish she sounded. 'I see you managed to restore that impeccable polish.' She motioned to his once more spotless shoes. He smiled shyly. 'Chuck has told me all about you,' she continued, breathless. 'Apparently you're "the best in the business".' That smile, and an awkward chuckle.

'I'm not sure about that . . . Mr Regas has a tendency to exaggerate—' He cut himself off suddenly, as if realising he had said too much. Even without the insight from Daniel, she could have guessed that American billionaires with names like 'Chuck' probably did tend toward aggrandisement. But she made a mental note: from that reaction and Vicky's reticence earlier, she concluded that the staff must have been prepped to remain tight-lipped.

'Well that's good to know.' She was teasing him really, her eyes twinkling with curiosity. 'What else does he have a tendency towards?' She caught Daniel's eye and held it. He squirmed under her questioning, burying his hands in his pockets and shrugging.

'I think that's your job, isn't it? To find out what he's like?' *Touché,* she thought.

'Yes, but also to ask questions,' she retorted.

The nervous chuckle again, and then he collected himself. 'Well there will be plenty of time for all that.' They stood for a moment, Ore hoping he might reveal something else, if only for something to say to fill the silence – but he wasn't caving.

Already she was feeling the buzz of adrenaline and raw curiosity that she thrived off whenever she was investigating a story. It also served to distract her from the lingering nausea and the jet lag.

After a beat Daniel decided on: 'Would you like me to give you the tour? I know Mr Regas wanted to meet you off the chopper and show you around himself but he's tied up in meetings until later this evening, I believe.'

That was twice now he'd referred to his employer by his surname, as Vicky had. Ore wondered if 'just call me Chuck' had different rules for his staff, or maybe in this case, the formality was just a symptom of Daniel's Southern upbringing.

'That would be great. I've been dying to take a proper look around,' Ore replied eagerly.

Chapter 4

Ore

Ore caught sight of herself in one of the extremely clean and extremely large windows lining the top sundeck, and she was not impressed by what she saw. She'd decided to pile her braids on top of her head, but the wind had already had its way, because half of them were now trailing down her back.

She looked washed out, her skin betraying her with the unmistakable green tinge and sweaty sheen of nausea. She was suddenly aware that the heeled boots she was wearing were wholly inappropriate for a boat, as was the white silk maxi skirt wrapped around her waist.

In truth, she was still exhausted from the journey, which had been both unbearably long and stressfully rushed. She had only given herself an hour for the transfer at Hong Kong and then once she landed in Sydney, she had been whisked first by private plane to New Caledonia and then hurried onto a helicopter, which dropped her off on one of the two helipads on board. A sullen-looking man had taken her bags and directed her to the deck to wait for Chuck.

It had only taken ten minutes for her lack of sea legs to make itself known, and then the handsome captain had found her.

'It's a pretty big boat, so I won't do a full tour today. You'll get to know your way around eventually. But this is the top deck and then as you look down it's the second deck, third, fourth, fifth et cetera.' Daniel spoke quietly but authoritatively as Ore followed behind him.

It was a welcome change, thought Ore, from all the men in New York who spoke loudly with no authority at all. She felt exceedingly conscious that she wasn't looking her best and then decided that Daniel was the sort of man who probably liked the 'girl-next-door type' – the kind of woman who felt effortlessly comfortable in a pair of old jeans and didn't wear impractical shoes. Someone who, like him, came across as sensible and straightforward, with a five-year plan and regular pension contributions set up.

Ore berated herself for getting distracted so easily. Pretty boys were her weakness. If she had met Daniel in a bar in New York, she would have found a way to get him back to her bed by the end of the night, and then most probably would have forgotten his name by the next morning. But, she reminded herself now, they weren't in New York, *and* he was sort of her subject. Her journalistic ethics would have to take precedence over her horny tendencies this time.

They circled three decks, and Ore was shown the second helipad, four lounges, the indoor and outdoor swimming pools, the gym, the games room, the dining room and the 'main' bar. She was finding it hard to keep up, and was sure that she would never be able to find her way around these labyrinthine corridors and narrow stairways.

Daniel seemed to have every last detail of the spec of the boat to hand, reeling off the square footage of each particular room as casually as if he were recalling what he had for breakfast. He was more than happy to answer a question about the type of wood used for the panelling in the library, but the moment she asked anything more prying he pursed his lips and said something evasive like 'I don't know about all that, miss'. But Ore was persistent.

'How long have you been working for Mr Regas?'

Daniel frowned, and Ore wondered how that could possibly be a controversial question.

'Technically, about a month, but I was just on retainer until last week', he replied finally. After a long pause, he added, 'I work through an agency, you see, and his usual captain . . .' She watched him as he seemed to realise he was digging himself a hole. Ore held her breath for a juicy titbit.

'Wasn't available,' he concluded.

Ore realised he was hoping to give nothing away, but in fact he had, simply by refusing to answer. His hesitance itself was suspicious. *Find out why the old captain left*, was added to Ore's mental list of mysteries to solve.

'I see,' she said lightly. For now she wasn't going to pry any deeper. It was clear he wasn't feeling chatty this evening and admittedly she had not made the best first impression.

Daniel checked his watch. 'It's probably time for me to take you up to dinner. We wouldn't want to keep Mr Regas waiting.'

'Yes, Captain!' She hoped he would respond to her enthusiasm – an enthusiasm her friends and family had described as 'infectious' – but, Daniel gave her a stiff smile and motioned for her to walk ahead of him. He would have to be put on the back burner. For now she needed to concentrate on the man of the hour: Mr Chuck Regas himself.

She heard him before she saw him, walking up yet another concealed set of stairs snaking up three storeys on the left side of the boat.

'Listen, Sandra, I don't want to tell you how to do your job, but this is a mess.' Ore felt sorry for Sandra. Chuck's tone was disconcertingly cheery, and it sent a shiver down her spine. 'Get back to me tomorrow with some new figures and we'll go over the numbers with the PR team a second time, OK?'

Ore couldn't make out the reply though she strained to hear. As she reached the top of the stairs, Chuck hung up immediately, beaming at her as if she were a long-lost friend.

'Ore! An absolute pleasure – so glad to have you on board.' She was not the only one who had done her research – he had pronounced her name correctly. He wore a plaid shirt over a navy T-shirt, a pair of cargo shorts and shoes that looked better suited to mountain climbing than yacht reclining. His hair was somewhere between blonde and white, almost beige. He was shorter than she had expected.

Before she could react, he was leaning in for a hug, and Ore went into autopilot, squeezing his shoulders and smiling widely. As they pulled away from each other, she became very aware of Daniel standing behind her. When she glanced over, she spotted him resolutely looking into the middle distance.

'Mr Regas, thank you so much for . . .' she was a little breathless, acutely aware that this man in front of her might be the making of her career '. . . all this,' she said, waving her arms around awkwardly.

'Please, please, call me Chuck. I thought we'd established this!' He sounded playful but there was a strange vacantness to his gaze that Ore found unnerving.

'Of course, sorry, Chuck,' she stumbled – she was nervous.

'Come, come, Carlos has cooked us up a feast, and he gets mad when I let it go cold.' He winked as he placed a hand gently on Ore's shoulder and led her into the dining room. Just before he closed the door behind them he called, 'Dan, let's talk after dinner please?'

It took a moment for Ore to process that he was talking to Daniel, who even in the short time she'd known him, did not seem like a 'Dan'.

'Yes, sir.'

Ore wondered if he would correct him, but the informality only seemed to flow in one direction. Chuck smiled and pushed the door closed.

Chapter 5

Daniel

Dan. He hated it when Chuck called him that. The very first time they'd met, he had been taken aback by the familiarity of it, the presumptuousness. No one had called him Dan since he was in middle school. But he hadn't had the presence of mind to correct Chuck then, and so now he never would. Daniel consoled himself with the fact that this was just 'one last gig' before he joined the Hartfords, and *they* always called him Captain Wilsons, which he appreciated.

Stood outside the dining room, he felt uncharacteristically curious about what conversations were happening on the other side of that door. Usually he prided himself on his ability to stay out of the guests' business. He hadn't gotten to where he was by meddling in other people's affairs. The mega rich did not like to hire snoops. But this time he was intrigued. Why would Chuck want a reporter on board? It seemed nonsensical. The whole point of yachting around these parts was to be unreachable, unobservable, surely?

He didn't like to admit it, but he was also thinking about Ore. He'd embarrassed himself earlier, assuming she was a stewardess. It was unlike him, to not know the ins and outs of everything going on aboard the boat. He had heard Agatha mention something about a journalist a couple of days back, but he'd not been briefed on any specifics. He'd have to have a word with her later. For now, he headed back down to the mess to find Vicky.

She was standing at the head of the long table addressing the gaggle of fresh stewardesses and deckhands in front of her.

'Personal laundry is to be done out of hours, so that's between 10 p.m. and 5 a.m. I don't want to have to worry about finding a musty pair of boxers among Mr Regas' linens.' A titter spread around the table, as one by one the new recruits realised they were allowed to laugh. Vicky raised a single discerning eyebrow when one of the girls – and they were girls, some barely out of their teens – raised her hand.

'Yes?' Vicky sounded stern, but Daniel knew it was all an act; as soon as she had terrified them all into compliance, she would soften up. They had all been on board for three days, whilst Vicky had been getting the hospitality crew ready, Daniel had spent most of that time with the engineers and his first officer, Ollie Dudley, getting to grips with the immensity of *Lady Thalassa*. It was easily the biggest vessel he'd ever captained.

Chuck had arrived that morning, so now it was time to make sure the junior crew were all up to scratch.

'I need to use a silk pillowcase, because my acne plays up otherwise, and I usually hand-wash it every afternoon so that it dries in time. Could I maybe just pop in quickly around three to do that?' Daniel was standing quietly in the corner, behind Vicky, but he imagined the withering look.

Vicky took a deep breath, and Daniel watched as the young stewardess realised her mistake and looked down.

21

'Let me get one thing straight, kids: this is not a holiday. You are here to work, and to be honest with you, from here on in, your time is no longer your own.' Vicky took off her rectangular, dark-framed glasses and ran a hand through her sharp black bob. 'The thing about people like Mr Regas is that they expect a certain level of service, the kind that makes him forget that you're all real people with lives and hopes and dreams, the kind of service where he comes to think of you as "the way to get XYZ done" as efficiently and pleasantly as possible. You are a means to an end for him, and if you're not around to get something done for him because you're holed up in the laundry room handwashing your silk pillowcases . . .' Vicky paused, allowing the silence to absorb the brunt of the bluntness '. . . that would not make him happy, and that's rule number one: keep Chuck happy.'

The bewildered faces began nodding fervently, and the poor girl who had asked the question picked anxiously at her cuticles.

'Vicky, can I have a word?' Daniel watched a wave of relief wash over everyone at the table. Vicky turned sharply, only just noticing him.

'Christ, Daniel, you really have a way of creeping up on people.' She put her glasses back on and turned back. 'OK back to work, everyone. Amanda and Nicole, be sure to check if Carlos is on track with the starters, and then one of you can take over from Oscar in the dining room.'

As the crew scattered, Vicky took a seat and leant back with her arms crossed. Daniel found himself thinking that she looked tired.

'What can I do for you, Captain?'

He pulled up a chair. 'Well, as you saw, I got myself into an . . . awkward situation this morning. I had no idea that the reporter was arriving today, and I mistook her for a stewardess.'

Vicky's eyebrows shot up. 'You thought that woman was here to work on a boat? She was wearing wedge heels for Christ's sake!'

Daniel was still getting used to Vicky's brashness, but he appreciated her straightforwardness.

'Well, now you mention it, I don't know what I was thinking,' he conceded, and thought he spotted a shadow of a smile flash across Vicky's face. 'But it would have been nice to be brought up to speed.'

'There's no point pointing fingers at me, Daniel, I had no idea what the plan was until she was vomiting in the hallway, either.' Vicky sounded defensive, but Daniel understood that, like him, she was frustrated about being left out of the loop. 'It seems like another one of Agatha's little surprises.'

They exchanged a knowing look. In such small quarters it was always dangerous to bad-mouth anyone explicitly. You never knew who was lurking. Having both worked on boats for over a decade, they knew the drill. And anyway, nothing needed to be said.

Daniel had only known Agatha for a couple of weeks, and only met her in person this morning, but he had immediately understood that she was a woman who knew what she was doing. She was not averse to power games, and she could play Chuck like a fiddle. Daniel was perversely impressed by it, although he had personally always found that the simplest way to get things done was to work hard and be honest.

'I don't understand why Chuck would agree to this?' Daniel mused, genuinely confused.

Vicky rolled her eyes. 'It's a puff piece. Agatha has probably just handpicked the least discerning journalist in America and fed her with a load of PR spiel.'

Daniel wasn't so sure. Ore seemed sharp and observant. He had felt agitated talking to her, those dark probing eyes and disarming smile perfectly primed to extract some damning comment from him.

'Hmm, I don't know, Vicky. We shouldn't underestimate her. Maybe Agatha's misjudged this one.'

'Well it wouldn't be the first time . . .' Vicky's tone was conspiratorial but Daniel had no idea what she was talking about. He decided to leave it, reminding himself that this was a last-minute gig. He wasn't invested in these people, and he should really not get involved in any drama. Vicky seemed to sense his unreceptiveness to the gossip and changed the subject. 'Anyway I would recommend saying as little as possible to her. Chuck, i.e. Agatha, is going to want to feed her the story, so it's best if we don't interfere with the "big scoop".' This last part she bookended in air quotes. 'None of it makes sense to me but the inner workings of the mind of a billionaire is not something that we mere mortals can ever hope to understand. He's impulsive, and Agatha is persuasive, so I'm sure they've come up with some kind of reason to convince themselves it's a good idea.'

Daniel sensed that Vicky had more to say. After a pause and a slightly unnerving amount of eye contact, she continued. 'I've been working on this boat for five years, and working in yachting for almost fifteen. I spent a long time questioning the whims of the people I've worked for, but in the end it'll drive you mad. Keep your head down, their glasses full and the beds made; that's my motto.'

He didn't know what to say. He'd seen so many people grow tired of this life, but for him, being out at sea was still as exciting as it had been a decade ago when he first stepped on a yacht as a green deckhand. Sure the clients could be crazy, but there was something about facing each day, not knowing what it would bring, but knowing that you could handle it, that made him feel proud. He liked being good at his job.

'I gave Ore a tour of the boat,' he said after a while. 'Do you think that was the right move?' He trusted Vicky's instincts.

'Keep your enemies close, eh?' was all she said. Daniel didn't know if that was exactly approval, but it reassured him to know that he was being upfront.

'This has been a lovely little chat, Captain, but some of us have work to do.' Vicky slapped her thighs emphatically as she stood up. As Daniel arranged the chairs exactly back where they had been, Vicky eyed him curiously. 'I think we're going to get along well, Daniel.' He smiled and she turned and walked out without another word.

Chapter 6

Daniel

Off the coast of Corfu, Greece
A month earlier

Daniel had been planning on travelling around Europe for a month before he began on board the *Nightingale* with the Hartfords. He had been on back-to-back charters for most of the last two years. Since he'd made captain, he was more in demand than ever. He was looking forward to spending more than a day on land.

He was googling 'best restaurants in Athens' when the agency called. He considered simply not picking up. He already knew they were going to ask him to do 'one last job' – that's how the job he was currently on had been sold to him.

Eventually he reached for the phone, and Natalie's mewling voice trickled through the speaker. 'Daniel, how *are* you? Still the best captain in town?' Daniel was a patient person, but he was also an efficient one and there was something about sycophantic small talk that rubbed him up the wrong way.

'I'm fine, Natalie. What do you want?' He immediately felt guilty for his tone, which had sounded more cutting than he'd intended. But Natalie seemed unperturbed, and she did get right to the point. 'We need you, *desperately*.' This last word was breathy and dramatic. 'We've had a bit of a situation on board the *Lady Thalassa* and we need a replacement before they set off for a six-week tour around New Caledonia.'

'As in, Australasia?' Daniel was feeling exasperated, but he tried to keep calm. It wasn't Natalie's fault, he had to remind himself. 'I'm around Corfu at the moment. Surely you have someone a little closer to the action?'

There was a long pause. Daniel was sure he could hear the cogs in Natalie's brain turning, and then he was struck by a pang of guilt. The agency could be unreasonable, sure, but he had been with them since he started, and they'd always got him work; maybe he could show his gratitude with 'one last favour'.

Natalie sighed. 'I guess maybe I could try calling Captain Mary out of retirement, although it does seem a shame, just when she seems to have settled into it . . .'

Natalie had, rightly, concluded that a guilt trip would be the most successful strategy.

Daniel held out. 'I would've liked a little wind-down before I go to the Hartfords, make sure I'm on top form.'

'Of course, I completely understand, and to be honest I wouldn't have asked if I didn't think that you could handle it. You are one of our most competent, discreet, professional, hardworking . . .'

'Fine, I'll do it,' Daniel interjected impatiently. If there was one thing that made him more uncomfortable than a sense he was neglecting his duties, it was flattery. Natalie squealed so energetically that Daniel had to pull the phone away from his ear.

'AMAZING! We'll get you on the flight from Athens on the 4th. Is that OK with you?'

Daniel sighed. His month break had just been reduced to forty-eight hours, but he was hoping he'd still get the time to squeeze in a visit to the Acropolis.

'Yes, that works for me. What's the job anyway?'

'It's a fun one! It's a mega yacht, which you haven't done much of, but I'm afraid I can't give you the name of your employer yet. I have to let him know that you're up for it and then he'll call and introduce himself.'

'Sounds intriguing,' Daniel said flatly, feeling distinctly un-intrigued. The mega rich always liked to act as though being in their very presence was grounds to make you sign an NDA. He suspected it was probably some paranoid oil guy, or maybe a Middle Eastern prince.

'And what happened to their old captain?' It seemed like an innocent enough question, but Natalie's response unnerved Daniel.

'Well, I mean I shouldn't really say . . .' she began. He knew full well that she had a weakness for gossiping. 'But it's some dodgy stuff, and well, let's just say they're in need of a *male* captain now.'

That did not sound good, thought Daniel, regretting having already agreed to take the job. But it was only six weeks, he reasoned. *Buckle down, get on with it,* and then he could sail off into the sunset with the Hartfords, and finally captain a boat he could call his own. Until then, he'd take the money and the goodwill and keep his head down.

'Right . . . OK, that's all I need to know. Thanks, Natalie. Send over the boat specs and flight info when you can.' He hadn't got to where he was today by asking questions he didn't want the answers to.

The next day he got the call from Agatha, who explained that 'her employer' was looking for someone discreet. Daniel knew the drill: *sign the NDA and don't go posting anything on social media*. He always found that request amusing; maybe it made sense to ask that of the Gen Z junior crew, but Daniel was a captain now. Surely they didn't really think he was in the habit of putting shirtless pictures of himself clasping a bottle of Grey Goose on the internet?

Sometimes he would remember, with a start, that many of the crew were not much younger than him. He supposed that it wasn't that insane to imagine that a twenty-eight-year-old might want to disseminate a 'thirst trap' every now and again, but Daniel had always been an old soul.

When his classmates were getting Facebook for the first time, he was buried in an aviation magazine, or a book about tractors. Anything with an engine had always fascinated him. His interest in boats specifically hadn't solidified until his later teenage years.

Agatha explained the staffing structure, which seemed a bit excessive for only three permanent guests: Agatha herself, her employer and his daughter.

'And before I go on, I did just want to confirm that you have understood the terms of your NDA? I saw that your agency returned the form with some amendments . . .' Agatha sounded irritated.

But this wasn't Daniel's first gig. He was more than happy

to commit to not revealing any personal information about his employer in public but the severity of this particular NDA seemed overzealous and he didn't like making promises he wouldn't keep.

'Yes, I'm just not comfortable with signing the section that prohibits "discussion of all details and particulars pertaining to the employer, the voyage, the crew and the guests, in all circumstances, including in private and with familiars".' He had memorised the phrase, prepared for the pushback.

Agatha huffed, 'Well it's standard stuff.'

Daniel knew they weren't in a position to find a replacement for him at this point, so he held firm. 'I'd just like to be able to talk to my own mom about my job at Christmas without fear that I'm about to be sued.'

A pause on the other end of the line. 'OK, well you've signed the most important clauses I suppose . . . no disclosure to the press, on social media, in public forums . . .' Agatha seemed reluctant to concede, but eventually she did. 'As long as you understand that Mr Chuck Regas deeply values his staff's discretion at all times.' With the emphasis that she placed on his name, Daniel understood that he was supposed to be impressed, but he had no idea who she was talking about.

'Of course,' Daniel said matter-of-factly. His understated response only seemed to annoy Agatha more.

Agatha tried again. 'That's Regas, of Pagonis.'

She might as well have been speaking in Greek; none of it meant anything to Daniel. 'Understood,' he replied.

Exasperated, Agatha continued with her spiel: 'At various intervals, Mr Regas will be flying out some associates and other friends, but none of that is your concern. Victoria, our head stewardess, will of course be in charge of managing the crew. I suspect you won't have many dealings with any of the staff apart from the first officer.' Agatha sounded dismissive when she said 'staff', which Daniel found interesting, considering she was technically part of that category herself.

'And Mr Regas will undoubtedly ask you to call him Chuck, but I would advise against that. It sets up a complicated dynamic, don't you think?' Agatha had the sort of piercing British enunciation that conveyed that she inherently knew 'how things should be done' and Daniel had no desire to upset the status quo.

'Of course – I understand,' he repeated, when Agatha was done.

'We very much look forward to welcoming you to the team.' The phrase sounded forced and stilted, but then Daniel's response was not particularly convincing either.

'Thank you, Agatha, I look forward to working with you all too.' He hung up the phone and sighed. For now, he had a docking to organise, so there was no time to dwell, but he was pleased to have kept himself out of the most binding restrictions on that NDA. He suspected much of the younger crew would not be so savvy.

Chapter 7

Ore

Ore hadn't been expecting the company. Chuck had not mentioned that his personal assistant and his teenage daughter would be joining them for dinner. They made for an unlikely gathering. Agatha sat bolt upright, her startlingly blonde hair tucked neatly behind her ears, and Chuck was opposite her, at the other end of the table. Ore was facing Melanie, whose exceptionally straight and slightly too long fringe covered her eyes.

The adults were all politely chatting about how delicious the scallops were, and Ore was frustrated that she wouldn't have the opportunity to talk to Chuck alone tonight. It was always much more complicated to catch an interviewee off guard when there was an audience. She guessed that that was the plan. Melanie hadn't yet said a word, apart from a giggly thank you to the stewardess who had brought the food.

'So, Chuck, what's it like running a company like Pagonis?' She thought it was a simple enough starter question, but almost before she had finished her sentence, Agatha jumped in.

'He's always busy, aren't you, Chuck? And that means I'm always busy too! It takes a lot of manpower to keep a place like Pagonis ticking over, and keeping all that manpower in check isn't an easy job either.' Agatha was a journalist's worst nightmare; she had that canny ability to say something without really revealing anything at all.

Ore smiled at Agatha, hiding her irritation, and then looked back over at Chuck, who was chewing on a sprig of samphire as though he had no intention of answering the question directed at him. *So this is how it's going to go,* thought Ore. She decided to change her tack.

'And what's it like being the daughter of Chuck Regas then, Melanie?'

The girl looked surprised at being acknowledged, and then a little flustered. 'Umm, it's all right, you know. I guess Pagonis isn't like the worst vibe out there, but it's hardly like a non-profit or anything.'

Agatha forced a dry laugh. A tiny vein throbbed just south of her immaculate hairline. 'Oh, that's just Melanie, our budding little socialist!' Her tone was verging on shrill. 'Teenagers, what are they like?' The phrase might have sat better had Agatha herself not looked so young. Maybe it was genetics, or maybe it was expensive face cream, but Ore would have assumed that they were about the same age, at least half a decade away from thirty.

Melanie looked back down at her food sullenly. Ore felt a pang of pity for the girl. Despite the unimaginable luxury, how deathly boring it must be to spend your summer holidays with only your dad and his employees for company.

Ore tried again, turning her whole upper body to resolutely address Chuck. 'And how long has the move into hardware been on the cards?' A sharp intake of breath from over her right shoulder and Ore knew that she was once again about to be bested by Agatha.

'Well it's been in the works for quite a while, but Chuck wanted to make sure that the company was in a solid place, financially, but also brand-wise before expanding into new markets.' Ore turned her head emphatically and met Agatha's gaze, hoping to shame her into an apology, or at least silence, but Agatha was not deterred. 'We're hoping that by developing our own batteries we can transform how efficiently and sustainably our servers are run, but in the long term we might look into making that product available to our competitors.'

Agatha was a walking, talking press release, thought Ore. In fact, she was pretty sure that most of the phrasing matched word for word.

'Interesting,' said Ore flatly, as she speared her last scallop. 'Maybe we could have a chat one on one at some point, Agatha?' It was clear that she had a lot to say; maybe Ore could exhaust her, and then try and get to Chuck.

'Oh, well maybe not, I'm pretty busy.'

Ore was not easily vexed. She considered herself fairly tolerant, happy-go-lucky even, but Agatha's smug smile riled her.

'Oh, well, no problem, I wouldn't want to impede you doing your job.' Ore knew it was petty, the tone, the mimicking of language, and the way Agatha's eyes sparkled, Ore also knew she had lost this particular joust.

Mel looked from one woman to the other and smirked. Even the teenager in the room was picking up on the childish atmosphere. Ore needed to get a grip. From then on, she stuck to small talk, commenting on the food and 'lovely weather'.

Chuck only piped up to ask Mel an absent-dad-coded question about how school was going. The rest of the time he got on with eating his meal, checking his phone occasionally but mainly staring placidly into the middle distance. Ore wondered how somebody who appeared to have so few thoughts had built himself a multibillion-dollar empire.

After the dessert was cleared by the stewardesses, Ore declined coffee. She felt suddenly exhausted, the stretch of the past thirty hours weighing down her eyelids. She strained to stop herself from yawning as she willed Agatha and Chuck to hurry up with their unfathomably tiny sips of espresso. Eventually everyone stood up, almost in unison, and Ore scrambled to her feet.

Agatha addressed the table as if she were holding court. 'Thank you all for a lovely dinner. I'll be taking myself off to bed now. Goodnight, everyone.' Ore was sure she even bowed her head ever so slightly before turning to leave.

Mel scuttled off in the opposite direction, and finally Ore was alone with Chuck. She summoned her last ounce of energy. 'Do you always let Agatha do all your talking for you?' It was an impertinent question – she knew that – but the mix of tiredness and frustration had lowered her inhibitions.

Chuck looked up from his phone, an eyebrow raised. 'Straight to the point I see, Miss . . .' He obviously couldn't remember her surname.

'Please, call me Ore,' she replied, and thought she saw the shadow of a smile tug at his lips.

'Of course, Ore – forgive me, I am a busy man and having someone like Agatha who can keep across everything is indispensable to me.' He looked down again and then back up. 'But I will say that for your profile you would probably be best speaking to my staff, rather than me. There is no worse judge of one's character than oneself.'

'Perhaps, but it's always revealing to know what people *think* they are like.' She was enjoying herself. The repartee felt good-humoured but a little daring.

Chuck laughed softly and put his phone in his pocket, offering her the rare gift of his full attention. 'I tell you what, spend the next couple of days talking to the crew and then I promise I will give you . . .' he looked at his watch, as if calculating there and then '. . .forty-five minutes alone, with me, on Sunday, how does that sound?'

Ore beamed. 'Deal.'

Chuck laughed again, shaking his head slightly, and left her alone in the dining room.

When she got back to her room, Ore collapsed onto the pristine, white sheets. As she groaned with exhaustion, she felt something digging into her shoulder. On closer inspection she saw it was a small packet of Kwells. Vicky must have left it for her to combat the seasickness. Luckily the strange vibes at dinner had distracted her from the nausea, but now she was lying down, the slight rocking was once more noticeable to her, and her stomach.

She got undressed and tried to go to sleep, but ended up crouched over the toilet bowl. It was going to be a long night.

Chapter 8

Daniel

Daniel caught himself hoping that Ore would have a good night's sleep. He was sitting alone in the captain's quarters. The first officer, Dudley, was taking over the night shift. He had to admit that it was nice not to have to be within flinching distance of the helm at all hours.

It had been an eventful day. Daniel told himself that the reason he kept thinking about the errant journalist was because of the absurdity of the whole situation: the mistaken identity, the vomit. But if he allowed his brain to wander into less rational territory, something he generally tried to avoid, he knew that he was also a little taken aback by how pretty she was.

All these years at sea, he'd seen relationships blossom and rot in front of his eyes. It was a tale as old as time: young strapping deckhand, playful pretty stewardess, a whirlwind, followed by a destructive storm. He'd taken the mantra of not mixing business with pleasure seriously, and it had served him well.

But now here he was thinking about how beautifully the sunlight bounced off the smooth skin of her shoulders, how her collarbones delicately crested out from beneath that totally impractical strappy top she'd been wearing and how her eyes twinkled when she smiled. He felt a little ridiculous and reasoned that infatuation was not beyond him. He'd once had a mind-numbing crush on his elementary school teacher, which had faded naturally. He'd even gotten over Alice, his ex-girlfriend, eventually, so this little crush was sure to dwindle.

It was just unusual for him to be struck so suddenly like this. Miss Rachel had been a pretty constant presence in his young life and he'd been in classes with Alice in high school for years before he realised his feelings were 'romantic'. They'd kissed once at a party when they were seventeen but it hadn't been until another five years later, when he was back staying with his mom between charters, that they'd run into each other at the grocery store. A few weeks of gentle courting, and then just before he left for another season, he'd asked her to be his girlfriend.

They managed intermittent long-distance for three years, before she came to terms with the fact that he'd never give up the seafaring, not for her anyway. Daniel had always been sure of the fact that they wouldn't 'end up together' but he thought it would be good practice to have a girlfriend before he had a wife. Alice was lovely, caring and understanding. She got on with his mom too. But she never made it into the version of the future he imagined for himself, however hard he tried to make space for her there.

Still, it had shocked him how bereft he'd felt when she finally ended things. He hadn't managed to eat anything for days, and even though he didn't cry about it, the dull but persistent ache in his chest took longer than he had expected to die down. Almost a year, in fact.

He was used to slow feelings, not whatever this was.

I wonder if she'll realise that the Kwells were from me. It was bothersome, the way his thoughts intruded so forcefully, when he was trying to concentrate on the seabirds episode of *Birds of a Feather*, the documentary series he'd put on to try and unwind. He hadn't put them there for the recognition, he reminded himself; he was only helping out a fellow traveller.

He had just managed to convince his brain to refocus on the diving sea puffin in front of him when there was a soft knock at the door. He checked his watch; it was just after midnight.

'Dan, you in there?'

Daniel was shirtless, and felt that Chuck might interpret that as some sort of masculine showdown.

'Just a moment, sir.' He scrambled for a T-shirt and was still pulling it over his head when Chuck pushed the door open. Chuck seemed taken aback to be met with Daniel's taut, sculpted torso.

'I see you work out, man.' Chuck chuckled nervously, and Daniel was glad that his skin was dark enough to conceal the hot flushing in his cheeks.

'A little,' he conceded, unsure whether to sit down in the armchair behind him or stand. In the end Chuck strolled over to it and took a seat, leaving Daniel to perch on the edge of the bed. He should have known he'd have no chance of winning any kind of showdown with a man like Chuck Regas.

'I need to ask you a favour, Dan.' Chuck was leaning back in the chair, hands steepled under his chin, and Daniel considered if he was *trying* to look like a movie villain. 'Could you take care of this Ore girl for me?'

There was no way Chuck could have known what he had been thinking only moments before – Daniel knew that – but still he felt like he had been caught out. He was aware of his sweaty palms.

'Urm, excuse me, what do you mean by that, sir?'

Chuck let out a bellow of laughter. 'Oh Danny, God, no don't get any ideas, although she is rather lovely isn't she?' This last part he mumbled to no one in particular, and then, remembering what he wanted to say, he carried on. 'I just mean I need you to keep an eye on her. I've told her she can speak to any of my staff but I'd like you to be with her at all times when she does so.'

He held Daniel's gaze intently. Daniel didn't know what to say, but Chuck continued. 'Of course it's not that there's anything to hide per se, I just like to know that my staff are being suitably discreet and they're more likely to remember that if there's a . . .' Chuck scanned Daniel up and down, and it made his skin crawl '. . . a captain in the room.'

Daniel had supposed that men with inordinate amounts of money and influence might worry about people feeling intimidated in their presence. Chuck seemed to enjoy it. More than the pure power play, he seemed to enjoy other people's discomfort as well.

'So what do you say?' Chuck smiled and Daniel broke eye contact and looked off into the middle distance, focusing on the bland seascape print on the wall.

'Whatever you need, sir.' Chuck stood up suddenly and patted Daniel on the shoulder as he walked past him.

'I knew I could count on you, Dan. I'll be in my office at the end of each day, and I'd like to keep track of her reporting . . .

contemporaneously. If that suits?' The question was obviously rhetorical because he didn't wait for an answer.

After he'd left the room, Daniel fell back on the bed exasperated. Why had he taken this job? He could be wandering around the Acropolis right now, and instead he'd been demoted from captain to babysitter.

He wasn't even sure exactly what he was supposed to be stopping Ore from hearing, although after that interaction he suspected there would be more than a few people on this boat who would have uncomplimentary things to say about Chuck Regas. It was going to be a long two weeks.

Chapter 9

Ore

Day 2

Despite waking up halfway through the night with her cheek melded to the marble tiled floor, before dragging herself into bed, Ore felt quite fresh when her alarm bleated into her ear. She took a moment to just lie there and take stock. This was her moment, her scoop, and she had to be on top form.

She mentally ran through the list of people she needed to speak to, to make the profile *New York Herald* levels of thorough. This was what she had been training for: no stone unturned. She also knew she'd have to be savvy about it. Ore was ruminating on the best order to do her interviews in when a sharp knock rattled her out of her scheming.

'Hello?' She rolled out of bed and pulled on the white towelling dressing gown that she'd left pooled at the end of her bed the night before. She always slept naked.

'It's Vicky. Chuck sent me to invite you to breakfast on the sun deck, served at 9 a.m.' Vicky was all business, and before Ore had a chance to open the door and ask where exactly 'the sun deck' was, she heard footsteps retreating down the hall.

Ore checked her watch to find it was already half past eight. She needed to get a move on.

First, a quick shower, which was a shame because it was glorious; the mega rich did not suffer poor water pressure. Next Ore had to decide what to wear. She heaved open her suitcase and rummaged frantically, realising that her packing was chaotic. Why had she packed a gold bikini? When exactly had she thought she might need a full-length indigo kaftan? The pac-a-mac was nonsensical and the pink neon visor seemed like the decision of a madwoman.

At 8.52, she settled on white linen trousers and a slim-fitting dark brown waistcoat. She thought it was suitably 'lady journalist' attire. The fabric was just a shade darker than the bare arms it showed off. Ore was hoping that after two weeks in the sun she might match it exactly. She left her braids loose, and added dashes of gold: earrings, rings and a thin chain.

At 9.02, she realised she wouldn't have time to re-lay her edges, and a slug of Vaseline was about all she could do for her face. Slightly flustered, she managed to find a second to admire herself in the mirror before grabbing her notepad and heading out into the maze of corridors.

Her plan was to wander around until she bumped into one of the numerous members of the crew on board. She went down two flights of stairs at the end of the hall and found herself in what she could only assume was a ballroom. Chuck did not seem like the type to dance, but she wasn't sure what else this huge space with three crystal chandeliers and a raised stage in the corner could be for.

She stopped to consider her options and then felt stupid for heading downwards. It was the sun deck after all. As she trotted back up the stairs, she came face to calf with that stiff white uniform. She looked up and grinned.

'Captain Wilsons, we must stop running into each other like this.'

He looked a little flustered by her overfamiliar tone. Ore was enjoying herself.

'Miss . . .' he began. 'I'm sorry I don't know your full name.'

Ore cocked her head to the side, genuinely intrigued by this rather beautiful man who seemed at once completely in control of himself and yet . . . nervous?

'Ballou-Adu.' She was in the habit of not bothering with both her second names. She found that it often turned into a back and forth, at least with most white people. Despite her pronouncing it out loud first, they would repeat it back with mangled vowels, and then she would find herself repeating it again. And so it would go like that until they either got it right or she gave up.

'Miss Ballou-Adu – it's interesting. Can't say I've ever heard that one before.' Daniel's pronunciation, despite his accent, was spot on. It made Ore feel surprisingly triumphant, like she had made a risky bet and it had paid off.

'Well it's half Haitian, half Nigerian.' She shrugged. Daniel nodded contemplatively, and Ore felt the need to fill the silence 'I'm actually looking for the sun deck.'

Daniel pointed upwards and Ore laughed. 'Yes I figured that out, eventually. Any more precise directions than that? Chuck is waiting for me.' She was quite late now.

'Past the gym and then up the set of stairs on the starboard.'

'Great thanks!' Ore squeezed past him on the narrow stairway before fully absorbing what she'd heard. 'Actually sorry, I can't remember what that last part means. I'm not the missing stewardess remember?'

She thought she saw a glint of embarrassment flash across his face but he quickly composed himself.

'Sorry, it means the right side of the boat, if you're looking forward towards the bow.' He seemed genuinely apologetic.

'Got it!' She turned, and then, never one to miss an opportunity, she turned back. 'Would you be up for having a chat after breakfast, just about, you know, life on board, your job and . . . Chuck?' She knew he'd see right through her but she had to try.

He chuckled. 'You mean an interview?'

She smiled, eyebrows raised hopefully.

'I don't think that's a good idea. It's better if you talk to Mr Regas about things.' His tone was deflatingly stern.

'Fair enough – worth a shot eh?' She winked at him. 'I better run.' He just nodded and she jogged off in search of her elusive breakfast.

Chapter 10

Ore

Chuck was sitting at the end of an obnoxiously long table, wearing a short-sleeve shirt with pink pineapples on it. Ore wondered if she should comment on it. It seemed like the sort of thing people wore so that other people had to acknowledge it. She decided against it; she was keen not to get caught up in 'the game' of Chuck Regas, and besides, she had little faith she'd be able to conjure up the sort of slanted compliment required.

The other thing she noticed immediately was that he was alone.

'Apologies, Chuck, I had a hard time finding my way.' Ore was slightly out of breath.

Chuck frowned ever so slightly as he looked up from his plate of pancakes. 'Oh, I sent Vicky to fetch you. Did she not escort you up?'

Ore didn't want to get anyone into trouble. 'No that's right, she did knock on my door, but I was running super late so . . .' She hoped he wouldn't notice that she hadn't exactly answered the question.

He did. 'That's not what I asked,' he said, and Ore was taken aback by the forcefulness in his voice, though he spoke quietly. For a moment they held intense eye contact. Ore was determined not to be cowed. Eventually his face cracked into a shallow smile, and he gestured to the seat opposite him.

She smiled brightly back at him. 'Well here I am, anyway!' she chirped, settling into the space where a plate and cutlery were laid out. She felt slightly shaken by the exchange, though she was not about to show it. As she spooned a heap of granola into a bowl, it occurred to her that perhaps he had planned it that way. To set her on the back foot, despite the breezy setting – this was an interview after all.

'Did you sleep well?' Chuck asked between two mouthfuls.

'Perfectly, thank you – the room is beautiful.' Ore took a sip of orange juice.

'I hate to be that crass American, but your accent really is delightful. Whereabouts in the UK are you from? I spent a couple of years living in Jersey about a decade ago and I used to love popping over to the mainland.'

'I was brought up in Margate, and then my mum and I moved to London when I was a teenager.'

'Margate? I'm afraid I don't know where that is – near the coast somewhere?' he asked lightly.

'Yes, that's right, but my dad is American, and I was actually born in the States . . .' She was aware that she was not supposed to be the one answering the questions, but she'd started now. 'And after I finished my undergrad in London, I went to Columbia for journalism school, and then stayed in New York after.' She took a bite, and felt the weight of the silence through the loudness of her chewing.

Chuck didn't seem to mind it. He wasn't jumping to fill the void with words that might reveal him. He was proving a more worthy adversary than she'd anticipated. 'But anyway, that's more than enough about me; what about you? You've never granted an interview of this kind. As far as I know, you've only ever spoken to the press about your work, so why now?'

Chuck sighed loudly and placed his fork down. Ore felt as though she was about to get a rehearsed response. A young man in navy shorts and a polo emerged from the French doors behind Chuck with a cafetière in one hand and a small jug in the other. Nobody said a word as the coffee was poured and Chuck gave only the slightest dip of the head to indicate wordlessly that he did in fact want cream. Ore followed suit with a shake of the head and the man disappeared without further acknowledgement.

Chuck continued seamlessly. 'I've been running Pagonis for a decade now and we've come an unbelievably long way, from a start-up in my father's garage in Oklahoma, all the way to the two-thousand-strong workforce we have today scattered over Silicon Valley.' She was right: he'd obviously been prepped by Agatha.

'And as we go into this new phase, away from software and into hardware, I think it's important to take stock of how far we've come.'

'When you say "we", what do you mean by that?'

Chuck laughed, and then in a tone that reeked of faux modesty he replied, 'Well, I guess it seems a little unfair to say that I did this all on my own. I've got a great team behind me.'

Ore resisted the urge to roll her eyes. 'But you're the founder, you're the CEO, ultimately the success of Pagonis is mostly your doing.'

He smiled, sincerely this time, and Ore made a mental note. Flattery was an effective strategy.

'So how far have you come? Tell me a little about how you got from that garage to well . . .' she held up her hands and looked around '. . . all of this?'

Chuck reeled off the predictable backstory. How he had come from nothing, was born and bred in Oklahoma, worked hard and eventually got into MIT on a scholarship. It was all stuff she already knew, public knowledge that was accessible on his Wikipedia page, nonetheless she took notes diligently. She wanted him to think that she was hanging on to his every word.

Occasionally, when she hadn't jotted anything for a while, he would glance down at her pad as he spoke, and she would dutifully scribble something like: *he is still speaking, and yet he is saying nothing*. He was too far away to read what she was writing, but he would smile a little smugly each time, apparently believing he'd said something of note.

Both cups of coffee were cold by the time Chuck had arrived at the 'end' of his story. He leant back and took a sip, wrinkled his nose, and then set his cup back down.

'So are we done?' Chuck asked. Ore had only actually asked that one question. The rest of the time had been spent on his spiel.

'Just a couple more things I'd like to ask you.' Up until that point Chuck had been making a point of looking relaxed and accommodating. Now he stiffened, visibly unhappy that she was planning on doing some actual journalism.

He looked down at his watch emphatically. 'Um, sure, but I have a very important call in half an hour so we'll need to wrap in the next fifteen.'

Ore smiled again, as though she hadn't noticed the condescending tone and totally unnecessary addition of *very important*.

If she only had fifteen minutes, she would have to be sparing. First things first. 'I was really hoping to speak to members of your crew, just to get some background, as you suggested yourself yesterday.'

He'd slipped back into looking like he was in total control of the situation. 'Of course, I have asked Dan to show you around, and take you to anyone you would like to speak to.'

Ore was a little surprised. 'You mean the captain?'

'Yes, why? Is that a problem for you?'

'No, not at all,' Ore fumbled. 'I just bumped into him on my way here, and he didn't seem . . . willing to talk particularly.'

Chuck Regas laughed softly and rattled the glasses on the table. 'Oh don't mind him – he seems a little stern but he's an easy enough nut to crack. You officially have my permission to speak to any and all of my staff, but as I said Dan will introduce you.'

'Do you mean to accompany me? Will he be present at the interviews?' Ore knew when she was being surveilled, but she wanted him to know that she knew.

'We're like a family on this boat, Ore. Anything they can say to you, they can say in front of the captain, and me for that matter! I have nothing to hide.'

There were two things that Ore had picked up in the year since she'd graduated, having worked both as a freelance reporter and as an office temp. One, that any job where they insist they are 'like a family' is toxic as hell. And two, only people that have something to hide tell journalists that they have nothing to hide.

Ore hadn't come onto this boat expecting to investigate anything; she was here to write a profile after all. But now Chuck had, unwittingly, intrigued her, and she wouldn't be able to let that sniff of a *deeper* story go.

'That's fine – thanks for arranging that,' Ore said sweetly, eager to avoid an interrogative tone. 'And my second question, and then we can leave it there, was just about this new venture that you're obviously very excited about: your new mega batteries. What made you want to get into that market?'

Chuck didn't look startled. Ore surmised that after last night Agatha had made sure that he was prepared with an answer to this question. 'Well firstly—' he held up his index finger, a teacher, explaining an equation to his enthralled class '—it is something that I believe we've relied for too long on Asia for. We need an American competitor to drive competition.' He looked over at the notepad again and Ore began writing on command.

'And secondly, I don't know if you know this, but I'm a bit of an environmentalist, and well, a philanthropist, and the way that batteries are produced now, it just isn't sustainable, and the human cost . . .' He trailed off, shaking his head slowly and looking down solemnly.

His empathy felt performative, but Ore chimed in. 'I know, it's awful, the children—'

'The children! Exactly, the children in the mines – it's just awful,' Chuck interjected as if suddenly remembering his lines. 'Anyway yes, that's why I've worked so hard to develop ethically and environmentally sustainable batteries, for the planet and, well, for the children.'

He looked at Ore as though he expected a round of applause,

but she had one burning question. 'So what *are* you using instead of cobalt?'

Chuck tapped the side of his nose conspiratorially. '*That*, I'm afraid, is top secret. Can't have everyone else stealing the family recipe now, can we?'

'But if the point is philanthropic, then surely it's better for the planet, and the . . . children.' She felt a little ridiculous repeating his slogans. 'Surely the rest of the industry would benefit from knowing how to circumvent the use of cobalt?' She knew she had pushed it too far even before she finished the sentence.

Chuck tensed and averted his eyes, pulling out his phone. 'I'm terribly sorry, Ore, I have to take this call now.' He stood up abruptly, throwing the napkin from his lap onto the table, and bringing the phone to his ear as he strode off. Ore berated herself for spooking him so soon. His phone hadn't been ringing.

Chapter 11

Daniel

Daniel was feeling apprehensive. He was a man who liked a plan, and a man who liked when things went to plan, but ever since his meeting with Chuck last night he was trying to come to terms with just how far from the plan this charter was beginning to veer.

He found himself wandering aimlessly around the boat, considering his life decisions. Eventually he settled at the crew mess and busied himself making a coffee. He didn't hear Vicky come in and take a seat at the table behind him, over the sound of the milk frother.

'Can I get one of those too?' He jumped and Vicky made a sound that could only be described as a cackle. 'You're never as alone as you think on this boat, remember?' Vicky always had time for a teachable moment.

'Hi, Vicky, yes of course – I brewed enough for two cups anyway.'

'Expecting company, are you? Maybe with a certain lady journalist you've taken a fancy to?'

Daniel felt heat radiate from his beating heart up his neck to his cheeks. Externally though, he tried to look unfazed, turning around and handing Vicky her mug with what he hoped was a bemused yet serene smile on his face.

'I have actually been tasked with chaperoning her, whilst she interviews the rest of the staff.' It was a trick he had learnt a long time ago, about deflection. The key was to pick up on the specific thing that the person had mentioned and then make a statement about that thing, without actually answering the question that was asked.

It worked. Vicky raised an eyebrow. 'That's not really in your job description, is it? Why can't Agatha do it?'

'Who knows?' Daniel thought on the question. 'I suppose Agatha is not really . . . everyone's cup of tea?' It was an absurd thing to say, and Daniel was not really in the habit of mocking people, let alone imitating them, but Agatha's Queen's English was a parody in itself.

Vicky burst out laughing, and Daniel felt a dash of pride, along with something else . . . a warmth in his chest. Usually he felt pretty isolated from the rest of the crew; his position demanded it, as did the very location of the captain's quarters. But here, with his highly competent second-in-command at the helm most of the time, he was free to, well, mingle.

Vicky collected herself, wiping a trail of smudged mascara from under her eyes. 'I suspect that Chuck has seen you two together and figured that you might be able to . . . seduce her into compliance.'

It was Daniel's turn to laugh, letting out an indignant snort. 'Because we're both black?'

Vicky considered for a moment. 'Well, partly yes, I remember once he had an investor of his, I think he was Indonesian, and he sort of sent him after me when I went to make drinks at the bar. I guess he assumed we'd bond over our shared culture.' Vicky let out a weary sigh. 'I've been working for the man for almost fifteen years and he still can't quite hold it in his head that I'm Vietnamese – not only that, I grew up in LA for God's sake.'

That last sentence was loaded with exasperation, a feeling that Daniel understood. On most of the boats he'd worked on, most everyone senior had been white. He had always felt like an anomaly; he guessed that must have been Vicky's experience too. But he wasn't used to commiserating with his colleagues like this.

'I hear you,' was all he could think to say.

After Vicky realised that was as good as she was going to get, she continued, 'But anyway, no, I meant more because you're both very attractive.' Her tone was steady, matter-of-fact, but Daniel could sense that this was a sort of challenge, and there were many ways he could fall into the trap.

'Well, I'm flattered, Vicky, but I'm not here for a romance, and I doubt that she is either. We both have jobs to do that would only be . . .' he searched for the right word '. . . compromised by that sort of thing.' Vicky didn't seem totally satisfied with that answer. She looked to be deciding whether there was more she should say.

'You know what happened with the last captain, right?' Daniel didn't, and he didn't want to know either; he preferred to avoid crew gossip at all costs, but it was too late. 'She basically got harassed by one of Chuck's big-time investors, and when she went to Agatha about it, I guess she was expecting some sort of *female solidarity*.' Vicky paused dramatically. 'Anyway, Agatha made her sign an NDA and sent her packing with a conciliatory bonus.' Vicky waited for Daniel to express shock, or even disgust, but he kept his face composed.

'That's all very unfortunate,' he said flatly, and saw the shutters came down behind Vicky's eyes. She seemed to realise that he had pushed the boundaries of their tentative seedling of friendship, and she had gone too far. Daniel felt sorry closing it down, but he didn't need to get involved in any drama.

Vicky stood up brusquely, her coffee only half drunk, and found an excuse to leave. Apparently there were some more rooms to ready before Chuck welcomed new guests on board. Daniel was left standing alone in the kitchen, wondering why he was suddenly feeling so down about keeping his distance on board. It had never bothered him before.

He supposed that Ore was probably done with breakfast by now and if he was going to show willing with Chuck, he should 'make himself available to her'. He felt deeply uncomfortable about the spying element of his new mission, but she was a journalist after all; she must understand how this all worked.

He found her on the sun deck, the gold flecks in her braids shimmering in the light. She was sitting on the edge of a lounger, hunched over her notepad, chewing at the end of her pen absentmindedly.

'Miss Ballou-Adu, how was your breakfast?' She looked up at him with that brilliant smile of hers.

'Captain Wilsons, just the man I wanted to see!' He wondered if she knew the effect she had on people, the one that made him feel like she really was delighted to see him. He suspected that she did.

56

'At your service.' Before he knew what he was doing, he was holding out his hand, a reflex perhaps. She looked down at it, bemused, but shook it firmly.

'Chuck said you will be . . . accompanying me to my interviews.'

Daniel baulked. He felt uneasy about being part of Chuck's deception.

'Well yes, I will introduce you to the staff.' Daniel floundered, not making eye contact. 'But everything said off the record will remain strictly confidential.' The moment he said it, he regretted it. Daniel was not a dishonest person, and he resented Chuck for putting him in this position.

Ore sighed with relief. 'Oh great, I kind of assumed that you'd been told to sort of report back on everything so that's really good to know, Daniel.' Now he felt even worse.

'No problem,' he said stiffly.

'So where shall we start?' She bounded up from the lounger energetically, hardly able to contain her enthusiasm.

What he did next, he had to admit to himself, was partly to relieve his own guilt. 'Why not with me? I can't promise I have that many useful tidbits to share about Mr Regas or Pegasus, but I'll do my best.'

Ore laughed. Daniel wasn't sure what about, but he couldn't help smiling at the sound.

'I'm assuming you mean Pagonis? Chuck's company, and the most profitable in the world?' Somehow her teasing didn't feel condescending, but Daniel was still embarrassed.

'Oh sorry, I'm not really into all that tech stuff; I still use a Nokia.'

'That's actually very Gen Alpha of you, ahead of your time.

57

I wish I was better at switching off from all that stuff to be honest.' Daniel thought of himself as someone who was decidedly behind on the times, so it was refreshing to hear Ore was impressed by this fact about him.

'Let's head down to my quarters? It'll be a bit more private than out here.' He realised how that sounded about a beat after Ore did. 'Or actually the control deck will do fine,' he added hastily.

She raised her eyebrows but said only, 'Lead the way.'

Chapter 12

Ore

They sat opposite each other, barely an arm's length apart, across a small exceedingly tidy desk in the captain's cabin. There was a glass door separating them from where another man in a uniform similar to Daniel's was sitting in front of a spread of flashing lights, dials and levers.

'Will we be heard in here?' Ore asked, gesturing towards the man.

'Oh no, it's pretty soundproof in here and First Officer Dudley is a pro; he'll be focused on the job at hand.' Ore was reassured, although she only now came to realise that she hadn't prepared any questions for Daniel, so sure had she been that this particular interview was never going to happen.

She scrambled through her notes, trying to look like she was identifying a specific page, and settled on the list of questions she had hoped to tackle with Chuck at breakfast. She'd have to ad lib a bit.

'So, Daniel, why don't we start off by you just telling me a little bit about yourself? How did you end up working for Chuck Regas?' Pen poised, she offered her most 'approachably curious' expression.

'There isn't much to it really. I work for an agency and they needed a last-minute replacement.' He seemed to hope that would put the matter to bed, but Ore wasn't about to be blown off again.

'Yes, you mentioned that. What exactly happened to the last captain?'

He shifted in his seat before answering. 'I'm afraid I'm not sure.' Ore was pretty certain he was lying.

'Right, so the agency didn't mention anything to you?' Even if she knew he wouldn't cave, it was worth a shot.

'No, miss, they just give me a call, tell me where and when, and I go.'

'That must be a lonely life for you.' It was meant to be a question but it came out sounding judgemental.

He was silent for a moment, and Ore noticed how still he was. No fidgeting this time. He looked away, out the window, and then answered, 'It can be, yes.'

'So how did you get into yachting? Not to sound ignorant but I had never imagined that the captain of a mega yacht might be black, and Southern to boot.'

'Southern to boot? You sound like a New Yorker. I grew up just outside Houston; it's hardly the Mississippi Delta.' He spoke calmly but Ore heard that familiar undertone of exasperation. She had heard it coming from her own mouth before, the defensiveness that came from an irrational need to prove you were not a token hire.

'I'm sorry, I didn't mean for it to come across like that. I'm just curious.'

Daniel looked at her placidly. She had some winning back of trust to do.

'Well, I grew up in Southern England, in a place called

Margate. It's a very white place, so my mum and I got used to being the only black people around most of the time,' Ore leant forward, and Daniel looked at her intently. 'Then I moved to London, which was great, and I got used to – you know – having "the community" around. It wasn't until I went to Columbia and started trying to make it as a journo in New York that I felt that feeling again, of being "the only one" and having to stand my ground when people asked questions about what I was doing in that particular room.'

There was silence. Ore leant back in her seat, wondering what other tactics she might have to get him to open up. The 'tell me about yourself' was supposed to build rapport, not completely shut it down.

'My mom was always broke,' Daniel said suddenly, though quietly. He looked like he was surprising *himself* by opening up. 'There were three of us. Terry is a year older and Maddy is a year younger – than me, that is.'

Ore didn't dare move or speak, lest she break the spell.

'My dad left when I was little and we didn't see him for years. Before I left, we'd started seeing each other again occasionally, and it turns out all that time he was only about fifty miles away, in Lake Jackson.' Daniel's gaze was focused somewhere off in the distance, and Ore had to resist the urge to turn around and follow it.

'I was always into vehicles: cars, trains, boats. Mom used to take us to the museum for an afternoon and leave us there while she did a shift. When she came back, she'd find me in the locomotive section, or the maritime history section or whatever.'

Daniel seemed to remember where he was just then, and

looked almost startled to notice Ore staring at him. 'Sorry, I don't know where that came from.' He began shifting in his chair again. 'You don't want to know about all that.'

'I do,' and she meant it. She knew none of it would be useful for her story, but she was invested now. 'Tell me more about that, Daniel.' He looked away again and she felt her chance slip away. 'Please,' she added, in barely more than a whisper.

'The thing with boats, and cars and trains, is that they're by and large reliable, and if they're not, then you know there's something wrong, and you can fix it.'

'There's no hidden agenda,' Ore cut in softly.

Daniel's eyes brightened almost imperceptibly. 'Exactly, they are straightforward and as long as you look after them they will take you where you want to go.'

'It sounds like you didn't always get a choice in where you wanted to go?' Ore was forgetting herself.

'I spent a lot of my life feeling like I was on a path to somewhere and nowhere, like I knew exactly where I would end up and even if I didn't want to, it was bound to happen.' Daniel shrugged. 'And then I won some build your own boat race competition and ended up at sailing summer camp, all expenses paid.'

'How old were you then?' Ore promised herself she would get to more questions about Chuck soon.

'Sixteen, and then I went back the following year, worked my ass off to pay for it the second time, and the third. And then I met this guy there, Jack, making some extra money over the summer, and he told me all about working on yachts, hooked me up with his captain and got me my first job as a deckhand.' Daniel exhaled, as if he had been holding his breath for a long time.

'That's quite the journey, and now here you are – it's amazing.' Ore wasn't exaggerating. She loved hearing about people who broke the mould that life had cast for them. She liked to think that's what she was doing too.

Daniel smiled shyly. 'I don't know about amazing, but I guess these days, it does feel like it all worked out how it was supposed to.'

Ore hoped he didn't think she was being insincere. 'No genuinely, that's a very cool origin story.' She made sure to look him directly in the eye when she said, 'Thanks for sharing that with me.'

Chapter 13

Daniel

He really hadn't intended to tell her very much of anything, and when he started with the life story stuff, it had mainly been a ploy to keep her off the topic of Chuck. It had got out of hand in the end; he couldn't seem to stop and she had seemed so enthralled. He did not think of himself as a natural-born storyteller. Mostly he liked to get down to the facts, let those speak for themselves.

He told himself that she was probably just very good at pretending to find people fascinating, but he couldn't quite bring himself to believe it. In the little time he'd known her he'd noticed that she was not that good at hiding her feelings, at least not in front of him. Maybe it was just the curse of an expressive face, or just plain old lack of practice. It surprised him – surely it was an important part of being a journalist? Daniel for one had been perfecting the art most of his life, and yet when faced with her disarming smile, he felt as though he were giving himself away somehow. The more worrying thing was that he didn't really mind.

'So if I can get back to Chuck . . .' Her voice brought him back into the room. He might have known that his distracting technique would only work for so long.

'As I said, I don't know much, but I'll tell you anything I do know.' There he was again, lying to her face. He still felt bad about it, but he noted that it was easier than last time.

'Do you like him?' It was so direct, and totally not what Daniel had been preparing himself to answer.

'Um, I . . . Um, what do you mean?'

Ore smiled devilishly. 'Do you like Chuck? As in, do you think he is a nice person with good qualities?'

Daniel took a moment, pretending he was thinking of something particularly insightful to say. He counted to ten, furrowing his brow, performing his pondering. 'I think that Chuck is a person who is good at what he does, and is pleasant to those around him.'

'Well, *that* was almost as convincing as Agatha's answers.' Ore was deadpan, and then Daniel spotted a tug at the corner of her mouth, and then she was trying to hold in a giggle and then they were both laughing a little too loudly. Daniel worried that he wouldn't be able to stop, as his eyes began to water. When First Officer Dudley turned to see what was going on, Daniel only bellowed louder.

Ore's eyes twinkled as Daniel got a hold of himself. He couldn't remember the last time he had laughed so hard, and he fought off a creeping feeling of self-consciousness. Suddenly he felt overly aware of how close to him she was sitting, and he had no idea what to do with his hands. Ore leant back and crossed her arms, a playful grin on her face.

'Just tell me one thing?' she pleaded softly. How could he refuse?

'Sure,' he said, a little nervous about what he was agreeing to.

'Does he make you call him Mr Regas? It seems strange to me that he's so familiar with you but you only address him by his surname.'

Daniel hadn't been expecting that. It seemed inconsequential really, so he didn't feel conflicted about answering. 'I called him Chuck once, when we first met and he insisted.' Daniel thought back to his first conversation over the phone, a couple of weeks earlier. 'And then both Vicky *and* Agatha suggested that I don't.' He could see Ore's curiosity pique; it was subtle, but her shoulders drew back slightly and she tilted her head down so she was looking up at him slightly, under her perfectly arched eyebrows.

'Why's that then?'

Daniel realised too late that he had entrapped himself. The truth was revealing, but he was here now.

'Vicky said that . . . that he had a way of using that kind of familiarity to his advantage.' He knew he had said too much, and what's more he had dropped Vicky in it too. What had happened to his plan to say as little as possible?

It was clear that Ore was not just a hapless puff-piece writer. He found he was a little hurt by the thought that their shared moment of merriment was a ruse to get him to open up.

'So it's a self-protection mechanism for you? To keep your distance from Chuck, so he doesn't come asking for favours?'

'I wouldn't say that.' Daniel was on high alert now.

'What would you say?' Ore was pushing, her tone a little forceful, but Daniel had said enough.

'I would say that I like to keep things professional.'

Ore must have sensed his reluctance, because she nodded slowly and closed her notepad, though she had not written anything down. 'Well thanks very much, Captain Wilsons, for your time.' The formality felt jarring.

'Please call me Daniel.' It sounded more pleading than he had intended, and strangely pointed after their conversation, but Ore smiled.

'Yes, Daniel, of course, I was kind of teasing.'

'Is that the great British sense of humour I'm always hearing about?' He had to admit that he hadn't been able to tell she was joking.

'The very one,' she said, winking at him. Daniel was glad the interview was over. He found Ore's presence disconcerting. He yo-yoed between feeling entirely at ease and feeling nakedly on display, and he was unused to both.

'So who did you want to speak to next?' Daniel was keen to move things along.

'It's got to be Vicky, right?' Ore chirped, a mischievous look in her eye.

With trepidation, Daniel replied: 'Vicky it is.'

Chapter 14

Ore

Ore felt triumphant. Daniel had cracked, if only for a moment, but he'd confirmed many of her suspicions about Chuck. Ore prided herself on being a good judge of character, and she liked being right.

She was still peeved about having to be chaperoned during her interviews but she believed Daniel when he said he was not a spy. Obviously his role was to mildly intimidate her interviewees into knowing they were being listened to, but she took him at his word that what was said would not go any further.

They walked through a series of identical corridors, Daniel weaving through doors and down stairs with the quiet confidence of a person walking through their own home. They ended up outside the mess.

Daniel knocked, and when Vicky answered the door, she looked bemused.

'You don't have to do that, this is your boat, Captain.' Ore glanced over at Daniel. He looked a little sheepish, and Vicky was wearing a wry smile. This was going to be interesting, thought Ore. Vicky didn't seem the type to be cowed by Daniel's presence, and from what he had said earlier, she was also discerning.

'Hi, Vicky! Would you mind if we sat down for a chat? I'd love to ask you a couple of questions.' She'd slipped into reporter mode.

Vicky turned and gave her a chilling once-over. There was an uncomfortably long pause before she said simply: 'Sure.'

She walked over to the table and sat down. Ore took a seat opposite and Daniel remained, disconcertingly, standing somewhere behind her.

'Just a moment.' Vicky inspected something smudged on the table in front of her, then with a huff she stood to fetch a cloth and wiped down the surface thoroughly. Ore lifted her notepad when it became clear her corner of the table would not be exempt.

'Right, that's better. Sorry, where were we?' Vicky sat back down, and Ore found herself thinking how many type A's must work on boats. Her life back in New York, and even in London, had been full of creative, liberal arts types. The sorts who would probably enjoy the aesthetic of a ring left on a wooden tabletop by a glass of red wine.

Ore suddenly felt nervous. Vicky was not a woman to shy away from eye contact, and Ore was under-prepared. She'd been imagining how these interviews would go on for days, at times hard to differentiate from a friendly conversation. They would be easy-going and subtly explorative. Now she found herself unable to think of anything to ask.

'Um, where are you from then, Vicky?' She picked up her pen, if only to have something to do with her hands.

Vicky looked over Ore's shoulder, throwing Daniel a look she couldn't quite decipher but it didn't seem generous.

'I'm from LA,' Vicky said flatly, now crossing her arms.

'Cool, sorry, um I just . . .' The slow warm-up wasn't working terribly well. *Get to the point.*

'Did you want to come back when you have some actual questions?' Vicky made to stand up and Ore felt her opportunity to gain Vicky's respect slipping away.

'No, I've got them here.' Ore's voice was firm this time, forceful even, and Vicky's demeanour changed, as though her curiosity was suddenly piqued, and she leant forward slightly.

'Obviously you know I'm here to write about Chuck, so I guess what I want to know is . . . What is he like?'

'To work for? Or as a person?' Vicky did not seem fazed by the prospect of commenting on either. Ore tried to contain her excitement.

'Either,' said Ore, before quickly adding, 'or both.'

'As long as you understand your place, by which I mean, the difference between his "guests", in his case, mostly his investors, and his "staff", he's as good to work for as anyone,' Vicky explained. Hardly a glowing recommendation, thought Ore.

'And as a person . . .' Daniel cleared his throat then, and Vicky's eyes flashed up once again, to somewhere behind Ore's head, and then back again.

'He's nice I suppose . . . generous certainly.' So Daniel's presence was going to be a hindrance; that was clear.

'And when you said, "the difference between staff and guests", what did you mean by that exactly?' Ore wasn't giving up.

'Well, I've worked in boating for fifteen years and as much as employers love to say differently, we're not a family. Some of us are here to serve, and others . . .' Vicky paused and held Ore's gaze, her dark eyes piercing '. . . others are not.'

There was silence and Ore wasn't sure if Vicky would say more, but she did.

'Those who confuse those boundaries don't last very long.'

'Can you give me an example?' Ore was poised over her lined pad. She heard movement behind her and then Dàniel was standing right by her left shoulder.

Vicky didn't look at him this time, though it was clear he was trying to get her attention.

'No, I cannot,' she said simply.

'OK, maybe you could explain what you mean by boundaries?'

But Vicky had already checked out. She shifted in her chair and uncrossed her arms. 'I've actually got a lot to get on with – apologies.' Without even acknowledging the question, she stood up.

'Oh well, I've got a couple more—'

Vicky cut her off. 'Sorry there's not more time, good luck with your piece.' Ore could only say 'thanks' to the door left swinging in Vicky's wake. That must be a new record, thought Ore, she'd managed *one* question. Well, two if you counted the wasted 'where are you from.'

She turned to Daniel, exasperated. She opened her mouth to say something, although she wasn't totally sure what exactly.

He cut in first. 'That went well.' Usually Ore was good at detecting sarcasm, but the accent and his placid expression was throwing her off. Either way it niggled at her.

'Really, Daniel? You think that went well?' She sounded whiny, rather than the combo of unfazed but self-aware she was hoping for. She was surprised to see his brow furrow with

71

concern. Maybe he had been sincere. She realised that she couldn't afford to not have him on side.

'Sorry, Daniel, I didn't mean to snap. I know you're just trying to be helpful. It's my job to get them talking after all.' She looked down, feeling a surge of something familiar course through her body, one she had been blissfully free of since that email from Agatha. It was a tightening in her stomach and a faint sense that she was outside of herself. She would observe the crouching figure, braids falling over her face, eyes set on the linoleum, painted nails picking at each other, foot tapping softly but rhythmically. That's when the refrain began, softly at first and then building into a din. *You really thought you could do this? A couple of little online articles and you think you're ready for a big scoop? You? A staff writer at the* New York Herald*? There's ambition and then there's delusion.*

The warmth of a hand on her shoulder pulled her back into her body, and the imposter syndrome chorus quietened, though it wasn't silenced.

She looked up to find Daniel standing close to where she was seated, with his palm laid upon her shoulder, inches from his belly button. She could feel the small space between them like she could hear the loaded silence, and both felt unbearable.

She stood up, and Daniel took an unsteady step backwards, his wayward hand finding refuge in his pocket.

'Sorry, I didn't mean to . . . I don't know what . . .' Daniel began. Ore had her own fumbling to do, so they spoke over each other.

'I better be going. I didn't want to . . .' She reached for her notepad, which was embarrassingly empty. They both giggled nervously as Ore turned back to Daniel.

Another silence. Ore felt the agony of guessing at his thoughts. *He knows you're a fraud now.* She shook her head instinctively.

'Are you OK?' The concern in his voice, like his hand on her shoulder, only added to her sense of shame so she plastered on a smile.

'Sure, just going to head back to my cabin for a little bit, regroup; maybe I can meet you later and we can try and talk to Ollie?' She only needed to get out of this room and then she could be alone and give that snarling voice a talking-to, like she had before.

Ore was already marching to the door when Daniel replied: 'Shall we say three o'clock?'

'Great.' Ore was breathless. With one hand opening the door, she swung herself round and witnessed herself in another out-of-body experience, lifting her other hand to her forehead in a salute and saying the words: 'Catch you later, Captain.'

Chapter 15

Daniel

Daniel stood in the kitchen for a few minutes after Ore left. He was, maybe for the first time in his life, wholly unsure what had come over him. He replayed the moment in his head, cringing to himself as he recalled his palm landing on her bare shoulder. He hadn't been thinking, another rare phenomenon, and he had seen something in her eyes that he recognised, although he couldn't put a name to it. She seemed scared and he had wanted to protect her from that feeling.

He had glimpsed the negative that made up the Technicolor Polaroid, and he had felt a little overwhelmed as though she was now sitting naked in front of him. Except he was at least worldly enough to know how to navigate a woman's naked body – not so much her soul laid bare.

Daniel was beginning to come to terms with what all of this meant. He had had crushes before and, much like this one, he always found them more disturbing than enjoyable. He reasoned that it was only natural for people, including himself, to be attracted to Ore. She was beautiful, bright, funny and easy-going. On his good days he thought of himself as being the former two, but the latter he was most certainly lacking.

He had suspected after yesterday that he might have some untoward feelings, but he'd thought himself more than capable of overriding those. The hand-on-the-shoulder incident seemed to suggest otherwise and he was going to have to double down on his efforts. It was all quite inconvenient really, to be faced with these unnecessary challenges, just as he had been hoping for an autopilot kind of gig – figuratively speaking, of course.

'Captain Wilsons to top deck.' The radio clipped to his belt crackled into life with Vicky's voice.

'Copy that.' He was glad to have somewhere to be.

As he walked up the stairs, he felt the now familiar vibration of the walls around him and heard a distant whining. The choppers were on the way, and that meant one thing: more guests arriving, which was not on the itinerary. He took the steps two at a time.

Vicky was barking out orders to the clusters of stewards and stewardesses who were coming, and then going, once they had received their instructions.

'Did you know about this?' Vicky strode over to him.

He held his hands up in surrender. 'Not at all.'

Vicky brought her forefingers to her temples and massaged them slowly. Daniel stood still waiting for what he suspected was her bridled rage to pass.

'Right, OK, well there's two choppers on the way, that's all I've been told, so that's anywhere between like eight and sixteen new guests.' Vicky looked up at him, as if he was supposed to provide sympathy at this point, despite the fact he was still waiting to hear exactly what all this had to do with him.

'That's a lot to ask, at such short notice,' he offered, and Vicky seemed satisfied.

'Oh, and they want to go to the Barrier Reef.' She delivered this line with an almost theatrical level of nonchalance, as if that wasn't going to mess up the entire navigation schedule and require Daniel to plot the reroute all through the night.

Daniel was unwilling to take the bait that Vicky was dangling in front of him. He sensed this was another one of her tests.

'I guess I'll go speak with First Office Dudley and we'll come up with a plan.'

Vicky didn't seem impressed but then again she didn't seem disappointed either. She merely nodded curtly and said, 'Thanks, Captain, I know it's not an easy ask, but I appreciate your level-headedness.'

Daniel was stunned by the compliment; he enjoyed passing tests.

'No time to lose then.' He smiled and was met with something similar, a slight upturning of lips at least, before she set her sights on another victim.

In truth, as much as this would mean changing course, he was keen to have something other than Ore to focus on. It was too much like hard work mediating his own feelings whilst having to spy on her. Maybe this also exempted him from a debrief with Chuck, which was another aspect of this scheme that made his skin crawl.

He radioed Ollie as he made his way to the wheelhouse. 'First Officer Dudley, do you copy?'

'Copy.'

'I'm heading over to discuss a new plan. Mr Regas wants to make a little detour.'

'How little are we talking?'

'He wants to go to the Barrier Reef.'

A click and then silence on the other end of the line. Daniel imagined that Ollie might have muted himself as he reeled off a colourful variety of expletives. Another click and Ollie was back, with a performatively calm: 'Copy that, Captain.'

Ollie was leant back with his arms crossed wearing an unamused expression when Daniel got to him a few minutes later.

'I heard the choppers and I knew it wasn't going to be good news.' Ollie had been working with Chuck on and off for about five years, so Daniel had come to understand that nothing about the billionaire's last-minute whims shocked him, even if they annoyed him immensely.

'The Barrier Reef though, they were only there a month ago; seems like we have a Chuck fixation on our hands.' Ollie sounded resigned as he turned to the ship's monitor and Daniel took a seat beside him.

They would have to turn around, and although Ollie was a great boatsman he admitted that he would rather they made it a two-man job.

'The last time we went it was Annie manning the ship . . .' Ollie had a strange distant look in his eye. 'I probably shouldn't have gone to bed.' He seemed to be talking to himself.

'Annie is Captain Harleston, I presume?' The old captain, the one who had been 'sent away' suddenly.

Ollie bristled at the mention of her name. 'Yes that's right. She was a great captain; it isn't fair really.'

Daniel had tried to stay out of it, but every crew member on this boat seemed determined to upset his blissful ignorance. He felt like Ollie wanted him to ask, so he obliged.

'What happened to her?'

Ollie scoffed. 'You really want to know?'

He didn't, and yet he said, 'Sure.'

'Let's just say that one of Chuck's buddies took a liking to her, and friends of Chuck do not like it when they can't have what they want.'

The memory of Chuck's leering gaze over his exposed chest and the ease with which he asked for favours flashed into Daniel's mind. In combination with what Vicky and Natalie had already told him, Daniel was totally unsurprised by Ollie's revelation.

'I see,' said Daniel flatly. He had not intended for it to come out sounding so cold. Ollie seemed taken aback – perhaps he had expected outrage. He looked as though he might have more to say and then thought better of it. Maybe he remembered that he was talking to his captain.

'Anyway, I've plotted the new coordinates. Are you OK to take over for the rest of the afternoon? I'll relieve you for a few hours tonight and then we can both be at the helm for the midnight manoeuvre.' Ollie was all business now.

'Sounds like a good plan. Thank you, Dudley.' Both men looked straight ahead as they spoke and when Ollie left the room, he did so in silence.

Chapter 16

Ore

Ore stood in front of the mirror and tried reciting her affirmations. *I am enough, I am capable, I am loved, I deserve to be here. I am enough, I am capable, I am loved, I deserve to be here. I am enough, I am capable, I am loved, I deserve to be here.*

Eventually, the *you're an impostor* voice recoiled back into the subconscious lair it had crawled from, and Ore's rational brain took over the reins. It had been a while since she'd had a bout of such overwhelming self-doubt.

There really is no harder thing than conquering one's own mind; that's what Kyle, her therapist, had told her. But there would come a time when what felt like the burdensome beating down of her unhelpful thoughts would happen pre-emptively, seamlessly, effortlessly.

This particular episode *had* felt pretty burdensome, but maybe it was the unfamiliar environment wearing down her resilience. For a moment she felt her mind wander, considering how much more overwhelmed she'd be at the *New York Herald*, scratching at the scab of inadequacy. She managed to pull herself back into the present before she went down that thankless path.

Instead she thought about her *toolbox of strategies*, as Kyle called it. When she was in the depths of *this*, back at the end of her first year at Columbia, she had found when she was stuck on a story or assignment it was freeing to do the most terrifying thing she could imagine, going back to the start. Retracing her steps but trying to follow them slower than she had laid them. That's when she would find the golden nugget of the story. It was in her nature to run towards things, but turning back would serve her well, he'd insisted.

What a difference it made.

That first year when her grades were coming back average, and her classmates seemed to be drifting through the course effortlessly as she slogged through eighteen-hour days, half studying, the other half bartending to pay her rent, she had drafted several emails to the dean to tell him she was dropping out – but she had never sent them. The voice had been the loudest it had ever been, telling her she wasn't good enough to be here, day in and day out.

She had collapsed in the library, and when she woke up in the campus infirmary they told her it was 'exhaustion'. She had been embarrassed, convinced it only confirmed that she wasn't cut out for this, that her admission had been a terrible mistake. Then she met Kyle, and he would turn out to be the first man in her life who would ever truly know her.

'Many overachieving children find themselves lost as they get into their twenties. For a long time they rely on validation from teachers and parents to build their sense of self-worth, and then once they end up in a milieu with equally high-performing peers, they no longer know how to understand their own value.' He had said it as though it was a throwaway observation, but Ore had felt seen, uncomfortably so.

She hadn't gone back for three weeks, and then one night after getting back from a particularly chaotic shift at the bar, she'd opened an email from Gail Fairweather, informing her that her latest assignment had been 'a disappointing read'. There had been tears, panic and shame in abundance. She booked an emergency next-day session with Kyle while crouched inside her wardrobe. Since she was little she'd sought out tight, dark corners whenever things felt like too much.

Over the next six months Kyle encouraged her to cut her hours, apply for more financial support and slow down. Whenever things got on top of her she was supposed to stop, not run faster – turn around and face the monster chasing her. Most of the time, it turned out, it was just a bogeyman, a figment of her overactive imagination.

What would Kyle say to me right now? She had the urge to call him, but she knew she shouldn't. Firstly because of the time zones they were respectively in, and secondly because he wouldn't answer. After the way they'd left it, it would be unwise for him to.

Slow down, take a step back, turn around, what have you missed while you were too busy steaming ahead?

Ore took a deep breath. *I am enough, I am capable, I am loved, I deserve to be here.* And then she added, *and I look hot,* because she did. Sometimes it soothed her to worry more about what she looked like, how others perceived her, than how she felt. That was something she had, counter-intuitively, always felt more in control of. She smiled at herself brightly in the mirror and marvelled at how convincing it looked.

Ever the master of fake it till you make it – another of Kyle's observations.

She laid out her pitiful notebook, with its half page of illegible scrawlings, on the small desk in the room. She found her other notebook sandwiched in between layers of clothing in her suitcase and then opened her laptop.

Methodically, she started at the beginning, with what she had found out about Chuck's childhood before she'd spoken to him. Not much, it turned out. He must have used his connections to scrub himself from the internet he so loved, she thought.

But there was a line in the student paper she'd come across, scanned into the MIT online archives that mentioned a boarding school in Europe. She had forgotten about that. On his Wikipedia page there was no mention of it and that morning he had only talked about his 'run-down shack of a schoolhouse' in Stillwater, Oklahoma.

Clicking through her folder of annotated articles, she landed on another obscure find. In one of the very few interviews he had done early on in his career he listed *fluent Flemish* as his 'surprise secret talent'. In the note she'd made, she'd written, *he's boring then . . .*

Now she tore out a page and sketched out a timeline. She wrote: *Born, 1982, Oklahoma, school approx. 1988–2006, some of that in Belgium? Some of that in Stillwater? MIT 2007–2012, Pagonis founded 2014–now.*

It wasn't much, but already she felt calmer. She had located at least one mystery to solve, and it was a bit of direction if nothing else.

From her interview with Vicky, she had almost nothing apart from the comment about Chuck being a bit of an arsehole boss, which even Daniel had alluded to, and she had basically figured out herself. *Chuck not a nice guy?* she wrote underneath the timeline, and then she wrote *boundaries* and *investors* and underlined both.

For good measure she decided to look up the majority investors in Pagonis and listed their names down the side of the page. If Chuck was in the habit of inviting them on board, she might even have a run-in with some of them and she wanted to know who she was dealing with.

Next she made a list of the crew she knew about and placed check boxes next to each name. Her goal was to talk to at least half the staff, across a range of roles. Maybe the younger, greener crew would be more loose-lipped.

Finally she was left with Mel and Agatha. The former she had decided she wouldn't talk to. It would be unethical to take advantage of a teenager's ire towards her parents just to get a scoop, even if she had to admit it was tempting. For Agatha, her plan was to try and catch her 'off duty'. Maybe a glass of wine would soften her hard edges.

She was lost in thought and scheming when she heard the walls begin to rattle, the abstract seascape above the desk thrumming in its frame. The vibrations became more intense and Ore felt a rising sense of panic, mixed with a tinge of nausea.

As the noise settled into a louder whirring, her brain settled on the conclusion that it must be a helicopter arriving.

She checked her watch: 15.06. Damn she was late again. She gathered her spillage of notes into a pile, splashed some water on her face, spritzed on her perfume, pulled on a cardigan and headed up to the deck to track down Daniel. She needed to get her head in the game. Her next interview would be better; it had to be.

Chapter 17

Daniel

Daniel too had lost track of time and was a little startled when Ore knocked lightly on the door. He stood to open it and through the glass was surprised to see that she looked uneasy. Even in the short time they'd known each other he'd come to associate her with natural confidence. Whatever had happened in the kitchen was obviously still affecting her.

'Ore, my apologies, I hadn't realised what the time was.' Her nervous energy was infectious; he felt as though he didn't know what to do with his hands, how to stand or where to look.

'No problem, I was also running behind.' They stood in silence, Daniel realising too late that he would need to step back to let her into the room.

Before he did Ore said: 'Sorry about all that back there.' She wasn't looking at him; instead she was fiddling with the end of one of her braids, her eyes trained on the grey carpet.

'No problem.'

Daniel stepped back to let Ore pass. Before she did, she looked up at him, her dark eyes brimming with something he couldn't decipher. He found himself compelled to ask her if she was all right. He opened his mouth, saw her eyes glint, and then lost his nerve.

'Come on in,' he said. She quickly looked away and walked further into the room. 'I'm afraid I won't be able to accompany you on any more interviews today or tomorrow.'

She had her back to him, first looking down at the control panel and then out to sea.

'Uh-huh.' She sounded miles away. 'That's fine, maybe I can just talk to Dudley on his own.'

'I'm not sure that's a good idea.'

She spun around, the soft sadness of her expression morphing into something harder. 'I assume that's because Chuck wouldn't allow it?'

He was a little taken aback by the harshness of her tone.

Almost immediately she looked contrite. 'Sorry, God I don't know what's wrong with me today. I guess I have a lot riding on this.'

He could understand that. 'There's been a bit of a change of plan, which I'm not totally happy with myself.' He didn't want her to think he was trying to make her life harder on purpose. At that moment he didn't want to think about why her opinion of him mattered so much.

'I'm guessing you heard the choppers arriving?' Ore nodded and Daniel continued explaining himself. 'That's a new batch of investors for Chuck to "entertain", and now we have to reroute as he wants to head towards the Barrier Reef, again.'

Ore nodded once more, thoughtfully, Daniel could almost see the wheels turning as she digested the information. 'Do you think he'll let me talk to them?'

'Worth an ask.' Daniel shrugged. He half hoped Chuck would refuse the request. He already had enough to be getting on with, without a new batch of interviews to chaperone. The other half of him was pleased to see Ore light up again with excitement.

'That would be really something . . .' She was muttering, talking to herself more than him. 'Thanks, Daniel.' She walked over and for a second he thought she was going to hug him. His body stiffened reflexively; he worried it would betray him.

Instead she turned and continued towards the door, and he felt a flash of disappointment.

'I'm going to go find Chuck and see what's going on, find out who's on board.' Ore looked determined.

'Sure thing, I'll be up most of the night so perhaps if you need to do some interviews tomorrow, we could arrange something for early afternoon?' He cringed. He sounded too eager.

Ore had one hand on the door handle. 'Yep, I'll let you know.'

As the door shut behind her, Daniel tried to dismiss the feeling that he was already looking forward to seeing her again.

Daniel got back to work. He'd have to plan a stopover straight after their detour, as the boat needed refuelling, and he was dreading having to go down to the kitchen and tell Carlos that he wouldn't be getting any new ingredients for five days.

He had just fired off a request to the port authorities in Cairns when Dudley burst in. He was beginning to learn that the first officer was prone to intense changes in mood.

Standing in the middle of the room, Dudley crunched over, with his head in his hands. *Pretty dramatic*, thought Daniel.

'Are you OK, Dudley?' he asked, although his instinct was to ignore what he thought of as attention-seeking behaviour. When Dudley looked up though, his face was red, as though he'd been crying, and Daniel felt bad for having assumed theatrics.

'I'm raging.' Dudley's breath was ragged, and he ran his hand through his hair exasperatedly as he tried to formulate a sentence. 'Vicky just told me . . . Told me that Claude is back on board. I can't believe it. I honestly . . . I don't know what hold he has over Chuck.'

Daniel was beginning to put the pieces together, but he needed to make sure he wasn't jumping to conclusions.

'Who is Claude, Dudley?' Daniel hoped his tone was calming.

Dudley huffed incredulously. 'Claude Van Der Bodem. That's the arsehole who . . .' He looked as though he might begin to cry again. 'The guy who messed with Annie.'

For the second time that day Daniel found himself trying to comfort someone. He approached Dudley slowly, deliberately, as if approaching a wounded animal. He put an arm around him and Dudley lowered his head. Daniel felt the soft jolts and damp spread of tears on his shoulder.

'The whole thing was so messed up. Annie was just trying to be nice, and he took it too far . . .' Dudley gulped. 'I just can't believe we all have to serve that guy as if nothing's happened.'

Daniel patted his back rhythmically, and Dudley's breathing evened out slowly. When he leant back, he seemed a bit embarrassed. 'Sorry, man, I know this is all before your time. I thought I could handle coming back, but it's a bit much, you know?'

Daniel didn't know; this was why he had always kept his distance from the rest of the crew. Getting emotionally invested in people only ever led to drama and upset.

'Do you need me to cover for us both? I'm sure I can manage if you can't face doing the overnight.' It was the only way Daniel could think to help. He wasn't very good with words.

'Are you sure? I'd appreciate that, Captain.'

The men nodded at each other and then, suddenly uncomfortable with how close they were standing to each other, they both took a step back.

Dudley mumbled something indecipherable as he left. Daniel took a seat and reviewed the day. He had been hoping for this one final agency job to be a simple one, yet already it was turning into something . . . complicated. Worst of all, and try as he might to avoid it, he had ended up where he hated being the most: involved.

Chapter 18

Ore

Ore found Chuck on the third deck, alone and on the phone. She hovered awkwardly a few paces behind him, not wanting to interrupt but also tempted to eavesdrop.

The wind wasn't working in her favour so she only caught snippets.

'Near the site . . . three days . . . Klauparten . . . reef.' It was an intriguing and utterly meaningless collection of words but Ore made a mental note, if only to flesh out her sorry-looking mind map.

Chuck abruptly ended the call and Ore leapt back before making as if she had just walked onto the deck. Still, he looked startled. 'Ore, what are you doing here? I usually like to be alone when conducting business.' He was smiling but Ore understood that he did not take kindly to being ambushed.

'I was just looking for you to ask what all that noise was about?' Again she figured it was best to play a little dumb.

'The choppers? Oh yes, a few of my friends and business associates have flown over to enjoy a little getaway.'

'Ahh so it's nothing to do with Pagonis then? I was hoping maybe I could speak to one or two, but if they're just on holiday I wouldn't want to intrude.'

'My dear, we're all far too successful to be afraid of mixing a little business and pleasure. I'm sure they'd be happy to speak to you.'

Ore laughed, if only because she had no idea what to say.

'And how have you and the captain been getting along?' Chuck continued, giving Ore a once-over that made her skin prickle.

She laughed again. 'Oh fine, he's been very helpful.' She kept her tone even and light.

'The two of you together make a very attractive pair.'

It's strange, thought Ore, *how the body can read a situation so much faster than the mind.* Before he had even finished the sentence her heart was beating faster and her muscles had tensed, ready to fight or flee.

'He's a very handsome man, but I am not even remotely successful enough to mix business and pleasure.'

Chuck held her gaze for a moment, and she knew that this was some sort of showdown. She was not about to whimper into the shadows. She held her ground and something akin to excitement seemed to flash across Chuck's face. A predator revelling in the thrill of the chase.

After what felt a beat too long, Chuck laughed. 'Well played, Ore. I'm sure my associates will enjoy your company very much. Come with me.'

He walked ahead and she followed, trying to ignore the gnawing in her stomach.

When they got to the top deck, the half dozen men already had drinks in hand, lazing around the huge glass-top table.

'Here he is at last. Keeping us waiting, Chucky?' One of the men – tall, red-headed and pink-limbed – stood to shake Chuck's hand.

'Treat them mean, keep them keen, eh.' This one was older, maybe in his sixties or even seventies, his hair surprisingly thick for its almost white hue.

'You call this mean? My wallet trembles at the idea of what you think generosity looks like.' This man received a hug from Chuck, and a hearty slap on the back.

One by one he made his way around, before turning to Ore from the head of the table. 'Richard, Gerry, Ousman, Freddie, Claude, Roger . . .' He gestured over to Ore. 'This is Ore. She's a reporter for the *New York Herald* and a very special guest of mine. Please be nice.'

Ore smiled and was glad that her flushing cheeks weren't obvious.

'Hello, all, very nice to meet you,' she said, trying not to sound intimidated but instead sounding overly formal in contrast to all that collegiate banter she'd just witnessed.

'A reporter! Aren't you worried about all those skeletons in the closet, Chucky?' It was the white-haired man again and when he turned back to Ore, he winked.

All the men laughed, although Ore noticed some more than others. Ousman was a serious-looking man, his bald head glinting in the sunlight. Claude too was not as jocular as the rest of them. He was stern, with an almost military-style buzz cut and the sort of pale grey eyes that made his face look otherworldly. He caught Ore's gaze as she scanned over the table, and held it for a moment too long.

'Ore has asked me if she might be able to speak to some of you for the piece she's writing. It's a profile.'

'As long as it's not of you.' The redhead's turn at being the joker.

91

'Unfortunately so.' It was clear from the irritability seeping from Chuck's response that this man did not have the same standing as the elder one. 'But let's not talk shop tonight. We'll do an island trip tomorrow maybe? Ore, you're welcome to join, and then there might be a chance to have a chat with a couple of these rascals.'

Ore was relieved to have an out for this evening – she wasn't sure how much longer she could handle the discomfort of all this male gazing. Maybe tomorrow, after a good night's sleep, she might have reinforced her resilience, and have a decent idea of what questions to ask them.

'That sounds perfect. Thanks, Chuck.' Ore tried to keep the unease out of her tone. 'I'm going to hit the hay, but I look forward to seeing you gentlemen tomorrow.' That wasn't exactly true, but they all smiled and nodded on cue. All apart from Claude, whose grey stare Ore could feel fixated on her.

'Have the kitchen send some dinner to your room, anything you like,' Chuck insisted. And then he added, 'Sweet dreams.' It was a strange thing for Chuck to say, and the way it elicited laughter from the men only made it stranger. After another nervous laugh in response, Ore had to stop herself from breaking into a jog as she retreated from the table and down the stairs. Food and sleep were the last things on her mind right now.

Back in the sanctuary of her cabin, Ore fell back onto the bed and stared at the ceiling. She'd only been on board for forty-eight hours and she felt unmoored. She giggled to herself in the silence thinking of it, the manifestation of that metaphor, lost at sea, losing her footing on unstable ground. All of it was laughably on the nose.

After a moment, her brain kicked back into gear. She needed to make notes, before she forgot those names Chuck had reeled off, or that hushed phone call. She laid them out on the bed, and cross-referenced the names with the list of investors she'd made earlier. *Richard Greenam, Gerry Porter, Ousman Alzahrani, Roger Alderton* were all there, and she guessed that *Freddie* must be Frederik Dolph, but there was no one by the name of Claude. She'd have to ask for his surname tomorrow, but for now she wrote 'on board' for the other names, and a question mark by Claude's.

She recalled Chuck's phone call on the deck. She wrote down 'clow-par-ten?', circled it and then wrote 'cloup-arten' and underlined it. Her brain felt as confused as the words on the page, but it also felt calmer for not having to be their sole guardian.

It occurred to her that it might be wise to keep all her musings in a safe place. After scouring the room and finding no safe, she thought about stuffing the papers under her bed. *And then what happens when the stewardess comes in?* A silly idea. In the end she settled on placing them between the folds of her beach towel. In retrospect it had been a complete waste of luggage space anyway, as if a billionaire's mega yacht wouldn't provide her with its own supply of towels.

As she got ready for bed, her mind wandered to Daniel. That incident in the kitchen felt like a lifetime ago already, but if she concentrated she could remember the heat of his palm on her bare shoulder with freakish clarity. Not only the physical sensation, but the immediacy with which it had brought her back into her own body, lassoed her dissociated mind back into place.

And then later, when she'd snapped at him about Chuck, she hadn't expected that wounded look. She also hadn't expected to feel so guilty. Daniel was nice, but she barely knew the man.

She wondered if she fancied him, thinking back to meeting him. She had been struck by his good looks, and she had enjoyed charming him, as she did most men. On paper he was certainly a catch, if you set aside the fact that he was a potential source. There was the small matter of him being totally unavailable to her, in the sense that he lived thousands of miles away, at sea, but her dating track record might suggest that that hadn't always been a deterrent.

But the problem was that she was wondering – usually she knew almost instantaneously if she would sleep with a man. That familiar fluttering in her stomach – she hadn't felt it with Daniel. She must not then, she concluded, fancy him, and yet . . . here she was worrying she'd hurt his feelings.

It was just another puzzle for her mind to obsess over, and she had enough mysteries to solve on this boat. It was time to sleep. Tomorrow was another day, perhaps to get answers, but more likely to discover yet more questions.

Chapter 19

Daniel

It was midnight, and Daniel was growing restless. Usually he enjoyed this time alone, with just his own company and the expanse of inky ocean, but tonight he couldn't relax into it. He had tried everything – tuning in to the country music show he liked, reading his book on the manufacturing history of the Apache helicopter, even casting that downloaded episode of *Birds of a Feather* – but nothing would calm his racing thoughts.

He was annoyed that everyone was hell-bent on confiding in him. Vicky, Dudley, Ore, even Chuck – everyone wanted him in their confidence and he found the role nothing but stressful. At around quarter to one he decided that it wouldn't hurt to leave the wheelhouse and stretch his legs for a little bit. The boat was on course and on autopilot. It wasn't technically allowed, but everyone seemed to be overstepping at the moment, so he would too.

Daniel wandered out into the night. It was cool and he took a moment to revel in the silence of the waves. The constant hush quieted the frantic thoughts in his head slightly. He wasn't a man taken to strolling without purpose, and so he decided to lap each of the three main decks and then head back to his post.

As he walked the perimeter of the second deck, he was

startled to find a figure hunched over the dining table. He would have to pass them if he wanted to complete the circuit, but he was reluctant to talk to anybody. As he dithered, the figure turned, the blue-tinged light from her open laptop shading Agatha's face a ghoulish grey.

'Sorry to interrupt – I'll leave you to it.'

Agatha was certainly not someone who would soothe his jangled nerves.

'No, don't apologise. I shouldn't be up anyway . . .' She sighed heavily, and Daniel worried that he was unwittingly inviting a confessional. 'How are you doing?' It had not been at all like what he had expected her to say next. He was momentarily stunned.

'Er . . . I'm OK, just having to man the boat overnight as we re-set course . . . for . . .'

'Ahh yes, the Barrier Reef; sorry, I didn't even realise that that would affect you like that . . .' She shook her head softly, her vacant gaze crying of exhaustion. 'I'm sure Chuck doesn't have a clue either – not that that would make a difference.' After a beat she seemed to register what she had just said. 'God, that was . . . you didn't hear that from me.'

She laughed nervously and looked up at Daniel, an almost pleading expression on her face. She looked young, thought Daniel. Her severe, dark-rimmed glasses were holding back her pencil-straight fringe, which was sticking up at odd angles, and something about seeing her face so exposed made her seem barely older than a teenager.

'It's OK, I'm not going to tell anyone. I have no interest in gossip.' He had meant it sincerely, but she laughed, and he felt like he had done a good thing. She shut her laptop.

Daniel stood awkwardly. He wasn't sure what the politest way out of this chance encounter was, but Agatha turned her chair, and then the one beside her, leaning back and looking at him expectantly.

'It's OK, I don't bite. I just . . . Would you mind just sitting with me for a moment? I feel like the only human company I've had recently is someone I work for – which doesn't count.'

Daniel took the seat, scooting it back and slightly further away from her. Before he had even settled, she began.

'I guess what I'm trying to grapple with is, will it ever be enough? Where does it end? If I do a bad job . . . Well that's basically not an option, and if I do a good job, that's just setting the bar even higher, and guess who has to clear it next time? Me.'

She folded her arms and huffed. Daniel felt that he was supposed to say something in response.

'How long have you worked for Chuck?' An innocuous enough question.

'Just under two years. I started straight out of uni . . . well as an intern originally and then he offered me the personal assistant role, which was not exactly what I had in mind but, well, I could hardly say no . . .'

'Why not?'

Agatha looked at him like he was deluded. 'You don't turn down a job at Pagonis; everybody else on my course would kill to work there.'

'Is working for Pagonis the same thing as working for Chuck?' As soon as he said it, he realised that it sounded pointed. He hadn't meant it like that – he was genuinely confused about corporate structuring.

Agatha looked so dejected, Daniel worried she might start crying. 'No, I guess it's not,' she said quietly.

Daniel's attempts to stay out of everything were failing. He could see that, and even if he didn't like it, he couldn't keep doing the same thing and expecting a different result. He'd read somewhere that that was the definition of madness. In the spirit of remaining solutions-focused he decided to try an innovative method. He leant in slightly.

'I didn't mean to upset you, Agatha,' he began tentatively, but as he saw her face brighten, he felt emboldened to keep going. 'But you shouldn't worry – you're obviously very bright, and doing very well for yourself. You're probably earning more than me.'

Agatha beamed, her mood transformed. 'Probably,' she said. Daniel decided not to dwell on the overtone of smugness. 'I just wish I was a little more appreciated.'

'If you don't mind me asking, how old are you?' It wasn't a wholly appropriate question, but his curiosity was getting the better of him.

'Twenty-four,' she said warily, 'but I'll be twenty-five next month.'

'You're still so young, Agatha, and I think that part of being that young, and in your first job, is that you have to pay your dues, often without much fanfare.' He remembered Jack, the first officer who had trained him as a bosun, saying something very similar when Daniel was feeling particularly impatient about proving himself.

Agatha shrugged. It was interesting, he thought, how she could be so formidable, so ruthlessly efficient and yet so childish.

There was a long silence. And then, almost in a whisper, Agatha said, 'Sometimes I'm not sure that Chuck is a good person.'

This was dangerous territory, for them both.

'I think it's quite normal to feel that way about your boss.' Daniel hoped his tone was reassuring. He leant forward further. 'Ore hasn't been receiving only glowing reviews about him, but I think people generally think Chuck isn't a bad person, just that he's . . . particular.'

Agatha looked Daniel in the eyes intently and offered a kind smile. She looked down momentarily, and when she caught his gaze again there was something he didn't expect to see in her eyes. He realised just too late what it was: longing.

Her lips only brushed his before his body caught up with his brain and he jerked away suddenly. For a split second they exchanged a shared expression of shock and then hers melted into embarrassment and his into vacancy.

He had overstepped, he had gone against his instincts, and he was paying the price. Of course she had misinterpreted his kindness.

This is what happened in the world of yachting. He'd seen it: the excessive drinking, the clumsy advances, the chaotic fallout. Drama, that's what he'd seen in his eleven years on boats, and up until this very moment, he had managed to exist in its periphery. Now he was in the midst of it.

He stood up slowly, wary that any sudden movements might be misconstrued. He needn't have worried. Agatha had lowered her head into her hands. She was completely still as he backed away.

'Good evening, Agatha,' he said. He could hear how cold

and formal he sounded, but it was for the best. And then, when she didn't respond, and he saw her shoulders begin to shake rhythmically, he added, 'I'm sorry.' Even then, the words were devoid of meaning, a triplet of silence-plugging syllables, before he turned and walked back to the wheelhouse.

Later when he was finally relieved from his shift by Dudley at 5 a.m., he found himself unable to remember anything specific from their interaction, apart from the fact that it had happened. He knew that he had spoken to her about Chuck and tried to comfort her, he knew she had tried to kiss him, but he couldn't recall the exact words or even what her face looked like up close. It was as though his brain had decided to simply erase this strange anomaly, as it was such an outlier.

Daniel was not a good sleeper. Most nights he would find himself reaching for his phone to play, ironically, 'ocean sounds sleep aid playlist'. The room had to be blacked out and still he would wear an eye mask. On this particular night though, he got into bed, turned the light off, and before he had time to think it all through, he was asleep.

Chapter 20

Ore

Day 3

Ore woke up with a start. She had the sense that she had been running, and as the cogs of her conscious brain began to whir she surmised that she must have been dreaming. There was, quite literally, nowhere to run on the *Lady Thalassa*. She stretched, rolled out of bed and pondered her reflection in the mirror.

She inspected her chin for stray hairs, her nose for open pores, her forehead for fine lines. Everything seemed to be in order, so she decided to move on to arguably more pressing matters. She earthed out her pages of notes – the sparse timeline, the investor list, the web page prints – and began writing down questions for each of Chuck's merry band of rich men.

When she was done, she bundled them up in her notebook, tucked it under her arm and bounded up the stairs. She was about halfway up when she realised she had no idea where she was meant to go. Presumably her solo breakfast with Chuck was not a regular thing.

She was dithering on the stairs when a man in chef's whites appeared at the top of them. She amused herself with the thought that she had magicked him into existence to cook her breakfast and then worried she was really losing it.

'Hello? Excuse me?' The man had an almost comically French accent. He came slowly down the stairs, until he was standing over her, a couple of steps up.

'Sorry, I . . . I don't really know where I'm going.' She shrugged.

He shook his head thoughtfully. 'In a way, that is a trapping of the human condition.' His tone was so sincere that Ore was at a loss for how to proceed.

They stared at each other for a moment. The man was probably in his late thirties, Ore thought, Middle Eastern maybe? Well French obviously, if the accent was anything to go by, but also brown. Eventually she landed on: 'I was just looking for breakfast actually.'

'Above or below deck?' He pointed first up the stairs, and then downwards as he spoke. Ore wasn't sure if he was being sarcastic. When he turned to look at her quizzically, she figured he was merely being very literal.

'That's the issue, I'm not sure.'

He thrust his hand towards her, palm outstretched in greeting, but the movement was so sudden that it made Ore jump.

'I'm terribly sorry, how rude of me. My name is Carlos, Carlos Aminé. I am the head chef.'

Ore took his hand, and he shook it animatedly.

'Ore, nice to meet you.' He was a good-looking man, with a beard so dark and sharply groomed that it could have been drawn onto his chin. His smile was wide and easy.

'I would personally recommend that below the deck is a better option for you. The men with Mr Regas, they are not always . . . easy company.' Carlos gave her a knowing look; Ore felt frustrated that she was not in on said knowing.

'In what way?' She cocked her head to the side and tried out her best curiously clueless expression. But it had the opposite to the desired effect. Carlos' smile stiffened and he just laughed nervously without answering the question.

'Come with me. I will take you to breakfast,' he said instead, and ushered Ore back down the stairs, down another nondescript grey-carpeted corridor and then, somehow, they were at the mess again, coming through a different door to the previous time. She was never going to get the hang of this place.

Inside, Vicky and the first officer were talking in hushed tones, stopping immediately upon seeing Ore and Carlos. On the table were remnants of breakfast, a couple of croissants, a large pan of solidifying porridge, a bowl of fruit salad, almost untouched, and a few rashers of bacon on a greasy plate.

Carlos turned to Ore. 'Sorry, my dear, I thought there would be more left.' He gestured towards the table, most of it covered in empty plates and bowls. 'And what are you two gossiping about?' This was directed at the pair in front of him.

'Haven't you heard?' The first officer – Ore couldn't remember if she'd been formally introduced to him yet – was the sort of conventionally attractive man that she'd seen her white classmates swoon over. Sandy wavy hair, a light stubble, a square jaw and, most importantly, an abundance of height. Ore got surfer vibes from him, but maybe that was just the Australian accent playing tricks. That's not to say that she was immune to his good looks, but she'd had her fair fill of white boys at Columbia and the novelty had worn off.

'Heard what?' Carlos asked.

The first officer shot Ore a suspicious look. 'I'm not sure I can say with . . . others in the room.'

'Oh I'm sorry I didn't mean to intrude.' It was clear that the majority of the people in the room did not want her there, but Carlos was having none of it.

'Nonsense! You must eat.' He ushered Ore into a seat and she took it awkwardly, picking up a pastry and trying to chew in a way that seemed appreciative.

Carlos nodded his approval and then turned his attention back to his crewmates. 'What is it that you're trying to say, Dudley? Spit it out.'

In response Dudley crossed his arms. Ore could feel the rage radiating off him. She had no idea who it was directed at, but it was palpably uncomfortable.

'It's the guy – he's back on board.' Vicky spoke up. Ore understood that the cryptic act was for her benefit.

'The guy?' Carlos was no more enlightened and Ore could see the frustration blooming across Vicky's face.

'The guy that . . . messed with Annie.' Vicky spoke slowly, cautiously holding Carlos' gaze until the switch flipped over to understanding.

'Ahhhh' and then, as the cogs kept turning: 'Oh no, that is very bad. I cannot believe Mr Chuck would allow that . . .'

'Carlos!' Vicky hissed and jerked her head towards Ore. He had revealed too much, apparently, but it was too late. Ore was determined to find out who Annie was.

Carlos waved his hand dismissively. 'You worry too much, Vicky. She is one of us – "below the deck", as you say.'

'She's literally a journalist, Carlos. Her job is to snoop.' Vicky looked over at Ore, having up until then acted as though she were not in the room. 'No offence,' she offered half-heartedly.

Ore smiled, hoping the exchange could be laughed off – 'none taken!' – but Vicky had already turned back to Carlos.

'I did not know,' he admitted, and then to Ore he continued, 'but you can promise all of this is uhh, how to say . . . off the recording?'

'Off the record? Yes, of course. I wouldn't reveal the sources for anything I publish to anyone without their consent.'

Carlos smiled triumphantly at Vicky, who rolled her eyes. Dudley remained silent and fuming in the corner, his eyes trained on the half-finished bowl of cereal in front of him.

Ore was used to people not liking journalists but the hostility in the room was growing ever more intense. She had at least learnt that Carlos would be a great person to interview, and that there was something dodgy going on with someone on the boat and a woman named Annie, which was more intel than she'd managed to gather from the whole previous day of interviews.

She quickly finished off her pastry and made her excuses. 'Thank you for breakfast, Carlos; maybe I can catch up with you later. I'd love to hear more about life on the boat.'

'I bet you would,' Vicky muttered under her breath, just loud enough for everyone to hear. Ore ignored it and Carlos nodded enthusiastically.

'Nice to meet you, Dudley.' At the mention of his name he seemed to snap back into reality.

'Yep, sure, you too.' It was unconvincing, but Ore was grateful that she'd at least elicited a response.

In her hurry to leave she went through yet another door leading out of the mess and found herself out on the deck.

Chapter 21

Daniel

The blare of Daniel's alarm reached him in the depths of unconsciousness, and dragged him to the surface. It was unusual for him, to feel like he had slept deeply. His limbs were heavy and the folds of his pillowcase imprinted on his cheek. He felt groggy.

He sat up and rubbed his eyes before remembering the events of the night before, at which point he froze. Perhaps in some vain hope that this too was some extended part of a dream, he pinched himself lightly on the wrist, and then felt ridiculous and reached over to turn off the alarm.

In the newly expectant silence of the room, he ran through his plan of action and realised it was simple: he was going to pretend nothing had happened. At first the idea of maintaining another lie fizzed a current of stress through his body, but as he settled into the idea that no was likely to ask him anything about last night directly, he calmed himself down. And then there was Agatha. She was young, sure, but he trusted her instinct for ambition would override any temptation to cause a scene.

As he showered and dressed, he managed to steer his mind back on course, planning for the day ahead. He would walk the deck, have something to eat, and take over from Dudley this afternoon. Daniel liked to do this, to walk himself through the day; he thought of it as getting a head start.

On his lap of the ship, he consciously avoided the deck where he had seen Agatha the night before. He knew, rationally, that it was highly unlikely she would be there again this morning, but he couldn't shake that disturbingly *irrational* niggling that he would be tempting fate if he went back to the scene of the crime. Instead he lapped round the bottom deck twice.

He saw Ore before she saw him, from the shadow of the awning over the dining table. He watched as she came out of the mess, walked across the deck and settled into the obnoxiously long outdoor sofa just outside the sliding doors into the salon.

She looked like she was writing something in the tatty reporter's pad she carried around. Bent over slightly and with her legs curled up beneath her, he found himself noting the glints of gold crowning her hair, and the way the sunlight seemed to make the angelic lines of her face glow.

Almost without thinking, he made his way over to Ore. When she heard him approach she looked up and smiled, and he felt his breath catch slightly.

'Hey, Captain!' She seemed genuinely pleased to see him, putting her notepad down on the seat beside her, though she did remember to close it first, Daniel noted.

'Sorry again about yesterday. I am around most of the day today though, if you need me.' He offered what he hoped was an easy smile.

'No worries at all, I was a little . . . all over the place yesterday anyway. Feeling more clear-headed today.' There was that candidness again, and she was unapologetic about it. Was he envious or put off? He didn't know.

107

'I'm speaking to some of Chuck's investors today, so I'm assuming at some point he'll ask you to "supervise me".' Ore winked at him playfully and once again he was pleased for the discretion his dark skin offered when it came to the rising heat in his cheeks.

'Although,' Ore continued – obliviously, hoped Daniel, 'I guess if you're manning this boat then someone else will take us out on the island?'

That caught Daniel's attention. He didn't like the idea of Ore going off with Chuck and his creepy investors on her own.

'I'm actually hoping to corner that Claude guy. He's so mysterious, I can hardly find anything about him online.' Ore had lowered her voice and brought her hand up to her mouth. As though she were following a stage direction, she darted her eyes from left to right and raised an eyebrow.

Daniel realised he was supposed to laugh, but he'd missed his chance and Ore cleared her throat a little self-consciously and leant back in her seat. Daniel's mind was racing in different directions and it took him a moment to catch up with the loudest one. *It's a bad idea for Ore to be alone with Claude.*

'Daniel, are you OK?'

He needed to say something. 'I'm sure Dudley can cover for me, then I can relieve the bosun and take you guys out on the tender myself.' Maybe if he was there, he could make sure nothing untoward went on. He resigned himself to inserting himself into 'the drama' but after what he had inferred about Claude from Dudley, he was sure that he didn't want Ore to face anything like the situation with Annie.

'Oh no no, don't bother yourself with all that, if it's a hassle to change plans now.' Ore was gathering up her notes.

'Mr Regas wants me there if you're interviewing people anyway.' This was not exactly a lie; he was expecting that Chuck would probably command his presence at the last minute for this day trip. But it was not exactly the truth either.

Ore shrugged. 'I guess that tracks. Anything you think I need to bring? I've never been on a speedboat before.' Ore's excitement was infectious and he decided to worry about his ever more problematic relationship to truth-telling later.

'You'll need a hat. This South Pacific sun is no joke, and maybe, you know, more generally cover up a bit.' He sounded so parochial, but she was wearing a tight khaki tank top with very thin straps. The ozone layer would not be forgiving. Neither would the gaze of a man like Claude. Daniel himself was finding it hard to banish the intrusive thought of what it would feel like to trace the tip of his finger along her collarbone. It was certainly not his belief that women were to be blamed for men's perverse brains, but in this scenario a long sleeve would be useful protection, in more ways than she could know.

'And maybe a packet of those Kwells if there are any left,' he added. The trip would not be long, but if her first day on the boat was anything to go by, it could get messy without seasickness medication.

She looked up at him then with an expression he hadn't seen before. Not cheeky, playful or borderline flirtatious, but something softer. A warmer version of the scared look she had given him in the kitchen after her 'episode'.

'That was you? I just assumed Vicky had left it.' Ahh, he thought, the look of sincere thanks. Again he felt a flush. Suddenly he couldn't look at her directly, so instead he fixed his gaze on the cuff of his jacket and picked at a loose thread.

'It was nothing – I have some left over.' He sneaked a peek at her face and she looked bemused.

'*You* get seasick?'

'Well, no, but I used to, when I started out. I'm a firm believer that you can grow sea legs. So when we get a new recruit, I always make sure to find the ones looking a bit, well, green, and offer them a couple of tabs of Kwells. I know what it's like to feel as if you don't belong – sometimes it can be as easy as knowing that you're allowed to need help, to start to feel differently.'

Ore nodded thoughtfully, holding his gaze in a way that made his palms sweat but that he couldn't break. 'I know exactly what you mean,' she said quietly.

It seemed to occur to her suddenly that they had been staring at each other in silence for slightly too long. She looked down, stood up and began mumbling about getting herself together. Daniel felt like he had been hypnotised, somehow unable to arrange his thoughts into working order.

'I'm just going to go change, you know . . . sleeves . . .' she laughed nervously '. . . and you know get questions together and . . .' When she caught his eye again, he just nodded. She laughed again and trotted off inside.

Daniel didn't move for a minute or so. He could think only of golden braids and supple shoulders. Finally a plan crystallised in his head; he needed to talk to Dudley and then somehow get Chuck to agree to let him take the tender out instead of the bosun, Fida. And then he needed to keep Ore away from Claude. That, he suspected, would be the hardest part. Ore wanted to get him alone, and Daniel couldn't really imagine anyone *not* wanting to spend time alone with Ore alone. At least he could keep an eye on things.

Chapter 22

Ore

Ore heeded Daniel's advice and donned a long-sleeved shirt and white linen trousers. She slathered herself in suncream and even dug out a baseball cap she'd jammed into her suitcase. With her sunglasses on, she looked like she was a fugitive in disguise, or at least a celebrity avoiding the paps.

Down on the lower deck, she found that she was also glad for the lack of skin on show in front of Chuck and his accomplices. She could feel their eyes on her as she walked down the stairs to greet them.

'Hello, Ore, how did you sleep?' Chuck walked over to meet her at the bottom of the staircase and for a dreadful moment she thought he was going to hug her. He seemed equally unsure of his own movements as he reached her and ended up awkwardly outstretching his hand for her to shake. Ore was puzzled to see him fumble; evidently he was not the confident alpha of this pack that she had assumed him to be.

Even more agonising than their exchange was that it set the tone for the other men, who filed past her one by one, offering their own palm-crushing handshakes. Each one mumbled a pleasantry: 'morning', 'pleasure to have you with us', 'nice to see you' et cetera. All except for Claude, whose grey gaze held hers for a minute too long and framed a smile that made the hairs on the back of her neck stand up. He didn't say anything, just waited until she broke eye contact and looked down, chuckling softly when she blushed.

Once they had all filed past, Chuck stood apart from everyone to address them.

'Richard, Ousman, Freddie, Claude, you guys are coming out with me on the boat, I gather. Agatha will be out in a moment to talk through the itinerary. Gerry and Roger have "too much work to do", apparently, and will be staying here.'

At Chuck's use of air quotes, Gerry chuckled, adding: 'Yes, securing you your next twenty-million-dollar injection!' All the men laughed, apart from Claude.

Chuck called for Agatha, and as though she had been waiting in the wings for her cue, she appeared almost immediately at the top of the stairs.

'Hello, boys!' she cooed. Ore had only ever seen Agatha in what she thought of as 'all business' mode. She usually wore a button-down shirt, a pair of neutral pencil-leg trousers and nondescript flats. Now here she was in a dress: above the knee, with the exact type of thin straps that Ore had been warned against, and in a bright shade of pink, all coupled with white trainers. Her usually pencil-straight platinum bob was tied into stubby pigtails at the nape of her neck. She looked like she was auditioning for the part of 'fun-loving sorority sister'.

Her reinvention was not going unnoticed. The men cheered as she came down to join them. Richard even pulled her in for a hug. Although she played it off well, Ore spotted

Agatha's look of bewilderment, quickly masked, as he did so.

'So, in about ten minutes we'll all head down to the boat. We'll be joined by Carlos, our head chef, who will be setting up a beach barbecue for us later on; Nicole, one of our lovely stewardesses; Oscar, one of our deckhands; and the captain himself, Daniel Wilsons, at the helm – so we're in good hands.'

Ore couldn't be sure, but she thought she heard an edge of something when Agatha said Daniel's name. All the same, she found herself quietly pleased that Daniel was coming along. There was something about his presence that made her feel . . . safer? Or maybe calmer? She couldn't quite explain it.

It was a strange thing for her to feel about a man. Her dad had never been around and she'd grown up with her older sister and mother, a true matriarchy. Being around women was what made her feel at home. Men were for adventure, excitement, and more than occasionally, for heartbreak. Kyle had been the first man she'd ever felt truly understood by. Theirs had been a relationship, if she could call it that, of intense mutual care. But there had always been a current of something electrically dangerous between them. Even though he had tried so hard to neutralise it, it was never fully extinguished.

Daniel though, despite the little time she had known him, made her feel steady, grounded. There was nothing dangerous about him. Ore was grateful for that here.

Everyone milled around as Agatha flitted off to ensure final preparations were complete. Ore drifted towards Richard, or 'Dickie' as he insisted on being called. He was probably in his mid-sixties, Ore estimated, with the deep tan of a rich white man who can afford to chase the sun around the globe. His fingers, which a little too often found themselves resting on Ore's shoulder, or elbow, or waist, were thick and encircled by silver rings. His watch looked as though it probably cost more than Ore's Columbia degree.

He was pleasant enough to talk to, laughing abundantly at her witty remarks on the state of US politics, asking her questions about her upbringing and education, only name-dropping a few times.

'Well when I holidayed with the Clintons in the 1990s it would have never occurred to me to worry about being seen with them – these days though with social media, it only takes one picture of you with the "wrong people" and suddenly you're enmeshed in a dozen conspiracy theories and your board is telling you to keep a low profile.' He shook his head solemnly. 'I guess that's why I value my time on board the *Thalassa*, nothing like international waters to shield you from the prying eyes of the public.'

Ore made the appropriate sounds in response, something akin to offering her condolences. She had spent time in similar circles at Columbia, with the moneyed parents of her classmates. She often found herself wondering if they simply forgot that she was not from 'their world', or if there was something about extreme wealth that sheltered people from the feeling that their life experiences were totally unrelatable. Maybe it was just what happened when you were so accustomed to having people listen to you. Maybe it was just natural to end up believing that everything you said was insightful and interesting.

Just as Richard began to wax lyrical about his time starting out in the London Financial District in the Eighties, Agatha came to Ore's rescue.

'Excuse me, Dickie, I hate to interrupt but we're all making our way to the boat now, if you'd like to follow me.'

'We'd better be off, after you, Miss . . . ? Sorry what was your name again? I'm terribly forgetful in my old age.'

Here we go, thought Ore. 'Ballou-Adu,' she said as they followed Agatha.

'How wonderfully exotic, and where are you from?' Richard paused, frowning slightly as he inspected her face for clues of her racial origins. 'Originally?'

Ore heaved an internal sigh, preparing herself for the choreography of this conversation. 'My parents are from Haiti and Nigeria.' She mirrored his pause, in a way she hoped was pointed without being confrontational. 'Originally.'

'Ah Haiti, such a beautiful place, what a shame it's turned out the way it has.' It was one of the more irritating responses Ore had contended with, but she plastered a smile on her face.

'I've never been, but yes I hear it's beautiful.' That seemed to satisfy him, the acknowledgement that he was both worldly and benevolent towards the less fortunate.

In her mind she had imagined the 'tender' to be a small speed boat, the sort of thing that you could fit half a dozen people into, where you'd be able to feel the mist of the sea on your face as you raced through the waves. What they were actually being herded onto looked like a yacht itself. A sort of younger sister to the *Lady Thalassa*.

The deck they walked onto had a large dining table set with ten places, and the requisite row of white loungers at the bow. She suspected there were even bedrooms on board, judging by the row of portholes. She held on to the railing tightly as she made her way over the gangway.

Ore didn't realise how tense she had been feeling until she spotted Daniel, welcoming the other investors, and her shoulders relaxed.

Chapter 23

Daniel

Ore looks good in white, he thought. Daniel was trying to concentrate on welcoming everyone onto the boat but he found himself instead mentally tracking Ore's whereabouts as the guests mingled on the deck. He held himself back from walking over to her, redoubling the effort when she looked over at him and offered up that brilliant smile. Instead he nodded a hello and busied himself at the helm. It was also a useful tactic for avoiding Agatha – he hadn't figured out quite yet how to navigate that situation. Luckily for him, her hot pink dress made it easy to keep tabs on her and avert his gaze as needed.

'I didn't think you would be taking us out today?' It was Chuck, standing in front of him with his hands stuffed into the deep pockets of his cargo shorts.

'Um, yes, sorry, I thought I'd leave Dudley to it. Makes more sense than switching him out.' Daniel kept his voice even. He was getting better at the whole 'half-truths' thing.

'Hmm, yes I suppose so.' Chuck didn't sound convinced, and Daniel avoided eye contact by fiddling with the levels in front of him. 'And you're sure it doesn't have anything to do with a certain someone joining us on board today?' Chuck raised an eyebrow and Daniel's composure began to slip.

'No, sir, I um . . . I just thought that . . .' he fumbled, and Chuck slapped him on the back with a chuckle.

'Don't worry, Wilsons, your secret's safe with me. I don't blame you at all; she's a pretty specimen, that's for sure, and dare I say the pair of you would . . . make a lot of sense together.' Daniel understood that Chuck was trying out some 'man-to-man' camaraderie, but the leer of his gaze as he looked over to Ore stoked a wave of rage in Daniel. He was also attuned to the subtle implications that came with Chuck saying that they 'made a lot of sense'. They were the only two black people on this boat, after all.

'I'm not sure what you mean, sir.' Daniel decided to play dumb.

'Of course you don't, Wilsons,' Chuck said with a wink. 'Anyway, anything I should know that came out of yesterday's interviews?'

'No, sir, everyone was very discreet.' It was true: nobody had really said anything of importance to Ore, but even if they had, Daniel felt less and less sure he would be feeding back to Chuck as he had originally intended to.

'Good to hear.' Chuck stood for a moment, as if he had something else to add, and then turned and walked back over to his guests.

Daniel peeked over to see Ore standing with Claude to one side. She was smiling and speaking animatedly whilst Claude stood stony-faced. Daniel bristled, but he had a job to do: getting the boat to the island in time for Carlos and the rest of the crew to set up their barbecue. Besides, Claude wouldn't dare do anything in broad daylight with everyone around him like this. Daniel comforted himself with that thought as he steered the boat away from the *Thalassa* and into open water.

Once on the waves, Daniel relaxed a little, as the sound of the wind in his ears and the sun on his face reminded him what he was here for. On mega yachts like Chuck's it was easy to forget you were even at sea. Sometimes he missed the early days of his career, back when he was up on deck all day, mucking in, outside, with the sea air both comforting and exhausting him. These days, he often spent the entire day sat inside the wheelhouse, separated from the breeze by a thick pane of glass.

He caught shards of laughter and conversation from the deck, where the guests were mostly leaning against the railings, holding drinks, chatting happily. Ore had her back to him, looking out at sea, the hulk of Claude by her side, standing a little too close. They didn't seem to be talking to each other. The loose linen of Ore's shirt rippled and Daniel thought of the fairy tern, a delicate white seabird with piercing dark eyes. Claude, in his mud-coloured cargo trousers and khaki T-shirt, embodied something more predatory. Daniel felt the same helpless distress he did when he watched what documentary narrators called the law of the jungle.

He peeled his eyes away and tried to focus on the horizon. A flit of pink across his eyeline caught his attention and he glanced over to see Agatha, uncharacteristically giggling at a joke from one of the old men. He wasn't sure which one it was; he presumed he was someone who had something that Agatha wanted. In the brief time he'd known her, it was clear she wasn't someone who wasted time with unbeneficial flattery. Suddenly she looked over, and Daniel's heart began beating with a surge of panic. As their eyes locked, he chastised himself for getting caught staring. What if she misinterpreted it as some kind of flirtatious exchange? Before he looked away, he caught a glimpse of something like triumph in her eyes as she snaked her hand up the old man's arm. This was a game for her, just what Daniel had feared.

He checked the coordinates for the island. They were making good time with the wind behind them. Focusing on the waves once again, another movement caught his attention. A khaki-clad arm in the midst of white. Ore was doubled over, her seasickness apparently not 'kwelled', and Claude was rubbing her back. Daniel had to fight the instinct to leave the wheel and drag Claude away from her. His reaction was so visceral, it took him by surprise, and when he looked down his knuckles were paling around the wheel.

Just then one of the stewardesses – Nicole, he thought her name was, a sturdy woman with a mop of tight auburn curls – rushed over to Ore. As she unclasped her from Claude's grip and walked her off the deck inside, Daniel felt himself calm. The predator interrupted just in time.

Ore didn't resurface for the rest of the short journey. Daniel slowed the boat as they approached the island and Oscar, the deckhand, helped him drop the anchor. Rather ridiculously, they would now have to get the dinghy in the water to get everyone to shore. The third and final seafaring Russian doll.

'I'm assuming you have experience with this kind of vessel?' he asked Oscar. Daniel was a little embarrassed to admit that he had barely interacted with any of the junior crew since he'd been on board, so his question sounded overly formal.

'Yes, sir, of course. I used to drive my father's bowrider every summer'. *Of course you did*, thought Daniel, taking note of Oscar's perfectly tousled hair and almost alarmingly white teeth. He had to remind himself, often, just how much of the world of yachting was rich kids looking for a couple of summers' worth of pocket money, before they turned in their polo shirts for tailored suits. He was the anomaly.

'Right, great, let's get the first load of guests on board then.'

Agatha strolled over to Daniel as he was talking to Oscar. 'Is there space for Dickie and I, Captain Wilsons?' She cocked her head to one side, a smug smile on her face and an arm linked through the old man's.

'Are you trying to get us preferential treatment, Aggy?' Dickie chuckled, and Agatha joined in, although hers was shallow and, to Daniel, unconvincing.

'Of course, Oscar, would you help Mr . . .' Daniel's mind went blank.

'Greenam,' Agatha said empathetically after a moment, as though wanting to catch Daniel out. Presumably Richard Greenam was the sort of name you should just know, in Agatha's mind. The kind of high-net-worth individual she made it her business to acquaint herself with.

'Mr Greenam, if you'd like to make your way over to the dinghy.' He bowed his head and gestured towards the galley. He could feel Agatha's gaze trained on him, willing him to look up, but he didn't until they had gone. After them the tall Scandinavian man, 'Mr Dolph', and the Middle Eastern guy, who everyone just called 'Ousman', clambered into the dinghy. A thumbs up from Oscar and they were motoring off towards the shore.

Daniel was aware that Claude was hanging back, and turned to him. 'I'm sure there is room for one more, sir.'

The grey eyes were unblinking, and Daniel felt a shiver run down his spine as they inspected his face.

After a beat too long, in which Claude held his stare, he finally replied, 'It is OK. I will wait for the next transfer.' Daniel could not place his accent. German perhaps, though his W's didn't sound like V's; then again, maybe that was just something they exaggerated in World War Two films.

Was he waiting for Ore? Daniel was driving himself crazy, totally unsure whether he was accurately reading into Claude's actions.

Chuck wandered out onto the deck, slipping the phone from his ear and back into his pocket. 'Sorry about that, folks. Are we there yet?'

'Yes, Mr Regas, just waiting for the dinghy to come back.'

'Good job, Danny boy.'

Daniel cringed. He hadn't thought it could get much worse than Dan, yet here they were.

'Where's our dear lady journalist?' Chuck asked, holding his hand to shield himself from the sun as he identified the five figures bumping over the waves.

'She's *zeik* . . . how do you say that in English?'

Chuck shrugged. 'Christ, Claude, I don't know, Flemish is hardly a universal language.' Chuck's tone was lightly mocking. He chuckled to himself, but Daniel noticed it falter quickly into silence in the face of Claude's piercing stare.

'Sick, she is being sick,' Claude said flatly. How strange it was to see Chuck embroiled in a power dynamic where he was not in the driving seat.

'Poor thing,' Chuck replied meekly. Claude said nothing, simply turning to look out to sea.

The three men stood, silently watching as the dinghy pulled up to shore in the distance, and the passengers got out. As it sped back towards them, Ore and Nicole emerged from below deck. Ore was looking worse for wear, ashen-faced with a film of sweat coating her forehead.

'We'll be on firmer ground soon enough, just one short little ride further,' Nicole said soothingly, as she guided Ore to where the men were standing. Ore looked like even the mention of 'one short little ride' was enough to make her vomit. But she nodded stoically.

'Are you feeling better?' The sympathy seemed alien coming from Claude's mouth, Daniel thought.

'Yes, thank you, Claude.' Ore managed a small smile, and Claude returned something similar, although it didn't warm his eyes like it did hers.

'Everyone ready?' It was Oscar, calling out from the boat.

Everyone apart from Nicole, who was helping Ore with hers, donned their life jackets and climbed in. It was a bit of a tight squeeze with five passengers. Ore was sandwiched between Daniel and Claude. As Oscar drove the boat towards the island, Daniel tried to think of anything but the overwhelming awareness that his arm and leg were pressed up against Ore's.

Chapter 24

Ore

Peristéri Island (property of Chuck Regas)

Ore felt awash with relief to be standing on dry land. Apparently there was a limit to how much seasickness pills could achieve, especially if you threw them up within half an hour of taking them. Daniel had helped her off the boat, and the concern in his eyes had embarrassed her. She was supposed to be working, not another one of Chuck's high-maintenance guests.

The island was almost obscenely idyllic. Ore imagined it couldn't take longer than about thirty minutes to walk round the entire perimeter of it. An oblong of luscious green encircled by a wide band of demerara sugar sand, tapering into shallow turquoise water. It seemed uninhabited, not a building to be seen. Ore concluded that Chuck probably owned it.

Agatha was sitting with a glass of what looked like champagne in hand, on a large picnic blanket. All three of the men sitting around her appeared to be amused by what she had to say. Ore was finding this personality shift from Agatha both bizarre and intriguing.

'There's drinks, nibbles and another blanket in the hamper. I'm going to head back to get Nicole and the rest of the supplies now, sir.' Oscar was holding both his hands behind his back as he spoke, his head lowered slightly. Ore found the subservient hierarchy of the boat uncomfortably feudal.

'Thanks, Oscar,' Chuck and Daniel said in unison. Ore cringed slightly when it was Daniel's turn to bow his head and say, 'Sorry, sir.'

Chuck seemed to find the whole thing amusing, slapping Daniel on the back and walking over to the rest of the guests.

Ore was standing to the side of them, a little way off, trying her best to flush away the nausea with big breaths of sea air. Daniel walked towards her, stopping at an awkward angle away from her and then turning so they stood side by side.

'How are you feeling?' he asked.

'I've felt better,' she admitted. 'Just as I got accustomed to the *Thalassa*, here you go testing my limits again!' She was teasing him but he looked so apologetic, she felt a bit bad.

'Sorry about that. I tried to make the ride as smooth as possible.'

'No, no, sorry, I didn't mean it as a comment on your . . . driving.' She wasn't sure what the right terminology was. He chuckled and she found herself smiling at his warm laugh.

'To be honest I'm just a bit stressed about getting this piece done. I've been here for three days and I haven't written a single word of the article yet. I'm not even sure what my angle is.' She wasn't sure why she was telling him this; something about his presence made her feel like she could confide in him.

'Angle? I thought it was just a profile piece? Don't you have enough from your chat with Chuck?' He was asking innocently enough, and the lack of eye contact made her want to open up. In truth it was a bit of a lonely experience, being out here, away from the bustle of her auntie's house, with its comings and goings. And usually she'd have her friends to talk to about whatever it was she was working on.

'Oh you know us journalists, there's always an angle. I just have this feeling that there's something more to it . . .' She couldn't quite articulate it. 'Something more, I don't know . . . going on?'

She glanced over at him, and noticed him tense, almost imperceptibly.

'It might be easier to just stick to the brief though, no? Write up your conversation with Chuck and just enjoy yourself for the rest of your time here.' His tone had changed into something more forceful.

'Is that advice or an order from up above?' she asked, motioning her head in Chuck's direction.

Daniel looked at her, his eyes almost pleading. He looked like he was trying to work out what to say next, but in the end he settled on: 'Neither. I'm not the writer; what would I know?'

Ore wished he would just tell her what was on his mind, partly because she sensed it might help her understand the 'something going on' and partly because it seemed to be burdening him.

'Anyway, duty calls. You should ask Nicole for some ginger tea when she gets here.' With that, he strode away. Ore wondered how on earth tea could be brewed on a desert island.

Soon the dinghy arrived carrying Carlos – who must have been stowed away somewhere on the bigger boat – Nicole and an unfathomable amount of 'supplies'. Ore wandered back over to the guests.

'Have a drink, Ore, it might do you some good to relax into it.' Chuck passed her a glass of something sparkling. She worried she might not be able to keep it down, but took a sip out of politeness. It turned out to be delicious, and next thing she knew, she had polished off another two glasses.

As the guests drank, the crew busied themselves setting up a marquee, dining table and what looked like a fully operational gas barbecue, which was hooked up to a huge canister. Ore marvelled at the power of money.

The conversation was mainly centred around Chuck, Frederik and Ousman talking about their MIT days; Agatha and Richard seemed to have their own repartee going about their time at Cambridge, albeit over fifty years apart. Ore sat quietly grazing on the delights of the mezze board and drinking more than she'd intended. She listened, and occasionally laughed politely, but she was becoming more aware that with every passing minute she was losing out on the opportunity to get answers.

Claude was sitting apart from the group, further up the beach, which nobody seemed surprised by. She resolved to buck up, stop acting like this was a holiday and go do some actual journalism.

She stood up and excused herself. 'Just going for a little wander,' she explained.

'Careful that you don't run into any big bad wolves in the forest.' Frederik had loosened up too, after a few glasses. 'Or one big bad wolf in particular.' He looked over pointedly to where Claude was sitting, and the other two men laughed.

'Why do you say that?' Ore kept her tone light, but her question seemed to dampen the mood. The laughter dried up.

Chuck looked at Frederik, with an expression that was hard to read. Frederik took another swig and Ousman topped up his glass of sparkling water.

'He's only kidding, Ore,' Chuck said after a moment, 'but don't be long. We'll be eating in about twenty minutes.'

Ore was no idiot, and she was a woman. Which meant that she understood that Claude was someone to be careful around. A lot of men were, and she resented that they assumed she was oblivious to his hungry gaze and wandering hands. Still, she needed, at the very least, a surname from him, if she had any hope of getting to the bottom of whatever it was that Chuck was mixed up in here.

'Not about to miss whatever feast Carlos is cooking up – don't worry,' she said breezily, dusting away the sand on her clothes.

Claude was sitting further away than it looked. The expanse of beach and clear visibility were deceptive. When she finally got to him, he looked up suddenly, although he must have seen her coming for a while.

'Ore, you have come to steal a cigarette?' He held a pack open for her to help herself. She was in the habit of smoking exclusively after midnight, usually when she was wasted. Today though, under the blinding sunlight, she thought it best to just accept his offer.

'Thank you.' She took a cigarette and sat down beside him. When he produced a lighter, it was clear that she was to lean in and light straight from the flame. She was keenly aware of how close his face was to hers and suddenly she wished she'd taken greater heed of Frederik's warning.

She inhaled, leaning back, and then blew the acrid smoke

into the air between them. 'I um, I wanted to have a chat with you today actually.' It came out sounding less assertive and more apologetic than she'd intended.

'A chat? Is that what the English say when they mean interview?'

She laughed, if only for something to do. 'I suppose so. Is that a problem?'

He turned to her, and she felt like he was testing her nerve with his silent stare.

Finally he shrugged. 'Go ahead.'

In that moment Ore's mind went blank. In the commotion of her seasickness she'd left her precious notepad on the tender. She took another drag of the cigarette to kill time and then it came to her: start simple.

'How do you know Chuck?'

At an painfully leisurely pace, Claude nodded and took out another cigarette, lighting it and inhaling slowly.

'Chuck and I, we were school friends,' he said matter-of-factly.

'Where did you go to school?' Ore's heart was beating a little faster. If she could get him to confirm the boarding school, then she would at least know that Chuck was definitely withholding, if not outright lying, about his childhood.

'In my hometown.' She was by no means surprised that Claude was not forthcoming, but it was still frustrating.

'Where is that?' She tried not to let the irritation seep into her voice; she suspected he'd only relish it.

'Geraardsbergen.'

'Is that in Belgium?' Ore wanted to be sure.

Claude rolled his eyes. 'Honestly, I thought it was an

American thing to be bad at geography; maybe it has spread now to the rest of the anglosphere.'

He wanted her to drop it; she could sense it. Maybe he thought that she would be shamed into retreat if he insulted her intelligence. But he had only given himself away: she was onto something.

'How old were you at the time?'

Claude shifted in the sand. 'I'm not sure, maybe like six or seven. How can I remember that?' His tone was as steady and monotone as ever, but she swore she could detect him getting just a little flustered.

'No problem, I don't need you to be exact.'

'So you are the sort of journalist who does not deal with exact facts.' Another dig, before he took a long drag. Ore said nothing. 'Have you any other questions? We should be going back for food now.'

Time was running out. It seemed she was doomed to collect only tiny fragments from everyone. She would have to do the piecing together in her own time.

'Does "klauparten" mean anything to you?' The moment she said the word, she knew she'd hit a nerve. Claude's head snapped around, catching her in another one of his iron stares.

'Where did you hear that word?' His eyes turned somehow icier. Ore felt a flash of fear. There was a menace there that she hadn't seen before.

'I . . .' she stumbled. She hadn't thought that far ahead, only wanting to make the most of this conversation before it was over. 'I can't remember, maybe something Chuck said to me in one of our chats?' She was lying, and he knew it.

Neither of them moved, and then the forgotten cigarette burned down into her fingers.

'Ouch!' She flung the butt into the sand.

'You should be careful not to make a habit of getting your fingers burned.' If ever Ore had heard a threat . . . Claude smiled, and, perhaps for the first time, Ore realised, deep in her bones, that she was messing with dangerous people. She needed to be more careful.

'Shall we head back?' Her voice trembled slightly, and it only made him smile wider.

'I think that would be wise.'

Ore clambered to her feet as Claude rose slowly. The walk back to the others was excruciatingly silent. The whole way Ore racked her brain for things to say, but nothing materialised. It felt like her body was too concerned with survival mode to be able to think of anything else.

When they reached the table, which by now had been set up with a stunning array of barbecued meats, fish and vegetables, she let out the deep breath she'd been holding in.

Chapter 25

Daniel

Ore looked scared as she sat down, and Daniel felt angry. He turned his gaze to Claude, who calmly took a seat beside Chuck and began pouring a glass of beer for himself. Daniel had been keeping an eye on them, and it didn't look like anything untoward had happened. He had been a bit surprised to see her smoking, and then he'd had to remind himself that he'd only known the woman for a couple of days, and really that meant he didn't know her at all.

Carlos tapped a teaspoon to his glass and ran the guests through the meal in front of them, but Daniel wasn't listening. He was too busy looking at Ore and trying to not be too obvious about it.

'Did you want a drink?' Nicole was standing over him with a jug of something.

'Um, no, I shouldn't,' he said, distracted. He shot a glance at Claude, but the man's expression was as ambivalent as ever. *What has he said to her?*

'It's not alcoholic,' Nicole continued.

'Sure, OK, thanks,'

Nicole leant over just as Frederik turned suddenly, and then

132

most of the jug of something was splashed over Daniel's white trousers.

'Shit, sorry.' Nicole was flustered, the jug still in her hand.

'It's fine, I'll just go clean myself up a bit. Apologies, folks, do start without me.' He gave Carlos, who had been cut off mid spiel, an apologetic look. Truthfully, he was glad to get away from the table for a moment to clear his head.

He took off his shoes, walked to the dinghy and fished out a cloth from the pile of supplies. He had dipped it in the sea and began dabbing when he heard a light splashing behind him.

'Ore?' She had rolled up her own white trousers and was wading towards him. 'What's up?'

'I asked Nicole for some sparkling water and she said there should be more in the dinghy.' Ore paused, as if wondering whether to go on. 'And to be honest, I also just needed to get away from that table for a bit,' she added shyly.

'What happened?'

Ore looked self-consciously down at her feet. 'I'd hoped it wasn't that obvious,' she said quietly.

'Oh no, it wasn't, I just . . .' Daniel knew it was unprofessional to say what he did next, but he also knew after today, he would find it hard to forgive himself if he didn't warn her. 'I know that Claude has a bad reputation when it comes to beautiful young women.'

It was only when she looked up at him, startled, that he realised he'd called her beautiful. It felt so obvious to him now that she was, that he'd forgotten it was an intense thing to say. Now it was his turn to be self-conscious.

'Well um . . .' Ore cleared her throat and busied her hands tying her braids into a ponytail, avoiding his eyes. 'I have to say that's hardly a revelation Daniel . . . him being a creep I mean, not that I'm um . . . that I'm beautiful or whatever.'

The sound of the water lapping around their calves filled the silence. Daniel was at a loss for words. He didn't know what he had expected her reaction to be, maybe he'd just wanted to 'save her', to be the hero who warned her about the dragon. It was pitiful really, as he couldn't seem to muster the courage to actually save her from the beast.

It was Ore who broke the stalemate. 'But something weird did happen.' It was almost a whisper.

Daniel threw the cloth back into the boat and faced her. Almost instinctively he reached out his hands, laying them on each of her arms. She looked up at him, her dark eyes deep with fear, and maybe . . . tenderness?

'Tell me, Ore.'

She hesitated for a moment and then: 'I think there's something . . . I don't know . . . sinister going on. I was asking Claude about his time at boarding school with Chuck . . .'

'Wait, I had no idea they were old friends. I thought he was just one of his investors . . .' Daniel mused.

'Well that's exactly it, there's basically nothing online about Chuck's early childhood, but Claude told me they were at some school in Belgium together when they were kids, and when I asked Chuck he said that he grew up in Oklahoma . . .'

Daniel was having a hard time keeping up. It seemed like a random detail to get caught up on. What the hell did it matter if Chuck went to some fancy school in Europe? And why was Ore so shaken up about it?

'. . . and I found this old clipping from the college newspaper where Chuck is talking about speaking Flemish as his party trick.' Ore's words were tumbling out now, her eyes wide and slightly frantic.

So was he only pretending not to understand Claude on the boat earlier? It was all so strange.

'And then I said this other thing . . . And he, I think he threatened me.' She looked for a moment like she had more to say, but then she dropped her head and began muttering to herself, inaudibly, her breathing shallow and fast.

Daniel's hands were still clasping her. 'Ore, look at me.' She did. 'Take a deep breath.' She did. 'And another one.' *I won't let anyone hurt you.* Soon her breathing had slowed and he watched as the anguish melted from her face. Her arms slid around his waist, and as naturally as if they had embraced a thousand times before, his arms enveloped her.

Daniel felt himself descend into a deep sense of calm. Standing there, in the shallows, holding her, with the heat of her breath rippling over his chest, it was impossible to imagine that the rest of the world was turning.

He had no idea how long they stood like this, and at a certain point he became aware that they were just within sight of the marquee. Maybe from a distance it wouldn't be clear what was happening, but they had surely melded into one singular figure, no longer distinctly two.

Daniel pulled away first, and then wished he hadn't. Ore looked bewildered and a little ashamed. 'Sorry that was . . . inappropriate of me,' she began.

'It wasn't . . . I didn't . . . It was nice.' A burning heat rose into his cheeks as he spoke.

'Yeah, it was nice.' Ore looked at him, and before they knew it, they'd both burst into a fit of giggles.

'God, is it always this intense? Boating, yachting, I mean? Maybe it's something to do with being out at sea. Don't they say it makes people go crazy?' Ore was smiling. She seemed happier, lighter than she had done. The realisation made Daniel glow with something like pride.

'I've heard it is yes, but usually I like to stay out of "the crazy",' Daniel replied.

'Doesn't look like there's much chance of that this time, I'm afraid.' Ore chuckled.

Once upon a time, not so long ago, Daniel would have been dismayed to hear that. Now though, he was almost excited by the prospect.

'I better head back anyway; they'll be wondering what's going on . . .' Ore turned to look back at the beach. 'They can probably see us from there, can't they . . .'

She reached into the boat and pulled out a bottle of water. 'Well I guess there's nothing to be done about it now. I have well and truly revealed my unprofessional colours.' She shrugged and began wading back to shore.

'You coming?' she called over her shoulder.

I think I would follow you anywhere. The thought popped into Daniel's head with such force and clarity that it alarmed him, but he hitched up his trousers and caught up with her anyway.

Chapter 26

Ore

No one had said anything when the pair of them appeared together and sat down, although Ore was sure she'd clocked something of a 'look' exchanged between Chuck and Agatha.

The food was delicious, but Ore wasn't hungry. The conversation with Claude had rattled her and then her *moment* with Daniel had left her all muddled up. Now she was having a hard time concentrating on the idle chit-chat around the table.

'Was everything OK?' Carlos frowned at the plate as he cleared it from in front of her.

'Yes, it was lovely. I just feel a bit . . .' She patted her stomach. 'I've not quite recovered from the journey, I guess.'

Carlos huffed, displeased.

'Would you ladies mind if we excuse ourselves for a moment? I'd hate to ruin the atmosphere by talking business.' Ousman spoke quietly, with the sort of indiscernible accent that indicated a childhood spent in international schools.

'Not at all,' Agatha said with a giggle. Ore suspected she was a bit drunk.

The 'men who want to talk business' stood up and walked up the beach, leaving Ore, Daniel and Agatha at the table.

'I'm going to help Oscar and Carlos load up the dinghy for

the first trip back. Let me know if you need me . . .' Daniel started and then shook his head. 'If you need anything,' he corrected himself, before leaving the table.

Ore was left with Agatha, who poured herself another glass.

'Having a nice time?' Ore asked. She'd meant to keep her tone light, but it sounded a tad accusatory. Agatha bristled.

'Yes, I am actually,' she said, taking a sip. Ore felt like she'd got off on the wrong foot. 'It seems you are too.'

It was a retaliatory jab. Ore knew that meant Agatha must have been able to make out something of Ore's exchange with Daniel from the beach.

'I love your dress by the way.' It was almost true. She liked the colour, but the cut was a little too cutesy for Ore's taste. It was more just something to say.

'Thanks.' Agatha looked like she couldn't decide whether she believed Ore. They sat there a moment, each wondering if it was worth trying to start over conversationally.

Ore took the plunge. 'It must be nice working for someone like Chuck. I mean, hell of an office, right?'

Agatha scoffed. 'Are you trying to interview me right now?'

Ore felt deflated. It felt so long since she'd had a normal interaction with anybody, why was everyone on this boat so on edge?

'No, sorry, I'm not trying to . . . I'm just trying to make conversation.'

Agatha stared at her for a moment, and Ore thought she spotted something akin to sympathy; then in a flash, it was gone.

'Well I'd be careful who you're making conversation with on this boat.' Another swig, and a look that dared Ore to ask more.

'Why do you say that?' Ore took the bait, expecting yet another warning about Claude.

'Well, you know there are spies everywhere.' Agatha turned to look at Daniel. 'I've been told that Chuck isn't too happy about what you've been getting the staff to say about him behind his back.'

Ore didn't say a word, but she was confused and a little irritated by the crypticness. It felt like schoolgirl gossip.

Agatha continued, 'I know that you think you have something going on with Daniel, but everything you've said to him, just know that he's feeding it back to Chuck.' She looked like she was enjoying herself.

Ore was surprised by the strength of the feeling of betrayal. She didn't even know if Agatha was telling the truth, but Daniel had promised her he was only supervising. He was the censor, sure, but he had assured her he wasn't a spy.

'I see,' she said. She knew enough about schoolgirl gossip to realise that the reaction was everything, and she wasn't about to give Agatha that satisfaction.

Inside though, Ore was reeling. She realised that whatever Agatha's motivations, Ore had been naive to trust Daniel so implicitly. What had happened to her journalistic scepticism? Why had she been so quick to believe Daniel's pure intentions? Because he was cute and because she suspected that he fancied her, and that was her weakness: her own damn ego. She'd reasoned to herself that she felt safe, that he was trustworthy, but where had that come from really? She barely knew the man.

She replayed the conversation they'd just had. She had basically revealed her whole investigation to him, and now he would tell Chuck, and she'd be off the boat in no time. She could kiss goodbye to her *New York Herald* exclusive and a contract job. All because of a handsome captain.

Ore was no longer interested in trying to talk to Agatha, so she was grateful when Nicole came to join them, chatting obliviously about the dramas of the day: how stressed Carlos had been, how they'd had to do three trips to the dinghy. Ore and Agatha made the appropriate interjections: 'oh, no!', 'really?', 'what a nightmare'. It was in this way that an awkward silence was kept at bay until the men returned.

Ore felt her pulse quicken as she spotted Claude and Chuck walking ahead of the pack, talking in furtive tones. When Claude looked up and caught her eye, her blood curdled and she quickly averted her gaze, fumbling to fill up her glass and appear nonchalant. Had he told Chuck? She held her breath when Chuck cleared his throat to address the party.

'I believe it is that time of day, everyone . . .' Chuck was smiling widely, but the men behind him groaned and Agatha rolled her eyes.

Nicole stood up and started clearing the table. Agatha turned to Ore. 'Did you bring a swimsuit?'

She didn't know what she had been expecting, but it wasn't that.

'Um, no, why?'

It was Richard who answered her. 'Chuck likes to embarrass everyone by making us play games . . . What is it called again?'

'Chicken fight, or shoulder wars.' Ore imagined Agatha in a classroom, hand ever outstretched, barely able to hold in the answer until the teacher picked on her.

'I'm sure we can make something work.' Richard winked at Ore, and she wondered how all these men had managed to make it to the pinnacle of their industries without being brought down by a slew of sexual misconduct allegations.

Chapter 27

Daniel

Daniel felt dazed, an intoxicating combination of a day in the sun, a tropical paradise . . . and Ore. As he walked over to Oscar and Carlos, he tried to remember exactly what her hair had smelled like, the feel of her palms resting on his back, the sound of the small sigh she had let out when he drew her close.

'I just think that it will spoil if you pack it without the ice.' Carlos was in a bad mood it seemed. There was a fine line with him between too much and too little praise for the food. Too much and he would accuse the Americans of 'lacking any culinary discernment'; too little and he would sulk that 'no one but the French and the Lebanese can appreciate good food if it slaps them in the face'. Today it was the latter that aggravated him.

'I'm taking it back on the first trip though, Carlos, and if I don't leave the ice, the guests won't be able to have cold drinks,' Oscar pleaded, holding a large bag of ice cubes and looking dismayed.

'Drinks, drinks, drinks, that is all they ever want to do; never mind the food, as long as you keep the guests drunk, they will be happy.' Carlos was waving his arms around in a way that seemed to Daniel comically European.

Oscar caught Daniel's eye, shrugging with exasperation.

'Let's keep the ice on the island and get the food back onto the boat and refrigerated as quickly as possible.'

Oscar dropped the ice, looking relieved for the timely intervention.

'Suit yourself,' Carlos sniffed, '*tu me trouvera, fumer une clope.*' He stormed off.

'Thanks, mate,' Oscar said. Usually Daniel would have corrected him – 'Thanks, Captain' – but right now he was feeling so giddy that he let it slide. Together they loaded the dinghy up – gas canister, barbecue, leftover food – drove it back to the bigger boat and unloaded it again.

As they shuttled back to the shore, Daniel could see the men walking back towards the marquee, and suddenly Daniel felt anxious to get back. He didn't like the idea of Ore facing Claude and Chuck alone.

'Can we pick up the pace a bit?' he asked Oscar.

'Are you in a hurry to get back for the games then?'

'What games?' Daniel had no idea what he was talking about.

'Oh yes, of course, you're new to this. Chuck has an obsession with what he calls "team bonding". I don't know what it's all about but he'll be gearing up for a few rounds of Chicken Fight right around now,' Oscar explained.

As they approached the shore, Daniel saw that Agatha had changed into a white one-piece swimsuit, which plunged into a deep V at the front. All the men, save Ousman, were now wearing swimming shorts and he found himself scouring the party for Ore. Eventually he spotted her; she was wearing a crew kit – red shorts and a white polo shirt.

'Captain Wilsons, just in time.' It was the old man – Richard. 'The games can begin.'

Daniel and Oscar secured the dinghy and walked over to the guests where Chuck was explaining the rules: 'It's challengers style, so the winner stays on. No clawing, no biting, no gouging.'

'Spoilsport!' Richard piped up again, and everybody chuckled indulgently.

Chuck continued: 'Last man or, excuse me, woman, standing wins. OK, team, pair up!'

Richard immediately turned to Agatha, Oscar to Nicole, and Chuck enthusiastically teamed up with Frederik. That left Daniel, Carlos, Ore and Claude. Daniel tried to catch Ore's eye. He was shamefully excited to touch her again, but she seemed to be avoiding his gaze. She walked over to Carlos. He gave her a little bow.

'My pleasure, mademoiselle,' he said and the two stood side by side with the other teams, Ore resolutely looking anywhere but in Daniel's direction. He didn't really understand what was happening, but then maybe it was a wise move, to try and maintain at least the pretence of a 'purely professional' relationship.

Daniel looked over to Claude. He was wearing dark grey trunks, which emphasised his compact, dense build.

'It seems it is you and me, Captain,' Claude said flatly.

'Top or bottom?' Daniel asked, although with Claude being no more than five-seven and Daniel towering well over six feet, it was more of a courtesy question.

'I will be on top,' Claude acquiesced.

As everyone waded into the water, Daniel jogged to retrieve

143

a pair of shorts, discarding his stained trousers. By the time he got back to the water's edge, Agatha was already clambering onto Richard's shoulders and facing off with Nicole and Oscar.

'Ready, set, go!' Chuck was giddy with strangely childish delight as he whooped and clapped. Agatha was an – unsurprisingly – competitive player, swiping at Nicole determinedly. Nicole and Oscar, though, were an agile team, ducking and swaying out of the way with ease. Eventually it was Richard who let the side down, not moving fast enough when Nicole got a hold of Agatha's arms and promptly yanked her into the water.

When she resurfaced, her blonde fringe plastered over her eyes, she looked annoyed. Daniel suspected she was not someone who was accustomed to losing.

'Who's next?' Chuck turned to Ore and Carlos, who dutifully took up their positions. They were an elegant pair, but it was Ore who won the round for them. As with her reporting, she was dogged, each wobble only making her more resolved. Nicole put up a good fight, but when she fell from Oscar's shoulders, Daniel joined in the cheer from the beach.

Next up was Chuck, teetering on Frederik's shoulders. For the amount of practice that he must have had, he wasn't much good, thought Daniel. He was mostly talk, playfully goading Ore, but ultimately splashing out of the game pretty quickly. Daniel thought he spotted a triumphant look on Ore's face as she watched Chuck fall.

And then it was his turn. Claude hadn't uttered a word, not a cheer or a clap, but now he turned to Daniel.

'Shall we eviscerate the opposition, then?' Claude's tone was, as usual, totally monotonous. Daniel worried there might be more intention behind that statement than simply winning this stupid game.

'After you,' he said. He didn't like the man, but it wasn't in his job description to make his opinions about the guests known. He followed Claude into the waves.

Daniel offered Ore a small smile as they got into position, but was met by a blank look. Was she just playing it cool in front of the crowd, or was there something else going on? She was looking at Claude now, and as Daniel studied her face, he saw a glimmer of the same fear he had seen flash across her face earlier, before she composed herself.

'Aaaaand, fight!' Chuck called.

It was a pretty even match. Despite himself, Daniel couldn't help but get into the spirit – he didn't like to lose either. Claude was mostly on the defensive, ducking and lunging out of the way of Ore's attacks. There was something fervent about the round. On the beach, no one seemed to be cheering or laughing. There was only the sound of grunts of effort and splashes of water. When Claude eventually made his move, reaching for Ore's elbow, it was her flinching that toppled her off balance.

'Ha!' Claude exclaimed, before sliding off Daniel's shoulders. 'Good team.' He held out his hand and gave Daniel's a crushing shake. When Daniel turned to see Ore rearranging her soaking braids on top of her head, she gave him a withering look. The effect was far more crushing. He felt confused. Surely this wasn't about the game? Maybe it was because he had teamed up with Claude, but that was only because she had chosen Carlos. She strode back to the shore, where they were met by a half-hearted round of applause. Even Chuck seemed to have lost his enthusiasm.

Daniel resolved to give Ore some space. He reasoned that today had been full-on – all in a day's work for a yachtie perhaps, but she was new to the world of catering to the whims of the super rich. Not to mention her conversation with Claude. She probably just needed a little time to decompress. Besides, he had been distracted by Ore all day. It would do him some good to concentrate on the job at hand, and stop letting his obsessive thoughts get the better of him.

When they returned to the marquee, the crew set about dismantling it and loading it into the dinghy. Ore, Agatha and the guests took to the picnic blankets. When Daniel snatched a glance in their direction, he saw Ore off to the side speaking first with Ousman, and then with Frederik. It seemed he was not the only one doubling down on getting the job done.

Chapter 28

Ore

Ore couldn't wait to get off the island. That morning she had dreaded the boat journey back, but now it couldn't come soon enough. The day had dragged, each fresh chapter of it bringing a new and bizarre twist that left her feeling more disorientated than the last.

The nausea, the drinking, the encounters with Claude, then Daniel, then Agatha. And to top it all off, a few rounds of spring-break-inspired tomfoolery. She was looking forward to getting back to the cabin, depositing the details into her notebook and unravelling some sense from it all.

At least she had managed to talk to the other investors, although neither Ousman nor Frederik had very much to say for themselves. They were both early supporters of Pagonis, back when it was run out of Chuck's MIT dorm, and it seemed that loyalty counted for a lot with Chuck. They had all made each other rich, a feedback loop of investment and ever larger returns. Ousman's remit was property and Frederik's was, oddly enough, pet food. They were both open, and unfazed by Ore's questions, a sure-fire sign that they were dead ends on the path to whatever dodgy stuff Claude and Chuck were involved in.

Richard had been drunk most of the day, so Ore hadn't bothered, but her instincts told her he wasn't 'in on it' either.

As they were bundled onto the dinghy, Ore made sure to keep her expression neutral as she sat across from Agatha and Daniel. Earlier he had been trying to get her attention, but now he seemed to have got the message, making no effort to engage with her. Agatha was looking a little worse for wear, like she was concentrating on keeping her lunch, and copious glasses of champagne, down. Her hair had dried into a frizzy shag, her perfectly applied makeup washed away by the seawater, leaving behind a patchier, slightly sunburned complexion.

Chuck and his friends had gone ahead, so this transfer was just the crew, Agatha and Ore. Nobody spoke. On the second boat, Ore feigned another wave of seasickness and hunkered down in the small kitchen. Sometimes making polite conversation with Carlos, sometimes just watching as he cleared away the pots, pans and various kitchen gadgets Ore had never come across before.

When they finally made it back to *Thalassa*, Vicky was waiting on deck with one of the other stewardesses. Amanda was her name perhaps.

'Welcome back, gentlemen. Dinner will be served in about an hour,' Vicky announced as they climbed the galley.

Ore shot Carlos a sympathetic look. It was relentless – after such a long day in the sun she couldn't even imagine mustering the energy to cook for a table of eight. Carlos seemed unruffled.

'Roast partridge with dauphinoise,' he announced, to a chorus of appreciative murmurs, once everyone had made it onto the deck. 'Will you be joining, mademoiselle?'

Ore admired his stoicism but she couldn't match it. 'Not tonight, thank you, Carlos. I think I'm in need of an early night.'

'Very well, Vicky will deliver a little something to your door.' Carlos strode off before Ore could object. She really didn't want to have any more intense social interactions today, and by the look on Vicky's face, it seemed Ore was caught in the middle of something that had little to do with her.

'Yes, Chef,' Vicky murmured somewhat bitterly under her breath as Carlos' chef whites retreated into the salon. In the next second, she had turned back to the guests with a smile convincingly stretched across her face, and Ore wondered if she'd imagined the terse exchange.

'If you'd like to make your way to the top deck, I have refreshments waiting.' Vicky began leading the group away and in the commotion, Ore slipped away.

Walking through the corridors, Ore was relieved to be alone. She ran to her cabin, and once inside, had to resist the urge to push a chair up against the door handle. She settled on locking herself in instead, and found herself rather dramatically sliding down the laminate wood until she was sat cross-legged on the floor.

She took ten deep breaths, closed her eyes, and for some reason a memory of Kyle slipped into her head.

Chapter 29

Ore

Their sessions were coming to an end. The university budget only stretched to six months of sessions maximum and Ore had exhausted her allocation. They were sat in his small office: her clutching the mug of tea he always offered, she always accepted and never drank; him leaning back and waiting for her to speak first.

This was their ritual. Kyle insisted that she set the tone of their discussion so she had to be the one to start talking. He would open the door, greet her and start boiling the kettle, silently handing her the mug and then simply waiting. Sometimes they would sit in silence for ten minutes whilst Ore tried to work out what she wanted to say, but it was never an uncomfortable silence; in fact it was often her favourite part of the week. It was a time when she didn't have to explain herself, or indeed defend herself; she could just be, and he wouldn't ask anything more of her.

On this particular Tuesday morning, Ore was preoccupied by the finite amount of time together they had left. She still felt like she had so much to say, like there were so many parts of herself that she wanted him to see and explain back to her.

Eventually, she blurted out something that had been lurking in the perimeter of her mind for a while.

'I've never felt about anyone the way I feel about you.' The heat rose to her cheeks as she spoke, so horrified was she by what she was daring to say out loud.

Kyle looked momentarily taken aback, and then collected himself. He shifted in his seat, and took a deep breath.

'What do you mean by that?' It was a classic therapist question of course, but Ore realised that maybe she'd been expecting a different response. What's more, she wasn't really *sure* what she meant. Kyle wasn't an unattractive man, but he was older, mid to late thirties by her estimation, and his hairline showed it. He was about as far from her usual type as you could get: skinny, sort of nerdy-looking with round tortoiseshell-rimmed glasses, white, a big fan of plaid shirts. All that was to say that her own feelings were confusing to her.

'I think . . .' she began without knowing where the sentence was going. She cleared her mind, like he had taught her to do, and closed her eyes, imagining she was reading from the teleprompt of her rolling thoughts. Another one of his tips. 'I think that I respect you, and I like spending time with you, and that you've saved me, and I don't know how I am going to cope once I can't see you anymore.'

She opened her eyes, one at a time, as though trying to mitigate the brightness of his face. But it was expressionless.

'And I also think that I fancy you.' This she added defiantly, finding that she was angry about his total lack of response.

Then he sighed, removing his glasses slowly and cleaning them with his shirt. 'Ore . . .' He sighed again. 'You know that

that's not appropriate. I'm your counsellor, but I'm inclined to respond to that comment by asking you why you think that? That you . . .' he stumbled, 'you have a romantic attraction to me . . . Ore, are you OK?' His face was etched with concern, but it was only when he stood up and sat on the sofa beside her, that she registered she was crying. Maybe sobbing would be a better description. Her shoulders heaved and her throat stung and the tears kept falling.

Through her jagged breathing she managed to stitch together a sentence: 'I . . . just . . . think . . . you . . . make . . . me . . . feel . . . so . . . safe . . .'

He pulled her into a hug then, and the smell of him instantly soothed her, the feeling of his fingers splayed across her back, the brush of his stubble on her bare shoulder. Her breath slowed to a steady rhythm and as he pulled away, she looked up at him. His eyes were a light hazel, and quite beautiful, she found herself thinking. She heard her heart beating in her ears as she moved her face towards his and parted his lips with hers.

When he didn't pull away, she circled her arms around his neck and pressed herself against him. His hands found her waist, fingers clutching at the fabric of her dress. Ore's mind went blank. She could only feel her own need for more of him. A soft moan escaped from her throat, and it seemed to shock him out of a trance.

Her hands were left empty; she panted at the empty space he left behind. When her brain caught up with her body, she dropped her eyes in shame, unable to look at the man standing over her.

'I think we should leave it there,' he said quietly. She wasn't sure if he was talking about just the kiss, this particular session, or the whole therapy thing.

'It's a shame we never got onto talking about your relationship with your father, and some of the lingering attachment dynamics at play here. Textbook "daddy issues", in layman's terms.' He said it so matter-of-factly that it took Ore a moment to register her own rage. When she looked up at him, he was cowed by the fury in her eyes.

'I'm sorry, Ore, that was . . . uncalled for. I don't know what came over me . . .' He ran his hand through his hair, which Ore noted was definitely thinning. 'I'm not really sure why I . . . This whole thing is . . .'

'I'm going to leave now.' Ore grabbed her bag and shoved past him, out of the door before he had the chance to say another word.

It had been agonising to try and comfort herself without his guidance. Just when she needed his calming presence the most, he was the very thing she had to avoid.

Every time she thought about cracking and giving him a call, she'd remember the daddy issues comment, and feel renewed anger.

Eventually, a couple of months later, he had reached out and they had met on a park bench on campus. As Ore sat down beside him, she wondered if he had chosen such a public spot in order to dissuade her from pouncing on him again. She felt embarrassed at the thought.

'Hello, Kyle.' They didn't look at each other as they spoke, just stared right ahead.

'Hello, Ore, how are you doing?'

'I'm actually OK. I wasn't for a little bit but I am now.' Ore realised as she spoke that it was the truth, and she felt proud of herself.

'I'm really glad to hear that.' There was a beat of silence before he continued. 'I wanted to see you to apologise. For everything. I don't know what came over me and I shouldn't have . . . reciprocated.'

Ore didn't feel like assuaging his guilt so she changed the subject. 'I've been thinking about that thing you said about my father.'

It was Kyle's turn to look embarrassed. Out of the corner of her eyes she could see him looking around, checking no one was in earshot.

'I didn't mean it,' he said softly.

'Yes you did,' Ore replied, equality softly. 'And I guess you're right. I think that the way I felt about you, safe and understood, I've never had that from a man in my life. It was confusing and . . .' she looked over at him; his expression was kind, and she felt her residual rage melt away '. . . overwhelming.'

'It's OK to need that, just . . . not from me.' Kyle shrugged apologetically.

'But wouldn't it be better to just rely on myself? Isn't that what you've been teaching me, with all that "toolbox" chat? That I need to fix my own problems . . . ?'

'Well yes, it's important to be able to rely on yourself, but there's nothing wrong with needing a guiding hand or a bit of support.' Kyle had slipped back into his 'therapy voice', quiet but authoritative.

'Just . . . not from you.' She hadn't meant it as a dig, but he hung his head.

'I'm sorry, Ore, I wish it could have been different.' Once

again, she wasn't sure what he was referring to . . . Did he wish that they hadn't kissed? Or that he hadn't been her therapist when they did?

Ore left their meeting with new resolve. She was going to kit out her toolbox, and dedicate herself to becoming adept at using them. And she wasn't going to let herself fall into the trap of thinking that she needed a man's help to do that. Men were for exciting love affairs, and fleeting dalliances. The work of straightening out her tangled mind, and toughening up her resilience, was hers alone.

It was that resolve that she had to tap into now, as she sat on the floor of her cabin, thoughts racing, and alone in the middle of the ocean. She had only herself to rely on. This was the test. She opened her eyes, scrambled over to her suitcase and began relaying all the strange happenings of her day into her growing pile of notes.

Chapter 30

Daniel

Day 4

Daniel slept deeply that night. The strangeness of the day had exhausted him. He didn't dream, and when he awoke the creases of the pillow had, once again left an indent in his cheek. He examined himself as he brushed his teeth. His hair was growing a little long, the neat peaks fuzzing into overgrowth, and he needed to shave.

They were about twenty-four hours away from the reef and Daniel was grateful to have something to occupy his thoughts that didn't involve Ore. In a bizarre way he was slightly relieved that she had stopped talking to him – for what reason he couldn't work out, but it gave him a chance to rearrange his priorities into a respectable order.

It was really none of his business what she got up to, and now that it seemed unlikely she would be alone with Claude again, he would do well to stay out of it.

Breakfast in the mess was a sullen affair; Vicky seemed to be in a terrible mood after being kept up to the early hours of the morning first by Chuck's guests and then by

Melanie who had had a meltdown about the partridges at dinner.

'She's a walking contradiction, that girl, calls herself an "environmentalist" but takes a dozen private jet flights a month, is vegan but has a designer croc skin handbag that costs more than my apartment!' Sometimes Daniel found himself wondering why Vicky continued to do this job. The ultra-rich seemed to infuriate her and yet she'd dedicated years of her life to catering to their whims.

'I still remember when she went through her Pingu phase. The girl was about eight; she'd watched a couple of episodes, but who had to organise for the yacht to sail all the way to Cape Town so she could go see the penguins?'

Dudley rolled his eyes as though he'd heard the story a dozen times before, but Amanda and Nicole gave the appropriate disapproving reactions.

Daniel was quiet, newly resolved to get on with his job. Vicky was having none of it.

'So how was yesterday then? Any drama?'

Daniel shrugged and Vicky turned her attention to Nicole, raising an inquisitive eyebrow. Nicole needed no more prompting than that.

She leant in conspiratorially as she spoke. 'Well . . . that reporter woman got suuuper sick on the boat out, and then at one point she went off with Claude.'

At the mention of his name, Dudley's head shot up from the bowl of cereal he was swirling with his spoon.

'Don't, Dudley.' Vicky gave him a stern look. *Don't say a word*, it seemed to say.

Nicole seemed confused. 'Anyway . . . So yeah she went off with him for a while, but they just looked like they were talking and having a cigarette, and then it was lunchtime and Carlos was in a terrible mood because everyone was a bit drunk and not finishing the food . . .' Nicole paused for breath. 'And then I spilt a drink down the captain . . .' She looked over at Daniel, blushing slightly.

'Don't worry about it,' he said flatly.

'And then like at one point it looked like . . .' She blushed again and Daniel willed her to hold her tongue.

'Do go on . . .' Vicky seemed to have a sixth sense for gossip. A sly smile crept across her face as she looked from Daniel's stony expression to Nicole's slightly nervous one.

'Well it looked like the captain and the reporter had a bit of a moment . . .'

Daniel glared at Nicole. How had he let his authority slip such that this stewardess felt comfortable enough to gossip about him in front of his face? He'd been too lax on this job; that much was clear.

Vicky was grinning. 'What kind of moment?' She turned to Daniel.

'It was nothing. She was just feeling a bit . . . uncomfortable about her interaction with Claude . . .' Daniel hoped that the mention of Claude might shut the conversation down but instead it just piqued Vicky's interest further.

'So you thought *you'd* comfort her?' Vicky's tone was suggestive of something untoward and suddenly Daniel felt like he was the one who had taken advantage of her. It struck him that maybe that was how Ore had interpreted it. Was that why she had been acting distant?

'It wasn't like that.' Daniel's denial sounded limp, even *he* wasn't sure he believed it.

'Well, Captain, I'm sure I don't need to tell you this, but you'd be advised not to mix business with pleasure.'

Daniel was mortified, and he shot Nicole a look, but she just shrugged. It was clear that this stewardess knew where her loyalties lay, and it wasn't with him.

'And then Agatha and Ore seemed to have a tense convo as well, not sure what it was about but the vibes were terrible.' Nicole concluded her rundown of the day and Daniel wondered what that exchange might have been about. Maybe Agatha had said something about that night on deck and Ore really did think he was some sort of predator? The stillness of mind he'd managed to cultivate that mourning had already evaporated, and before he'd even finished his eggs.

'By the way, Daniel, Carlos told me to tell you that he's agreed to speak to Ore today, so you'll need to make some time this afternoon.' Vicky sounded like she was annoyed at having to relay this information, but Daniel didn't have the energy to try and figure out why.

All he knew was that he wasn't in the mood to play chaperone again today, but he didn't really have a choice.

'I told her to come find you in your quarters. Dudley will take over at noon.'

It really was Vicky running the ship, thought Daniel. Wasn't he supposed to be in charge? The question was obviously written all over his face because Vicky added, 'Don't give me that look, Captain. I'm not trying to undermine you; I'm just trying to make sure we all get the stinking fat tip we deserve.

My retirement villa in the south of France is not going to buy itself after all!'

It was strange to imagine Vicky retiring, not just because she could only have been forty years old at the maximum, but also because she was always ten steps ahead of everyone. Daniel couldn't imagine her ever just stopping. As if to prove his point, she got to her feet and was out of the room, flanked by Nicole and Amanda, before he'd finished chewing his mouthful.

Daniel spent the morning in the wheelhouse flinching at every creak of a floorboard, imagining Ore standing on the other side of the door and feeling both thrilled and horribly anxious at the prospect. He tried to remember himself before he met Ore, which was only four days ago. That version of him – detached, cool, rational and level-headed – seemed totally out of reach to this version of him.

The moment he had stilled himself into something resembling calm, he heard her outside the door. He found himself drawn to the sound of her voice, and despite himself, trying to concentrate on what she was saying. Here again, she was having a strange effect on him: Daniel, the man who hates gossip, eavesdropping on a private conversation.

'I've had some luck. It's just really hard to get people to open up.' She must have been on the phone, because Daniel couldn't hear any replies.

'No I totally get that, Henry ... yeah I know, but I'm almost there, just on the brink, I can feel it.' She sounded stressed, and Daniel found himself resenting whoever this Henry guy was.

'No no, yeah yeah, profile I get it. I'm not trying to break anything ... It's just that there's definitely something ... No

I hear you. You're right. OK thanks, Henry, I'll try and get you something by end of day tomorrow, a first draft at least.'

A long pause and then: 'OK, bye, speak soon.'

He heard her let out a long sigh, and concluded Henry must be her editor. In a way Daniel found it hard to imagine anyone being Ore's boss. She seemed a person who never answered to anyone.

She knocked on the door and he made a point of walking over slowly to open it. He didn't know what he'd been expecting, but Ore's pleasant, easy smile disarmed him.

'Hello, Daniel,' she chirped breezily, her white, straight teeth, dazzling. She had to be faking this nonchalance, he thought, and she was disturbingly good at it.

'Oh, um, hello, Ore. Let me just get my jacket and we can go and find Carlos.' Daniel tried to match her bright tone.

'Great,' she said, flicking through her notebook. The only hint of any inner turmoil was her slightly ragged cuticles.

On the walk to the kitchen, they didn't speak. Ore strode slightly ahead, and Daniel wondered when she'd become so confident navigating the boat.

Carlos was perched on the counter top with a pencil in one hand and a cookbook in the other, a deep frown furrowing his brow.

'Is this a good time?' Ore asked when he didn't acknowledge their presence in the kitchen. He looked irritated for a moment and then flashed a big smile.

'Ore, yes of course, mademoiselle, let us have the interview!'

Carlos bundled them through the long narrow kitchen and through a swinging door. His 'office' was a tiny space, barely big enough for the two chairs and small desk crammed into it. Carlos gestured for Ore to take a seat, and Daniel wedged himself into the only available corner as Carlos took the other seat.

'I had heard about the chaperone from the others, but this is a little bit imposing, no?' Carlos pointed at Daniel as he spoke, and Ore laughed. It sounded a little too high-pitched.

'Yes, and remember he's a spy too!' Then it was Carlos' turn to laugh, but Daniel knew she wasn't joking. That it was meant for him to hear, to know that she knew.

As Ore opened her notebook, Daniel felt hot, and extremely claustrophobic.

Chapter 31

Ore

It was game on. She had no time to mess around anymore. Henry hadn't been forceful on the phone but he had made himself clear. No article, no staff job. She'd let herself get distracted by Daniel, and where his loyalties lay, as though it wasn't damned obvious that they resided firmly with the billionaire paying his wages. She needed to stop trying to be everyone's friend and buckle up. He could report back to Chuck if he wanted; she'd deal with that when the time came.

'So, Carlos, thanks for speaking to me. First of all are you happy to go on the record or is this on background?'

Carlos shrugged, opened his mouth to say something then seemed to decide better of it and instead said, 'Let's play it safe and say on background.'

It was to be expected, thought Ore. 'Right, OK, well let's start nice and easy. How did you end up working for Chuck?'

'It's a very long story . . .' Carlos began, and he was right, it was. It started with his childhood in Beirut and ended with him living hand to mouth as a private chef in Paris. That was where he happened across one particularly rich-seeming guest.

'What do you mean by "rich-seeming"?' Ore probed, having surmised that he was talking about Chuck.

'Oh you know, he was dressed terribly, and in Paris if you're being invited to those kinds of private functions, and you turn up wearing cargo shorts, you must have the bank account to compensate, you know. And then there was the fact that he was an American, and everyone around the table was French, but speaking in English, just for him! Imagine!' Carlos was so animated, Ore couldn't help but giggle.

'And so after dinner, while the Parisians were on the balcony smoking, I went and spoke to Mr Regas, and he complimented me on the food, and well, as you say, the rest is history.'

'And what do you think of Mr Regas now? Is he a good boss?' Ore held her pen poised over her notebook, anxious that Carlos was about to clam up, as the others had done.

'He is a fine boss – like most rich people he can afford to be nice, most of the time, you know what I mean?' Carlos paused, his question not rhetorical, it seemed.

'Not really . . .' Ore wanted to know more.

Carlos rolled his eyes at what he saw as Ore's naivety. 'He does not need to shout at people to get them to do what he wants. Everyone understands the power of money implicitly. It is like the cargo shorts, you see – he has nothing to prove, because the billions in his bank account do the talking.' Carlos leant back, seemingly very pleased with his insight.

Ore furrowed her brow and waited for him to feel the need to further explain himself. He took the bait.

'So for example, the other captain, Mr Regas never asked her to give Mr Claude a private tour. Claude said he would like a tour and then Captain Annie, she offered, and Mr Regas only said that that was very thoughtful of her, but I am sure he knew that Mr Claude is a . . . a pushy man.'

164

Ore tried to keep her expression composed, as though Carlos had not just said out loud what everyone else seemed to have been whispering behind her back since she arrived on the boat. Maybe it was the cramped quarters but she was sure she could feel Daniel tense up behind her. She soldiered on before Carlos caught on that he was overstepping.

With an even tone she asked, 'And what happened to Captain Annie in the end?' Without Vicky in the room, Ore was determined to make the most of Carlos' loose lips.

'Well she had to go. Claude is one of the biggest investors for Mr Regas as you know.' Ore nodded as if she did; she didn't want to spook Carlos, as she furiously took notes. 'So when he tried it on, I think Annie had a bit of a . . . uh . . . struggle on her hands.' Carlos looked down as he said this, visibly upset. Ore felt bad for digging, but that was the job, so she leant forward, laid a hand softly on his and waited for him to recover himself.

'She ran down to the mess actually and Vicky was there, and then Dudley and myself got there too. Then she went straight to report it to Agatha. I think Annie thought that she could speak woman to woman.' Carlos huffed indignantly at the memory. 'Of course Agatha went straight to Mr Regas.'

Daniel coughed loudly from behind Ore, and she knew that her time was running short. 'And then what happened?'

'Oh well, she was made to sign a DNA . . . no . . . what do you call it . . . damn . . .'

Carlos waved his hands around agitatedly and Ore interrupted impatiently. 'An NDA?'

Carlos clapped his hands excitedly, the sound reverberating around the cramped space and making Ore jump. 'Aha! Yes that is it, an NDA, and then twenty-four hours later she was flown off the boat.' He shrugged and then his expression dulled and he suddenly looked sad.

Ore had one more question: 'Thanks for sharing that with me, Carlos. I just have one more question for you, does *Klauparten* mean anything to you?' For the first time during the interview Carlos looked wary. He shot a look over Ore's shoulder in Daniel's direction but whatever response he got seemed to reassure him.

'I am not totally sure, but from what I can gather . . . and this is off of the record as you say?' Carlos was getting nervy.

Ore nodded emphatically.

'It is the name of Claude's company, although I am not sure what it is. It seems to make him very much money. That is all I can say. I really must be getting on now!'

And with that the interview was over, but Ore was buzzing. It was the most headway she'd made since she got on the boat. 'Thank you so much, Carlos, I really appreciate it.'

'Yes, yes no problem. I will show you out; I have prep to do.' Carlos ushered them out of the office and back through the kitchen. Once they were standing in the corridor with the door still swinging, Daniel turned to Ore.

'I didn't know about the NDA stuff,' he said quietly.

Ore wasn't sure whether she believed him anymore. 'Are you going to tell on Carlos?' Ore was surprised by how wounded he looked by the question.

'No, of course not. Listen, Ore . . .' She was looking at him expectantly when he cut himself off. 'Not here.'

He grabbed her by the hand and led her down a flight of steps and across the bottom deck. She thought about pulling her hand away at first, but despite herself, his touch felt comforting.

'Where are you taking me?' Ore asked, a little breathless from the pace.

'Kit cupboard number 6,' Daniel replied. As though that actually explained anything.

It turned out it did. It was a bit bigger than a cupboard, but it was full of kit, life jackets, water skis, one of those big blow-up banana things, though in its deflated state. The number 6 was painted on the door.

Inside, there was just about enough space for them both to stand between the shelves stacked with various iterations of neoprene.

'Why are we here, Daniel?' Ore felt exasperated and she wanted to get back to her pile of notes.

'I wanted to speak to you in private, and I feel like there's nowhere private on this boat.' Daniel seemed flustered as he looked down at her hand, which he was still holding. He dropped it suddenly. 'Oh God I'm sorry, this is actually so inappropriate. I've brought you to this weird cupboard and now you probably think I'm trying to . . . I don't know . . .' He went to reach for the door, but Ore grabbed his arm. She hadn't seen him lose his cool quite like this, and it was kind of endearing.

'It's OK, Daniel. I'm OK. I don't think you've lured me here to "do a Claude" or anything.' She cringed; it was probably too soon to be making a joke of that, but Daniel laughed nervously and appeared to calm down.

'I actually feel very safe around you.' It came out of nowhere. She hadn't believed she felt that way until she said it out loud.

But it was true. 'Although I was naive enough to think I could also trust you, so maybe I'm not the best judge of character,' she added quickly.

There was that wounded expression again. 'I didn't mean to lie – it's actually very unlike me. I don't know why I did. I think that maybe I wanted you to . . . and in the end I never actually reported back anything that you . . .' Daniel trailed off, breaking eye contact and standing up straighter. 'Sorry, this is not your problem, I just wanted to bring you here to say that I'm not going to say anything to Chuck, and you don't have to believe me but I'm saying it anyway.'

Ore was undecided; her body was so treacherous when she was around him. Everything about his presence made her feel calm and trusting but she couldn't get Agatha's words out of her head. 'Agatha said I can't trust you. She said she knew about the stuff I've been getting people to say about Chuck; she said he's not happy about it,' she said bluntly.

Daniel sighed heavily. 'Ah, so that's what she told you on the island.'

There really were spies everywhere apparently. 'Yes.' Ore was standing with her hands on her hips, waiting for his explanation.

'Agatha and I . . . we had . . .' He stalled again, searching her face for something, which he seemed to find. 'We had a strange night. I can barely remember it . . .'

'Oh God, Daniel, it's OK. I don't need to hear this; it's none of my business.' Ore was trying to stay level-headed, but her heart was beating too fast, and something like dread was coursing through her veins. *Why was she having such a strong reaction to this?*

'No, no it's not like that. Well it sort of is, but . . .' Daniel sighed again.

Ore was trying to concentrate on keeping her breathing steady.

'Basically she was complaining about Chuck and I told her that she wasn't alone and that a lot of people you had spoken to insinuated similar stuff . . . I was trying to make her feel better . . . and then she tried to kiss me.' He spoke with such earnestness and the room was so stuffy.

Ore felt disorientated. She didn't know if she felt like laughing or crying. Every time she thought she was getting to the bottom of something, some other detail would emerge. She felt her heart slow, as she regained her composure. 'I see.' So it was Agatha who couldn't be trusted? Or maybe it was both of them? Or everyone. She looked up at Daniel's face. His deep brown eyes called to something in her, and she knew she was doomed to have faith in this man, in spite of any evidence that urged the contrary.

'So you won't tell Chuck about Carlos' interview?' Ore heard the pleading vulnerability in her own voice.

'I promise,' he whispered, and once again, she believed him, hoping with her whole heart that she wasn't making a huge mistake.

They had gravitated even closer to each other in the small space. The intensity of their exchange pulled them to within touching distance, and Ore felt the urge again, to be held by him. The feeling was not excitement, like she usually felt with the men she was attracted to; she was not overcome by lust. It was something heavier, a grounding sensation. It was the same feeling she had had with Kyle.

They gazed at each other for a moment, and she thought she saw a glimmer of something in his eyes, something that she recognised. She imagined what it would be like to lean in, and cup his face in her hands. And then he took a step back.

'That NDA stuff is dodgy,' he said suddenly, looking away and bursting the bubble.

'Yeah totally.' She took his lead; this was not the time to get caught up in some romantic fantasy. The memory of Kyle's rejection flashed through her head. She was doing it again, looking for comfort in others when she should be finding it in herself.

'I mean Claude obviously has some hold over Chuck . . .' she was musing out loud.

'It can't just be the money, but then they did go to school together so maybe it's just an old friend's loyalty?' Daniel offered.

'I mean how easy is it to find a new captain though? Surely it's got to be a lot of hassle.' Ore wasn't sure how all that worked. She couldn't imagine it was the sort of thing where you just put up a LinkedIn ad.

'It is. The agency was lucky that I had some time booked off, and I could jump in to replace Annie at the last minute.'

'I think that's the missing link. I need to work out what Claude is offering Chuck that's worth all that hassle, not to mention the bad blood it's created with all his staff . . .' Ore felt sure this was the key; she just had no idea how to work it out.

'What do you know about his Klauparten company thing?' Daniel asked, and Ore was quietly impressed that he had followed the interview so intently.

'I couldn't find anything when I googled it, but I'll have another look tonight.' They stood for a moment in silence, each mulling over the puzzle.

'I think we should get out of this cupboard now; sorry it's all so cloak and dagger. I'm probably overreacting.' Daniel made for the door.

'You don't strike me as the sort of man who overreacts, Daniel, and you know this world better than me, so maybe we should try and only talk about this stuff when we're alone like this.' Ore felt a thrill at their newfound camaraderie.

'OK, well if I hear anything, I'll knock on your door, and then we can meet here to discuss it.'

'So you're a double agent then?' she said teasingly. 'Turning on your former spymaster to work for the enemy?'

But Daniel looked serious as he responded, 'Honestly? I wanted to stay out of it all, but if I am going to get involved, I want to be on the right side . . . with you.'

Ore felt heat rising into her cheeks. 'Well, glad to have you on board, Captain Wilsons, if you'll pardon the pun.'

He laughed, and it made Ore feel less alone.

Chapter 32

Daniel

'I'd better be getting back to the wheelhouse.' In truth, he knew Dudley had taken over by now, but he was beginning to feel like he couldn't trust himself in this small space with Ore standing so close to him.

Moments before he had almost lost control. Her dark eyes, doe-like and almost liquid with feeling, had pierced through something. It had felt like the lulling of the boat and gravity itself were conspiring to test his resolve. And then when he stepped away he thought he saw disappointment on her face and it made his heart beat even faster.

'How far away are we from the reef now? I'd almost forgotten that's where we were headed?' Ore was making her way out of the cupboard, throwing the question back over her shoulder nonchalantly. Daniel tried not to fixate on how much he yearned for them to be closer again, close enough for him to feel the heat radiating off her body.

'Umm—' he checked his watch '—about twelve hours. I was supposed to rest up until I relieved Dudley for the night shift.' He shrugged. 'But I guess I . . . got distracted.' As Daniel said the words it occurred to him that they were more flirtatious than he'd anticipated. He had been referring to the interview with Carlos, but from the way Ore suddenly looked down and smiled shyly, he guessed she had taken it differently.

'Sorry about that,' she said quietly, peering up at him through lashes. Just as that heaviness began to settle between them again, Ore turned suddenly and threw the door open. The blinding midday sunlight flooded in. The smoggy gatherings of their intimate huddle dispersed into the wind.

'I'm heading this way.' Ore pointed vaguely in the direction of the lower deck.

'Right well I'm heading up to the top deck to check in on Dudley . . .' Daniel pointed up, and then felt self-conscious about mimicking her gestures. Ore giggled and they both stood there for a moment. Daniel felt like a kid again, at a loss around a pretty girl.

Eventually it was Ore who turned on her heel, offering him a salute and a wink before heading below deck. Daniel didn't move and when she disappeared down the stairs he let out a big sigh.

'What the hell is wrong with you, man?' he said to himself, out loud, before looking around to check no one was there to witness his descent into madness. He shook his head forcefully, as though that might dislodge the growing sense that he already couldn't wait to see her again.

He hoped that he had regained her trust, but he was worried about where this story was going. The stuff with Claude, it was fishy for sure, but he found himself hoping that Ore would let it go and focus on Chuck. Claude was not a man you wanted to get on the wrong side of. He determined that the best thing to do would be to make sure he was up to date with Ore's investigation, and keep an eye on Claude and

Chuck. If he knew that Ore was digging into this mysterious Klauparten and he could keep an eye on Claude to make sure he wasn't getting wind of anything, maybe he could keep her safe.

He didn't particularly feel up to reflecting on exactly why he was so compelled to do so, because then he'd also have to face the fact that her touch made his blood run hot, and that earlier in the cupboard he'd felt a stirring. He hadn't gotten inappropriately hard since he was a teenager, and it felt embarrassing that he couldn't control himself.

He'd try and catch up with her after his afternoon shift, see if she'd discovered anything else, and hopefully try and gently persuade her to stick to the profile, and forget about Claude, for her own good. In the meantime, he needed some rest before he took over from Dudley.

Back in his room, Daniel slipped on his tracksuit bottoms and an old T-shirt, before sliding into bed. With his eyes closed, he found it impossible to fight the urge to relive the moment in the kit cupboard. And as it had at the time, it made him hard.

He imagined her hands, slender fingers and soft palms, curling around him, coaxing him and stroking him. He wished he could bottle the smell of her, and inhale it now as his hand pumped faster and the ache in his groin intensified. Jasmine and peppermint and something indescribably heady, like ripe flesh. He thought about the crease between her thigh and hip that he'd spied when she was on Carlos' shoulders in the shallows. He thought about the glimmer of her collarbone peeking out of her linen shirt. He thought about her mouth, slightly agape as she gazed at him in that cupboard. And then

174

he was tumbling, shuddering, thundering back into his bed. His breath heaving, and his hand wet.

He laughed to himself as he cleaned himself up in the bathroom. He didn't think of himself as a horny person. He had enjoyed sex with his ex, but since they had broken up, he had found himself surprisingly satisfied with celibacy. The odd hook-up in his home town on the rare occasions that he went back were enough to sustain the months on board. He rarely even touched himself, and when he did, it was, as with everything else in his life, efficient, more a way to get himself to sleep than something he took pleasure from. This was something different. He looked in the mirror, and found himself smiling – he looked younger.

Conveniently it did also have the effect of sending him to sleep, and when his alarm went off, he was once again dragged from an unusually deep slumber.

Daniel put on his uniform and headed up to the wheelhouse to relieve Dudley.

'I'm glad you're here, Captain. Take a look at this.' Dudley pointed to the whirl of dark grey hovering over the map on the screen in front of him. 'I think we need to go around it . . .'

Daniel leant in to take a closer look, and sighed heavily. The last thing he needed on his plate was a cyclone. 'I'll talk to Chuck.' It was one of his least favourite parts of this job, but needs must.

Chapter 33

Ore

Ore was sure she was getting the hang of the place, but somehow after going down what she could have sworn were the same stairs and corridors she always did, she found herself at an intersection that she had never come across before. She kept wandering, choosing turnings at random.

If she was being honest with herself, she was preoccupied with the revelations from Carlos' interview and the ones about Daniel and Agatha. If she was even more honest with herself, she was currently only preoccupied with the latter, and in particular about Daniel.

It was an interesting departure from how she usually thought about men. Her thoughts were not anxious or swirling. She didn't feel wrongfooted, misunderstood or gaslit. In fact, she was settling into a quiet certainty that Daniel liked her. Not just that he fancied her, but that he wanted the best for her, that he cared for her. That was not something she was accustomed to getting from men. As Kyle had so tactfully put it, it was textbook daddy issues.

Ironic, she thought, that he'd so successfully needled his way into her heart off the back of those very 'issues'. She'd told herself she wouldn't let that happen again, not until she was 'ready', not until it made sense. In her mind that meant not until she was at least, say twenty-eight, with an apartment of her own, and a staff contract to pay the rent. She was nowhere near any of those milestones, and that was before you took into consideration that Daniel was a yacht captain who literally lived on the other side of the world.

So even though she was finding it increasingly hard to deny that she enjoyed Daniel's company, and that in the kit cupboard today there had been a moment when she wanted to kiss him, she recognised that it was the same impulse she'd had in Kyle's office: a yearning to be cared for, to be looked after. And as nice as the feeling was, she wasn't sure it was the same as love. Nevertheless it was a nice change from the chaotic, head-spinning liaisons she was used to having back in New York.

She was lost in thought, and meandering through the belly of the boat aimlessly when she heard a noise from a door left ajar. Where was she? She noticed that the carpets were plusher here, and that the doors were further apart than they were in crew quarters.

The sound crystallised into distinction: someone was crying. She considered turning around, finding her way out of the warren another way, but something about the cries resonated in her, pulling at her heartstrings. She approached the door, recognising the particular wails of adolescence. She knocked quietly.

'Come in.' The words were muffled between sniffs and sobs. Almost without thinking Ore pushed the door open to find Melanie, Chuck's daughter, sitting on her bed, her knees drawn up to her chest, eyes puffy and hair scraped off her face into a strangled ponytail.

'Oh . . . it's you.' The disappointment was palpable. Ore felt immediately embarrassed. Why had she felt the need to intrude on such a private moment?

'I'm so sorry. I don't know why . . . I'll go . . .' Ore began retreating.

'No,' Melanie said forcefully, and then, more sheepishly, she added quietly: 'No, I . . . I thought it was my dad.' Something in her expression once again sent a pang of pity through Ore.

'Are you OK?' Ore instinctively moved towards her, sitting gingerly on the edge of the huge bed. She couldn't help scanning the room quickly, and noticing that it was even more luxurious than her own. Designer sunglasses were strewn across the large mahogany dressing table, and a set of multicoloured swimming costumes were hung up on a clothes rail in the corner, each still on one of those hangers shaped like a woman's silhouette and adorned with a thick bundle of tags. Melanie herself was wearing a pair of excessively distressed, stonewash jeans that looked like they could have been found in a Camden charity shop – though Ore couldn't be sure if that was by very expensive design – and an ACDC band T-shirt that hung off her slim shoulders like a poncho.

'I just thought maybe he'd notice I wasn't around and come and find me. I don't know.' She shrugged and tried on a nonchalant expression, scrubbing at her eyes with a balled fist. It didn't last, and when the determination melted back into quiet sobs, Ore inched closer and tentatively laid a hand on her shoulder.

'It's OK. It's not your fault; dads are just useless.'

At that, Melanie let out something between a snort and a giggle. Ore joined in, and after a moment, Melanie's heaving shoulders had calmed and her breathing fell back into a steady rhythm.

'You know he said that this trip would be a great opportunity to hang out?' Melanie said suddenly, her tone harsh, mocking. Ore understood the substitution: away went self-pity and out came disdain.

'Like, I wanted to go to Bali with Emily and our other mates, but he like, insisted, like basically begged me to come, and then like the moment we get here, he's invited all these other randoms, like that creepy mate of his, and all the other money guys and like you . . .' She paused and shot Ore an apologetic look. Ore batted the comment away and Melanie carried on. 'And Agatha like won't even let me talk to him most of the time, like I'm just getting in the way of the all his business deals or whatever, but really she just cares about her bonus!'

Melanie had worked herself up again.

'Just breathe,' Ore said calmly, taking in a deep breath and then slowly letting it out, then repeating the exercise until Melanie joined in.

Ore found herself marvelling at how universal some 'issues' were. All the money in the world couldn't save you from a shitty dad. Ore hadn't really thought about hers in a long time, at least not in detail. These days he was more of an abstract concept, a font of all evil, a bogeyman that could explain away all of her neuroses. She hadn't seen him in person for about five years, and she had to admit that she hadn't made an effort to change that. Eventually he'd given up trying. Maybe she'd wanted to punish him, for all those years when she was the one yearning for him, and he was nowhere to be found.

Ore wondered if one day Melanie would find herself in the

same position, attributing all her woes to the failings of this one man. It felt strangely karmic that as she had been lost wandering the halls, mulling on her own relationship with her father, here was Melanie, ten years behind, only at the beginning of her journey into the world of unsatisfactory men.

'I'm sure he does want to spend time with you, Melanie,' Ore began.

'Mel . . . call me Mel. I hate Melanie . . . Only Agatha calls me that.'

'Sure, Mel, I . . .' Ore tried to think back. What would she have wanted to hear, back when she was sixteen, torturing herself about what made her so unlovable, so beneath notice to a person who had literally bought her into being? 'I think . . . I know that he does want to. He just . . . he probably doesn't know how.'

Mel sniffed, her big green eyes welling. 'Why? Why doesn't he know?'

Ore's heart ached. 'Maybe he was never shown how.'

Mel was quiet for a moment. 'He never speaks to his dad,' she said softly. 'I've only met him once, and Mum always says that their relationship is whack.'

'Well there you go. I think often people need to be shown how to love, you know?' Ore couldn't help but pry a little further. It was probably unethical to use Chuck's teenage daughter for deep background, but she reasoned that that hadn't been her intention.

'Do you know what happened between them?'

Mel shrugged, staring at the bed covers with a distant look in her eyes. 'Well Mum says it's because he got shipped off to boarding school when he was a kid, but like, who knows. It's not like he would ever talk to me about it. All he ever asks me about is school. You know sometimes I go and like hide in the cinema room like all day, just to see if he'll notice? He never does. He doesn't even know about Emily.'

Ore was getting out of her depth, but despite herself she felt a jolt of excitement for having verified the boarding school fact.

'Who's Emily?' Ore asked softly. She didn't want to spook Mel, but she looked up suddenly, that defiant expression returning to her face.

'Emily is my girlfriend.' Mel's tone was combative, and Ore sensed that this was a sentence that had been practised in the mirror, rehearsed a million times in her head.

'And you think he'd have a problem with that?' Ore was having to tread carefully.

Mel rolled her eyes, 'no, obviously not – he's just never asked.' Mel was quiet again for a moment. 'Like isn't it ridiculous that you basically know more about my life than he does, and like you're basically a stranger? No offence.'

'None taken,' Ore reassured her, but Mel was on a roll.

'I've literally wanted to go to the Barrier Reef for forever on this stupid boat and it's only now that stupid Claude is here that Dad finally wants to go. He's only interested in his stupid business, like now that Claude wants to go, all of sudden it's got to happen right now.'

Ore felt a tingle run down her spine. Why would Claude want to go to the Barrier Reef so badly? And what did their business have to do with it? It could just be a red herring, but Ore had a gut feeling that it was at least worth adding to her bundle of notes.

'Well, it might still be fun to go to the reef?' Ore offered lamely.

'I guess.' Mel lowered her chin to her knees and sighed. After a minute or so of silence, Ore began to feel awkward.

In true teenage girl fashion, Mel's own barometer for discomfort was pretty sensitive. 'You can like, go, you know?' Ore knew that the sneery remark was defensive.

Ore stood up from the bed. 'You should tell Chuck about Emily. He might just be waiting on you to open up a bit; maybe he's afraid of overstepping?'

'Maybe, whatever.' Mel was looking out the window, and Ore took her cue to leave. As she reached door, Mel turned her head, and almost inaudibly she said, 'Thanks.'

Ore nodded, mirroring Mel's own sad smile, and shut the door gently behind her.

Chapter 34

Ore

Back out in the maze, Ore was eager to be reunited with her pile of notes. She headed upwards and then once she made it to the top deck she figured out her way back to the room, trotting all the way.

She passed one of the stewardesses first, offering up a benign smile, and then at the bottom of yet another flight of stairs, she spotted a figure she was determined to avoid. It was Claude, walking up towards her calmly. Ore's heartbeat quickened as he approached, and she couldn't be sure if she was going to fight or flee. For now it was freeze, as she stood motionless at the top of the stairs. Once he reached her, she stood to the side and he passed without a word, his expression impregnable.

As Ore's pulse returned to normal, she took a deep breath. *You're overreacting*, she told herself, as she bounded down the stairs, trying to expel the nervous energy from her body.

Once outside her door though, she stopped cold again, noticing immediately that the door was not entirely shut. The lock hadn't clicked into place, as though someone had left in a rush but made sure the door closed quietly behind them. An image of Claude flashed into her mind, his hand easing the door closed behind him as he checked no one was coming.

Or maybe it was someone else altogether, on their way in . . . Ore's heart was back to racing as she tentatively pushed the door open.

There was no one inside, *obviously*, she thought, and wondered when she had become so paranoid. She had probably been the one in a rush that morning. She laid her bag, with this morning's notes from Carlos' interview, down on the bed, and went into the bathroom.

She looked at herself in the mirror, admiring the new sun-kissed shade of her arms and face. She tried to centre herself. It had been a long day, and she realised she hadn't eaten anything since breakfast, and that had been a rushed affair – she'd snuck into the mess for a slice of toast before the crew came in for their food because she hadn't fancied another terse interaction with Vicky.

She'd go and find Carlos to see if he could send some food to her room again. She splashed her face with water and reached for her perfume bottle, instinctively, with her left hand. Ore was not a particularly tidy person but she was a creature of habit. Wherever she stayed she'd keep her favourite bottle of jasmine oil and orange blossom scent on the left side of the sink.

Her hand landed clunkily on the porcelain. The bottle wasn't there. She frowned; she was sure she'd put some on this morning. In the bedroom she checked the bedside table, but there was nothing. Back in the bathroom she stood with her hands on her hips and rotated slowly, scanning every surface. Finally, she reached for the mirror and pulled. It was one of those slim cabinets and behind the glass on the middle shelf, was the squat, pear-shaped bottle.

She stared at it, almost afraid to touch it, and then closed the cabinet again. Her reflection looked back at her, scared. Someone *had* been in her room. She rushed over to her suitcase and rifled until she found her notebook, still nestled between her laptop and a pair of trousers. They didn't look like they'd been disturbed. Ore took a deep breath.

The thought of Claude looking through her things made her feel sick. She scoured the rest of the room but nothing else seemed out of place. Granted it was hard to tell, as she'd left a fair amount of her own mess.

Why would he have moved her perfume bottle? It felt like some sort of psychological warfare, like he just wanted her to know he'd been there. She shivered. She'd have to find a better hiding place for her notes. If he'd come once and failed to find anything, surely he would try again.

In the meantime she triple-locked the door, even going as far as to push a chair up against the handle. On the one hand it felt dramatic, but on the other, she had no idea really who she was dealing with. She opened her laptop, and for good measure she plugged in her little-used dongle. She wasn't about to risk doing any more research on the boat's Wi-Fi; she was up against tech entrepreneurs for God's sake. She couldn't believe she'd been so careless up until now.

She was glad that she'd followed Gail, her old professor's advice about paper notes – 'always keep a physical copy, and preferably keep it on you, at all times.' Gail had been talking about reporting on black op sites during the Iraq War. Ore hadn't expected to need to follow her guidance on a luxury mega yacht, but then again, in a couple of ways it wasn't so dissimilar: a void of legal jurisdiction and a powerful enemy with almost unlimited resources . . .

Ore was trying not to panic when the phone rang, and she almost jumped out of her skin. With shaking hands she picked it up.

'Mademoiselle, I am calling to see if you are coming to dinner or you want room service?' It was Carlos. Ore sighed with relief, and then felt a little silly about allowing herself to indulge so entirely in the horror movie version of her own life.

'Ahh, Carlos, you read my mind.' Ore's stomach grumbled in agreement. 'Could I get dinner in my room again? Sorry if that's more work for you. I don't think I can face any more socialising tonight . . .'

'No problem at all, I'll make you something special. Leave it with me!' Carlos' breezy tone calmed Ore, and as she put the phone down, she began to consider the possibility that maybe she had absentmindedly put the perfume in the cabinet, or maybe whoever cleaned her room had? She decided to try and believe this version of events, for the sake of her own sanity.

Ore crawled under the sheets and turned the TV on, flicking through channels mindlessly, until her racing thoughts slowed. She settled on a reality TV show with a premise she couldn't quite fathom and soon enough had fallen into a deep sleep.

Chapter 35

Daniel

It was getting dark and the sea was unusually calm. It usually was before a storm, as the saying went. Daniel stood on the top deck looking out at the expanse of silver. The sun was beginning to dip behind a forebodingly dark smudge of clouds on the horizon. He checked his watch. Chuck was supposed to have met him fifteen minutes ago, but it seemed he was, as usual, running to his own schedule.

When Chuck did eventually come up the stairs, he seemed totally unrushed. His phone was nestled in the crook of his shoulder, and as he approached Daniel, he was wrapped up in the conversation. 'The thing is, Derek, that he'll need to see the site. Well that's not exactly right, he wants to see the site, before he invests the equipment, and the rest of the money . . .' Chuck looked up at Daniel and rolled his eyes, making a motion with his hands that meant 'I'm trying to wrap this up' as he leant against the railing.

'Sorry, Derek, I have to go now. I'll keep you in the loop, but stop worrying – this is in the bag; we just need these last moving parts to slot into place.'

It was funny, thought Daniel, how 'business speak' was so particular and yet so vague. Chuck wasn't really *saying* anything. 'Copy that' seemed perfectly suitable and far more efficient to Daniel.

'Sorry, Dan, my bad – running a bit behind today.' Chuck slid his phone into his pocket. 'You know how business is?' He turned to Daniel, a single eyebrow raised.

This was why Daniel had been dreading this encounter. Chuck was a master at making him feel somehow inadequate and a little flustered. Both were feelings he had been relatively unused to before this job. Between Chuck and Ore, Daniel was watching his carefully constructed composure splinter away.

'Not particularly, sir, but not to worry. What did you want to discuss?' Even when Daniel did manage a neutral answer, it felt like Chuck was mocking him.

'Right, Captain, OK, straight to the point as usual – that's what I like about you.' Daniel did not feel like this was true.

He just nodded in response. He wanted this interaction to be over as soon as possible.

Chuck held Daniel's gaze for a moment too long, narrowing his eyes slightly, as if willing him to speak. Daniel held firm. It always felt like a conversation with Chuck turned into an unspoken power struggle.

'Right well, I wanted to talk about resetting course this morning. I'm not sure what that's about.' Chuck was smiling, an expression of faux curiosity on his face. 'And I don't remember approving it.'

Daniel ground his teeth, trying to contain his annoyance. *He* was the captain. He understood that Chuck was his boss, and that the very wealthy are accustomed to having things go their way, but Daniel was new to this level of micromanagement.

He had never had his boating experience questioned before. Usually his boss and their guests were happy as long as meals were served on time and the pool towels were restocked regularly.

'Sorry, sir, as I explained in the memo . . .' Daniel had slipped the note under the door of Agatha's office that morning '. . . there is some really bad weather forecast for tonight and we need to go around it.'

Chuck frowned and looked petulant, as if he was considering who he needed to call to get the weather in line.

'What happens to the itinerary if we go round?' Chuck asked finally.

'We'll be about twenty-four hours behind, so we won't get to the reef until the day after tomorrow,' Daniel said flatly.

Chuck huffed, and then ran his hands through his hair exasperatedly. 'And if we go through, we can stay on schedule?'

'Well, in theory yes, but we can't go through, sir, it's a cyclone.' Daniel had assumed that would put an end to the matter, but Chuck persisted.

'What category?'

Daniel was surprised that he knew to ask the question, and felt himself fumble. 'Well, er, it's category one . . . but er, I wouldn't recommend—'

But Chuck was already waving his hand dismissively. 'Category one! Is that all? Annie steered us through those all the time – sometimes I really miss her tenacity.' Chuck shot an accusatory look at Daniel and then stared almost wistfully into the middle distance.

'And yet that is the very reason you fired her?' It slipped out before Daniel could stop himself, and as he watched the shock wash across Chuck's face he imagined his own was probably fixed into a similar expression.

'Excuse me, Captain?' Chuck's tone grew icy and menacingly quiet.

'My apologies, sir, I don't know what came over me.' Daniel felt the heat rising into his cheeks and he dropped his head.

'You better make sure it doesn't come over you again, Captain. As Annie found out, I am generous, but I am not forgiving.' It sounded like a threat, and by the look on Chuck's face, he meant it to.

'Those I hold close, those I trust, I will go a long way to protect, but those who betray me, they often come to regret it,' Chuck continued, his voice totally devoid of emotion.

Daniel found himself saying 'yes, sir' and keeping his head bowed.

There was silence for a moment and then Chuck changed the subject. 'So have you got any updates on our lady journalist?'

Daniel got the distinct feeling these two thoughts were not really disconnected at all. Chuck was putting his loyalty to the test.

'Not really, sir, the crew are pretty discreet, although I did see she had the opportunity to talk to Claude and the other investors the other day, which I was not privy to.'

Chuck stiffened, almost imperceptibly, and for his next question he re-engaged the friendly tone he had had before. 'You don't need to worry about that. Claude and the others wouldn't have had much to say . . .' Chuck smiled at Daniel. 'Unless she's mentioned anything to you?'

'No, sir,' Daniel answered a little too quickly, and berated himself as he watched suspicion flash across Chuck's face.

'Right, well, as I've mentioned, it would be deeply . . . unfortunate if you weren't being straight with me, Dan, and if Ore were to publish anything . . . unsubstantiated, it would be detrimental to her career as well. I have a few friends in the papers who think of me as a very good judge of character.' The litany of threats was delivered with nonchalance, but Daniel understood the severity of them. If Ore published something Chuck didn't like, she wouldn't work again, and neither would he.

'I understand, sir,' Daniel said, finally looking up to meet Chuck's intense gaze. For a moment they were locked in, neither wanting to back down. Eventually it was the ringing of Chuck's phone that cracked the tension.

'Let's stay on course please, Captain – the only way is through!' Chuck said before answering the phone and heading back the way he came. 'Sandra, hi, talk to me . . .'

Chapter 36

Ore

Ore woke up with a start and an immediate sense that something was wrong. At first she couldn't work out where she was and the static sound of the TV added to her disorientation. *Right. Yes, I'm on the boat.* But that realisation was not comforting in the least. It meant that the room swaying was most probably not in her head. She scrambled for the robe on the back of her door, but lost her balance as the cabin jerked suddenly, sending her shoulders plummeting into the plush carpet. She decided crawling was best.

Next she made her way to the windows, pulled the curtains, and then immediately wished she hadn't. Through the glass, which now didn't seem at all sufficient, a black and angry sky stormed intermittently. The nightmarish scene was punctuated by washes of ink. It took Ore a moment to compute that that was the sea and when she did, she felt sick to her stomach. She was no expert but she was pretty sure the waves shouldn't have been reaching up that far; she was on the mid deck . . .

Ore had never been in a situation where the possibility of death felt so looming. No longer was her brain at the wheel; instead she felt like a passenger in her own body, a body that was hell-bent on staying alive.

The floor see-sawed erratically but she managed to get to the door. All the lights in the corridor flickered a ghoulish green and it was eerily silent. She laid her hands flat on the wall for support but a sudden sway sent her flying sideways and there was an almost deafening shattering sound as she hit the ground. Confused, she rolled herself onto her other side. Her white bathrobe was soaked in blood. For the first time since she'd woken up she felt a cold sweat of panic prick the back of her neck.

She gingerly ran her hand up her side and winced as she hit a tender patch on her side. She pulled back the robe, but there was only a small scratch on her belly. It only occurred to her in that moment to look at what she'd fallen onto. Seeping into the threads of the carpet were trails of oozing deep brown liquid, and then nestled on top, a steak.

Ore laughed out loud and the sound bounced off the walls. That must have been her dinner. She guessed Carlos had left it outside her room when she was asleep. It was not her blood soaking the robe, but that from a medium-rare ribeye. It looked delicious, she thought, before another violent tip brought her back into the moment. On closer inspection the scratch seemed the result of the smashed plate scraping across her skin. It wouldn't be this that killed her, she thought wryly.

Ore began dragging herself along the corridor. In moments of calm she would get to her feet, still keeping her body low to the floor in a sort of crouch, and try and cover as much ground as she could before the boat was thrown once again by the waves. As if on autopilot, she made her way up to the top deck. The stairs were particularly perilous, and it took what felt like an age to get to the top.

Finally she found herself outside the door of the wheelhouse. Her body had sought out the safest place on the boat, as close to Daniel as she could get.

She braced as the impact on the left side of the boat sent the wall to her right into a horizontal lunge, and then moving with the momentum on the way back up, she lurched for the handle and fell through the doorway.

'What the hell!' It was Dudley, and he sounded agitated. Worse than that, he sounded scared.

From her position on the floor she could see Daniel, sitting at the helm, eyes trained straight ahead and seemingly calmly adjusting various dials in front of him.

'Who is it?' he asked, not turning round, and without a hint of Dudley's panic in his voice.

'It's our errant reporter,' Dudley said dismissively, before turning his attention back to the small screen in front of him.

'Ore,' Daniel breathed, as if in a sigh of relief, 'are you OK?' He was still looking straight ahead, but Ore reasoned that it was definitely for the best. She was about to answer when a sheet of whistling black sea washed across the entire pane of the windshield.

'Holy Christ, mother of God,' Dudley exclaimed. 'How the hell have we found ourselves in the middle of this, Captain?'

'It'll be fine, Dudley; we just need to ride her out.' Daniel's voice was steady, but Ore was sure she could detect an edge to it, as though he were trying to convince himself as much as Dudley.

'Why are we even in this mess? Weren't you in charge of charting? Annie would have never got us into this situation.'

'Annie isn't here.' Daniel's tone had turned steelier. 'I am in charge of this boat now.'

Dudley huffed, exasperated, but he didn't answer.

A radio crackled to life. '*Thalassa*, do you copy?' The voice sounded distant, and Ore felt acutely aware of how far away from anything they were. In the middle of the ocean, in the middle of the night. What had possessed her to accept this assignment?

Dudley lunged for the radio. 'Copy, we're at minus 18.2871, 147.6992, sailing through violent storm.'

That didn't sound good.

'Charting east,' Dudley clarified.

'You're around fifty-five nautical miles from the reef. Chart west to reach calmer waters,' came the urgent voice.

'Captain?' Dudley turned to Daniel, who remained silent. 'Captain!' Dudley repeated. 'This isn't some ego test; you don't have to prove anything to Chuck. You need to get this boat to safer waters.' Dudley was pleading now.

Ore kept her eyes on the back of Daniel's head, the whole room holding its breath.

'Copy, charting west,' Daniel said finally, and Dudley let out a loud sigh.

For a few moments the only sounds were the waves crashing and Dudley typing. Ore didn't dare make a sound. Maybe she'd been wrong to come here. She scooped herself into a ball on the floor, hugging her knees to her chest, and focused on her breathing. She looked up at the clock hanging in the corner of the room: 2.31 a.m.

Chapter 37

Daniel

Daniel was berating himself for letting Chuck convince him of this insane plan. But it wasn't until Ore was in the room that he knew he had to abandon the madness. He hadn't dared to look at her, partly because he really needed to focus on the task at hand, and partly because he feared that if he looked into her deep dark eyes he might melt. Right now, it was only adrenaline and a dash of dissociation keeping him in control and he imagined that a warm smile from her might break him down into a blubbering mess.

As it was, her presence had calmed him, and it wasn't until she had burst through the door that he'd realised how worried he'd been about her.

'Captain Wilsons.' It was the radio again, but the internal channel this time. Even Vicky sounded stressed. It must be bad.

'I'm hunkered down in the salon on the lower deck with all the guests. Well most of them . . . Ore is unaccounted for.'

Dudley interrupted. 'She's with us.'

'How the hell did she get up there? Anyway . . . that's great, but we can't find Mel . . .' There seemed to be some commotion in the background and the line cut out.

It took a moment for Daniel to even remember who Mel was. He hadn't seen her in days. She usually kept to herself, slinking around the boat from her room to the gym to the pool and back.

'I really hope she's all right.' Ore's voice came from behind him.

Then Vicky was back. 'Chuck is going out of his mind. I don't know what to do.' She was speaking quietly, defeatedly.

Just then, a wave flung itself over the cabin again, the clock smashed to the floor and a chair from the corner of the room slid across the floor and slammed into the wall.

Ore yelped.

'Are you OK, Ore?' Daniel couldn't resist anymore. He spun round in his chair. The sight of Ore made his blood run cold. She was huddled in a white robe, and her left side was drenched in what looked like blood. Despite his better judgement, he got out of his chair and knelt in front of her, his eyes wide and full of fear.

'What happened?' He reached out for her instinctively, laying his hand on her shoulder and leaning in to look at the wound.

'It's OK, Daniel, it's not what it looks like . . . It's just, it's um, steak juice?' She looked up at him and the absurdity of the moment was overwhelming. He burst out laughing and soon enough she'd joined in.

'Guys, I think that this cute moment is going to have to wait until we're not in the middle of a cyclone.' It was Dudley, but when Daniel looked over at him, he could see a smile tugging at the corner of his lips as he spoke.

'A cyclone?' Ore's laughter evaporated.

'It's not technically a cyclone; it's just a violent storm.' Ore's face fell and it dawned on him that for those not versed in shipping terminology 'violent storm' didn't sound that reassuring. It was definitely better than a cyclone though.

'We're charting out of it now, so in an hour or so, we should be in calmer water.'

Ore nodded, still looking nervous.

'Don't worry, you're in safe hands,' Dudley piped up.

'I know,' Ore almost whispered looking into Daniel's eyes. The air between them stilled, and Daniel felt his heart ache.

'Not as safe as Annie's but still . . .' Dudley muttered under his breath, breaking the trance of the moment.

Daniel was crouched in front of Ore, and another crash knocked him off balance.

'Daniel!' Ore reached for him.

'I'm fine, I'm fine,' he said, dragging himself back over and into his seat. He was a bit embarrassed, but more than that he was touched by the concern in her voice.

Over the next half an hour the violence of the waves calmed. Daniel decided to check in with the rest of the boat.

'Vicky, how's everything down there? I think we're out of the worst of it.'

'We're OK, still no sign of Mel though. I would try and find her, but I need to stay here and keep everyone calm. Some of the greener crew are totally traumatised.'

Daniel could sympathise. He remembered his own first big storm, back when he'd been a deckhand. It was really the first time he had understood all that talk of the ocean as a 'cruel and unforgiving mistress'. That was when he'd come to terms with the fact that she could never really be controlled. It had terrified him and seduced him. He was a man who strove for control in all things, and here was one thing he could never tame.

'Any idea where she could be?' Daniel asked.

'I sent Oscar out to scout the obvious places, but this boat is bloody huge, Daniel. It's hard to know where to start.' Even through the distortion of the radio, Daniel could hear the exhaustion in Vicky's voice.

'I think I know where she is.' It was Ore, speaking like she'd just had a revelation.

'How would you . . . ?' Daniel began but before he could finish the sentence Ore was stumbling to her feet. He stood up just in time to catch her as she lost her balance. The swaying was less severe, but the boat was by no means sailing smoothly.

'Thanks.' Ore steadied herself. 'Just trust me,' she said and locked Daniel in a stern gaze. Finally, he nodded.

'We're going to find her,' he reported back to Vicky. And then he turned to Dudley. 'You got this,' Daniel said and before Dudley had time to protest, he was leading Ore out of the wheelhouse, the door slamming behind them.

'I think she's in the cinema room,' Ore said and then frowned. 'Although I have to admit I have no idea where that actually is.'

'Lucky I've memorised the entire layout of the boat,' Daniel said.

'Of course you have,' Ore replied, rolling her eyes. 'Please, Captain, lead the way.'

Despite the seriousness of the situation, Daniel smiled to himself, pleased to be the beneficiary of that much famed English 'teasing'.

Chapter 38

Ore

They found Mel cowering in the corner behind the third row of seats. The room really was a 'cinema' room, complete with red velvet upholstery, cupholders and long horizontal speakers built into the walls.

It had been a less treacherous journey than the one to the wheelhouse, but on a few occasions Ore had found herself falling into Daniel's arms. It was almost comical how he always seemed to be right there whenever she stumbled.

'Mel, there you are. Everyone's been looking for you.' Ore knelt down. Mel had been crying and she instinctively leant in for a hug. Ore was slightly taken aback but settled into it.

'I couldn't sleep, so I came down to watch a movie but then the boat was rocking so much and I tried to get up the stairs but I fell and hurt my ankle.' Mel's voice was muffled in Ore's shoulder.

'Let's have a look.' Ore pulled back and looked down. Sure enough Mel's foot was swollen; the side of her ankle had already begun to bruise.

'Can you walk on it?' Daniel asked, his voice calming, to Ore at least.

Mel shook her head.

'That's fine. We'll just stay with you here,' Ore said reassuringly and Mel gave her a small, sad smile.

'Your dad is really worried about you.' Daniel knelt down too.

'Really?' The hope in Mel's voice was a little heartbreaking, thought Ore.

'Of course, he's been looking for you everywhere,' Ore added. It wasn't quite true but she supposed that for a billionaire, sending your staff to look for your lost daughter was akin to a normal person doing it themselves.

Daniel got out his radio. 'We've found her.'

Vicky's reply came immediately. 'Oh thank God, where are you?' Before Daniel could answer they heard Vicky relay the message – 'they've found her, Mr Regas' – and then in the distance Chuck's voice: 'They've found my baby?'

Mel's smile got a little brighter.

'We're in the cinema, she's hurt her ankle so we're going to stay with her until everything's calmed down a bit,' Daniel explained.

'Copy that. Good work, Captain.'

'It was Ore who found her.'

There was a beat, and then, with an edge of reluctance Vicky replied, 'Thanks, Ore.'

'Don't mention it,' Ore called back as she settled down beside Mel.

Vicky didn't elaborate; the radio crackled into silence.

Mel incrementally lowered her head onto Ore's shoulder. Daniel sat on the other side of her.

For the next few hours, the three of them sat there, huddled in the corner, intermittently relaying their experiences of the night and then falling into long, comfortable silences.

It was hard to keep track of time in the dark, windowless space, but Ore supposed it was nearing morning when she heard footsteps approaching. Mel was snoring softly. At some point in their exhausted state, Daniel and Ore's hands had found each other, and when the door opened, she pulled her palm from under his suddenly.

Vicky was the first to march in, closely followed by Chuck.

'Oh, sweetie,' he cooed, rushing over to Mel and scooping her into his arms. It was a disconcerting sight, to see him express such fatherly tenderness, and Ore, Daniel and Vicky all lowered their gaze away from the intimate moment.

'Dad,' Mel started, before bursting into tears. 'I was so scared.' Chuck gathered her into a tighter hug.

'Oh, pumpkin, I'm so sorry. They told me you hurt yourself? Let's get you to Gerry; he hasn't practised for years but I'm sure he knows his way around a sprained ankle.'

Mel nodded meekly and the pair made their way out of the cinema, Mel limping and propped up by Chuck's arms around her waist.

Vicky let out a huge sigh and for a terrible moment Ore worried she might cry. She didn't. Instead she turned to Daniel and Ore, hands on hips.

'Well that was an absolute nightmare. You two look terrible. I suggest we all get a little bit of shut-eye before we have to be at breakfast.' Ore couldn't tell if she was joking; surely the crew wouldn't be expected to carry on the day as normal after this?

'Agreed,' said Daniel. Vicky turned and left without another word.

Ore felt shell-shocked. Daniel leant back against the wall.

They were sitting shoulder to shoulder and Ore was suddenly extremely aware of that. They didn't speak and after a while their breathing matched pace.

'I'm so sorry,' Daniel said finally, quietly.

'About what? You couldn't have known about the storm.'

Daniel didn't reply straight away and then: 'Actually I did, but I let Chuck talk me into going through it. He's completely obsessed with getting to the reef as quickly as possible, God knows why. I swear I'll never listen to him again.'

He looked so determined and serious that Ore snorted at the earnestness of it all. 'Well, that seems unlikely, but yeah, maybe when it comes to risking the lives of everybody on board . . .'

Ore had meant it to sound teasing, but when Daniel turned to look at her his eyes were brimming with pain and remorse.

'Oh, Daniel, sorry, I was just kidding. Too soon I guess?' She smiled, trying to lift the mood, but he dropped his head.

Now her heart was aching for him. She lifted his chin up to meet her gaze. 'Daniel, it's not your job to protect everyone, but for what it's worth, without you here, and your insane ability to keep your cool in the midst of chaos tonight, this could all have ended very badly . . .'

'I've put you in danger, Ore . . . I need to tell you something . . .' Daniel looked up at her, his eyes full of sorrow, and something inside of her snapped. She pressed a finger to his mouth to stop him saying any more.

There was a split second where she knew that she had the chance to lean back, to choose an awkward apology over the crossing of a line, but she didn't. His lips met hers softly, and she melted into him, her hands moving to cup his face, to pull

203

him in closer. He let out a sound like a whimper and the pressure of his mouth on hers deepened. She felt a jolt deep in the pit of her stomach, and the warmth of his breath felt as though it was enveloping her whole body.

He pulled away suddenly, and in the soundproofed room, their jagged breathing was the only thing she could hear. She had a sense that his better judgement might be kicking in, but she wanted one last taste before it took over.

She reached out, and pulled him back to her, pressing her body against his and sighing with something like relief when his arms snaked around her waist. She realised that she had been waiting for this, maybe not consciously, but now that they were here, it felt inevitable and somehow fated. She had never felt this way before, a combination of desire and total serenity, something both foreign and divine.

Her arms encircled his neck and she found herself suddenly horizontal, her back arching against the plush, dark-carpeted floor. Daniel's hands glided down her side, hooking around her thigh as he settled his weight on top of her. They were entangled with writhing limbs and hot breaths. Ore had lost sense of where hers ended and his began. Time became languid, her thoughts crystallising into simple desire. As he trailed kisses down her neck, she found herself thinking about how new this feeling was. Her body was excited, she was turned on, but she was also calm, comfortable, unrushed, able to fully indulge in the tingles of pleasures that were erupting all over her body. She felt safe.

She nestled her face into his neck and inhaled the sweet mix of him: hints of cocoa, musk and something like sea salt; it was dizzying and startlingly familiar.

She heard herself moan as his fingers began fumbling with the buttons on her shirt. Her head tilted back, to give him better access. And then his hands retreated. For a moment she thought maybe she was about to wake up from a dream, that this was a fantasy her own brain had concocted and was now overwhelmed by. She kept her eyes closed, wanting to hold on to this moment for a few seconds more. Her breathing slowed and she felt the weight of him disappear.

As she floated back into the confusion of reality, she realised what was happening. Finally she worked up the courage to open her eyes. Daniel was kneeling, just out of arm's reach, his gaze trained to the floor in front of him. She got the sense he was trying very hard not to look at her. Sheepishly, she sat up, curling her knees under her chin. She felt mortified.

After what felt like an eternity of silence he said softly, 'Sorry, Ore, I'm not sure what came over me. I think it's been an . . . intense night . . . maybe we should try and get some sleep.'

His words echoed around her head, but they felt meaningless. He might as well have been speaking in ancient Greek. She was aware that she was nodding, and though they were resolutely avoiding eye contact he must have sensed the movement because he stood up and awkwardly laid a lumpen palm on her shoulder before walking out of the room.

Ore didn't know how long she stayed in that room. The stillness of the soundproofed air was a safe haven away from what she assumed was the chaos above deck. It was the furious buzz in her back pocket that finally roused her from her dazed state.

'Henry, hi.' She tried to hide the exhaustion in her voice.

She realised with a jolt of terror that she had promised Henry a first draft today.

'Ore, how's it going?' He was also trying to hide something, but his thinning patience was obvious in those few words.

'Well actually we had a pretty mad night, a cyclone.'

'Christ, are you OK?' Henry's voice was momentarily tinged with concern and Ore was grateful that the drama of the previous day might buy her some sympathy – and some time.

'Listen I just wanted to check in, in case you wanted to talk anything through before you send over the first draft . . . tonight.' Ore was feeling overwhelmed. She took a deep breath and managed to reason that if she went to bed now she could probably sleep for a few hours and still have time to send something a little rough over to Henry later.

'Sure, Henry, tonight.'

'Great.' Ore could hear the relief in his voice. She hung up without saying goodbye and dragged herself back to her cabin.

Chapter 39

Daniel

Day 5

Daniel's brain had a canny way of compartmentalising. Much as he had after the 'Agatha incident', Daniel pushed the encounter with Ore to the back of his mind as he climbed the stairs back to the wheelhouse.

Dudley looked exhausted. The bags under his eyes had developed an alarmingly purple hue. He didn't even seem to have the energy to greet Daniel when he walked in; instead he just dipped his chin in greeting.

'Dudley, go to bed. You look terrible.' Daniel was hoping he sounded compassionate but the order was a little too clipped, a sign of his own tiredness.

Dudley didn't need any more encouragement though. He grunted in agreement as he pulled himself to his feet and almost stumbled out of the room. Daniel settled into the empty seat and busied himself getting the boat back on course. They'd had to take a considerable detour and now, they'd be behind schedule. Chuck would just have to deal with it. It was mad really how Daniel was still worried about Chuck's judgement even after he'd put the whole boat in danger with his obstinance.

Still, Daniel had to bear some responsibility – he was the captain after all.

It was about midday by the time Dudley came back. Daniel had been awake for almost twenty-four hours and was feeling delirious.

'Now *you* look terrible,' Dudley said dryly. Daniel made a sound somewhere between a snort and a giggle, and Dudley looked almost alarmed.

'I think you need to go to bed, Captain – you're starting to lose it.'

Daniel had to admit that his faculties were waning. He was having trouble remembering the order of the last day. He heaved himself from his seat and lumbered out the door.

It wasn't until he lay down in bed that he remembered he still needed to warn Ore about his conversation with Chuck, warn her to stay away from the story she was intent on digging up. The madness of the storm had gotten in the way. He had tried to tell her when they were down in the cinema room, before she leant in and . . . everything got out of control.

The rest of what happened had blurred now in his mind. He knew he had wanted her, badly. That he'd almost convinced himself that maybe he was back in his own bed, fantasising again. The mix of fear, adrenaline and white-hot lust, all of it had messed with his judgement. He'd let himself go, egged on by the receptiveness of her body to his touch. He'd indulged and pulled away too late, the damage done. He could recall clearly now the look on her face, unmitigated desire and utter vulnerability. It had terrified him.

Daniel didn't sleep well that night. He dreamt of his father for the first time in a decade. A friend had told him that he'd spotted Leroy parking his pickup in the driveway of a condo in Lake Jackson. Daniel hadn't believed him. There was no way his dad could be so close and never have visited. It didn't make sense. He had stopped believing his mom telling him that his dad had gone on a top-secret government mission, at about ten, the same time he discovered Santa Claus wasn't real, but he always assumed his dad was at least far away. Lake Jackson, that was a fifteen-minute drive.

In the dream, like in real life, Daniel drove up to his address, passed his house dozens of times. Whenever he was leaving town he would detour to drive down that road and see his dad's truck for himself. Once he spotted an old man, with his back to the road, sweeping the drive, but it wasn't until later that his brain made the connection – that the old man was probably his dad, just fifteen years older than the last time he'd seen him.

In the dream, unlike in real life, Daniel walked up to the front door. He knocked three times and waited. He fought the instinct to run away and when the door finally opened, the man who answered looked exactly the same as the day he'd walked out. For a moment the men locked eyes and Daniel started to smile, but then the door swung shut again and just as it slammed into the frame, Daniel woke up with a start.

Chapter 40

Ore

Day 5

Ore only managed about three hours of fitful sleep before she gave up on the idea. She was in turmoil. She needed to send that first draft, but she couldn't stop thinking about Daniel. This was why men, sex and feelings weren't supposed to mix. Had she learnt nothing from Kyle? Was she doomed to continually confuse closeness and care for attraction? Now she'd lost the only person on this boat she'd felt like she could trust.

On top of that she was nowhere near done with her investigation and Henry was expecting a draft from her any minute now. She had to push the Daniel stuff to the back of her mind and focus on her job.

She took a while to get settled, as she always did when a deadline was looming. Her brain got ahead of itself and insisted on completing any other task that had also been neglected. That's how she found herself hanging all her clothes in the empty wardrobe, a whole five days into her stay. As she tidied the bathroom, she remembered with a start the strange goings-on in her room from the day before. She'd wanted to discuss it with Daniel, but then everything had gotten crazy and now that probably wouldn't happen. She put it out of her mind.

Finally she made it to the desk. For the next hour *she* started a draft of the article she wanted to write. She soon realised that a series of suspicions did not a story make. There were serious holes. She'd followed up on Klauparten, but the company seemed to be a shell, registered in 2000, with no employees and owned by someone called Derek Foley. Derek, after some quick googling, appeared to be a South African ecologist. He was kind of handsome, tanned and blonde with exceedingly symmetrical features and an easy smile. She had no idea how he fit into this thing.

So the only facts she had were that Chuck's origin story was at worst a fabrication and at best some massaging of the truth. That Chuck had gone to school in Belgium with one of his now serious investors, who didn't seem to actually exist: Claude. She also knew that the previous captain, a woman named Annie, had been assaulted by that very same mysterious Claude, paid off and silenced by an NDA. But she didn't have any on-the-record sources to back up those allegations or any real proof. She tore up the sheet of paper she'd been scribbling on and lowered her head into her hands. *Billionaire has dodgy friend and covers up sexual assault*, sadly, in this day and age, wasn't a headline.

So Ore relented, and wrote the story that everyone wanted her to write, the one Henry was expecting. It was basically a regurgitation of Chuck's spiel that very first day at breakfast with a little bit of colour added in, the odd unattributed quote from Vicky, another from Carlos. Some overly verbose descriptions of the interior of the boat, and a couple of lines

211

about Chuck's doting reunion with his daughter. Defeated and deflated, she hit the send button.

She leant back in her chair and stared at her pile of notes, all useless now, and fought the urge to cry. She wasn't sure if it was the exhaustion catching up with her or general emotional deregulation but even though she understood she should be happy, that a job at the *New York Herald* was probably now in the bag, she felt empty. Like she'd somehow betrayed her journalistic integrity.

Ore crawled into bed, and was about to drift off, when there was a swift knocking at the door. She didn't move. She didn't have the energy to speak to anyone right now.

'It's Daniel . . .' The voice was soft and deep and unmistakably his. She held her breath.

'I don't know if you're in there . . . ?' he continued, and then let out a big sigh. She watched as he tried the door handle, and was relieved that she had locked herself in, as she had started doing since the previous night. 'I guess not,' came the voice, and then another sigh.

He laughed to himself, a sad laugh. 'I don't know what I was going to say anyway . . .' He turned silent for a moment and Ore waited, expecting the sound of retreating footsteps. But none came.

'I guess I would say that I am sorry, for what happened earlier, that I feel like I've lost my mind since I met you, which is somehow only five days ago.' He chuckled to himself. Ore imagined him with his back to the door, maybe sitting on the carpet. She smiled at the thought of it, this man baring his soul like a dramatic, heartbroken teenager.

'I used to be practical, rational, routine-driven, and now, I don't know, I don't seem to care as much about everything being in the right order, in the right place; instead I find myself wondering when I'll get to see you again.' His tone was soft but Ore could hear the frustration in it too, like he'd been wrestling with this new wayward version of himself.

Ore wondered if she should speak up now, but she felt suddenly sleepy, calmed by his murmurings, and unwilling to break this liminal spell.

'I realised today, just now in fact, that I run away from things, or maybe that's not quite it. I just never even walk towards them in the first place, because, well, maybe because I think that the things I really want, they'll reject me, slam the door in my face.' Ore strained to hear him, as his voice grew quieter.

'Ironic really, that I'm saying all of this to an empty room from the other side of a locked door . . .' He trailed off and then Ore heard him clear his throat, and shuffle his feet, as though he had suddenly broken out of this confessional trance.

'What the hell are you doing, Daniel?' he scolded himself, and before Ore could decide whether she should finally respond, she heard his footsteps retreating and she almost immediately fell into a deep, dark sleep.

Chapter 41

Ore

Day 6

When Ore woke up in the morning, she wasn't totally sure what had been a dream and what had been real. Almost automatically she checked her emails; Henry's name was sitting at the top of her inbox:

Hi Ore,
Great start – maybe we need a bit more about the daughter? 'Chuck Regas, the father' is a nice angle and something a bit new. Would be good to get Melanie on the record. Let me know what you can arrange.
H

'Great start.' Ore groaned. That was editor speak for 'I want more'. Ore reread the email. An interview with Mel about what a great father Chuck was – that was going to be tough. She'd also need to ask Chuck's permission to interview Mel on the record. Her only hope was that her and Daniel's heroism from the night before might buy her some good favour. She might even be able to wrangle another interview with Chuck himself if she played her cards right.

Ore recited her usual words of affirmation in the mirror, took a shower and felt surprisingly upbeat as she got dressed. As disappointing as it was to find the nib of a story and not be able to follow it through, she was almost relieved that the matter was out of her hands. She had another week on board to gather a couple more interviews, and then she could relax, avoid Claude, and maybe take a leaf out of Mel's book and make use of the pool and gym until they docked in Sydney and she could fly back to New York.

The phone on Ore's desk began to ring, interrupting her daydreams of late summer back in Queens. She picked up. 'Hello?'

'Chuck wants to talk to you. He's asking that you meet him for breakfast in half an hour.' It was Vicky, straight to the point, as usual.

'OK, right, any idea what he wants to talk about?' Ore asked.

'Unlike you, Ore, I'm not paid to ask questions.' And with that Vicky hung up. Ore found herself wondering what had made Vicky this way. Maybe a working life of pretending the 'customer is always right' had convinced her that everyone was in fact, always wrong.

Ore changed into a summer dress. It was a dark terracotta, with long tulip sleeves and a neckline that sat just below her collarbones. She twirled her braids into a bun on top of her head and rubbed some jasmine oil on each wrist.

When she walked onto the top deck, the sun was shining brilliantly. The sea was an exquisite turquoise and it was hard to imagine that it was the very same water that had been inky black and furious as it tossed the boat around two nights ago.

Chuck was dressed in his usual fare: cargo shorts and a short-sleeve shirt, but Ore almost didn't recognise Daniel sitting next to him.

She realised she had only ever seen him in his captain's whites. Now he sat in a khaki linen shirt with the top two buttons undone to reveal the glint of a silver chain and a curl of chest hair. In front of him sat a thin cream envelope.

'You look magnificent, my dear.' Chuck gestured for her to take a seat and Ore found herself sitting opposite Daniel, who gave her a shy smile. She felt herself blush and tried to avoid direct eye contact. She was still trying to work out how she felt about him in light of the past twenty-four hours. It wasn't helping that he looked particularly hot right now.

'I've brought you both up here this morning to extend my gratitude for looking after my darling Mel the other night. I doubt you can ever really know what it means to me to have her safe and sound, but I would like to extend a small token of my thanks.' Chuck nodded towards the envelopes in front of them and leant back with his hands steepled in front of him.

Gingerly, Ore and Daniel both opened them at the same time. Ore gasped. It was a cheque for $50,001. It was hard not to immediately spend that money in her head. She imagined moving out of her aunt's and renting an apartment in Manhattan. It would be modest, one, maybe two bedroom max. And maybe she'd get a car, for getting out of the city on weekends. *What's that one extra dollar about though?*

It was Daniel who cut through her daydreaming. 'Thank

216

you, Mr Regas, but I absolutely cannot accept this.' Daniel pushed the envelope into the middle of the table.

'Nonsense, consider it an advance tip.' Chuck's smile grew tighter.

'I'm more than happy to wait until the end of the job, with the rest of the crew, sir,' Daniel said sternly.

Ore's bubble burst, she knew that she had to do the same. How would it look to accept 'gifts' from the subject of her pieces?

'Thanks, Chuck, but I also have to refuse. It's not a good look for my journalistic integrity.' Ore laughed nervously as she too pushed the envelope back.

'So the two of you are just selfless good Samaritans, I see.' The words were complimentary but the tone was sneering. Chuck snatched the envelopes back and stuffed them into a pocket.

But Ore wasn't about to waste this opportunity to ask for a favour, while he was at least pretending to be generous.

'One thing I would appreciate, Chuck . . .' Ore began sweetly.

Though Chuck's expression had hardened, he managed to turn up the corners of his mouth as he responded, 'Anything, my dear.'

'Could I trouble you for another interview? I'd also love to speak to Mel on the record. My editor is keen to get an insight into "the family man"?'

Now Chuck's smile loosened into something broader and more genuine – she'd tickled his ego. 'Of course. That's a lovely idea. Actually, why don't you both come along on our little excursion tomorrow?'

'Excursion?' Ore wasn't sure she could stomach any more island trips.

'Well I was going to take Mel to the reef. She's been wanting to go for ages. Some of the other guests might tag along too, but it'll be a once-in-a-lifetime opportunity to see the Barrier Reef up close. We'll have scuba equipment on hand if you want it?'

Ore couldn't actually think of anything worse than being underwater, weighed down by a tank of oxygen on her back, but if this was her only chance for that interview she supposed she'd have to endure another boat trip. She couldn't imagine that they'd actually cajole her into the water.

'I'd be delighted, thank you, Chuck.' Ore knew that Chuck would not take kindly to having his 'generosity' refused twice this morning.

'Right, well that's settled then, and I'm sure the captain wouldn't want to miss another opportunity to see you in your bathing suit.'

Daniel choked on the mouthful of water he'd just sipped and Chuck seemed to find the whole thing hilarious. Ore thought she could spy a subtle reddening of Daniel's cheeks, but she understood men like Chuck; he got off on power trips, of all different sizes, from $50,001 cheques all the way down to making a grown man blush.

Chuck slapped Daniel on the back gleefully. 'Now now, Captain, I'm only joking, but you will come, won't you? Suffice to say you've put in a pretty decent shift to get us there – time to enjoy the spoils.'

'I need to man the ship, sir.' Daniel's voice was raspy and even to Ore's ears it was an unconvincing rebuttal.

'Nonsense, what the hell do I employ Dudley for if not to be able to treat my favourite captain to a day off . . . ?' Chuck's eyes were twinkling. He was back in control and wielding his power freely, exactly as he liked it.

Chapter 42

Daniel

It wasn't even a day off. He was going to have to drive the tender after all. Daniel had never met anyone who could get under his skin quite like Chuck.

'I'll be ready to set off at nine then, sir, and be sure to have Carlos set us up with lunch to have on board.' It was pointless to argue with the man.

Chuck grinned. 'You don't mind if I leave you to have breakfast together? I actually have to hop onto an important call.' It wasn't really a question; Chuck was already turning away by the time he got to the end of the sentence.

Daniel stole a glance in Ore's direction. He was sure she was becoming more beautiful by the day. They sat opposite each other at the very end of a large rectangular glass table that could comfortably fit around twenty people, lord and lady of an empty manor. The rest of the deck was still cleared of its usual adornments, no loungers or drinks table. The huge gas barbecue and the bar were still bundled up in tarps to protect them from the storm.

An awkward silence settled between them, thankfully broken by the appearance of Nicole with two large plates heaped with steaming pancakes.

'Morning, you two!' Nicole chirped cheerily. Either she was totally oblivious to the discomfort that lingered in the air or she was compensating. Regardless, it was some welcome levity.

'Hello, Nicole, how are you doing? What a crazy couple of days hey?' Ore smiled as she chatted to Nicole, and Daniel wondered when exactly he'd turned into the sort of person who noticed how delightfully sunlight reflected off a woman's face.

'Literally insane, I mean I've only been doing this for a couple of years, but I've never seen a storm like that. I thought I might actually, like, die, you know?' She shot an apologetic look at Daniel. 'Not that I like doubted you or anything!'

Daniel waved away her apology. 'Please, Nicole, don't worry about it. It was a misjudgement on my part and I'm really very sorry you were scared. It shouldn't have happened.' Daniel hadn't meant to bring the mood down, but his sincerity skewered the remaining joviality.

Nicole bowed her head. 'I'll get you some coffees,' she said quietly before scuttling away.

'Twenty-year-olds aren't very good at earnestness, Daniel.' Ore's tone was lightly teasing, and Daniel felt awash with relief. Until that moment he hadn't realised how much tension he'd been carrying. After their last encounter in the cinema room, he'd feared that she might hate him, or worse, totally lose interest in him.

'Yes, it seems the misjudgement keeps on coming . . .' He dared to look directly at her and her face took his breath away.

Her brow furrowed slightly. She was waiting for him to say more. When he just smiled and looked away, she leant in, pushing her plate to the side and placing her clasped hands in the middle of the table between them.

'Daniel, look at me.' Her voice was barely a whisper. Daniel felt the hairs on the back of his neck prick. She was close enough that her breath brushed his face. He did as he was told.

'It is not your fault that we were in that storm.' Daniel gave Ore a small smile. He knew she was trying to make him feel better, but she didn't understand what it meant to captain a ship. It meant accountability, responsibility.

'It's my job to keep everyone safe, Ore.' He was surprised to hear his voice crack.

Approaching footsteps. Ore leant back suddenly as Nicole served the coffee.

'Thanks, Nicole,' Daniel said in what he hoped was a cheery tone, but Nicole just nodded nervously as she turned to go.

'I think I've spooked her.' It was an offhand comment but when Ore giggled, Daniel grinned.

Ore started on her mountain of breakfast and Daniel followed suit, chewing in a now comfortable silence. When she was done, she pushed the plate away and took a sip of coffee. He watched her as she worked up the conviction to say something.

'I was in my room last night, like, *all* last night.' His chewing slowed as he absorbed what she was telling him. Eventually he swallowed and took a large gulp of water to buy himself just a few milliseconds' more time.

As he put down the glass, he met Ore's gaze. 'And why didn't you answer the door?' He was stalling, trying to remember exactly what he'd said.

'I was about to fall asleep, and I was worried about who it might be,' Ore said matter-of-factly.

'Who were you worried it might be?' Daniel felt himself getting agitated; he hated the idea of Ore being scared.

'Well, I had this weird thing happen in my room a couple of days ago. I thought someone had been in there and moved some of my things . . .' She paused, wary. Daniel nodded almost imperceptibly: *go on.*

'Well I thought for a crazy moment maybe Claude had been in there, like looking through my notes or something, but I'm *definitely* just being paranoid.'

Daniel's expression must have changed as his blood boiled because Ore's turned to concern.

'I mean I am probably being paranoid, and my notes hadn't been touched so . . .' She reached out her hand again, this time laying it on his forearm. Almost instantly his rage dissipated, a calm radiating outwards from her touch.

'Please, Ore, call me next time, if you're worried about anything like that. I think it's right to be a little wary of men like Claude, and Chuck for that matter . . .' He took a deep breath. 'I meant to tell you about my conversation with Chuck, before the storm . . .' Daniel looked around. 'But maybe not here.'

'Now *you're* paranoid. Shall we say, kit cupboard 6, after your afternoon shift?' Her tone was nonchalant but Daniel thought he spied a mischievous glint in her eye. He told himself to stop imagining things.

Her hand was still resting on his arm and she suddenly pulled it away self-consciously. Daniel felt a little bereft as Ore continued: 'It doesn't really matter anyway. I've sent a draft to Henry already, the straight profile, and he's said he wants more on the daddy-daughter angle, so the investigation is off . . .'

'Oh right, I kinda thought that was just a ploy to get another interview with Chuck, but honestly I think it's for the best. I think Chuck is more dangerous than he looks.' Daniel was relieved.

Ore crossed her arms, and Daniel got the sense that he'd annoyed her. 'I mean, that's usually the sign of a good story, Daniel, one that powerful people don't want you to tell, but I guess you're more in the habit of leaving closed doors as they are.' Her comment stung and brought back into sharp focus the memory of the night before. The dream, the irresistible urge to go to Ore's room, the mix of disappointment and relief when she didn't answer, the soliloquising into the empty corridor.

He was embarrassed, ashamed of the truth in her words. 'You're right,' he said quietly, defeated.

Ore sighed loudly and when he peeked over the table, she seemed agitated, rubbing her palms restlessly over her face and neck.

'What's wrong, Ore? I didn't mean to minimise your work. For what it's worth I think you were on to something; I just don't want to see you get in trouble. We're in the middle of international waters with a narcissist billionaire. It's best not to rub him up the wrong way.'

Ore laughed at that, and once again it made Daniel smile.

'So you're more perceptive than you look, huh? I'm sorry for being snappy. That's not how I wanted to talk about . . . that night . . . I guess I'm feeling a bit confused after . . . what happened the next morning.'

Chapter 43

Ore

There, she'd said it. She'd straddled the elephant in the room and marched it into the glare of daylight.

Ore waited for Daniel's response and when it didn't come, she soldiered on. 'When we kissed in the cinema room, and then you ran away.'

There was a long pause, but Ore resolved not to say another word until Daniel responded. A silent battle of wills ensued.

Finally, Daniel spoke: 'I wanted to stay, I wanted to . . . do more. I just think that maybe it's a bad idea.'

Ore waited again for his reasoning and when it wasn't forthcoming, she prodded, 'Why?'

Daniel threw his arms up in the air with such energy that it made Ore jump. She'd never seen him so expressive. 'Oh I don't know, Ore, take your pick. There's a million reasons why. Because I'm a boat captain, and I spend eighty to ninety per cent of my life in the middle of the ocean and you're only on board for another week and then you're flying back to the other side of the world.' What had started as a burst of fury petered to a whimper by the last word.

Ore hung her head. He was right. It was selfish of her to demand his affection because she needed it right now. She was lonely on this boat, scared, out of her depth, literally and metaphorically. He was an escape, a welcoming port in a storm, and it was unfair for her to nestle herself in his warm embrace only until she was ready to go back to her real life, with her real friends, and her hook-ups and her new job. She would leave him behind; she had to, and he knew that.

'I'm sorry, Daniel.' And she was, for all of it. When she looked at him, he hastily swiped a single tear away from his cheek, and she felt her heart break.

Daniel silently stacked her plate on his and then balanced the coffee cups on top. 'I'll take these inside,' was all he said as he disappeared through the sliding doors and into the salon.

Ore sat staring at her reflection in the glass of the table. Why did she insist on only developing feelings for men she could not have? Her therapist, and then the captain of a boat she was only staying on for a fortnight. Her friends would probably say that it was 'classic avoidant behaviour'. Maybe it was, but if the goal was to avoid hurt, she was definitely doing something wrong.

'Oh sorry, I didn't realise there was anyone out here.' Ore looked up to see Agatha, hands up in a gesture of surrender, retreating backwards. She looked tired and almost bewildered. Ore realised that she hadn't seen Agatha since the day on the island and wondered what she'd been up to.

'It's fine. I was actually just about to leave.' It wasn't a lie, except Ore had no idea where to go. Usually she spent her days chasing the story and being trailed by Daniel. The hours of the day stretched out before her. Agatha seemed to understand her look of hesitation as she made to get up from her chair.

'You can stay, I . . . I just wanted to sit in the sun and I don't know . . . chill? For a moment?' Agatha managed something that was almost a laugh, but was too scratchy to be completely convincing.

'I didn't take you as the type to chill.' Ore was a bit thrown off by Agatha's casual tone. She sounded like her actual twenty-four years, as opposed to the Chuck Robo assistant 3000 schtick she usually had going on. Ore thought back to that picture she'd found during her research, of Agatha in her final year at Oxford, taken only two years ago.

Agatha's voice was raspy when she spoke. 'It's been pretty full-on . . . I've barely slept since the island. Chuck has had me up all night preparing business models for all the investors and then . . .' Agatha's pale blue eyes watered. She opened her mouth to continue but instead of the end of the sentence, a sob escaped.

For a moment Agatha seemed horrified at herself, eyes wide with shock and disgust. She brought her hands to her face just in time to meet a second escaped wail, which turned into a third and fourth. Ore was paralysed with surprise. Sitting opposite her now Agatha seemed so young, so vulnerable, a million miles away from either the formidably stony persona Ore had met on the first night, or the determinedly 'fun' Agatha from the island trip.

It was strange to be sat in such an outrageously serene setting, floating in the middle of the ocean, basking in the almost over-clarifying light of the Australasian sunshine, opposite a crying companion – for the second time in twenty minutes.

Ore weakly reached over the table, her fingertips gingerly

resting on Agatha's shoulder. The contact seemed to bring her back into the moment.

'Goodness, I'm sorry, I don't know what's wrong with me.' Agatha scrubbed at her swollen eyelids.

'You look tired,' Ore offered.

Agatha scowled. 'Thanks.'

'No, I didn't mean . . . I . . .' Ore felt too emotionally drained herself to say anything more comforting. She pulled her hand back.

After a moment of silence Agatha sniffed and then said, 'I guess you and Daniel are the golden couple now.' Her tone was sneering.

'I definitely wouldn't say that.' Ore was wary. What did Agatha know, and how?

'Chuck is shipping you guys so hard that I find myself wondering if he wants to jump into bed with you both himself.' Ore was a little stunned. This was a very questionable opinion for Chuck's primary PR representative and executive assistant to be voicing.

And there was more: 'After you two saved the day with Mel, he won't stop going on about it, and who gets it in the neck for "losing her" in the first place?'

It was a rhetorical question but Agatha paused long enough that Ore felt the need to shrug in response.

'Me, I get it in the neck.' Agatha's tone was accusatory.

'That wasn't my intention, Agatha. I had no idea . . .' Ore began.

'No of course not, just like you had no idea that you've trained Daniel into your little lapdog. When you say jump, he says how high, right?'

227

Ore had no idea what to say. Agatha was working herself up into a frenzy.

'You just swan onto this boat, with your frankly absurdly long legs, and your razor-sharp cheekbones and your perfect bum, and your stupid little notepad and your article for the *New York Herald*, and everyone swoons, and the rest of us just have to get out the way.'

Ore understood that she was meant to feel attacked, but it was hard to keep a completely straight face. Agatha's face had turned an unsettling shade of crimson as she got angrier, and despite the venom in her voice, her insults were absurd.

'Agatha . . .' Ore said softly, as through trying to soothe an agitated pet. Agatha's breathing slowed, as she climbed down from the peak of her rage.

'Despite . . .' Ore searched for the right word '. . . appearances . . . I do not have my shit figured out, like, at all.' Ore sighed heavily. 'To be honest I thought I was onto something, I don't know, bigger here, but what I'll end up putting out is just another puff piece about Chuck Regas, hardly Pulitzer-prize-winning journalism. I'm selling out to pay the rent, just like everyone else.'

Agatha's expression was impassive for a moment, and Ore held her breath, worried she'd said too much. Why did she tell Agatha, of all people, that she was digging for a bigger story? She scolded herself for getting caught up in the moment.

Agatha took a deep breath and wiped the smudged mascara from under her waterline. Then she looked Ore straight in the eye. 'There is,' she said calmly.

Ore was confused. 'There is what?'

'Something bigger there.' It took a moment for Ore to register what she was hearing: someone from within Chuck's inner circle confirming her hunch.

Agatha let out a thin laugh. 'And you know, if you find out what it is . . . there might even be a Pulitzer in it for you.' With that, she stood up suddenly and marched back inside, leaving Ore, once more that morning, trying to process a bombshell revelation.

Chapter 44

Daniel

Daniel hadn't meant to get emotional; in fact he'd surprised himself with his reaction. Walking down to the kitchen, coffee cups trembling on the dirty plates in his hands, he replayed the scene on deck and didn't recognise himself. Who was this man? Who poured his heart out and cried in broad daylight? This job was supposed to be plain sailing but it had turned into the stormiest of rides.

Bursting through the swinging doors, he caught Carlos off guard. '*Mon Dieu!* Attention, Capitaine!' A stainless-steel ladle clattered to the ground.

'My apologies, Carlos, I didn't mean to startle you.' Daniel's tone was even as he laid the plates down on the side but as he straightened up he noticed Carlos giving him a suspicious look.

'Is everything OK, Capitaine?'

Daniel did not know what it was that had betrayed him; maybe his eyes were red? Or something about his brusque movements. He berated himself. He was usually so good at maintaining at least the appearance of serenity.

'I'll pick that up.' Daniel gestured to the ladle on the floor, in part hoping to change the focus of the conversation.

'On this occasion, I think it is more imperative that you pick yourself up, Capitaine.' Carlos turned down the heat on whatever was bubbling on the stove and walked towards his tiny office. At the doorway, he turned and motioned for Daniel to follow him.

Daniel felt exhausted, both reticent to embark on another emotionally draining interaction and too feeble to resist.

The two men squeezed into the rickety chairs either side of the small, battered desk. Its surface was strewn with photocopies of recipes, seemingly unfinished lists of ingredients, and a scattering of black and white photographs of exotic-looking fish.

Carlos caught Daniel staring. 'Sometimes I wake up very early and cast a line out, to see what I can catch. It is always an exciting surprise to find out what the colours of the fish are in real life.' Carlos laughed at Daniel's concerned expression. 'Don't worry I do not cook them. I just like to look at them, and then I always throw them back.'

'Why bother?' Daniel remembered going fishing with his dad once, when he was very young, too young probably. They'd sat for hours, not speaking, just waiting. Daniel had found it boring, but at least they'd eaten fresh fish for dinner that night.

'Oh you know what they say, the beautiful things deserve to be free.' Carlos looked wistful.

'I'm not sure that's the saying,' Daniel said quietly.

'And it is not just for fish,' Carlos continued, ignoring the interjection, 'it is for feelings too . . .' Carlos trained his eyes on Daniel until he looked up. Daniel managed a small, dismissive laugh.

'It is no laughing matter, Daniel. You must learn to express yourself. You are so . . . what is the phrase . . . buttoned up!' Carlos threw his hands up in the air exasperatedly.

'It's just the way I have always been, Carlos. I am not . . .' Daniel paused, for fear of offending '. . . French, like you.'

'Pah! I am not French, Daniel, I am Lebanese, but that is beside the point. What I am trying to say is that just because it has always been, even if it has always worked, it doesn't mean that it *should* always be, and in fact, exactly *when* it stops working, that is when it is time to change.' Carlos folded his arms triumphantly, as though he had said something truly profound. Maybe he had, but Daniel was too tired to work it out.

'Right, thanks, Carlos, noted.' Daniel made to get up, but Carlos reached for his arm across the table to stop him.

'To deny your feeling for Ore will eat you from the inside out.' Carlos said this with such certainty that it unnerved Daniel.

'I don't know what you're talking about,' Daniel mumbled feebly, pulling his arm out of Carlos' grip. Carlos let go and gave him a sad smile.

'Sit down a moment, Daniel. What is the rush?'

Daniel sighed and lowered himself back down.

'Why do you never come and spend time in the mess? You're always up in the wheelhouse, or in your cabin?' Carlos sounded concerned, and his tone irritated Daniel. Carlos was probably about a decade older than him, but Daniel was still the captain and he didn't appreciate being lectured about his social habits.

'Is that a question, Carlos? I like my own company. What's wrong with that?' Daniel asked evenly.

'Nothing, Capitaine, except that it feels like you're hiding.'

Carlos was trying to be sympathetic, friendly even. Daniel understood this, but it wasn't making the exchange any less maddening.

'Well you're entitled to your opinion, Carlos. I really had better go now . . .'

'What is your hobby, Capitaine, when you are not working? What do you do with your time?' Carlos seemed to sense he was pushing for time.

Daniel sighed and then said: 'I like sudoku.' Carlos raised an incredulous eyebrow. 'And birds, I like birds. Out here I only really get to see seabirds, but I like all different kinds,' Daniel continued, impatient now.

Carlos smiled. 'Ahhh, well it makes sense why you like Ore so much then.' Daniel bristled, but Carlos wasn't deterred. 'She is like a bird, beautiful, majestic even, free and curious, flying wherever she pleases, and unwilling to be caged . . .' Daniel fought the urge to roll his eyes.

'I suppose,' was all Daniel said in response. He was eager to get out of the cramped space, and away from the philosophical musings. As he stood up he added, 'I'll come to the mess for dinner tonight.' He hoped it would at least quieten the scrutiny.

'We look forward to it!' Carlos said cheerily as he waved Daniel goodbye.

Chapter 45

Daniel

Back up in the wheelhouse that afternoon and left with his own thoughts, Daniel reflected on the morning. With a little distance he considered the possibility that Carlos might be onto something. Where had that outburst at breakfast come from if not some pent-up, neglected emotion that he seemed incapable of processing himself?

He had felt so angry with Ore, for hinting at the possibility of something between them, even though it was the very same thing he had longed for, perhaps from the very moment he'd met her. The logical conclusion might be that he was actually angry with himself. For developing these feelings whilst knowing deep down that they were unfulfillable and completely impractical.

He had always had a plan. He was twenty-eight now, the youngest captain he knew of, and, if he did say so himself, raking in a pretty decent paycheque, all untaxed of course. Another seven years, and he'd have enough to retire on. He'd move home, build his mom a new house, maybe help his brother Terry buy somewhere. Maddy was sorted already.

He'd find someone to settle down with, and maybe do a couple of charters a year to keep a bit of income rolling in;

maybe he'd just volunteer at the museum that had set him on this path to begin with. Four bedrooms, two kids, a garage – that was the plan.

And he was on course. Captaining the *Nightingale* for the Hartfords was a good gig. He'd worked for them a couple of summers back. They were fair and generous, with tips, which was common, and time off, which wasn't. He'd have a chance to travel. Only a six-week stopgap with Chuck Regas, and he'd be well on his way. And then Ore turned up, and his carefully laid plans were starting to seem, well, comparatively boring. Maybe that was what he was angry about.

All of a sudden, waiting seven years to feel at home, to feel loved and held, it felt like an eternity. He'd had a tiny taste of belonging, and it wasn't in the suburbs of Houston, it was in Ore's presence.

He looked out to the expanse of ocean before him and decided that was more than enough introspection for one day. He turned his attention to the job at hand, checking and double-checking the plotted course to the reef. It would be his last bit of complex manoeuvring. After tomorrow he could relax for the home stretch; maybe it would give him enough time to get his thoughts in a similarly straightforward order.

When dinner time rolled around, Daniel decided it was time he make use, once again, of the boat's autopilot programme for once and dutifully headed down to the mess to eat with the rest of the crew. Partly he went out of fear that Carlos might subject him to another therapy session, but another part of him hoped that a bit of company might serve as a welcome distraction.

The mood sounded jovial as Daniel approached the door.

'It was totally awkward, I mean why was he completely naked? Is that a thing English people do on the toilet?' It was Nicole and she was met with rapturous laughter.

'I think it's more likely something perverts do on the toilet,' Vicky interjected dryly. Daniel pushed the door open and was slightly dismayed by the hush that descended across the table.

'Captain Wilsons, hello, is there a problem?' It was Oscar, one of the deckhands.

'No no, I just thought . . .' Daniel was losing confidence in this idea, just as Carlos jumped in.

'I was telling the captain that he absolutely must join us for dinner more often. Come, Captain Wilsons, take a seat.' Carlos stood to pull up a chair next to his, scooting Amanda and Nicole along to make room.

'Please, call me Daniel.' Carlos smiled, but Daniel noticed the rest of the table exchanging looks. It had felt like the right thing to say, but it now dawned on him that he'd not been called Daniel by any of his crew since becoming a captain. He hoped he wouldn't regret it.

'Daniel . . .' Carlos said, as if trying it out. 'Come, sit, sit.' Daniel squeezed in next to Carlos. He felt uneasy, and wished that he'd changed back into his casual wear from this morning, instead of coming straight down in his captain's uniform.

'Please, don't let me interrupt.' He tried flashing what he hoped was an easy smile.

'Nicole was just telling us about her experience cleaning Richard's room this morning,' Vicky said before taking another mouthful.

Amanda passed Daniel a large bowl, and Oscar chipped in: 'Which one's Richard again?'

Dudley, who had been eyeing Daniel somewhat suspiciously, clarified, 'The old guy, Dickie with the bad combover. He's always drunk and chasing after Agatha.'

'Oh yes, well there's your answer, maybe he was just pissed, got undressed to go to bed and then never made it and fell asleep right on the toilet!' Oscar's ruddied face suggested he too might have had a glass or two with dinner, but the table laughed obligingly.

'And what do you think of Mr Regas' guests then, Captain … umm I mean Daniel?' It was Dudley and Daniel felt like the question was a test. An anticipatory silence awaited his answer.

'I don't mind Ousman, Frederick is a bore who thinks he's more good-looking than he is, Roger and Richard are both raving alcoholics with a superiority complex, Claude is a complete creep, and I think there's another one who is so beneath notice that I can't even remember his name.' There was an agonising beat where Daniel feared that he'd blown it; simultaneously jeopardising his level-headed reputation and not even getting a laugh out of it.

But it was Vicky who broke the spell with a wry chuckle, and then one by one the others joined in. A steady build that reached a crescendo of hysterics. Nicole clutched her stomach, Carlos slapped his thigh, Dudley wiped tears from his eyes and Amanda began hiccuping. Daniel looked around and glowed with pride, and something else, something warmer and comforting. Maybe he had been hiding.

Chapter 46

Daniel

For the first time in a long time, Daniel lost track of time. It was nearing midnight when the junior crew began clearing the plates. He thanked Carlos for the food and everyone else for the company and excused himself.

He headed downwards, towards the deck where the tender was kept. Oscar had been tasked with checking over it earlier that day, but Daniel knew himself well enough to check it over with his own two eyes. He'd only find himself tossing and turning in bed otherwise, trying to dispel recurrent thoughts of an empty fuel gauge, or a faulty drive belt.

As he descended into the lowest part of the bow of the boat, down a particularly narrow staircase, two voices grew ever more distinguishable. They must be coming from inside the garage, thought Daniel. Almost automatically he softened his footsteps; there was something about the tone of the conversation that sounded furtive. Maybe it was Ore's influence but he found himself drawn in, compelled to eavesdrop.

'I know we're a little behind schedule, but tomorrow, tomorrow is the day.' It was Chuck speaking, and strangely he didn't sound in control; he was the one trying to impress, rather than needing to be impressed.

Claude's voice responded in a monotone: 'It is not ideal. We had wanted to get the images of the site and the dive plans back to Derek and the team tonight. Our engineers need to get started if we're going to have the operation up and running by the end of the year.'

'Of course, and I appreciate your patience. The good news is that the authorities don't seem to be patrolling tomorrow, according to my sources, so we should get all the time we need.' Chuck sounded nervous.

'Well my guys are ready, and the chopper is picking them up soon? I think I'll stay up and brief them, show them the drill prototype, so they can familiarise themselves with it.'

Daniel's head was spinning. This discussion was definitely not meant to be overheard. Less than a week ago, he would have retreated up the stairs silently and pushed all this clandestine-sounding shit to the back of his mind. The new Daniel though, the one infected by Ore's curiosity, *he* couldn't help but stay exactly where he was.

'So this prototype drill, it's already powerful enough to cut through the reef bed? And it's what? Handheld?' Chuck's voice grew excited.

'Well it is just that – a prototype – and it's only for surface exploration, to see if the cobalt responds to an obsidian drill underwater in the same way it does on land.' Claude sighed, as though he'd explained all this a thousand times before. 'Of course when we scale this, it won't just be surface drilling, we'll aim for the whole face of the reef and maybe even come at it from the underside. That'll mean we need to ship in a few subsea collectors, but we can't do that until we have these "authorities" on side.' Daniel couldn't see the two men, but he could hear the air quotes.

'Great, great, I mean, this is all amazing stuff. I think deep sea is the way forward for sure. When I looked into sourcing that kind of cobalt on land . . .' Chuck whistled out a lungful of air to emphasise just how painful that kind of expenditure would be before continuing. 'It's just that these batteries, they're basically pure cobalt.' Claude only grunted in response. It was clear that he didn't share in Chuck's enthusiasm for the finished product.

'But the efficiency of them, you wouldn't believe – they can run like, ten, twenty times as many servers with like, a fraction of the electricity needed to fully charge them. It's a revelation. Once we have an underwater sample and we can be sure that it's just as effective, we're on our way.' Chuck's tone was full of awe, but Claude seemed to be growing impatient.

'Yes, very good, Chuck, well I'm going to head upstairs and wait for my men. No need to join me. I will see you in the morning.'

Daniel had been so engrossed, and concentrating so hard to try and make sense of what they were saying, that it took him a second too long to compute that the conversation was wrapping up. As Claude's footstep approached the doorway that Daniel was hiding beside, panic took over.

Instinctively Daniel clambered up the stairs behind him. By the time Claude opened the door, crossed the threshold and turned to his right, Daniel looked like he'd just begun to descend the stairs.

'Oh, Mr Van Der Bodem, how are you this evening?' Daniel's heart thumped against his ribcage. He kept his hand on the banister, for fear of the adrenaline betraying him a tremor.

Claude turned to look back into the garage behind him

with those dull grey eyes of his and then followed the stairs up to where Daniel was standing. It was the action of a suspicious man, but his demeanour remained eerily calm, as did his voice.

'I am well, thank you, Captain. I trust you have come from . . . ?' An innocent question loaded with an opportunity for confession.

'Dinner,' Daniel said, trying to walk down the stairs as nonchalantly as possible, 'with the rest of the crew.'

Just then Chuck emerged. He seemed startled to see Daniel, nowhere near as good at keeping his cool as Claude.

'Captain Dan! How are you? I was just showing Claude the tender. He's been dying to take a look.' Chuck spoke just a little too quickly.

'You didn't feel you had a sufficient chance to take a good look when we went out to the island?' Daniel wasn't sure why he'd said that. There was something about Chuck that made him act irrationally. He always found himself pulled into the weird mind games. He'd wanted to catch Chuck in a lie, but now as Chuck's expression turned sour, he regretted pushing it.

'It is not really the same when there are so many people on board. I like to have a closer look at things.' It was Claude who cut in, utterly unflustered by the exchange. 'I am going now – goodnight,' he added bluntly, before making his way up the stairs.

Daniel and Chuck remained. 'Excuse me I just wanted to check a few things before the morning,' said Daniel, making for the garage door. But Chuck put out an arm to block him.

'I hope you haven't forgotten our little conversation, Danny.' Chuck's tone was sickly sweet, like rotting fruit.

241

Daniel stood up straight. 'Sir?'

'About my feelings when it comes to generosity and betrayal? I do so value . . . discretion.' The threat was so thinly veiled that Daniel wondered why Chuck even bothered. Why not come right out and say it? *If you repeat anything you heard, you're toast.*

'Of course, sir, understood.' Daniel held his ground, meeting Chuck's gaze. And then suddenly the standoff was over.

'Great.' Chuck was smiling again. 'Well in that case I'll see you tomorrow!' With a slightly too hard slap on the back, Chuck was off, marching up the stairs.

The moment he was out of sight, Daniel let out a deep breath. He felt frozen in place, unsure what to do next. *What would Ore do?* He wasn't sure that he wanted to tell her what he had just heard, what with Chuck's threats to him and Claude's to Ore, it was obvious that neither man would take kindly to any of this information being reported on. The idea of putting Ore in danger made him feel sick, but he knew she would never forgive him if she found out he'd kept this from her. Not to mention that he was invested now, and the only way to get to the whole truth was to dig deeper.

He'd sleep on it. There was no point telling Ore tonight. He had to admit that his checks of the tender were cursory. He was impatient to get back to his cabin and write down everything he'd heard before he forgot any potentially vital detail.

Chapter 47

Ore

Ore had spent the day trying to relax, which was no mean feat when she had her career, her love life and her sense of self to re-examine. She'd been a little disturbed by how seductive Chuck's offer had been to her. How quickly she'd spent that money in her head. Daniel hadn't even considered it, even though a 'bonus' from an employer would be far more legitimate than . . . well whatever her money was for: saving Mel? It didn't really make sense, but then Chuck's motivations were often nonsensical, to Ore anyway. Even his decision to invite her here in the first place had never made any sense to her.

After a couple of hours by the pool, where she was completely undisturbed except for the fifteen minutes that Oscar spent cleaning it, she'd gone to the gym. Then the library, which was filled with the sort of leather-bound books that seemed more like set dressing than actual reading material. She'd bumped into one of the investors at the bar – Gerry was it? Or Roger? They'd exchanged pleasantries about the weather and then he'd excused himself to take a phone call, large gin and tonic still in hand. If she was being honest with herself, Ore felt directionless, and bored. She was almost looking forward to the excursion, even if it did mean dosing up on Kwells.

By the time dinner rolled around, Ore had been sitting in bed catching up on that incomprehensible reality TV show that had sucked her in for a few hours. Right on time at 6 p.m., Carlos called to ask her where she'd be eating.

'Un autre diner au lit?'

'Carlos, I'm ashamed to say, five years of learning French at school and none of it has stuck. For the monolingual, English please . . . ?'

'Dinner in bed again, mademoiselle?'

'I don't appreciate the "again",' Ore scolded him, 'but yes please, and I don't always eat it in bed, sometimes I sit at my desk,' she added quietly.

Carlos tutted. 'You and Captain Wilsons, two peas in a pod, always working, always on your own. Why don't you come to the crew dinner? I believe he might come . . .' Carlos' voice had taken on a theatrically nonchalant tone.

For Ore it was settled, she definitely wouldn't be going to dinner now. 'Does Daniel not usually eat with the crew?' Ore asked, always curious to know more about him.

'Almost never! You know how he is, very withdrawn, not very chatty, keeps himself to himself.'

'That's not been my experience . . .' Ore muttered, speaking as if to herself, but Carlos was all ears.

'Aha! As I suspected, you are the sunshine to his morning bloom then. It is only for you that he is his most beautiful self.'

Ore giggled. Carlos was certainly a welcome course of levity in her day and as clichéd as it was, his accent did make everything sound even more poetic. She wondered if her and Daniel's attraction to each other was embarrassingly obvious or if Carlos was just particularly perceptive. She didn't have the energy to deny it, and it felt harmless, fun, not like when Chuck made uncomfortable remarks about her and Daniel. Then again maybe it was just always better received from someone who wasn't white.

'I'm not sure about that, Carlos; I don't think Daniel is my biggest fan right at this moment.'

'*Oh non! Pour quoi!*' Carlos sounded so dismayed that Ore was taken aback, though she wasn't sure what he'd said. Thankfully he clarified: 'Why? Ore, what happened?'

Ore sighed. She wasn't sure that Carlos was the right person to bare her soul to, but after a week of isolation from her friends and family, she needed someone to confide in.

'I'm not sure. We had a . . .' She wasn't sure how to put this. It was one thing talking about a make-out session with a girlfriend; it was another with a relative stranger, and a man nearing his forties, albeit a very friendly one. 'A moment, yesterday actually, and then he sort of ran away. I tried talking to him about it and he got upset and said there was no point because I'd be leaving soon . . . which is also a fair point.'

There was silence on the end of the phone line. Ore felt a flush trickle up her cheeks. 'Sorry I don't know why I said all that. It's really not your problem at . . .'

Carlos cut her off. 'No, no I am just thinking about what you're telling me.'

Ore waited as he pondered.

'I think that he is a man who has for a long time not felt

his feelings, and he is not sure what to do with them now he feels them.' Ore didn't have the heart to tell him that this insight was not particularly revelatory to her.

'And I think that you are both too young to worry so much about the future. Take it from me, this kind of connection does not come around very often, so when it does, you should try and embrace it, even if it is fleeting. Take the time to admire the full beauty of the fish before you throw it back in the ocean.'

Ore had no idea what the fish metaphor was about, but she understood the general message. They were both so worried about the fallout that they couldn't seem to enjoy the moment. It just was such high stakes when real feelings were involved.

'Definitely something to think about. Thank you, Carlos . . .' Ore's belly rumbled, demanding a change of topic. 'Could I get something a bit stodgy, comforting, pasta maybe?'

Carlos scoffed. 'What is this stodgy? It sounds very English; it sounds like the sort of food I do not make. I will send over a beef Bourguignon.'

'Sure.' Ore laughed. 'Sounds great, and . . . Thanks, Carlos.'

'No problem, it is my pleasure to see the lovebirds fly towards each other,' and without another word he was gone.

Ore decided that she would prep some questions for Mel and Chuck, whilst she waited for the food. She'd started a new notebook, and banished her pile of mad ramblings to the very bottom of her suitcase. When the light knock came, Nicole handed over her plate without a word, and Ore was grateful not to have to engage in small talk.

She must have been exhausted because when the sound of the choppers woke her up, the lights and TV were still on. She found herself wondering who was flying in or out at this time of night as she drifted back into sleep.

Chapter 48

Ore

Day 7

It took a moment for the banging on the door to register first in Ore's subconscious and then pull her into waking.

'The tender is ready and Captain Wilsons wants to head off in twenty minutes.' It was Vicky's voice, and Ore understood immediately that she had overslept.

'Yep! Thanks, Vicky.' Ore scrambled out of bed and before she even made it to the door, Vicky had walked off.

She set about getting ready. What exactly did one wear to go not scuba diving? She decided covering up was probably the best tactic, as they'd be out in the sun most of the day.

By the time she got down to the garage, everyone was already there, waiting for her. Chuck and Mel, Daniel, once again disarmingly not dressed in his uniform, Claude and another three men she didn't recognise.

'Hello, all, so sorry . . . I . . . I have no excuse really. I overslept,' Ore offered by way of sorry explanation. Mel giggled and when Ore caught her eye they exchanged a shy smile.

Chuck didn't look impressed. 'OK, well now that our lady journalist has deigned to join us, we really should get going.'

It was only 9 a.m., and Ore wondered what the rush was. The last excursion hadn't set off until well after breakfast.

The last time she'd come down to the garage she'd already been feeling so sick that she hadn't properly taken it in. It would be hard, she thought, to describe the scale of it in her article. It was basically a marina, built into the mega yacht that sat at sea level, which itself was big enough to house the tender, and a small speed boat. The side of the 'garage' as they called it, opened up completely to allow the smaller boats out into the ocean. 'Smaller' of course was a relative term; the tender had its own indoor salon and two bedrooms as well as a kitchen.

It was surreal really to watch the boat being loaded up, within a boat. Daniel went about helping everybody get on board, instructing the three nameless men to carry their huge crate on first. As he did so he caught Ore's eye. She wasn't sure how to interpret his expression, but when he suddenly cast his eyes down towards the crate as it passed him, it clicked: Klauparten Inc was written in stout white lettering across the side of it.

Ore felt a little flustered. She'd been trying to put the strange details of that unfinished story to the back of her mind but now, with another tantalising clue, she felt that familiar buzz of investigative excitement.

'Ladies first.' Claude motioned for Ore and Mel to get onto the boat. Both did as they were told, settling down on the top deck. The men took the crate down below deck, Claude following behind them. Chuck came to sit beside his daughter and Daniel was last on. Oscar appeared out of nowhere to help cast off and then the huge wall of metal in front of them began to whir open, and they were on their way.

Ore impressed herself with the strength of her stomach as they rode across the waves. Only a week ago, she'd have chucked her guts up. Now she was almost enjoying herself, although she was not looking forward to the wind fuzzing up her edges.

After about ten minutes, Chuck stood up and motioned for Ore and Mel to follow him into the salon. The boat had obviously been designed and decorated by the same people as *Lady Thalassa*, because the interiors were almost identical: lots of grey velvet and expanses of white.

'I thought we could do the interview now, since we have a bit of journey time to kill. Is fifteen minutes OK?' Chuck took a seat at the slightly-smaller-but-still-huge glass table in the centre of the room. Fifteen minutes. It wasn't enough to interview two people, and honestly Ore had hoped she could conduct them separately, but she supposed she'd have to just take what she could get.

'Sure, is that OK with you, Mel?' Ore conceded. Mel nodded and slumped into a chair next to Chuck. Ore took the one opposite them both.

'Right well, as I explained to Chuck, my editor really wanted to dig a little bit more into your relationship. What is Chuck like as a father?' Ore kept her eyes on the notepad in front of her as she asked the question. When she finally did look up to meet Mel's eye, the expression of incredulity was exactly what she'd expected and hoped to miss.

Chuck seemed confused by the loaded pause, turning to Mel with a nervous chuckle. 'Well Melly Belly, go on, tell Ore what you think.'

'Daaad, please don't call me that. I'm not like five anymore.'

She rolled her eyes and then dropped them to her lap. 'He's a great dad, I guess. We have lots of fun together.'

Ore didn't think she'd ever heard a less convincing answer and she had to stifle a giggle as she diligently transcribed Mel's answer.

'And . . . What kind of fun things do you do together?' Ore persisted.

Mel groaned, 'Oh I don't know!'

'Mel! Answer the nice lady's questions properly please.' Chuck turned to Ore apologetically and then back to Mel, pleading with his eyes.

'Sometimes when I beg and beg and beg, he takes me scuba diving, so I can finally see the Great Barrier Reef.' Her tone was sarcastic and once again Chuck laughed nervously.

But Mel wasn't done: 'But even when we do finally do the super fun things I've been begging him to do for aaaages, we still have to bring his weird friends, or whatever they are – I don't really get it – along with us, and sometimes even like the press so they can write a profile about what a great, successful guy he is . . .'

Mel folded her arms and leant back, looking jubilant. Chuck ran his hand through his hair exasperatedly. 'No offence or anything,' Mel chipped in.

'None taken.' Ore wasn't sure if she should write any of that down. The way that Chuck was now scowling at the notepad in front of her, she decided to compromise: 'Shall I just say "scuba diving"?'

Chuck was quick to reply. 'Yes please, I think maybe Mel is still recovering from her fall. You haven't been sleeping all that well with the pain have you, darling?'

'My ankle is literally fine, Dad,' Mel retorted.

'Well it can't be that *fine*, if you made such a big fuss about it only a couple of nights ago and had everyone up worried and searching for you? Or was that a bit of an attention-seeking stunt?' Chuck's tone had turned sneering and mean. Ore felt she should look away. She couldn't bear to witness the flash of hurt that flew across Mel's face.

Chuck cleared his throat in the awkward silence that followed. 'Maybe we can have a chat about how Mel here inspired me to find ways to make Pagonis more sustainable? It was really Mel's passion for the environment that set all this in motion.' He waved his hands around vaguely.

'All what exactly?' Ore thought it was an innocent enough question, but for a split second Chuck's face fell.

He regained his composure so immediately, that Ore wondered if she'd just imagined his reaction. 'Well you know, this, generally speaking. I mean like Pagonis' green transition to sustainable energy consumption.'

'Right.' Ore wrote down his answer, and then underlined it. 'And, Mel, how much has he told you about this new top-secret battery he's making? Are you the key to all those industry secrets?' Ore knew she was pushing it a little bit, but she was mainly watching for Chuck's reaction he showed none.

'As if – he doesn't tell me anything. I basically know as much as you, apparently these new batteries last longer or whatever but I keep saying like, how can it be sustainable if it's not renewable? Like it still needs electricity to charge and stuff.' Mel shrugged.

'She's smarter than she looks that one.' Chuck looked like he might try and ruffle Mel's hair and then seemed to think better of it. 'But she makes a good point – eventually we'd hope that with these super-efficient batteries, we could also find a renewable source of electricity to power them. That's a little way off just yet though.' Chuck tapped the side of his nose theatrically and leant back in a way that seemed to signal that the interview was over. Ore checked her watch; they'd managed seven minutes.

Chapter 49

Daniel

From the wheelhouse Daniel had watched Chuck, Mel and Ore disappear from view and head inside. He spent a moment worrying that Ore might push it on Klauparten with Chuck and then talked himself down. Ore was the professional after all; she knew what she was doing.

It hadn't been until that morning when he'd practically seen the cogs turning in her head upon noticing the branding on the crate that the divers carried in, that he'd concluded that he really couldn't keep the revelations from last night to himself. He resolved to tell her once they were safely back on board the *Thalassa* and far from prying ears. He for one now knew how jeopardising careless conversation could be.

It was a short trip, and after twenty minutes, they arrived at the edge of the reef. There were already a few other boats around, all packed with tourists, eagerly gathered around diving instructors.

Daniel had cut the engine and was about to drop the anchor when he saw Chuck jog back out onto the lower deck and up the stairs towards him. He seemed agitated.

'Hi, Dan, how are you?' Chuck's pleasantries were rushed. Daniel didn't even have time to respond before he continued.

254

'Is there anywhere we can go? Somewhere that's, I don't know, a little less crowded?'

'Less crowded, sir? On the Great Barrier Reef?' Daniel tried to keep his tone even but Chuck picked up on the hint of sarcasm and bristled.

'Yes, Dan, I understand that it's a busy spot, but I was hoping that . . . Mel could have a more . . . unique experience and see a part of the reef that wasn't plagued with day-trippers.'

Rich people really hated company it would seem. It wasn't enough that they could spend three weeks of the year isolated in the middle of the ocean on their own private mega yacht, they also wanted one of the seven wonders of the world to themselves. It wouldn't surprise Daniel if Chuck had already tried seeing if there was a private hire option.

'Well we're on the north side at the moment, which is one of the most popular sites.'

'Well why have you brought us here!' Chuck was incensed, and Daniel got the feeling this was far more to do with his plans for whatever dodgy stuff he had planned with Claude than it was about Mel.

'Well, sir, it's popular because it has the greatest variety of marine life on the site. I thought Melanie might enjoy—'

Chuck cut him off. 'Let's try the southern end instead.'

There was no room for discussion as Chuck marched out of the room and back down to the deck. Daniel watched as he approached Claude and the three divers who'd gathered outside. Chuck leant in to whisper in Claude's ear.

Claude looked up suddenly and a shiver ran down Daniel's back as the man's grey eyes met his. It should have been impossible through the glare of the glass that separated them, and yet . . .

Claude nodded tersely, and looked away, huddling with the divers, who by now were wet-suited up, with neoprene arms dangling by their sides, muscled chests out and black swimming caps glinting in the sunlight. Each emblazoned with a bright white 'k Inc'. It was hard to tell the three apart; all had an identical build.

Daniel set a new course for the other side of the reef. It would take them over an hour to get to the southern end. As the sun grew hotter in the sky, Daniel amused himself by considering that those wetsuits would be getting mighty sweaty.

Chapter 50

Ore

Mel was not happy. Ore hadn't clocked that what she'd seen in the interview was Mel in a relatively good mood. Now she could almost see the deep dark storm cloud hanging over her head.

'I just want it to be perfect for you – you don't want to have to share your experience with dozens of tourists? Surely?' Chuck's tone was pleading, verging on whining.

Mel had opted for the silent treatment now, and Ore wished she was anywhere else but in this room with them. She should have made a run for it when Chuck first came back in, shoulders hunched and preparing to grovel.

'Sorry, Melly Belly, it's going to be a little while longer . . .' he'd begun. Mel had been looking at her phone as he spoke. She'd stopped scrolling but kept her eyes trained on her hands.

'You want me to hate you, don't you?' Her voice was quiet and cutting.

'Of course not! I just didn't realise there would be so many other boats here! That's just not how I imagined it!' Chuck sounded hysterical. He was not a man who took well to losing control of a situation.

'You want to know how I imagined it?' Mel looked over at

Chuck then, her hazel eyes twinkling with unshed tears. 'I never even thought about who else would be there, because the whole point was that it would be me and you, Dad, doing something we'd both remember forever.' A single tear escaped down her cheek. 'You asked me to come here. To join you on your stupid boat and you promised we'd see the reef. Why? You obviously would rather spend all your time with your investors!' Mel had grown louder; she was almost shouting now.

'You obviously don't want me here! Why is Claude here? Why are those weird men here? I hate you!' It looked like Mel might storm out, but then an eerie calm seemed to descend over her and the silent treatment started.

Chuck tried every tactic in the book: denial, apology, reasoning. Ore felt like they had both forgotten she was in the room, still sat at the table. Mel had settled herself on the large couch in the corner of the room, and Chuck had positioned himself just out of lashing distance from her.

Ore eyed the door; maybe if she just got up quietly, they wouldn't notice. But then again, she was hoping that Chuck might actually answer Mel's questions: *who were those men?*

When Chuck got no response, he sighed, as if defeated. 'OK listen, the three guys out there, they work for Claude and they also want to see the reef, for business reasons.'

The absurdity of it drew Mel out. 'They want to see the Great Barrier Reef "for business reasons"?' Her voice was dripping with disdain. 'I should have guessed. That's the only reason we're even here right? Nothing to do with me at all.'

Ore almost felt sorry for Chuck at this point. The wrath of a teenage girl was not to be suffered lightly, but then again, he'd brought it on himself. Ore had never had the chance to shout at her father, which she now considered might have been for the best.

Mel waited for a response and when Chuck hung his head and none came, she quietly got up and left the room. Thirty seconds later, a door slammed shut.

Chuck looked up and finally turned to see Ore. 'Before you ask, no, I'm not willing to expand on which business reasons.' He sounded subdued. He stood up and hesitated for a minute. 'Would you mind if I asked you a personal question?' He laughed dryly to himself. 'As you've borne witness to the intimacies of my familial relationships, it only seems fair?'

'Umm, sure,' Ore said cautiously.

'How do you get on with your father?' He seemed genuinely interested.

'I don't really know him. He left when I was very young,' Ore said plainly, shrugging.

'Hmm, well you seem to have turned out OK; maybe he made the right decision,' Chuck mused.

Ore felt a pang of anger. 'With respect, Chuck, I'd have to disagree with you, on both counts.'

Chuck laughed. 'And you're funny!'

Ore stretched a tight smile across her face as Chuck left the room.

She sat alone for some time, unsure where to go. She didn't fancy hanging out on deck with creepy Claude and his band of not-so-merry men. She wasn't in the mood for a sulky teenager or up for another round with the eccentric billionaire. That only left two choices: stay put or go and find the handsome captain.

She knew what she wanted to do. Ever since their tense breakfast yesterday she'd wanted to clear the air. And then after she'd spoken to Carlos, she wondered if they'd both got a bit ahead of themselves. Maybe they could just enjoy each other's company for the time she had left and not overthink it.

Before she'd even consciously decided, she found herself halfway up the stairs to the wheelhouse. She paused for a moment outside the door, admiring his silhouette through the glass window. He hadn't spotted her, and she felt slightly giddy at the chance to observe him in his natural habitat.

He was in his civvies, a dark brown T-shirt this time, and a pair of navy slacks. With his gaze straight ahead, the lines of his face caught the sunlight. His strong nose and heavy brow, his square jaw dappled with dark tight coils of stubble, his full lips. Ore was entranced, and when he turned suddenly, she jumped. He smiled at her reaction and she felt awash with relief. She'd worried that after yesterday he might never gift her with that lovely smile again.

Chapter 51

Daniel

She looked sublime, *as always*, he thought. She smiled back at him and his heart jumped. It was so easy and free – he'd worried that after yesterday she'd never look at him like that again.

He opened the door to let her in. 'Hey,' he said, shyly.

She stepped into the wheelhouse. 'Hey, I hope I'm not disturbing you.' She too looked bashful.

'Not at all.' Daniel turned back to the sea and she stood silently beside him, both of them staring straight ahead.

'I wanted to apologise . . .' Daniel started as Ore spoke over him.

'I just wanted to say, about yesterday . . .'

They turned to each other and giggled. They were nervous.

'I'm sorry about yesterday, Ore, and about the cinema room. I get in my head sometimes . . . and it's hard to . . .' He struggled to find the words.

'To get out?' Ore offered. Daniel nodded. 'I get that,' she added. 'I heard you though, and you're right, this . . . us, it doesn't make logical sense.'

She was only agreeing with him, but her words still made his chest tighten.

'But,' she said quietly, 'I just wanted it on the record that I like you, and it doesn't happen to me that often so . . . I just . . . wanted you to know that.'

Daniel felt two successive waves of emotion: the first unadulterated joy and the second, a crushing sadness.

'I like you too,' he replied 'obviously.'

Ore laughed. 'Well now that we've got that cleared up, on to more pressing matters.'

He shot her a look and she gave him a cheeky smile. The change in tone gave him a bit of whiplash but he was grateful not to wallow in the tragedy of their unhappily ever after.

'What's with those Klauparten crates?!' Ore asked in a loud stage whisper.

'Sshhhh.' Daniel looked around, increasingly paranoid. 'We shouldn't talk about this here, Ore.'

The smile slipped from her face instantly. 'OK.'

'But we *do* need to talk . . .' Daniel paused. Once he crossed this line, he wouldn't be able to uncross it. After a deep breath he continued. 'Meet me at our spot tonight? I overheard Chuck and Claude last night, and it's some pretty crazy stuff there.'

It was Ore's turn to look around now. 'Can't you just tell me now?' He could sense her impatience.

'I've written most of it down. We'll go through it all later, but for now, try and keep an eye on those divers; that's all I'll say.'

Ore seemed to contemplate pushing it, and then decided against it. 'OK fine, I'll wait for you in kit cupboard 6 after dinner tonight.' She winked at him. 'I must say that you seem to be getting a taste for all this "investigative journalism" stuff . . .'

Daniel smiled. 'I think I'm getting a taste for you.'

'Cheeky!' Ore grinned at him playfully, and Daniel felt his cheeks grow hot. He'd thought he was being romantic, but he had been told once that Brits had a hard time taking that sort of thing seriously.

Ore seemed to sense his embarrassment. 'I'm sorry, I can't help myself. If it helps, I'm getting a taste for you too . . .' He turned to her and she brought her hand to his cheek. It was a good thing that he didn't have time to register what she was going to do next because his heart might have beat out of his chest.

Her lips were so soft it took his breath away. He pulled her to him, his hands grasping for her, unable to get hold of quite enough. She moaned and his body responded instantly, that familiar ache that came with unbridled wanting. His fingers traced down the back of her neck, holding her in place to dip his mouth into the furrows of her collarbones and then grazed on the smooth planes of her heaving chest.

Unlike the last time, the knowledge that this was maybe, probably, a bad idea wasn't strong enough to drown out the thunder of his desire. It was Ore who came to her senses.

'Daniel.' She whispered his name against his lips, as if afraid to spook him. He pressed on, unwilling to let the moment end.

'Daniel, darling . . .' The words chimed in his ears like a siren call as he pulled away, dopy with want. 'We can't do this here.' She smiled, running a thumb across his cheek, as if wiping away an invisible teardrop. Her eyes were liquid again, warm with feeling.

'Does that mean we can do it somewhere else?' He wasn't himself, but he was being honest.

'I don't know.' Ore bit her lip, and Daniel had to restrain himself. 'Do you think that's a good idea?'

He didn't know; right this moment he didn't care either. He shrugged.

'Well, have a think. I don't want you to do anything you'll regret; I don't think I'd be able to forgive myself.' Her tone was light, joking even, but there was a tenderness there too. She straightened her shirt. 'I think I should head back down . . . And stop distracting you.' Another wink, and more whiplash. Daniel couldn't keep up.

'I'll see you around?' It was a strange thing to say but Daniel felt out of his depth, and he was still nursing the afterglow of something hard between his legs.

'I'm certain of it, Captain.' Ore gave him one of her goofy salutes and left.

Chapter 52

Ore

Ore was breathless as she bounded down the stairs. As she passed Claude and his men she kept her eyes to the floor, afraid they might be able to see some sort of evidence of what had just happened on her face.

Claude had resolutely ignored her since their exchange on the island, and she was glad of it. Today though, as much as she hated the idea, she needed to try and keep an eye on him. It was frustrating not to have the full story from Daniel yet, but she could make an educated guess that Chuck was somehow involved with Klauparten Inc.

It was clear that whatever the company actually did, they didn't want anyone to know about it. The branded diving equipment suggested that Chuck was telling the truth about this being some sort of business trip, and that said business was to take place, at least partially, underwater.

It struck Ore that maybe this whole plan, to come to the reef in the first place, was nothing to do with Mel's love of marine wildlife and all about Claude, as Mel herself had suspected. That also explained why Chuck had insisted on sailing through that insane storm and was so eager to 'set off early' this morning.

What she didn't understand was why he had invited her

and Daniel to come along. If they were up to some dodgy stuff then why invite a journalist?

By the time the boat arrived at its new anchoring spot, Ore still hadn't come up with a credible theory.

As the anchor was lowered, Ore went out onto the deck. The three men had fully suited up now. Not an inch of skin could be seen. What looked like blacked-out goggles covered their eyes, and they had breathing tubes in their mouths.

'You guys look like aliens.' It was Mel, who was now standing behind Ore, with her hands on hips. 'Is that what I'm going to wear too?' Despite her best efforts, she sounded excited.

Claude turned to face them, and Ore caught his gaze. A glance at the icy grey was enough to have her trying to find anywhere else to look.

'You are going with the captain; these boys are going on their own expedition.' Claude tried a smile, but the result was unconvincing.

Chuck appeared on deck just in time for Mel to turn her questions to him. 'So are you coming with me and Daniel then?'

'Um no, sweetie, I don't know if I fancy it. I thought I'd stay on board with Claude, but Ore will go with you, won't you?' So that's why she was here: to babysit. She was slightly offended that Chuck regarded her as closer to a nanny than an actual reporter.

In all honesty, Ore was totally horrified by the idea of scuba diving, but the combination of Chuck's not so negotiable insistence and Mel's self-pity pushed her to say, 'Sure . . . would you like that, Mel?'

Mel glared daggers at Chuck, and then shrugged at Ore.

'Well that's settled then. You and Mel and the captain will

266

go to the reef!' Chuck grinned, triumphant. It was interesting, thought Ore, that a man so accustomed to getting his own way was still so thrilled by it.

In response Mel stormed back inside. Chuck gave Ore something of an apologetic look and went over to join Claude. Ore wanted to stay put and try her hand at eavesdropping, but it was too obvious so she followed Mel instead.

She'd retreated to her spot in the corner of the large sofa, and was texting someone furiously. She looked up momentarily when Ore entered and then went back to her correspondence.

Ore hovered awkwardly, unsure how to proceed. Should she change? What on earth was she going to do with her braids? Mel was wearing what looked like an expensive, Lycra baby-grow, similar to what the men outside had under their wetsuits. Hers though, was that sort of trendy shade between green and grey, she wore it with the hood down and the gloves dangling from her wrists. Ore certainly hadn't brought anything like that. At the last minute she had stuffed an old black Speedo swimming costume into her bag, for fear of getting caught out like she had at the island. But it occurred to her now that she'd probably need far more sun protection . . .

It was Daniel who broke her out of her fretting. She hadn't heard the sliding doors open behind her, but when he laid a hand softly on her shoulder, she didn't jump. The warmth of his palm spread a calmness over her, but it also sent the vivid memory of those same hands grasping at her waist not twenty minutes before, flashing through her mind. Her breath caught in her throat.

'Sorry to startle you,' Daniel said softly, misinterpreting her reaction, for which she was grateful.

'No problem!' Her voice was strained with faux casualness. When the two of them caught eyes briefly, they both looked away at the same time. Ore was reassured that it wasn't just her who felt thrown by their passionate encounter upstairs.

'So Mr Regas just informed me that it's to be the three of us out on the reef today. Is that right?' Daniel was directing the question at Ore. He seemed to have surmised that she wasn't the 'underwater type'. In particular he eyed up the braids that trailed down to the bottom of her back.

'Yeah, he's not coming because he hates me.' Mel didn't look up from her phone.

'Right . . .' Daniel appeared unsure how to respond.

'But we're going to have a great time together anyway, aren't we, Daniel?' Ore was determined to cheer Mel up. Partly because she genuinely felt bad for the girl, and partly because spending the day with her in this mood, made the whole babysitting gig even more unappealing.

'Sure we are!' Daniel said, right on cue. Mel shrugged. 'So shall we go get some kit on and learn the basics?'

Mel looked up at Daniel then, her expression incredulous. 'The basics? I'm literally a certified scuba instructor, Dan. I completed my training in Belize last summer.'

'Please don't call me Dan.' The sharpness in Daniel's tone took both Ore and Mel by surprise. So much so that Mel even put her phone down.

'Oh, sorry.' Mel looked contrite. 'I just, I've heard Dad call you that and I thought . . .'

'It's OK, I didn't mean to snap, I . . .' Daniel didn't seem to understand his reaction himself. It was his turn to shrug.

'He calls me Melly Belly and I hate it, so I totally get where you're coming from,' Mel offered, and the pair of them shared a conciliatory, if a little awkward, laugh.

'Um, sorry to cramp your style, but I unfortunately have no idea at all how to scuba dive,' Ore interrupted.

'Well, Melanie and I could show you the basics and then maybe you can try going under for a little bit, or if you're not comfortable with that, you can hang back while we go out together?' Daniel suggested.

'It's Mel, actually, and no that's silly – why don't we just snorkel it? I have no idea why my dad was so obsessed with bringing all that scuba gear anyway. You can literally see everything cool from just below the surface, and that way Ore doesn't miss out.' Mel had perked up. She even seemed a little excited, and Ore was touched by her efforts to include her.

'That's very considerate, Mel. Are you sure though?' Daniel asked.

Mel beamed at the compliment. 'Yep, no problem, I'd hate to have to leave Ore here with creepy Claude and Dad anyway; that's literally no fun.'

'I'd hate that too, Mel. I think we should definitely try and avoid that.' Like most teenagers, Mel seemed to enjoy being spoken to like a grown-up. She grinned at Daniel's tacit agreement of her character assessment of Claude, before turning to Ore.

'Well you'll need a sun suit. I know you're black and everything but the sun around here doesn't mess around, and anyway you don't want to like age prematurely.'

Ore was bemused by Mel's directness. 'Do you think you have something that might fit me?' Ore was about the same

269

height as Mel, but she'd grown out of that adolescent waiflike shape a while back.

'I think there's probably an old one of Mum's lying around here somewhere . . .'

Chapter 53

Daniel

Near Lizard Island, Great Barrier Reef

Suited up, they all splashed into the astonishingly clear water. When they'd gotten to a good spot, or rather where Mel wanted to stop, they headed below the surface. Daniel had to admit, although he'd been scuba diving and snorkelling a number of times, that it was an awesome sight under there. Schools of outrageously bright colours darting between strange and otherworldly towers of coral. Daniel found himself thinking that Carlos would have loved it.

After a short while, even Ore, who was apprehensive at first, seemed to be enjoying herself. It was hard not to be wowed by this underwater metropolis.

'The thing is, once I can actually see what's going on, the fear just evaporates,' she explained to Daniel breathlessly before diving back under.

It brought Daniel a serene satisfaction to see Ore having fun. Time passed loosely and, very uncharacteristically for Daniel, he lost track of it. It was nearly 4 p.m. by the time he thought to check.

'Ladies, I think we should head back. We've been out here

for hours,' Daniel called. Both Mel and Ore were floating on the surface inanimately.

He swam over and gently lulled them out of their observation posts with a shake of the shoulder. They swam back to the boat, Ore a little faster than the other two. Back on the swimming platform, shedding their gear, all three were quiet, awed by what they had just seen.

Mel scrambled to her feet. 'Well thanks, Mum and Dad, I actually had . . . a lot of fun,' she conceded. 'Also you two are kinda cute together you know . . .' she added and before Ore or Daniel could mumble some unconvincing objection, Mel strode off.

Ore laughed nervously, turning to Daniel. 'Thanks for well . . . letting me experience this with you; it was beautiful.'

Daniel felt something rise up inside him, settling tightly in his chest, in a way that was almost uncomfortable. It took a moment for him to register that it was joy, mixed with pride.

'You are more than welcome Ore, I am . . . so happy you enjoyed yourself.' They sat beaming at each other. A thought flew through Daniel's mind: *is this what true love feels like?* He shook his head, as if to banish it.

'Are you OK?' Ore sounded concerned. Her brow furrowed endearingly.

'Yeah, I just . . .' Daniel had no idea what to say. It was new to him, this lightning-bolt feeling. With his ex it had taken months for them to build what he used to call 'a loving connection'. But with Ore, it was all so heady, so immediate, he felt giddy. 'I just, really like spending time with you.'

She smiled, and, to his surprise, reached for his hand, lacing her fingers between his. His pounding heart steadied and that lump in his chest softened into something warm.

'I really like spending time with you too, Daniel.' She laid her head on his shoulder and they looked out at the waves. It was a cliché, thought Daniel, but it really felt like they were the only two people on the entire planet at that moment.

Chapter 54

Ore

The splash was a way off, but in the tranquillity of the scene it caught their attention.

'A fish?' Ore asked, turning to the expert.

'I don't think so. It looked like a flipper . . .' Daniel squinted, and then there was another splash, and a third. His expression turned from confusion to understanding in an instant. 'It's Claude's guys.'

As though they were following the steps of a prepared plan, Ore and Daniel silently gathered their own equipment and made sure to dry their footprints from the wooden decking of the swimming platform. Daniel led the way as they quietly headed up the stairs on the side of the boat to get to the top deck and into the wheelhouse. Daniel motioned for Ore to drop the equipment. At the back of the wheelhouse was a door, about a foot off the ground. Daniel opened it and stepped through, holding his hand out for Ore to follow.

They found themselves in yet another small cupboard. It crossed Ore's mind that he had another make-out session in mind, but then he reached out and removed a panel from the back of the cupboard to reveal a small window.

'The sun's pointing in our direction so they won't be able

to see us past the reflection.' Daniel whispered, and then Ore understood. This was a stakeout.

Through the tiny pane of glass, Daniel and Ore watched as Chuck and Claude walked out onto the deck to meet the three men now hauling themselves and their scuba tanks onto the small platform. Claude looked around, then looked up towards the wheelhouse window. Ore's heart quickened as he shielded his eyes from the sun and squinted up at where they were hiding. A second ticked by slowly and when Claude turned back to the gathering on the deck, Ore let out a deep breath.

'Told you,' Daniel whispered teasingly.

They couldn't hear what was being said, but Ore could see that the discussion was animated, and positive. Chuck was smiling and slapping one of the divers on the back. Another of the divers had something in his hands.

'Can you see what he's holding?' Ore asked.

'It looks like a small black box . . .' Daniel trailed off as he craned his neck to see. 'Yep . . . it looks like they've opened a lid, but I can't see what's inside.'

'Damn.' Ore felt like the key detail was just out of reach. The five men continued talking for a minute or so, and then headed inside. Ore felt frustrated. 'What the hell does this all mean?'

Daniel looked reticent for a moment. 'I'm pretty sure what I overheard last night explains it all.'

'Can't you just tell me now?' Ore didn't understand why Daniel was insisting on withholding vital information.

'I'd really rather wait, and anyway, I left the notebook back on *Thalassa*.' Daniel had made his mind up.

'You're such a tease,' Ore replied, more than aware of the double entendre. They were doing that close-proximity thing again, bodies within touching distance, and the space between them becoming thick with unrealised expectation.

Ore held off making a move, and Daniel didn't either. She could understand that it was more difficult for men to stop their desire from becoming . . . noticeable, and no doubt Chuck would be marching over at any moment to demand an update on their route home.

Ore took it upon herself to defuse the tension, opening the door and stepping back out into the wheelhouse. Daniel followed her out, but she was sure she spotted a tinge of redness in his cheeks.

Almost right on cue, Chuck burst through the door. He stopped in his tracks when he saw Ore and Daniel, his eyes flitting to the open door behind them.

'What are you doing up here, Ore?' His tone was laced with suspicion and Ore panicked.

'Um . . . err . . . We were just . . .' Ore looked down at her feet, and felt a bead of sweat roll down the back of her neck. The silence was heavy.

'Ore and I were just . . .' Daniel had a go but he too stumbled.

'Oh,' said Chuck knowingly, 'I see.' Ore forgot how to breathe. She peeked up at Chuck; a lazy smirk settled on his face. 'I knew you two had a thing going on.'

On this occasion Ore was relieved by Chuck's strange obsession with their relationship. She'd always found it strangely racially loaded, but right now it was a useful explanation, and it wasn't even a wholly untrue one either.

Daniel laughed nervously, and Ore worried he might deny it. She knew him well enough by now to know that he took his 'professionalism' very seriously.

'We were just . . . talking,' Daniel said finally, and honestly. But the vagueness worked in their favour.

Chuck winked at Daniel. 'So that's what you kids are calling it.' On this round of nervous laughter, Ore joined in, wishing with all her might for an opportunity to flee this mortifying situation. Chuck obliged.

'Well if you don't mind, Ore, I need to have a chat of my own with our dashing captain . . .'

'Not at all, I was just heading back down,' Ore said slightly too quickly. She was already halfway out of the room. She heard Chuck offer up another back slap and a 'I don't blame you, Captain. If I was ten years younger . . .' as she scuttled down to the deck.

The journey back was uneventful. Ore sat in the salon willing the hour to pass faster. She needed to know what Daniel had to tell her. Mel had reverted back to sullen teenager mode and ignored Ore the whole way, seemingly texting non-stop, most probably messaging her girlfriend.

Claude and his men were nowhere to be seen. Ore imagined them squirrelled away somewhere below her, hunched over that mysterious box and exchanging ideas on how to take over the world.

Back inside the hull of *Lady Thalassa's* marina, Mel was the first to disembark, notably not acknowledging Chuck as she climbed onto the gangway and raced off. Chuck waited for Claude and the pair watched as that same crate was loaded off the boat by the divers, before they too got off.

Ore hung back, and when Daniel appeared she kept it brief: 'What time?'

Daniel was lithely hopping on and off the boat, tying various ropes to various hooks lining the dock. He barely looked up from what he was doing, and despite herself Ore took a second to admire his athleticism.

'Usual spot, twenty-one hundred hours?' Daniel suggested.

All this sneaking around was kind of exciting. 'Copy that, Captain,' Ore said, resisting her incessant urge to salute.

Chapter 55

Ore

Back in her room, Ore checked the clock incessantly. *How is it only six thirty?* She was pacing the room when her phone rang. It was Henry. She screened the call. She'd ring him after she knew more; there was no point pitching him half a story.

At seven thirty came Carlos' call. She was too anxious to eat, so she asked him to surprise her. When the bubbling moussaka arrived though, she could barely manage a mouthful, and she felt bad as she watched it cool and congeal.

After what felt like an eternity, 9 p.m. rolled around, and Ore almost ran to the middle deck. The door to kit cupboard 6 was slightly ajar and Daniel was already inside.

'Close it behind you.' He sounded agitated; she did as she was told.

The light inside the cramped space was weak but warm as Daniel pulled out a small notepad.

'Quite the budding journalist I see,' Ore teased, hoping to ease the intense atmosphere.

'If I had it my way, I'd never have been involved in any of

this,' Daniel fretted. Ore reached out and pulled his chin up to face her.

'I really appreciate all this, Daniel. I know it goes against literally all of your natural instincts,' she said with sincerity.

Daniel gave a tiny nod and opened the notepad.

For the next three minutes Ore's jaw hung open, as Daniel read out what might as well have been a transcript of the conversation he'd overheard. When he was done, Ore was speechless. He'd cracked it, the whole story; if she hadn't been so grateful, she might have been a bit envious.

'So what do you think?' he asked nervously.

'I think you've uncovered an environmental crime, fraud and a corruption scandal at the heart of one of the highest valued companies in the world, Daniel.' Even as she spoke Ore was still processing, thinking out loud. 'So Claude is helping Chuck to excavate cobalt from the sea beds right next to and even on the Great Barrier Reef, with plans to pay off, or lobby the Australian authorities into allowing him to set up a permanent deep sea mine. All the while he's touting this new battery as some innovative, *sustainable*, new leap forward for the tech industry . . .' Ore shook her head, in disbelief. She didn't know what she'd been expecting, but it was nothing on this scale.

'He's a crook,' Daniel said plainly, and Ore had to laugh because that *was* what it all boiled down to. Daniel seemed surprised by her reaction, but after a moment he joined in.

As the laughter died down, something heavier replaced it. Ore wasn't sure if it was the build-up of frustration throughout the day, or the ecstasy of putting together the pieces of this puzzle. Maybe it was the adrenaline coursing through her body, or the want that was creeping into his gaze. It could have been the smell of him, or the curve of his jaw, the pinkness of the inside of his lip that she could just make out in the dim light.

It was impossible to know exactly, and it was also impossible to fight it.

Chapter 56

Daniel

They crashed into each other, and his body was ablaze. The match had been lit and engulfed them both. He wasn't sure which moans were his and which were hers as they clawed at each other's clothing. He pinned her against the wall, and something fell off the shelf above their heads.

Daniel wasn't sure where to start. Her mouth was delicious, warm and wet and soft like sodden silk. She pressed herself into him, grabbing at his shoulders, and he ran his hand down her sides, grabbing at her ass to pull her even closer. She threw her head back as he kissed hot breaths down her neck, using his teeth to find his way through the lace of her bra to her nipple.

He stopped for a moment, admiring her panting curves, the skin of her breasts smooth and dark, and then puckering in anticipation of his tongue. She looked down at him, her gaze demanding, and he indulged her, taking the hard nib in his mouth. At the sound of her moaning, he could feel himself tightening against the seam of his flies. Her hands had travelled to his chest now and then her fingers were trailing lightly over the ridges of his abs and downwards. The stirring intensified, and Daniel's mind fogged, seemingly overwhelmed by the multiplying points of contact. Everywhere she touched him, his skin prickled, all of him standing to attention.

As she arrived at his waistband, it was his turn to groan, and the vibrations seemed to travel from his mouth through her body, as it quaked in response. He wanted more. He wanted to make her quiver; he wanted to watch her come undone.

He dropped to his knees and caught her gaze again as he unzipped her skirt. The aubergine-coloured fabric pooled at her feet. Face to face with the triangle of cloth, he took a jagged breath. 'Please,' she mouthed. Who was he to deny this magnificent woman?

He hooked his thumbs about the scant strips of fabric circling her hips, and slowly pulled her underwear down. 'Such a tease,' she whimpered breathlessly. He was enjoying taking his time. He brushed his lips over her hip bone, and planted a light kiss on the soft flesh of her stomach. Her breathing grew louder, raspier. He lifted her leg over his shoulder and found that crease, the one demarcating her thigh from her abdomen. As he ran his tongue along it, the throbbing between his legs grew louder and heavier.

When he finally tasted her, she exhaled with something like relief, her fingers digging into the muscles in his shoulder. The smell of her was intoxicating, and Daniel found it hard to maintain any concept of time passing, each new present building on the previous high. Her thighs showed the signs. Daniel felt them trembling in his hands, as her breathing quickened. He followed suit. Her hands clenched into fists and he felt her hardness, her pleasure swelling under his tongue, he used a finger to dip into her and was overcome by her readiness for him. He groaned into her again, and it tipped her over the edge.

As the tremors soaked through her body, Daniel did not relent. He wanted to venture to the very limits of her, and then take one step further. She breathed his name like a prayer and he forged further until she reached the peak again and then came tumbling back down to earth.

He was there to catch her when she landed, waiting patiently for those liquid pools of bronze to open. She kissed him softly and he stroked her cheek with his thumb. She purred against his lips. 'Would you be offended if I told you I wasn't expecting that from you?' she asked quietly, though there was a sparkle of mischief in her eyes.

'I would,' he said good-humouredly, 'but I'd try and take it as a backhanded compliment.'

'Please do,' she said but the last word was swallowed by his mouth on hers again. A moment of respite and then the furnace roared back to life. She was frantic now, and his buttons were the casualties, though he found himself totally unbothered as he heard one rattle to the floor. His shirt followed close behind and then she moved on to his belt. It was almost too much to bear, as she struggled with the buckle. She pushed him away, her hand flat on his chest, and he felt bereft.

She giggled. 'Don't look at me like that – I just need to get a better look at this . . .' She bent to take a closer look at the fastening, and her proximity made him even harder. He winced as her hand grazed over him, the lightest touch, an overdose of anticipation. Ore pulled at his waistband, and he studied her face as she exposed him. Was it surprise? Fear? Admiration? She looked up at him and his heart almost stopped beating. It was hunger.

Chapter 57

Ore

She'd never really thought that naked men were that attractive – not that she wasn't attracted to them, more that the aesthetics of the male form had always been relatively underwhelming to her. Daniel's body was a different matter. It was sculptural in its construction, each part of him harmoniously in tune with the other. His skin was so smooth and toned that her fingers sent confused, flustered messages back to her brain, as though they were expecting to feel the coolness of marble, rather than the warmth of flesh. In her right mind she might have taken time to marvel at it.

In this moment though, there was no time for that. Her body had taken the reins and her mind could only come along for the ride – an exhilarating one at that. She was crouching in front of him, facing the hard, taut, quite-a-bit-more-than-a-handful of him. She knew she was ready for it, and when their eyes met, he did too. He pulled her up and pushed her up against the wall. She hooked her leg around him and found herself staring into his eyes, transfixed by them as he slid inside her. Eye contact during sex was untrodden territory for her, but the intensity of it was exquisite.

With each thrust she felt a slow unfurling of something,

deep within her. Like her body was welcoming him in, like he wasn't merely a guest, but a cherished old friend. The edges of her began to blur. She could no longer determine where she and he ended, and the rest of the world began, their pleasure smudging the contours of things. She had an overpowering sense of herself as a mass of vibrating atoms and as the waves grew taller and taller, and she waited for the crash, she feared she might come apart entirely, that he would finish and find a mass of quivering matter dripping off his hands.

The graze of his teeth on her earlobe brought her back into herself and she focused on the smell of him to keep her there. She wanted to be present. The thrumming in the pit of her stomach had reached a fever pitch, but she didn't want to reach the summit without him. She grabbed his hips and slowed him down, whispering in his ear, 'Let's get there together.' He groaned into her neck and they found a new, delicious rhythm.

It was deliberate, what they were doing now, not frenzied like in the beginning. Ore didn't think she'd ever experienced anything like it before. Sober, for a start, and considered . . . He had navigated her body like a pleasure garden, admiring the blooms, stroking the petals, burying his nose in the bouquet. She was no mere object, but a living breathing constellation of new experiences, and they were on that exploration together.

She opened her eyes to find him again, and he was already there, his lips parted slightly. Each plunge dove deep now, caressing a part of her she didn't know was there. She realised the panting was hers and with the slightest of nods, his pace almost imperceptibly quickened. 'I'm almost there,' she breathed and he brought a hand to her face, his thumb slipping into her mouth.

'I'll see you at the top . . .' he whispered before his own breathing turned carnal. Ore wasn't sure if he had actually spoken or if she was reading his mind, but as her mind frazzled at the edges, she surrendered to him, body and soul, and was no longer convinced of any distinction.

At some point, as she floated out from somewhere deep within her body, he shuddered and she held him tightly for fear he might collapse. Her senses returned slowly, one by one. The roughness of the panelling against her back, the smell of neoprene and sweat, the sound of the waves, the taste of herself from his mouth, and then finally, the beauty of his face, beset with a smile that made her feel like she had finally found home. She realised too late that the hotness on her cheek was a tear.

His brow furrowed. 'Are you OK, Ore? I . . . I'm so sorry . . .' He sounded panicked.

'Shhhh,' she soothed him, bringing a soft fingertip to his lips. 'I'm just happy, Daniel, like I've been rummaging around my life looking for something I've lost, and I've just found it, and it's even more special than I remembered.'

In her postcoital state, she was being careless with her feelings, she knew, but the words tumbled anyway.

'You have such a beautiful way with words, Ore.' He smiled softly. 'I don't think I could have described it better.'

She laugh-gulped back another stream of tears and Daniel just buried his head in her neck. She let them fall then, splashing into his hair, and kept holding him as tightly as she could.

Chapter 58

Ore

At a certain point, the heat they'd generated started to dissipate and their naked bodies grew colder. It was Ore who noticed first. They had fallen into a sort of fugue state, not speaking or moving, but simply being, trying to hold on to the moment for as long as they could. Outside of this time, this cupboard even, they had no idea what awaited each of them, let alone their future together.

'I think we should probably go to bed . . .' Ore said quietly. 'Will you come to bed with me?'

He looked at her with sadness in his eyes. He was already mourning their moment, beginning to think about the 'after'.

'I don't know if that's a good idea, Ore. I would love to, I just . . . if anyone finds out, it doesn't look good for me.' Ore's heart sank, her elation replaced by the heavy weight of realism.

'I mean it's hardly a good look for me either, Daniel, but maybe I just care less about other people's opinions.' She was hurt and lashing out. She was pushing him away before he could reject her. It was textbook stuff.

Instead of replying immediately, Daniel stroked her cheek, until she looked up at him again, and when she did the tenderness in his face made her want to cry again.

'I do really want to, and I think you know that it is different for me – you get to leave this world, but this is the world that *I* live in.' His voice was deep and calming.

She nodded, soothed, reassured, but still desperately yearning for a different outcome.

'I understand – I'm sorry,' she muttered, and in response he planted a soft kiss on her lips.

'Now we should probably get some clothes on,' he said, and then waited, as though not wanting to make the first move and initiate the disentanglement. Ore nodded again, and with her agreement he pulled himself out and away.

Ore gathered her clothes, having to scout for her bra, and they dressed themselves in silence. She wasn't sure what to say. The whirlwind of feelings she'd experienced in the last hour were too muddled to articulate.

When they were both fully clothed, Daniel made for the door, opening it up slowly, to check for the all-clear, and then striding out onto the deck. Outside, the air was cool, and the moon's reflection glistened amidst the inky waves.

Ore leant out against the railing and took a deep breath. 'You know I didn't even take a Kwell today, and I was fine,' she said.

'You're finally finding your sea legs.' He came up behind her and hovered, as if unsure whether he could touch her outside of their hideaway.

'I think I get it, you know, why you might choose this life. There's something so free about it,' Ore mulled out loud.

'An old friend of mine always says it's like the circus, for people who are either chasing something or running away.'

'Who's the friend?' It occurred to Ore that they'd had very

few conversations like this – really she knew almost nothing about him, other than what she'd told him in that first interview. All they ever talked about was the investigation.

'Captain Jack Carter, but he was a first officer when I knew him. He fast-tracked me through my bosun years.' Daniel smiled fondly at the memory.

'Bosun?' Ore wasn't familiar with the terminology.

'It's like the third rung down: captain, first officer, then bosun. I was his right-hand man,' Daniel explained.

'And which one are you doing then? Chasing or running away?' Ore probed.

'I don't know. For a long time I thought neither. I thought I was one of the few people who knew exactly where they were going. I have a plan to get there . . .' He trailed off, and then corrected himself: '*had* a plan.' Ore kept her eyes trained on the indiscernible horizon. She wanted him to keep talking.

'But recently . . . *very* recently, I've been thinking that it's actually both. That I'm running and chasing, and I didn't even know it.'

'Well well, who's got a way with words now?' Ore could have said nothing, but she wanted him to know she was listening.

'Yeah, I guess. I seem to spend a lot of time *thinking*, at the moment. It's horrible. I don't know how you do it.' He was matching her lightened tone, but there was truth there too.

Ore yawned, suddenly exhausted.

'Oh geez, am I boring you?' Daniel chuckled.

'No! No I love talking to you. I just think I need to sleep now. It's been . . . an eventful day,' which was quite the understatement, thought Ore.

She turned to face Daniel. They stood awkwardly for a second, and then Daniel pecked her on the cheek and with a chirpy 'Goodnight!' he marched off. Had she had more energy, Ore might have been left reeling; as it was, she headed downstairs, seduced by the siren call of her bed.

Chapter 59

Daniel

As Daniel shut the door of his room behind him, he immediately regretted leaving Ore. He paced the room, trying to make sense of the loneliness he felt. His own company had always been a comfort but now there was a distinct lack of something. He changed into his pyjamas, brushed his teeth and got into bed.

Every time he closed his eyes, she was with him again, the softness of her skin against his and the whisper of her voice in his ear. He tossed and turned, but sleep eluded him. He checked his alarm clock; it read 2 a.m.

He sat up, willing his brain to compartmentalise, a task it was usually so good at. He needed to be up in four hours. He needed to rest, but the whole of his mind was consumed with only one thing. Before he could talk himself out of it, he got out of bed. As he had two nights previously he walked down the corridor on autopilot until he got to her door.

He knocked lightly, half hoping she wouldn't hear, half praying that she would. Or maybe his dream would recreate itself and she'd slam it in his face. But then she was there, standing before him in a white dressing gown, her hair wrapped in a scarf, bleary-eyed.

'Did I wake you?' he asked.

'Yes,' she replied with a sleepy smile, 'come in.' He crossed the threshold, shutting the door quietly behind him and watched, mesmerised, as she dropped the robe to the floor and climbed back into bed. Her naked body an invitation, dark amongst the bright white sheets.

Her gaze was transfixed on his face as he removed his pyjamas and when he lay down beside her she pulled him into an embrace. Their noses lay tip to tip, and he encircled her with his arms. She closed her eyes and sighed. He didn't think he'd ever seen anything more beautiful. Slowly his own eyelids drifted shut, the steady sound of her breathing coaching him to join her in a calm and deep sleep. He felt utterly at peace.

Chapter 60

Daniel

Day 8

He awoke to the smooth slope of her shoulder rising and falling gently. He couldn't resist pressing his lips against the nape of her neck. She let out a contented sigh and pulled the hand that was resting on her stomach up to her own lips. They lay there for an indescribable length of time.

Ore stirred, lazily clambering out of sleep, and the movement of her body, the slight repositioning of her hips, stirred something else. Suddenly he was wide awake.

He trailed his finger down from her mouth, over her neck, her chest and down her belly, bringing it to sit on that restless hip of hers. Her breathing changed almost instantly. Spurred on by her immediate response, he reached between her legs, which she parted obligingly. The wetness against his fingers set him alight. She moaned softly as she turned onto her back, to give him better access. Her eyes fluttered open, and he wondered if the want in his eyes was as carnal as the hunger he saw in hers. When she called his name, and convulsed under his touch, he wondered how he would ever let her out of his sight again.

When he sunk himself inside her, lost in the folds of her, he felt the shift, away from running, to chasing, and hoping one day to have. His body tightened, and every inch of him felt hot – her touch, her smell, pulling him towards release. A flash of ecstasy at the summit and then they plummeted together, landing back in a tangle of sheets. He never wanted to let go.

He came back to himself in a daze, and she snuggled into him. 'I for one am very glad you changed your mind . . .' she said between a smattering of light kisses across his chest. She propped herself up on her elbow, gazing at him.

'I don't know how I'll ever be able to sleep without you again,' he said quietly, and she gave him a sad smile. She made to get up and he pulled her back. He needed another taste of her. She giggled against his mouth and then leant back. 'Don't fly away just yet please,' he added.

'Fly away?'

'Like the magnificent seabird that you are.' He was giddy, talking nonsense.

She laughed. 'I have no idea what you're talking about, but we do probably need to get out of bed at some point. She reached for her phone. 'It's like nine o'clock.'

Shit. He was late. She had a habit of throwing him off schedule. 'I'd better go.' He was flustered suddenly, rushing out of bed and pulling on his discarded pyjamas. She watched him, head cocked to the side, curiously observing.

'So where do we go from here, Captain? I doubt any of this is part of your big plan?' She was cross-legged on the bed, and Daniel found it hard to concentrate on getting ready while she sat there naked, let alone think beyond the next day. She was right; none of this was part of his plan.

'Come to my cabin tonight?' He had already thrown his caution to the wind; why stop now? What was it Carlos had said? Something about things that have always worked, not working anymore, and changing? He couldn't remember exactly but he understood the gist of it now; denying his feeling for Ore just wasn't a viable option anymore, so it was time to change tactics.

Ore grinned. 'Great, I'll see you later.'

He leant in for one last kiss, and then hurried out.

Chapter 61

Ore

Ore really was not in the mood to work, but there was another missed call from Henry on her phone. And she was behind schedule for the next draft. She'd planned to write it last night, but then . . .

No she didn't have time to get lost in thoughts of Daniel. She was a grown woman; she could wait until tonight. Other people managed to work alongside falling in love. *Wait, do I love him?* No, she didn't have time for this! She willed herself out of bed and into the bathroom. In the shower she lingered over the parts of her that he had touched, smiling to herself. No, she had to write this article.

Staring at herself in the mirror, she noticed that her braids looked pretty dishevelled and then something in the corner of her eye made her blood run cold. The perfume bottle. It was back on the side of the sink. Hadn't she moved it into the cabinet last time? She tried to keep calm and get ready as usual but that niggling paranoia was back.

She rushed back into the bedroom and pulled her robe back on, suddenly uncomfortable with her nakedness. That's when she spotted the manila envelope on her desk. It hadn't been there when she left her room yesterday morning.

She approached it cautiously, looking around for any other signs of things out of place but could only scold herself for her messiness; it was impossible to tell. With shaking hands she picked up the envelope and pulled out the contents. A bundle of papers that looked like . . . bank account statements.

At the top of the page, INVOICE FOR SERVICES PROVIDED BY KLAUPARTEN INDUSTRIES. She held her breath as she read through the transactions: hundreds of thousands of dollars paid in by something called 'Greenloop' for 'resource exploration and excavation'. Ore was clued up enough to know that that meant 'mining'.

But that wasn't all – there was also a page that listed the board of trustees: Richard Greenam, Gerry Porter, Ousman Alzahrani, Roger Alderton, Frederik Dolph. And then there right at the top: CEO, Claude Van Der Bodem. Chuck was listed as a 'majority shareholder', and that Derek guy as the COO.

So all the men on board, they were all part of this, and she now had evidence tying Chuck to the company and confirming Claude as the true power behind the throne of Klauparten, as well as proof of their fraudulent business records. The shell company was not such a shell, what with at least four million dollars of income listed in the last year alone. This was enough to go to Henry with. Before she'd had a story, but it was built on hearsay; now she had a scoop.

After a quick Google search, she discovered that Greenloop was a 'non-profit conservation enterprise' whatever that was, and that Chuck was one of their main donors. They claimed to 'conduct research on sites of outstanding natural beauty and suggest policy proposals for protecting them'. If that was true, why were they paying Klauparten for mining services? The only explanation: the whole thing was a front, to allow Klauparten access to all the most protected places in the world.

One burning question now remained: who had left this envelope for her? Maybe one of the investors had had a turn of conscience? Or it could be one of the crew? If Daniel's eavesdropping situation was anything to go by, it was likely enough that someone working on board might come across a piece of such incriminating evidence totally by accident.

Ore was lost in thought when her phone rang. It was Henry. She answered the phone breathlessly.

'Ore, hi, are you OK? You sound like you've been running?' came Henry's New York drawl.

'Hi, Henry, no I'm just . . .' Ore tried to catch her breath, her mind buzzing with adrenaline. 'I was actually about to call you.'

'About time – what have you got for me?'

Ore braced herself. 'You're not going to believe this, Henry, but just hear me out. I've found something, something big, really big, about Chuck and this guy Claude and this company Greenloop and . . .' Ore was struggling to get her words out in order.

Henry cut her off. 'Let me stop you right there, Ore.'

'I'm sorry I know I'm not explaining this very well.' Ore was frustrated at herself.

'It's OK – you don't need to explain,' Henry said firmly, and then sighed. Ore was confused.

'In fact, please don't explain. I don't want to hear any more. This isn't what I commissioned you to write, Ore.' He sounded agitated.

'I know, but, Henry, this is huge, I just stumbled across it and . . . well not stumbled . . . but—'

He interrupted her again. 'Ore, stop.' She waited. 'Chuck Regas is a very powerful and very rich man. And in some cases, like this one, it might be best to . . . let sleeping dogs lie.'

'But, Henry, this is like proper dark stuff. We're talking fraud, corruption – there's even some dodgy NDA sexual assault stuff . . .'

'STOP!' Henry's sudden anger made her jump and stunned her into silence. 'Write me the profile I commissioned and leave it at that. For your own good, Ore.' And with that Henry hung up. Ore took a shaky breath as the dial tone rang in her ear.

Ore placed the phone down on the desk in front of her slowly. She knew she wasn't going to listen to Henry, but she was going to heed his warning. It was clear that anything she wrote about Chuck would come with consequences and she needed to think very carefully about how to play this.

What would Gail Fairweather say? Firstly, *you know you have a good story if no one wants you to publish it.* So, if anything, Henry's reaction was sort of encouraging. Secondly – *don't underestimate the tools at the disposal of your opponents; consider them all.* In the case of Chuck there were many: truckloads of cash, the best lawyers in the world, a trove of favours from people in high places, connections with the sorts of dubious and dangerous people you meet in the world of illegal mineral mining. *Thirdly, think about who the story is for, and where it will have the most impact.* On the former point she worried it would be too grandiose to say 'everyone' but she also felt it was true. On the latter, the *New York Herald* was clearly *not* the place, so she'd have to go back to the drawing board with pitching.

If she did decide to write the story for a competitor though, that was the staff job out the window. It would be hard to wave goodbye to the promise of that kind of security. She didn't know what to do.

What would Kyle say? *Slow down, take a step back, turn around, what have you missed, while you were too busy steaming ahead?*

So she did. And looking back, she couldn't help but marvel at how far she'd come in just over a week. She still had five days left, and maybe just when every bone in her body was telling her to run faster, she could take Kyle's advice once again. Give herself time to think and process. The right path would make itself known eventually, and she had a better chance of choosing if she wasn't blinded by impatience.

Wait and see, then. That was the plan, as radical as it felt. Ore sensed it was the right decision. She would finish off the article that Henry wanted and then write the story she wanted to write, and keep them both until she was off this boat. Maybe once she was back on solid ground, literally and metaphorically, and out from under Chuck's thumb, she would have a better sense of her next move.

With an unusual sense of calm, she opened her laptop. 'Chuck Regas, the man, the myth, the father.' She began typing the words with proficient detachment and before she knew it, she was done. She formatted, and spellchecked, and saved the document. But she didn't send it to Henry, not yet.

Ore's stomach rumbled and when she realised it was midday, it struck her that she hadn't heard from Carlos, who usually rang her for breakfast requests, if she didn't turn up to the mess. It seemed she'd have to venture out of her room if she wanted to eat.

Chapter 62

Daniel

Daniel was about as close as you could come to having a skip in your step, without, well, actually changing the way he was walking at all. This time the legs kicking under the surface of the gliding swan were doing a merry jig.

He was late to relieve Dudley, but he didn't care. The sunlight that drenched the top deck seemed to infuse the colours of the day with more vibrancy than usual. The gulls overhead squawked melodically, the brisk wind almost carried him up the stairs. For the first time in his life, Daniel felt the urge to whistle, which he resisted.

He felt sure that nothing could dampen his mood, but as he rounded the corner, he heard voices coming from the main salon.

'You work for me, Carlos, not her. She needs to grow up and come to breakfast when I ask her to, not hide away in her room. If I had behaved like that as a child . . . honestly I can't even imagine how my father would have responded to the insolence.' It was Chuck speaking, and he sounded angry, unapologetically so.

'I'm sorry, Mr Regas, I just thought that as she is eating in her room most days, it would not be an issue.' Carlos' voice was quiet, and Daniel cringed to hear him sound so contrite.

'Are you trying to tell me I'm a bad parent? Is it my fault she eats in her room? That is just how teenagers are these days! But I've had enough – no more mollycoddling, she needs to grow up.' So they were talking about Mel. It struck Daniel as unfair that it was suddenly Carlos' fault that Mel had grown used to getting her own way. 'I don't want you to send her food anymore. If she wants to eat, she'll have to come and actually interact with me at the dinner table!'

'If you think that is best, but having a teenage girl myself, I find it is not best to try and control them, much better to talk head on,' Carlos explained plainly.

Daniel couldn't see the exchange but he could almost taste the tension. He imagined Chuck turning purple in the loaded silence.

When he replied, Chuck's tone was ice cold. 'I will not be accepting parenting advice from my staff, thank you very much, Carlos, and most certainly not from absent fathers.'

Daniel felt the force of Chuck's disdain from the other side of the wall. He listened as Chuck's footstep faded away and then found Carlos perched on a bar stool, his head in his hands.

Daniel wasn't sure whether to admit to his eavesdropping. It was becoming a bit of a habit, and not one he was proud of. He decided to be straight with Carlos.

'I heard how Chuck spoke to you and I just wanted to say . . .' Daniel realised he had, in fact, no idea what he wanted to say, so instead he just reached out his hand and laid it on Carlos' shoulder.

When Carlos looked up, he had tears in his eyes. 'But he is right about one thing, I am absent. I haven't seen my Claudia for six months and when I did, she only wanted to spend a single day with me.' Carlos swallowed a sob, and Daniel felt suddenly out of his depth.

'I think the only thing you can do is make sure that she knows that you want to see her, and hope that one day she'll understand why you couldn't.' Daniel wondered if his own father had ever felt so torn up about not seeing him or his siblings. What advice was he given?

Carlos nodded thoughtfully and wiped at his cheeks with the sleeve of his chef's whites.

'Also Chuck can talk – he and Melanie hardly have the best relationship,' Daniel continued. Carlos gave him a strange look, a mix of caution and admiration.

'You should keep your voice down,' Carlos said, as if to illustrate the point, in a whisper. 'There are a lot of persons on this boat who report back to him . . . Luckily for you I stopped doing that some time ago.' Carlos hung his head again. 'And I have certainly paid the price . . .'

'What do you mean, Carlos?'

Carlos looked from side to side, theatrically gesturing for Daniel to lean in closer. 'Well when I started for Mr Regas, he would often reward me with unexpected tips for sharing information about others on the boat.' Carlos sighed. 'But after a while it started to get me down, and I did not feel I could get close to anyone, so I stopped, and the money stopped. I mean the pay is obviously still very good but the generous tipping, that was done. Now I have less to send to my ex-wife, and less to visit my daughter. He controls people with money, Daniel, to make them speak, to spill their secrets, but in the end it is to silence them . . . Whenever there is money involved, Chuck Regas has something to hide. Remember that.'

Daniel thought about the envelope with $75,000 dollars in. And then he thought about Ore's.

Carlos went on, 'So when you take the money, then you are in the trap and he will make you sign the DNA agreement in order to receive the transfer. He buys people's voices.'

'NDA,' Daniel corrected.

Carlos ignored him; he was on a roll. 'Even someone like Vicky is on the payroll. It was her who told Chuck about what Claude had done to Annie.' Daniel nodded along, trying to keep all the connections in his head. 'And she had overheard Annie talking to Agatha about it. By the time that Agatha did tell Chuck, he already knew and Annie was no longer on board.'

Daniel must have looked confused, as Carlos continued, 'Agatha has been trying to get back into Chuck's . . . um . . . good books is it?'

'Yes, yes,' Daniel confirmed impatiently, before coming to the end of the thought on his own, 'and that's why Agatha and Vicky don't get along.'

'*Exactement*,' Carlos said sadly, 'and that is his other tactic: divide and conquer, making everyone suspicious of each other. It's an ugly business.'

Noticing awkward social dynamics was not Daniel's strong suit. He'd thought that everyone seemed to get on reasonably well. Now with this new information to consider, he recalled Dudley's tightly wound temper, Vicky's standoffishness, Nicole's skittishness, Agatha's unprompted outpouring and sudden advance, the sudden hushing whenever he walked in on a conversation . . . In retrospect it seemed like everyone on this boat was on edge.

'And the money and silence is the best option – let me tell you that. I heard, well overheard, from Vicky that Chuck gave Annie two options: sign the NDA and take the money, there was a lot of it, or never work again. You'll know better than most that the world of the super rich is a small one, and a bad word goes a long way . . .'

Daniel was lucky this was a temporary gig for him; soon he'd be with the Hartfords, and he could leave all this behind.

'I'm really sorry, Carlos. Might I recommend you look for another job?' Daniel couldn't understand why anyone would stay working for Chuck.

'Pah, I would, but Chuck won't let anyone leave until he wants them gone; as I said, he is not afraid of giving a bad reference.' Carlos shook his head, defeated by his own indictment of the situation.

'There is always a way out, Carlos. A wise man once told me something about things not always needing to be like they've always been, and how when they're not you need to change . . . or something like that.'

Carlos looked up, and both men laughed softly. 'Well maybe this is my first step, of doing something different, to tell you, to break the silence. I trust that you will do the right thing with this information.'

Daniel was touched, if a little wary of the responsibility. 'I will try.'

'You do that, Capitaine, and in the meantime I've got lunch

to make.' Carlos pulled himself to his feet and slapped Daniel on the back on his way out. It was the first time Daniel had seen Carlos look his age.

Chapter 63

Ore

Ore was finally getting the hang of the layout and headed straight towards the kitchen. Inside, Carlos was nowhere to be found, but she helped herself to some of the fresh fruit in the fridge and sliced off a hunk of cheese to nibble on. Looking around the kitchen, Ore was awed. She was the kind of city dweller who often relied on the wealth of takeaway options available to her; being able to make a meal from scratch was a bona fide superpower in her eyes.

She hung around for a while, flipping through recipe books and looking through the cupboards, hoping that Carlos might return and save her from her hunger. When the door swung open though, it was Agatha standing before her, equally surprised.

'Oh hi, sorry I was just waiting for Carlos . . .' Ore explained.

'Um, yeah, I'm looking for him as well . . .' Agatha crossed her arms, but Ore thought she might try an olive branch, in the name of solidarity for the impractical and starving.

'I sort of came in here with the intention of "whipping something up", and then had to confront the fact that I can't even boil an egg.' Ore laughed nervously, and was relieved to see Agatha crack a smile, even if it was a small one.

'When I was younger my older sister cooked all the time, but I usually did the cleaning and then when I left home I always ate in the college dining room,' Agatha offered, still apprehensive.

'Well sounds like you two were a parent's dream. My mum literally did everything for me and my sister when we were little; I was more of a hindrance than a help.' Ore noticed a change in Agatha's expression straight away; gone was the glimmer of warmth.

'I didn't have a choice. My mum wasn't really around. We didn't have any money growing up, so she had to work all the time. We were very poor.' Agatha said bluntly.

Ore was taken aback. She hadn't expected that from Agatha – both that she had grown up poor, and that she would volunteer that information to Ore, of all people.

'I er . . . I had no idea, Agatha. I'm sorry – that must have been tough.'

'Yeah well, how would you? This haircut cost more than Mum used to make in a week, so . . .' Agatha was looking down at her feet, as though embarrassed by her outburst.

The obvious signifier of class wasn't just the haircut; it was Agatha's voice, her clothes, even her makeup. All of it quietly luxe, as though imbued with money unstressfully spent. If it hadn't been a sad spectacle, Ore would have been mostly impressed by how successfully Agatha must have studied the moneyed in her time at Oxford. Her attention to detail could not be faulted.

'It was part of the reason that Chuck hired me, said something about "working class grit".' She laughed but it was a hollow sound. 'That was before I realised how much he'd inherited from his grandfather. Did you know about that? Chuck's father was disinherited, so all the money skipped a generation. It's funny huh, how much rich people love to bang on about how poor they used to be? But if they really had been, I know they'd never want to think about it again; it's like thinking about death on the happiest day of your life – morbid.'

Ore was at a loss for words. What was driving this confession? Agatha continued, 'And then I guess I realised that he actually wanted me to be poor so I couldn't leave. Because that's the real difference isn't it? Between us and them? They deal in control while we scramble for petty cash . . .' Her eyes blazed. 'Be careful, Ore, watch your back because he has more people on his payroll than you can even fathom.'

'What exactly do you mean by that?' Ore spoke gently. Agatha's unpredictability was unsettling.

'Always with the questions – you don't believe me?'

Ore shrugged, something told her that despite Agatha's hostility, she wanted more than anything to talk. But Ore hadn't forgotten about Agatha's strange meddling with Daniel, she knew now that there was always some other agenda at play.

Agatha crossed her arms, threatening silence. Finally though, she cracked. 'Fine, well I'm just going to say that Chuck has a very good friend called Henry, who is also a journalist, I believe, an editor in fact . . .' Agatha trailed off, waiting for Ore's reaction.

Ore took a moment to catch up. 'Wait, you mean like Henry from the *New York Herald*, Henry Black . . . I'm confused, if they know each other then why did Henry commission me to . . .'

Agatha was exasperated. 'Henry is in Chuck's pocket, Ore; he does whatever Chuck wants. Did you know that he's funding the fellowship that will pay your wage at the *Herald*? This is what I'm trying to tell you . . . He is pulling all the strings. You've just been hired to write a puff piece. It's a publicity campaign.' Agatha's voice was getting louder. 'He decided he wanted you on board and I sent the email inviting you.'

'But why me?'

Agatha's eyes glinted with something like pity. 'Because he thinks you're inexperienced, that you're desperate for a job, that you'd do whatever you were told, but he underestimated you . . .'

Suddenly, Agatha took a step towards Ore, boiling with a quiet, white-hot rage, and then stilled, seeming to calm herself. Ore could feel the intensity dissipating as Agatha regained herself. And there was something else too, a familiar smell . . . jasmine.

Ore's eyes widened with sudden comprehension. 'It was you, who left me those documents,' Ore said softly.

Agatha looked stunned for a second and then nodded, almost imperceptibly.

'You have great taste in perfume. I must get some myself,' Agatha said coyly before looking over her shoulder and dropping her voice, leaning in. 'I don't want to be named.'

'Understood. I am not in the habit of outing my sources. The evidence stands alone . . . But if you would do an interview, even off the record . . .' Agatha held up her hand before Ore could finish.

'I've done as much as I can. Please don't ask me for anything else, but do it for all of us.' Agatha's eyes swelled with angry tears. 'And bring the bastard down.' She turned and left, the kitchen door swinging in her wake.

Ore wondered what else Chuck had done. And who was 'all of us?' Did Agatha realise that even if she wasn't named, Chuck would soon work out who had leaked those statements. Ore found herself hoping that Agatha would find the strength to leave and resolved to get in touch with her to help her put together an exit strategy, the moment she was off this boat.

The revelation about Henry left Ore shocked, but she found she wasn't surprised; at least it explained his strange behaviour on the phone. She was also glad that he had cut her off before she went into too much detail about what she'd found out. Although even what she had said could put her in danger. She just had to hope that Henry wouldn't relay it all back to Chuck before she was back on dry land and out of his clutches.

She was deep in thought when Carlos burst in. His eyes were red and swollen but he smiled broadly when he saw Ore.

'Oh hello, how are you, darling? I am so sorry about breakfast. I got caught up with . . .' He looked down at his feet solemnly but the smile was back in place by the time he looked up again.

'It's OK, Carlos, I was just seeing if there was anything I could scavenge,' Ore admitted.

'Did you find anything?' Carlos asked, busying himself with an apron.

'Lots more than I expected,' Ore said.

'Great, then you don't need me to cook you anything?'

'No, thanks though.' Ore made to leave and then had the urge to turn and say, 'Also thanks for your advice, about Daniel.' She smiled.

314

'I am glad that you and the captain have found each other; now you are out of your cages, you can fly freely, and side by side.'

As usual, Ore didn't entirely understand Carlos' metaphors but it sounded nice, getting out of the cage. Side by side though, that would be harder. She had no idea what would happen in five days' time, when they docked in Sydney . . . She shook the thought from her mind. She was planning on living in the moment until then.

Chapter 64

Daniel

Daniel spent the entire day counting down the minutes until he could see Ore again. Usually he relished his time alone in the wheelhouse, just him and the sea and the sky, but he was eager to recount his conversation with Carlos. In fact, he found that these days he wanted to get her perspective on everything.

Finally, Dudley knocked softly at the door. He looked tired. 'All right, Captain?' he mumbled as he took his seat.

'Yes thank you, Dudley, how are you?' It wasn't just pleasantries, to his surprise Daniel actually wanted to know.

Dudley seemed to sense the sincerity, because he turned and sighed and answered candidly. 'Honestly, not great – no reflection on you at all, but I miss Annie. Sorry I mean Captain Harleston.'

'It's OK, Dudley, you don't have to use her titles. We're just . . . chatting.' Daniel cringed at himself. He wasn't adept at this whole heart-to-heart thing. Dudley looked a little uncomfortable at the prospect as well, though he persevered.

'As I was saying, I miss Annie, and I keep trying to get in touch and waiting to hear back, but nothing.' Daniel worried he'd pushed the topic too far when he spotted the glisten of tears. Luckily for them both, Dudley held it together 'Maybe I misinterpreted things.'

He gave Daniel a wary look; staff fraternisation was generally frowned upon. Although it was endemic, most captains operated with a 'don't ask don't tell' policy – Daniel included.

But on this occasion he nodded encouragingly. 'You and Annie, were you an item?'

Dudley blushed. 'Yeah, I guess, whatever – we were together, or something, I don't know now. I haven't spoken to her since she left.'

Daniel felt a horrible sense of foreboding. This could be him soon enough. What if Ore left and he just never heard from her again? He forced the thought to the back of his mind, and willed himself back into the present. This was about Dudley, and what's more, Daniel knew why Annie hadn't been in touch. How had he ended up in this position? The gossip-averse, keep-the-crew-at-a-sensible-distance captain turned the holder of so many secrets.

He looked over his shoulder, an ingrained habit he seemed to now share with everyone on board. 'I'm going to tell you exactly why she hasn't been in touch, Dudley, but you cannot ask me how I know this information.'

Dudley's eyes grew wide with a mix of hope and dread. He nodded eagerly.

'Annie was forced to sign an NDA when she left the boat. I don't know what the terms were but I assume she cannot discuss any details of . . . what happened, which is probably a hard thing to do if she speaks to you.'

Dudley looked relieved, and then angry, and then desperately sad. When he eventually spoke, his voice was very quiet. 'Thanks for letting me know, Captain, much appreciated.' He turned back to the navigation screen and Daniel took it as his cue to leave.

Daniel made his way back to his cabin. The time was 8.30 p.m. Ore would be coming over soon. He was giddy as he took off his uniform, showered and then doused himself in aftershave.

Looking in the mirror he found himself admiring his own face. Vanity was not something that came naturally to him, but it was as though he was seeing himself through Ore's eyes. And he had to admit, it wasn't a bad sight.

Despite his anticipation, the knock on the door still made him jump. He tried to calm his breathing. He was reluctant to let her see this effect she had on him, the way she reduced him to an excitable schoolboy. He smoothed the fabric of his T-shirt and counted to five before opening the door.

She was dressed in a colour he wanted to call purple, but that wasn't quite right. It was the same colour as the crests of the clouds when they meet an orange sunset. It was the mist of dawn, the blue of sky mixed with the soft pink of nascent sunlight.

'You look beautiful,' he gushed, the words falling from his lips before his brain could catch up.

'Thanks, handsome.' She winked. 'Now let me in before anyone spots us. This place is full of spies . . . I have a lot to catch you up on.' She slipped under his outstretched arm and into the room. Before he could get his bearings she was off.

'I don't even know where to start. Like after you left all sorts of crazy stuff just started happening . . .' She told him about the perfume bottle, the envelope of damning documents, the call with Henry and the conversation with Agatha in the kitchen. He was having trouble keeping up, as she recounted it all breathlessly.

'Wait, so it was Agatha that left the documents?' He was sitting on the edge of the bed now, as Ore paced back and forth in front of him.

'Yes . . . which makes me think she'd not as soulless as I first suspected. Oh and I didn't even mention that her whole posh thing, it's totally an act. She grew up, in her words, "very poor".'

Daniel wasn't sure what the relevance of that really was, then he remembered how obsessed English people were with class.

'And she's like a class warrior now. I don't know but she seems to hate Chuck?' Ore was musing.

'Well yeah I mean he treats her pretty badly, like she's massively overworked and probably way too qualified to be his PA,' Daniel added. Ore gave him a quizzical look.

He felt a flush of embarrassment at the thought of how he'd come across those revelations. 'We were having a bit of a heart-to-heart, you know before she tried to . . . kiss me,'

'Urgh, don't remind me.' Ore rolled her eyes.

Daniel smiled. 'Are you jealous?' he teased. The thought that Ore might have to worry about his attraction to someone else seemed absurd to him, and a little flattering.

'No!' She swatted at his arm playfully, and he pulled her into him. They fell back on the bed, gazing at each other for a moment in mutual wonder. When their lips met, the rest of the room melted into static. Daniel couldn't fathom that anything other than Ore existed. One hand slipped into the curve of her back and the other cupped her cheek. She pulled away, giggling softly, and stood up again.

'Daniel, please, we have work to do. There'll be plenty of

time for all that once I get to the end of what Agatha said to me.' He must have looked disappointed because she came over to him, stood between his knees and took his face in her hands. 'You're my sounding board, and I couldn't make sense of any of this without you, so please, hear me out?'

He nodded. It made his chest ache with pride to know that she needed him.

'So where was I? Oh yes, so Agatha was going on about how Chuck controls everyone with his money and then she revealed that Chuck and Henry know each other, well that Henry is on Chuck's payroll somehow as well!'

'Henry, your editor?' Daniel swallowed down a creep of dread. He didn't like the idea of Chuck's influence over Ore extending further than this boat.

'The very one – something about my whole staff job contract being funded by Chuck, through this fellowship programme.' Daniel could tell that Ore was trying to put on a brave face. Her enthusiasm for 'getting to the truth' was waning in the face of this particular realisation.

'So, I guess I can stop worrying about pleasing Henry now. I'm obviously not taking that job.' The tone of defiance barely stretched to the end of the sentence.

Daniel pulled her back into his arms. 'You'll find another, better, job, I promise,' he whispered into her ear. He felt the heave of a sigh against him, and then she was restored, pushing back against his shoulder and standing again.

'Yes, well, that's a problem for future Ore, but for right now, do you have anything to report?'

'Well actually . . .' He paused, repositioning his hands behind him and leaning back, building the suspense. It had the desired effect. She giggled again, crossing her arms and arranging those luscious lips into a pronounced pout.

'Such a tease! Tell me!' she demanded.

'OK, fine, seeing as you asked so nicely . . .' Despite everything, he was enjoying himself. What they were discussing was serious, bordering on dark, but with Ore, in the cocoon of his cabin, he felt like they could take on the world, and laugh raucously while doing it.

'I came across Chuck telling off Carlos today,' Daniel started.

'Not Carlos! How could he!' Ore's outrage was touching. It mirrored his own at the time.

'I know, he's a lovely man, but Chuck was scolding him for taking food to Mel's room because apparently that was the reason she wasn't coming to sit at the table with Chuck and all his investors . . .'

'Yes, as though it's Carlos' fault that Chuck finds parenting so much less exciting than dodgy business deals,' Ore cut in again.

'Exactly, and anyway afterwards I went to check if Carlos was all right . . .'

'Was he?'

'Yes, he was.' Daniel wondered if he would ever get to the end of the story. 'And he was telling me a similar thing to what Agatha told you: that Chuck pays all his employees to spy on each other . . .' Daniel realised too late what he'd walked into.

'Did he . . . pay you?' Ore wouldn't look at him as she asked the question.

'No, although it's probably worse that I did it for free.' Daniel was ashamed of himself but he had to remember that he hadn't known Ore at all then, as crazy as it was that that was only

321

about a week ago. 'I do think that that is what that $75,000 cheque was for though.'

'Well I only got offered fifty, well 50,000 and a dollar to be precise, and I really wanted to take it . . . maybe you should have taken it, Daniel . . .'

He pulled her chin up so they were face to face. 'That money was my reward for betraying your trust, Ore. I could never have taken it.'

'That's very romantic, Daniel, but not very financially savvy.' She was teasing him now.

'Also, if *you* had taken it, you would have to sign a document to actually get the money . . . I'll give you one guess . . .'

'An NDA,' Ore said immediately. 'Well that would have been my piece dead in the water . . . .'. She paused, as though her brain was just catching up with what she'd just heard 'and of course, that's why no one will talk to me.' Ore had still been standing in front of him; now she went back to pacing. Daniel watched her intently.

'So does the fact that you *are* speaking to me mean you haven't signed anything?' Ore was once again not looking at him as she spoke, trying to sound nonchalant, and the dread returned. He knew what she was going to ask him next. 'Would you be a named source in my story?'

His stomach dropped. He would do anything for this amazing, beautiful, curious, fascinating, intelligent woman in front of him. Well, almost anything. Even if he'd somehow managed to get out of signing the NDA, would he have had the courage to publicly go up against Chuck? As it stood, if he agreed to be named, he would lose the only other thing he would do anything for – his job, and with it his whole life, his *plan*. Who was Daniel Wilsons without his captain's uniform? There was no doubt in his mind that Chuck would blacklist him. One call to the Hartfords with a bad reference and he was done. Not to mention the financial ruin that would come with being sued by America's second richest man.

Ore knew his answer before he finally voiced it.

'I can't, I had to sign the NDA to get onto the boat like the rest of the crew, although I did push back on some of the more severe clauses, that's why I can at least *talk* to you, unlike the others' he said plainly, after a beat he added, almost as an afterthought 'although Carlos doesn't seem to have read *his* very thoroughly.'

'I understand,' but she looked disappointed as she walked back over to him. 'I don't know how possible it'll be to get the story published with no names on the record, but maybe there's an editor out there willing to take that kind of risk.'

His heart ached to see her resigned to failure. Without thinking he whispered, 'Can I think about it?'

In an instant the hope returned to Ore's face. Daniel basked in the glow, pushing away for a moment the weight of pragmatism weighing down on him. He *would* think about it, but deep down he already knew that the conclusion would be the same: career suicide for a woman he'd known for eight days; even the delusional haze of Ore's presence couldn't obscure the madness of that.

'Can you let me know what you've decided on my last day? That way we can just enjoy the time we have left.' Ore leant in and kissed him. Another jolt from his aching heart, this time at the thought of what was to come after that time. Another thing to push to the back of his mind.

For now he gave into the oblivion of her, burrowing his face into her neck to hide from the future. She was his right now, and he'd never been more on board with 'living in the moment'.

On any other night he might have struggled to get to sleep, but after they had spent themselves, diving in and out of their own and then each other's pleasure, with the warmth of her breath dancing over his bare chest, he slipped into his dreams with ease.

Chapter 65

Ore

Day 9

She woke up to the soft sounds of Daniel getting dressed. The murmur of fabric pulled over skin, the pang of elastic settling around an ankle, the jangle of a fastened belt.

Even though her eyes were closed, she could place him in the room, as he went about his morning routine. She stirred and turned to see him pulling and tugging at the peaks of his hair in the mirror. There was something intoxicatingly intimate about observing him in his solitude. There was no self-consciousness in his movements.

He caught sight of her spying in the mirror, and, very uncharacteristically, poked out his tongue at her. She giggled. She wouldn't have believed that stern Captain Wilsons had any goofy tendencies at all, much less that she would find them so endearing. That was the sort of thing that should have given her the ick – it had taken far less in the past. With Daniel though, she was enthralled by his quirks, his 'flaws', his 'awkwardness', even his 'cringey' declarations made her feel giddy with curiosity. She wanted to see everything, know everything, understand everything about him. Not just pick at the scab, but examine it under a microscope.

'Morning,' she mouthed back into the mirror.

In response he turned and dove onto the bed. She yelped as he landed on top of her, smothering her with the covers. She really could not stop herself from the girlish giggles as he comically rummaged through the layers of fabric until he found her face. She quietened then, only the sound of their breathing audible.

I love you. The thought was sudden but not intrusive, like it had revealed itself rather than burst onto the scene. Ore had been in love before, but it had always felt like a bit of a contest. When she was a teenager, she had agonised about whether she was more in love with them than they were with her, and then at Columbia she'd had a short fling, just before the Kyle incident. Both had proved to her that the lover was usually the loser, better to take everything a little less seriously. She'd had a couple of confessions come her way since then – men she'd dated in New York, one even exclusively – and she'd revelled in the power of being loved a little more than loving. The way they looked at her adoringly, and she could look back with something closer to 'interest', the way she could enjoy the upper hand.

Now though, right here, *she* was the one gazing adoringly; she was the one doing the loving. It wasn't the first time she'd done those things, but it was the first time she'd done them fearlessly. She wasn't sure what it was about Daniel that made her feel so untouchable, but lying there in his arms, she found that it didn't matter to her if he loved her 'as much', or maybe even at all. It only mattered that he was there, with her.

When he dipped his head to meet her eager lips, she wished that she could stay in this moment forever. Blissful and weightless and loving.

'I better get to work,' Daniel murmured against her mouth. Instead of letting him go, she held on tighter, scattering more kisses all over his face. It was his turn to giggle. 'Ore, really, poor Dudley has been up all night . . .'

'OK fine,' Ore conceded eventually, releasing him from her embrace reluctantly.

'But I'll see you later? At your place?' he asked with faux nonchalance.

'Sure thing, swing by whenever you're done with work,' she replied gamely.

'I'll pick up some dinner on my way.' He pulled on his jacket and planted a peck on her forehead. Ore felt she might burst with joy, but as he gave her a small wave and shut the door gently behind him, a swirl of sadness laced through her contented mood. The domesticity of this scene, the plans after work, it was a fantasy, and worse than that, it was one that could never become real.

No, she was living in the moment; she had no doubt that leaving Daniel would be nothing short of heartbreaking so why pre-empt it now? Better to exercise a healthy dose of denial, at least for the next five days.

For the next three Ore and Daniel fell into an enchanting routine. Whilst Daniel manned the wheelhouse, Ore would enjoy a slow morning, go for a swim, maybe lounge in the sauna for a while, and then locate Carlos. He'd whip her up a simple lunch, which they'd taken to enjoying together, usually straight from the hob, forks in hand, leaning against the counter tops. She'd put in their dinner order, something she and Daniel had agreed upon the night before. The afternoon was for writing and avoiding Chuck and Claude like the plague.

As the piece came together, Ore became more and more convinced that she needed at least one named source to go on the record. Otherwise she was just opening herself up to an unwinnable libel case. Chuck's team of formidable lawyers was one thing, her having no actual proof of where all the accusations had come from – that was a fool's mission.

Apart from that one huge missing piece of the puzzle, the article was actually shaping up pretty nicely. There was no shortage of allegations, and the interviews she'd gotten with the crew and Mel painted a damning picture of a man drunk on delusions of his own power. Some moments she felt energised by the scope of the wrongdoing, and others she felt depressed by the prospect that he would most likely never be held accountable for them.

At around 6 p.m. she would close her laptop and go for her 'walk', which consisted of a few laps of the yacht. She was beginning to feel the effects of cabin fever. At night, she would dream about strangely mundane things, like driving down the highway, or running through Central Park.

On her 'rounds' she might come across another guest or a crew member. Now that she'd decided to stop 'reporting', she found that everyone was much more chatty. One particular run-in with Richard lasted almost an hour, and ended with an invite to have a 'private dinner' with him in his suite – she politely declined.

As 8 p.m. drew closer, she would feel the butterflies in her stomach stirring. She might have a shower or try to distract herself with some TV while she waited for the knock on the door. At the sight of his face, the butterflies would quell themselves, lazily basking in his sunny smile.

'Hello, beautiful.' Daniel would sweep her into his arms and give her a kiss that was somehow both an exciting promise and a steadying hand.

At some point food would arrive, but Vicky got into the habit of knocking once and leaving a tray outside. Often, neither Ore nor Daniel would hear; they were too far away, dancing naked on the surface of that very hospitable planet where only they existed. Sometimes the food was cold when they checked but by the time they checked on it, but they didn't care.

They ate in bed, feeding each other even the most impractical of meals, daring mouthfuls amidst the white sheets. After they had replenished their energy, they would feed the other hunger again, and then maybe one more time for luck after that.

As they dozed to sleep, Daniel might tell Ore about a rare bird he saw that day, and she might recount her conversation with Carlos in the kitchen. One of them usually fell asleep first, in the lull of the other's voice, but soon enough a light snoring was coming from both bodies.

Chapter 66

Ore

Day 13

Ore had one more night on board *Thalassa*, before they docked in Sydney. It was the first time she'd woken up before Daniel. He was definitely an early bird. The light was grey and mauve, glowing through the thin gauze of the curtains. Ore had not only come to tolerate the endless swaying of the waves below, but to enjoy them. How would she sleep with the sound of sirens, and the vibrations of the subways under foot back in New York?

She hadn't felt this well rested in years. It struck her that she hadn't touched or thought about alcohol since they'd been on the island. She guessed that sleeping with a captain on duty was probably a good influence on her metropolitan drinking habit. She'd also been eating well, thanks to Carlos, and definitely getting her fair share of aerobic exercise: swimming, walking and . . . all the other stuff too. She smiled to herself, pleasantly surprised by her ability to take satisfaction from something other than *achieving*.

Her professional life was in tatters; she'd been ignoring all of Henry's increasingly urgent emails and messages about the profile, and she wasn't interested in that sham job offer. She'd spent the past two weeks chasing a story that was probably unpublishable, and she had no other prospects, having let her other regular freelance writing slip by the wayside.

And yet, here she was grinning, content, happy. Maybe Carlos had a point with all this 'living in the moment' stuff. And she didn't have much moment left. She nestled her face into Daniel's back and he shifted awake.

'Morning, beautiful.' He smiled dopily, and she planted a kiss on each of his drooping eyelids.

'I wish I could wake up to this every morning.' The words were out of her mouth before she could stop them, piercing through their embryonic cocoon of denial. She felt the tension seize his body almost immediately, and her own stiffened in response.

She'd have done anything for one more minute in the 'before' but it was too late now. The bubble was burst, and the world outside it needed to be faced.

They were both quiet for a time, bodies pressed against each other in the dawn light.

'I'm going to miss you.' Daniel's tone was disarmingly matter-of-fact.

Ore pulled his face to hers, and when she spoke, her lips almost brushed his. 'Me too, Daniel, but I'm sure we'll see each other again . . .' She hoped with her whole heart that that was true.

'I don't think you can ever know how profoundly you've changed me, Ore.' His eyes blazed. 'Before I met you, I was on a treadmill, sometimes walking, sometimes running, consistently into my future. But with you I learnt how to fly. And hopefully . . .' he betrayed himself, the composure cracking with a break in his voice '. . . after you, I can keep doing that, high enough so that I can see how beautiful everything is.' She stroked the tear away from his cheek.

'Honestly,' she said, her voice low, 'it sounds like that's more Carlos' influence than mine.' His tears were swallowed into a chuckle then. Ore tried to capture the moment in her mind's eye. The dark, hot form of him against the cool light. The tiny gap between his two front teeth, the particular shade of pink of his inner bottom lip, the rays of his laughter lines fanning out from those dark, molten jewels.

'We still have an hour,' she whispered, sinking her fingers into his hair.

'It won't be enough, but I'll take it,' he murmured, closing his eyes again and resting his forehead against hers tenderly. And that's how they lay, for the next fifty-nine minutes, the seconds ticking away unceremoniously until Daniel pulled himself away and quietly got dressed. Ore stayed as she was, eyes closed, and pictured him moving around. If her imagination was going to be her only access to Daniel soon, she'd better start practising.

The door shut softly behind him as a silent hot tear rolled down her cheek. After an unknown while she got herself up, and slowly moved around her cabin, gathering her things, folding some, scrunching others, and then piling them into her suitcase.

They would dock in Sydney in the early hours and she would be far too groggy and grumpy to pack then. When all traces of her, apart from her toothbrush, were cleared from the room, she sat on the unmade bed and stared at her reflection in the mirror opposite. She was nervous about going back to her old life, where, ironically, she had felt so unmoored. By some strange logic her time on *Thalassa* had been intense, but also grounding. She was a more certain person than she had been two weeks ago. No job waiting perhaps, but a stronger sense of what she wanted, what she believed, her skills as a journalist and her ability to rise to the occasion.

Her phone buzzed her out of her introspection. It was an email from Henry.

> On second thoughts, we've decided that the first draft you sent last week was actually some great copy. So let's run with that. The rest of the team and I are really looking forward to working with you on a permanent business. Congrats!
> All my best,
> H
> P.S. see attached ;)

Ore was unnerved by the tone it was so jovial, as though their last conversation had never happened. And that winky face . . . She also found herself rereading the first few words over and over again: 'our end', an image of Chuck reading the article a few floors above where she was sitting, and nodding along approvingly made her feel nauseous again, for the first time in days.

She clicked on the attachment. EMPLOYMENT CONTRACT FOR MISS ORE BALLOU-ADU. She skimmed over it. It was an outrageous deal. Thirty-five hours with enforced overtime pay, twenty days' leave, unheard of in New York, and a signing bonus of . . . $50,001. She closed the document and threw her phone across the bed, a shiver running down her spine. Chuck *wanted* her to know that he was behind this. Was the cheque in the envelope all part of his plan? To make her understand just how deeply his claws were dug into her life? If she hadn't been so disturbed she might have been impressed by the foresight of it all. It was really giving 'evil genius'.

She would have to reply to Henry soon if she wanted to block publication, but she had at least until the end of the day, and for now she wanted to get as far away from her phone as possible.

She made her way up to the pool. Maybe a swim would help clear her head. She rummaged for her swimsuit and grabbed a towel.

She had grown accustomed to having the pool to herself but this morning another black-bikini-clad swimmer was doing lengths of front crawl. They were fast as well. It was hard to tell who it was until the goggled face emerged and removed its cap. Elbows splayed on the pool's edge, Mel gave Ore a surprisingly broad smile.

'Hey,' she said as Ore approached. 'I was hoping I might see you before we all get off this floating prison . . .'

Ore chuckled. 'So you're getting off at Sydney as well?'

Mel clambered out of the pool as Ore settled on the edge of a lounger. 'Well we all are, the guests I mean. I think that the crew stay on for a few more days and then have to go moor it up the coast somewhere.'

Ore realised that she'd sort of imagined she might be safe

334

from Chuck if he was endlessly floating around the ocean. Silly really – you were never safe from a man like Chuck. Mel must have misread the expression on her face, but her conclusion was still accurate.

'You're going to miss the captain, aren't you?' Mel wrapped herself in a beach towel and sat down next to Ore.

'I am,' she admitted. 'Very much.'

'Well I'm sure you can still, like, see each other, like he can fly to New York and you can visit him when he's got time off from work?' The hope in Mel's face was touching. Ore recognised herself, in her more naive moments.

'Maybe,' Ore said with a sad smile, 'but that kind of travelling is pretty expensive.'

Mel hung her head. 'Damn, yeah, sorry, that was like, super privileged of me to say.'

'Nah don't worry about it, you were only trying to help.' Ore had grown to like Mel.

'Like I did when I showed your article to dad, and told him what a great journalist you were, and then he basically invited you to be a glorified babysitter. Sorry about that . . .' Mel looked genuinely contrite, but Ore was only just catching up with the first part of the confession.

'Sorry, what article did you show him?'

'The one you wrote in i-POP magazine about sustainable practices in the Casper Donran factories.' Mel had begun wringing water from her hair.

Ore had written that piece whilst she was still at Columbia. It had earned a much-coveted 'excellent work' from Gail Fairweather, exposing the toxic dyes used in the factories that made CasperD clothing. The real sting had been that it was

335

mainly manufacturing their 'environmentally conscious' range. The hypocrisy.

'I totally stopped buying anything from CasperD after that,' Mel continued proudly. 'I think Dad thought I'd be super thrilled that he invited you on board, but like, I was into that article like two years ago, no offence.' Mel shrugged, rolling her eyes as if to say: *you know useless dads*.

'None taken,' Ore replied, on autopilot through their familiar exchange as what she had heard sank in.

Not only had her job offer been a set-up incentive for her to write the piece he wanted, but Chuck Regas had even hand-selected her. Ore guessed he hadn't even bothered to read the article, just assumed that anything his teenage daughter read in a magazine was probably written by some second-rate, PR puff-piece kind of journalist who would write down anything she was told to. He had underestimated them both. She was sure that someone had also pointed out that it might be good optics to give an exclusive interview to a young black woman. How liberal and magnanimous he would seem. The boil of anger quickly solidified into something else: renewed determination. She would find a way to expose him for the hypocritical, narcissistic manipulator that he was. Somehow she would find a way.

'Mel, if I trust you with a little secret, would you promise not to tell your dad, at least not for a few weeks . . .' Ore was hatching a plan.

'Sure.' Mel's eyes glinted with the excitement of conspiracy.

'If I give you my number, would you give it to your mum and ask her to call me? I'd love to use you in an article I'm writing, but I need a parent's permission and well . . .'

'You can't ask my dad, because it's about him,' Mel concluded. *She's a bright one*. 'Exactly.'

'Just promise me one thing in return?' Mel put out her hand.

Ore was wary but agreed.

'That you won't let him get away with his lies, because he will totally deny everything, so you have to like stand up for the truth and not let him bully you into backing down,'

Ore shook Mel's hand firmly. 'I will try my best.'

'That's not quite a promise, but I'll take it. Also Mom will definitely call you; she's always going about how much he lies, but she's not allowed to say anything, apparently.'

Patricia Regas, now that would be a get, although it sounded like she'd also signed a damn NDA.

'Thanks so much Mel.' Ore stood up, and to her surprise Mel did too, pulling her into a soggy hug. Ore's hands swung awkwardly at her sides. Mel was a little taller than her and it felt perverse to encircle her bare waist.

'You know I think I wanna be just like you when I'm older,' Mel gushed into Ore's shoulder. Ore was taken aback by the sincerity. 'Like maybe a journalist, but like super nice and also hot.'

Ore couldn't help but giggle. She was flattered. She pulled herself away. 'Well if you ever need any advice . . .' Ore wondered what on earth might make her qualified as an emotionally turbulent, unemployed twenty-five-year-old to give any advice to anybody, but Mel nodded enthusiastically and retrieved her phone from her bag and handed it to Ore to put her number in it. 'I'll totally hit you up,' she chirped before picking up her towel and plodding back inside.

In the silent churn of her lengths Ore thought about the implications of using the sixteen-year-old daughter of the subject of an exposé as a named source. It wasn't a good look, but she was probably the only person in Chuck's life who wasn't gagged by a pesky legal document. Without Mel, there would be no piece at all. She'd speak to Patricia. Ultimately it would be her decision, and she could only hope that Mel's mother held her daughter's best interests more firmly in her mind than Chuck.

After her swim Ore headed to the kitchen. Carlos was already crying by the time she swung through.

'Oh my darling, how I'll miss you.' He wrapped his arms around her and pulled her close, sniffing into her ear.

'I'll miss you too, and your food!'

He gave her a playful slap on the arm. 'That's all I am to you, a cook!'

'A chef!' Ore corrected and then at his not quite faux wounded expression she added, 'And a friend.'

Another hug and this time Ore wasn't sure she was going to keep it together. They had their lunch, as usual, bent over the hob.

'So how is the story coming along?' Ore had noticed that Carlos was the only person who didn't lower his voice when he asked questions like that.

'It's fine. It's sort of done . . . well my editor seems to think so anyway,' Ore said evenly.

'Sort of done?' It seemed that nothing could escape Carlos' intuition.

'I'm not sure I want to publish it. And well, there is another story, a better one, but I don't think I have enough to prove anything.'

'Hmm.' Carlos furrowed his brow in concentration. 'What do you need to prove these things?'

'I need people to go on the record,' Ore said plainly.

Carlos nodded gravely. 'And no one can because of Mr Regas' secret contracts.'

'Bingo.' Carlos looked confused, and Ore corrected herself with a: 'Yes that's right.'

'You've spent too long in America, Ore.' Carlos shook his head theatrically and Ore laughed. She really was going to miss him, but she couldn't resist one last push.

'Would you mind taking this?' She dug into her pocket and handed him her card. 'In case you change your mind?'

Carlos looked at her apologetically. 'I really can't afford to lose my work Ore.'

'I know, I'm not . . .' Ore sighed, and made to put the card back, but Carlos picked it from between her fingers before she did. She looked up at him hopefully.

'Don't get ahead of yourself – it is only to send you some recipes, so you do not have to live off takeout when you return to New York.' He winked, tucking it into his apron. Ore smiled. It had been worth a try.

The rest of the day dragged on. Ore didn't have anything else to write, so she wandered around the boat aimlessly, counting down the minutes until Daniel clocked off. At eight she let herself into his cabin with the spare key card he had made for her.

She settled into his bed, first resisting and then succumbing to the urge to bury her face in the pillow that smelled of him. She scrambled to stand as she heard footsteps approaching.

Chapter 67

Daniel

Daniel hadn't quite realised how encompassing his state of denial had been. That trick his mind was so good at, compartmentalising, had buried the fact of Ore's departure so successfully that it hadn't been until that morning that he'd actually come to believe it would happen.

How was he supposed to be with her for another night, now that the ache of loss had already started darkening his heart?

In the wheelhouse, he managed to distract himself for most of the day, plotting their way into the harbour, calling all the relevant officials to double and triple-check that their docking spot was reserved and ready. In the midst of his work, he revelled in the sense of order, the predictability of it all. He was in control, for what felt like the first time in days. When he was with Ore, sometimes the feelings were overwhelming, like he had lost mastery over his own mind.

He was deep in concentration when the radio cracked to life. 'Captain Wilsons, do you copy?' It was Vicky.

'Hello, Vicky, yes, in the wheelhouse, copy.'

'Roger that, on my way.'

It wasn't a promising sign. Daniel wondered what crisis he might have to avert, what last-minute outlandish request

Chuck had made now. They were so close to the end of the trip, Daniel found himself preparing his repudiations before Vicky had even walked through the door.

'We're on course, and I'm afraid there's absolutely no changing it now,' he said when she entered the room, not bothering to turn around.

'What are you . . . ?' But she was only confused for a second. 'I'm not here to relay some absurd message from Chuck. Don't worry, Daniel.' The tone of Vicky's voice made Daniel turn around. It was strangely warm. That and the use of his first name made him sure this was not about to be the conversation he'd imagined.

'Can I sit?' Vicky gestured towards Dudley's empty chair next to him.

'Sure.' Daniel turned so they were facing each other. He couldn't help but feel like they were slightly too close to each other. 'What did you want to discuss?'

Vicky took a deep breath. 'I know that you and Ore are . . . seeing each other.'

Daniel felt his cheeks flush hot, but was grateful for Vicky's wording at least. 'Well . . . umm . . .'

'There's no point denying it, Daniel. Who do you think is dropping off the food every evening? And let me tell you that the walls are not as soundproof as you assume they are.' Daniel's embarrassment grew blistering. Vicky seemed to enjoy that, and she smirked before continuing.

'And I also know that you and Carlos have been gossiping about the various . . . arrangements on board.'

Daniel had learnt enough from Ore to remember that he should fake cluelessness. 'Arrangements?'

Vicky shifted in her seat. 'I had Dudley come to me last night, in hysterics, asking if I knew about Annie signing an NDA. Information he sourced from *you*, Captain. I told him that I did, and that I encouraged her too and now he won't speak to me. Apparently it's all *my* fault that Annie got banished from this boat. Honestly, Captain, I preferred it when you knew to stay out of this sort of thing,' she said evenly.

'And it *wasn't* your fault?' It came out more accusatory than Daniel had intended.

Vicky scoffed. 'You think that I did a bad thing to get Annie off this boat, away from a sexual predator with a huge payout?' She shook her head. 'Men never get it.'

'And you also got a payout from Chuck though right? For the information you passed on?' Daniel probed.

'So what if I do? With men like Chuck, it pays to be on their good side, and it hurts, like really hurts not to be. Do you know what happened to the last girl Claude touched up? Chuck threatened to fire her, with immediate effect, and blackball her in the industry for making up lies about his "esteemed friend". She had to beg and plead for her job, even after almost ten years of service and then she had to promise to be his eyes and ears, to get close to her staff and then betray them over and over again . . .' Vicky's voice cracked and she stopped abruptly.

Daniel knew the answer to the question he was about to ask, but he needed to be sure. 'Who was that girl, Vicky?'

Vicky gave him a look, pleading with him not to make her say it out loud. Then she relented, slumped down in her chair as though the force of the confession had winded her. 'It was me, Daniel, but I didn't come here to tell you any of this, well

I didn't think I had; I came to say be careful. I don't know for sure that you're doing all this digging around for Ore, but if you are, stop, for your sake and hers.'

She leant forward now, urgently. 'Chuck is a cruel, dangerous and powerful man, and if you cross him, if she writes something he doesn't like, she's finished. He knows everyone, every other powerful man in New York for a start, and if Ore doesn't want whatever story she's writing to be the last thing she ever publishes, she needs to stop, leave this boat, forget everything she's heard and write the puff piece he wants.' She paused for a moment. 'And as for you, I'll just say that Elizabeth Hartford is a close family friend. She and her husband take Chuck's . . . character references very seriously.'

'Is this threat coming from you, Vicky . . . or Chuck?'

'Does it matter?' she said, suddenly sounding exhausted. 'It's real. That's all you need to know. Take it from someone who knows – he has no qualms about ruining people's lives.'

Message delivered, Vicky stood up and headed for the door. Daniel grabbed her hand as she walked past. 'I'm sorry, Vicky, you should never have been treated like that.'

Vicky snatched her hand back. 'Just get Ore to drop it,' she said without turning back.

Vicky's words swam around Daniel's head for the rest of the day, whilst he went through the motions of manning the boat. Dudley's arrival surprised him. He was losing track of time again.

'OK, Captain?' Dudley said as he took his seat. 'You look a little out of it.'

'I'm fine, thanks, Dudley,' Daniel replied, though he avoided looking at Dudley in the eye as he walked out. He didn't have the stomach for another heart-to-heart. That now familiar dread had resurfaced with a vengeance. He needed to see Ore, but he also didn't want to lose his head again. He knew the conversation he needed to have wasn't going to go down well. As he opened the door to his room, he half hoped she wasn't on the inside.

Still, the sight of her was a balm – at least for a moment.

'Hello, beautiful.' It was strange how something could become a habit so quickly.

She smiled at him and then kissed him forcefully, but it only made him sadder. Something icy in his veins reached his heart and encased it. *Self-preservation*, he thought. As if sensing his resistance she took a step back from him, wrapping her arms around herself protectively. He wanted to go to her, unfurl her and kiss away the bewilderment in her eyes.

'I'm sorry,' she said. He wasn't sure what she was apologising for. He suspected she wasn't either.

'It's OK.' He could hear how cold he sounded, how detached. He could see the twinge of hurt in her eyes before she looked down at her feet. If this was how it was going to go, he thought, he might as well get the whole job done. 'I've been thinking about your article, and your request.' His tone was brusque, businesslike. 'I've given it some serious consideration and . . .'

She looked up at him then, the liquid of her brown eyes pooling, but her expression defiant. She uncrossed her arms and stood a little straighter. 'You don't want to be named. I get it,' she said coolly, her voice unwavering but he could sense how hard she was trying not to cry.

'I appreciate that.' They were standing at an awkward

distance. Daniel remembered he was still wearing his captain's hat. He removed it.

'I also wanted to say something else.' He braced himself for impact; she didn't react. He continued, 'I don't think you should try and publish it at all. I think you should take the job, file the original piece and just try and forget about everything else.' Vicky probably knew Chuck as well as anyone ever could, and he couldn't bear the idea of Ore putting herself in danger or harpooning her entire career before it had even begun.

Ore's expression turned from disbelief, to bemusement and finally to rage. As it settled, it lost its heat and morphed instead into something frozen, impenetrable.

Ore brought her arms back across her chest, and shifted her gaze downwards. 'Well thanks for the advice, Daniel. I really *appreciate* you taking the time to tell me how to do my job. It's pretty clear to me now where your loyalties lie, and maybe I was just the stupid, naive, inexperienced hack you and Chuck seem to think I am, for falling for all this . . .' She gestured at the space between them.

The lump of ice wedged inside Daniel's chest hardened. She thought he was a spy, a double-crosser, a liar. But he was worse than that; he was a coward. He was scared of Chuck, for himself, but more than that, for her. More than he wanted her to like him, to *love* him, he wanted her to be safe. He wasn't as brave as her; he also wasn't as foolish.

'Ore, it's for your own good . . .' he started, but she cut him off.

'You sound like Henry.' And then with a sneer, she asked, 'How much did he give you? More than the original $75k? I'd love to know how much your silence is worth.'

Maybe if she thought he was on the payroll, she would start to understand how far-reaching Chuck's power really was. She'd realise it was a futile battle. So he said nothing, let her believe what she already seemed to believe.

'Right, well, there's quite literally nothing else to say, is there, Captain?' Her raised eyebrow conveyed devastating disdain. He moved to the side to let her pass, and she slammed the door behind her.

Chapter 68

Ore

Day 14
Sydney Harbour

After the fight with Daniel, Ore was in a daze. He had played her, wheedled his way into her heart, gotten her excited about her journalism again, for just long enough that he could sleep with her. And then once that was not an option anymore, all of a sudden his true colours revealed themselves, or maybe re-revealed themselves. She felt a fool for trusting not once, but twice. Who knew how much he'd told Chuck. She was in a fight against the clock to get this story finished and published before it got smothered by gag orders.

That last night, she'd cried herself into a dreamless sleep. At dawn she'd gathered her things and waited in the main salon right next to where the gangway would emerge. She wanted to get off as soon as humanly possible. She wondered if it was Daniel guiding the ship into the harbour from above, and she seethed at the idea of him sitting there, calmly getting on with his job as though he hadn't broken her heart.

It was Oscar who popped up to heave the large red lever

into place and open up the side of the boat. 'Eager to get off, are we?' he quipped between huffs of effort.

'Yes I am actually, being on this boat is making me sick to my stomach,' Ore replied dryly.

'Never did find your sea legs then, miss?' Oscar pulled on the large metal door and Ore felt a relief wash over her with the morning breeze.

'It appears not. I thought that maybe I had settled into ocean-faring life for a minute there, but I was wrong,'

'Right you are, miss . . .' Oscar pressed a button and they both watched as the gangway unfurled itself shakily. Oscar blithely hopped onto the swaying mesh walkway and tied its wavering end to a metal bollard on the dock.

'Whenever you're ready, miss, dry land awaits,' he called.

Don't look down, Ore told herself as she stepped out. Arriving on the chopper had been terrifying in its own way, but on balance this was worse. Somehow she made it to the marina. She waited impatiently for Oscar to collect her bags and then made a hasty exit. As the rumble of her wheels thundered across the wooden planks underfoot, she shot nervous glances over her shoulder, paranoid that someone was following her. She wouldn't be able to shake that feeling for days.

When she arrived at the airport, the check-in desk informed her that she had been upgraded to business class 'courtesy of the *New York Herald*'. Her late-night, hastily compiled email turning down the job and withdrawing her consent for the profile piece to be published obviously had not yet reached the New York office – the wonders of time zones. She was grateful for this one last perk of the job she'd never have.

She landed in JFK groggy and sleep-deprived, and almost

burst into tears to see her Auntie Laurie waiting in arrivals. She folded herself into the familiar warmth of her arms.

'Let's get you home,' Laurie said, stroking her head softly. 'You must be exhausted.' They barely spoke on the drive back to Queens, and Ore was thankful for it as she dozed in and out of sleep to the Nineties hits of WBLS.

The next day Ore woke up to a response from Henry, and five missed calls. The email read:

> Hi Ore, I'm not sure what prompted this change of heart, but I would urge you to reconsider, give me a call and we can discuss everything.
> All my best,
> Henry

Ore was even more unsettled by the pleading Henry than she had been with chirpy Henry. She didn't reply and blocked his number. After some digging around she found the tip line for the *New York Tribune*. In her pitch she made it sound like she had already secured Mel as a named source. For the next few days she checked her missed calls and inbox incessantly.

Chapter 69

Daniel

Daniel had watched Ore pull her case along the marina from the wheelhouse and he'd felt numb.

He hadn't been able to sleep after Ore had left his room the night before. For the first few hours he had gone back and forth, wondering if he should run after her, explain everything. But what would have been the use? She wouldn't have cowed at Chuck's threat, and besides, whether she left the boat believing him to be 'the bad guy' or not, she would still be leaving. And it was sort of easier in a way, knowing that she hated him. That was something he could bury and add to his list of reasons why he should have 'stuck to the plan' and 'not gotten involved in the drama'.

And so instead of going after her he headed upstairs, to take up his post and remind himself that before everything else, he was a captain.

He stayed holed away in his sanctuary of the wheelhouse all day, watching as each guest filed off the *Thalassa* over the course of the day. Mel was the next to leave after Ore, with Oscar in tow to help with her caravan of monogrammed luggage. She was wearing sunglasses and large headphones under her hoodie, and almost leapt into the waiting taxi, so eager, it seemed, was she to get back to her 'normal life'.

The trail of investors disembarked in pairs, fully kitted out in their loafers, chinos, quarter zips, mobile phones pinned to their ears. Finally Daniel watched as Claude and Chuck, followed a few steps behind by Agatha, stepped off the gangway and back into the world. They were deep in conversation as they marched across the dock. Daniel dreaded to think what destructive plot they were engineering next.

Down below him, he knew the rest of the crew were hard at work, stripping beds, scrubbing floors, cleaning windows. They would remain on board for the rest of the day and then head down the coast to Wollongong to anchor the *Lady Thalassa* in the morning. As rich as Chuck was he was still too tight to pay Sydney's docking fees.

As the sun went down, Daniel wondered if there was a way he could avoid the 'party'. It was tradition, and one that he usually tried to get out of. He'd never understood why, after cleaning the boat all day, anyone would want to mess it up again and then repeat the process the following day on a hangover.

He did need to eat though, so reluctantly he headed down to the mess once all the paperwork was done. He would just grab a few bites and then make his excuses and head to bed. Inside, Carlos was laying down dishes piled high with Lebanese delights: baba ghanouj, tabbouleh, sfeeha, falafel and shawarma. There were colourful salads littered with pomegranate jewels and topped with glistening pickles. But despite the feast, the general mood was glum, nothing like the carnival like atmosphere he had experienced on other charters on the last night. Vicky, Nicole and Amanda were all slouched over their phones; Oscar was picking at his cuticles.

'Ahhh, Daniel, come come, I have made enough for a small army.' Carlos smiled warmly and pulled out a chair for Daniel.

'This looks amazing, Carlos, and so different from what you usually make,' Daniel noted.

'Well Mr Chuck likes to remind me that he hired a French chef . . . not a Lebanese one, but I am a multitude, as they say.' Carlos chuckled and his joviality seemed to lull everyone else round the table out of their low spirits.

'Thank you, Carlos,' they chimed one by one as they helped themselves.

'How was everyone's day?' Daniel heard himself say. He felt somewhat responsible for the low morale, it was customary for the captain to call his staff in for a congratulatory speech after the guests had disembarked. Daniel just hadn't been able to work up the enthusiasm for it.

'Busy,' Vicky said bluntly, before spooning some couscous into her mouth.

'Mr Regas' guests were up very late last night, so we're all a bit tired,' Nicole explained.

'Well I appreciate all your hard work. You've been an excellent team; it's been my pleasure to work with you all,' Daniel said stiffly. The reaction was muted, and he couldn't blame them – he hardly believed himself.

Vicky gave him a withering look. 'Well from what we've seen of you, Captain, it's been an absolute blast.' Amanda stifled a giggle and then a brittle silence descended over the table.

As usual it was Carlos who dared to break it. 'So how was your goodbye with Miss Ore?' he asked, turning to Daniel casually as though asking about the weather. Daniel spluttered in surprise. The others also looked up at Carlos, with a mix of intrigue and bemusement.

'Um . . .' Daniel's immediate impulse was to reprimand Carlos, but he didn't have the energy or the support of the crowd. 'It was . . . we actually didn't leave it on good terms to be honest, Carlos.'

Carlos' face fell. 'Oh no! What happened to my beautiful lovebirds?' he said in dismay. Daniel wasn't sure he could feel any more mortified, but after tomorrow he would most probably not see any of these people again, so he decided to be honest.

'We had a disagreement. Ore has very strong . . . ideals, about what the right thing to do is, and I suggested that she might try and be more . . . practical in her choices.' Daniel shrugged, avoiding eye contact with Vicky, whose gaze he could feel on the side of his face.

Carlos was shaking his head. 'Is this about her journalism story? Because no one would talk to her on the record?'

Daniel was taken aback by Carlos' utter lack of discretion. Vicky too seemed shocked.

'What story is this?' Amanda asked quietly. Daniel wasn't sure he'd ever heard her speak before.

'About Chuck and his bad ways,' Carlos said matter-of-factly.

'Carlos!' Vicky reprimanded him.

'Oh, Vicky, why do you keep defending this man? He is bad, and we all know it – you most of all!' Vicky blushed, or fumed, it was hard to tell, but she fell silent.

'So why would you not go on the record, Captain? I know our reasons – we all work for the man – but why not help Ore yourself?' Carlos asked sincerely.

At that moment, Daniel found it hard to articulate an answer. He took a moment to think and then he replied: 'Because Chuck is a powerful man and it would be dangerous for both of us to be on the wrong side of him.'

Out of the corner of his eye Daniel saw Vicky nodding along, as though he was reciting her pre-prepared script.

Carlos sighed. 'Ever the follower of your head, Captain Wilsons. Not even Miss Ore could convince you to follow your heart, I suppose.'

The mood was once again tense. Daniel looked around the table. It really was a miserable scene; he had never seen a crew so dejected. The spectre of Chuck loomed large, even though he was likely halfway to San Francisco by now. And then it struck him; Chuck didn't need to be on the boat because he had planted agents everywhere. All of them were keeping each other in line, despite what they might want, or actually believe; everyone had convinced themselves that what was in their best interests, was what was in Chuck's best interests.

This was how he got away with everything: *silence*, reinforced not just directly, but indirectly. With a combination of bribes and threats he could convince anyone that it was the 'practical' thing to do as he said. And how could you overcome that? It would take someone with unshakable principles, and a heart stronger than reason. It would take someone like Ore.

The clatter of Daniel's cutlery on the plate got everyone's attention.

'You're right, Carlos, I need to follow my heart.' It was a cringey thing to say out loud, but Daniel needed to build up the courage to say what he was going to next.

'And I will be putting my name to the story.' He ignored the flash of panic on Vicky's face. 'And what's more, I think you all should too.

'Chuck rules this boat with an iron fist, and the worst thing is he is rarely even pulling any punches. We're all just so scared that he will, or that he'll close up his wallet, that we do what he says, or what we think he *might* say. I've only been working for him for two weeks and I've already been brainwashed into believing he is invincible.' Daniel shook his head, as the realisation sunk in. 'Chuck has convinced everyone that he is some sort of god, because on this boat, he sort of is . . . but there's a big old world out there, where people even as powerful as Chuck can, and should be held to account.

'I realise now that that was what Ore could see that we . . . I couldn't because we're so used to this life at sea, where it's guys like Chuck, the owners, the billionaires, who call the shots, and all we're allowed to respond is "yes, sir". We think that's the only way it can be. But maybe if we all stand together, if we all speak out, we can change things, for ourselves and for each other.'

Daniel wasn't sure where all of that had come from. He was panting with the effort of scouring it from the unknown depths of himself. The table was stunned.

Carlos sniffed, wiping a tear from his cheek dramatically. '*Vive la revolution*,' he muttered, as though to himself, and then: 'Count me in, Capitaine, I too will put my name on the record.' Daniel smiled, overcome with sheer relief.

'I will too,' Nicole added.

'And me.' Oscar stood up in excitement and then lowered himself back into his seat gingerly.

'I have some stuff to say—' it was Amanda '—and I know Dudley will want to speak out as well,' she said shyly.

They all turned to Vicky, who was leant back in her chair, an expression of incredulity on her face.

'No way,' was all she said before standing up abruptly and leaving the room.

Daniel's heart was beating hard, adrenalised by the camaraderie, and now that Vicky had left the room, he finally dared to explain what he and Ore had discovered. The mining operation, the shell company, the corruption. All of it.

As he spoke, the anger in the room grew and then settled into indignation.

'So how can we get in contact with Ore?' It was Nicole asking and the realisation that he didn't know the answer winded Daniel, his excitement suddenly collapsing in on itself.

'I . . .' Daniel began and then hung his head, defeated.

Carlos reached into the pocket of his apron, a smile spreading slowly across his face. 'I had a feeling that my lovebirds might need a little help to be reunited . . .'

Chapter 70

Ore

Queens, New York

The first call came from Carlos and he got straight to the point. 'I want to go on the record, Ore. I have given it some thought and I have decided that Chuck needs to be brought down.' He never explained what had made him change his mind, but after the calls from Dudley, Nicole and even Amanda, who Ore couldn't remember ever having even spoken to, she assumed that Carlos had campaigned on her behalf. When the promised call from Mel's mother came through, Ore was happy to explain that she wouldn't need Mel's testimony anymore.

'Mel will be very disappointed I know, but I for one have to say I'm a bit relieved. I hope you know what you're going up against with Chuck . . . Take it from me, he's ruthless in court,' Patricia warned sternly.

By the time that the *New York Tribune* got back to her, the 'named sources' she had promised were a reality and they agreed to commission the piece. She was put in touch with their investigations editor, who was none other than her idol, Gail Fairweather. Sitting opposite her in her window lined, penthouse office, Ore fought the urge to pinch herself.

'This isn't going to be plain sailing, Ore. I hope you know that,' she'd warned sternly. Ore chuckled at the apt turn of phrase and then had to assure Gail that she was indeed taking this very seriously.

'Going up against a man like Chuck Regas, we need watertight evidence,' she continued, and Ore wondered if she was doing it on purpose. 'And we'll have to get legal to go over it with a fine-toothed comb.

'The only problem is that all your sources are speaking to Chuck's character, terrible as it is, and backing up the NDA, the dodgy sexual assault cover-up, but apart from those documents and well hearsay, we don't have enough to publish the bigger, Klauparten, mining bit of the story,' Gail went on.

Ore had known this was coming; without Daniel or Agatha, there was no one to corroborate those claims. 'I'm working on it,' she lied. She couldn't face trying to contact Daniel and when she had tried to email Agatha on her Pagonis account, it had bounced back.

'Well, keep working on it,' Gail said before hanging up.

Ore spent the next few days writing up a version of the article that only included the bits she could back up. It was still explosive, but the idea that Chuck would get away with launching his new 'eco' battery, making millions in the process and probably being lauded as a sustainability hero made her blood boil. And if the world had taught her anything it was that men accused of sexual assault rarely faced any real consequences, let alone those only accused of covering it up.

It was the middle of the night when her phone rang and Agatha identified herself on the other end of the line.

Ore scrambled for a pen and her recorder. 'Hi, Agatha, how are you? I'm so glad you called.'

Agatha was in no mood for pleasantries. 'I've left Pagonis. I'm founding my own company; I'm sick of working for someone else.'

'That's great, Agatha, congratulations!'

'And I didn't take a payout. I even left before my last paycheque.'

Ore was confused as to why she was telling her this, and then it clicked.

'So, you haven't signed an NDA?' Ore asked tentatively, her excitement building.

'Nope,' Agatha replied bluntly.

Ore was beside herself, but she tried to keep her voice even. 'What made you decide to leave?'

'I'm assuming you're recording this?'

'I'm not right now but if you're giving me your consent to do so, I would love to start.'

'Yep, that's fine.' Agatha paused, whilst Ore set up the recorder, and then almost as though she could sense that it was time, she started talking. 'I left Pagonis because Chuck Regas is a bully and a liar, but worse than that, he's a hypocrite . . .'

It was a sorry tale. Agatha had been scouted straight out of Oxford and promised a job in the coding team, only to end up being used for her youth and prettiness instead as Chuck's executive assistant.

'He told me it was just for six months, whilst he found a place for me on the team, that it would be a good opportunity to get an overview of how the whole company worked, that it was a privilege, and don't get me wrong, he paid me very well, but I was basically just a pretty face to reply to his emails and collect his dry cleaning and flirt with his investors. I didn't get a double first just to sit on Richard Greenam's lap and laugh at his jokes.

'So I'll be your whistleblower. You can say the documents came from me, if I don't end up in court, at least it's good publicity for my new company.' She chuckled wryly.

'I can't tell you how much this means to me, Agatha, thank you so so much,' Ore gushed.

'You know that when you came on board, I hated you?' Agatha cut in.

'I sort of gathered,' Ore admitted.

'And it wasn't some sort of jealous white-woman thing, well maybe a little bit, but mostly it was how easily you carried yourself. Sometimes I've had to be a cold bitch to get anyone to take me seriously, and other times I've had to pretend to be a bimbo to get them to like me. You just turned up, being you, and Chuck was nice to you, and the crew liked you, well more than me at least, and Daniel . . .' She trailed off.

'The point is, you had principles and talent and you wouldn't let anyone convince you otherwise, and that's what I want to prove to myself: that I can do that too. So this is my first step.'

'It's a very brave one, Agatha, and I appreciate all of it.' Ore was touched.

Agatha seemed too uncomfortable to dwell on the sentimental. 'OK, well if you have all that on record, I better be off.'

'Bye, Agatha.'

The dial tone clicked and Ore stopped the recording,

immediately downloading it onto her laptop and scouring through the transcript for the best quotes. She couldn't wait to update Gail in the morning.

'Impressive stuff, Ore, this really takes the investigation to a whole new level.' Ore beamed at Gail's glowing review. 'Have you tried Captain Wilsons again? We could probably publish without him, but it would be the cherry on top, or one of Claude's victims maybe?'

The question brought Ore crashing back down to earth. She should have remembered that Gail was relentless; there was always something that could be better. 'I haven't had any luck getting hold of his contact details and Captain Annie doesn't want to talk,' she said gingerly.

'You're an investigative journalist, Ore, do some digging. Surely the other crew you're in touch with have his number?' Ore hadn't told Gail about Daniel. She'd felt embarrassed that she hadn't kept things strictly professional.

'No totally, I'll try and get hold of him.'

Instead she spent two days tinkering with the article and finding things to do that were exactly not speaking to Daniel. She knew what his answer would be anyway so she didn't really see the point.

Another unknown number call came through while she was getting ready for bed. She braced herself, as she had been doing recently, in case it was Chuck's team. She was growing ever more paranoid that they might have gotten wind of the story. When the voice came through, Ore didn't recognise it.

'Is this Ore?'

'Yes speaking, who is this?'

'It's Vicky, from *Lady Thalassa*.'

A beat of silence as Ore prepared herself for the threat.

'I want to go on the record.' It was not at all what Ore had expected her to say. And she began to wonder what had happened on the boat after she left. Who had managed to turn all of Chuck's tight-lipped staff into whistleblowers?

'OK, let me just set up a recording,' Ore said, still cautious.

Vicky explained everything, revealing another litany of cases when Chuck had silenced mostly women to protect himself and his friends. Annie of course, but also his ex-wife Patricia, a handful of younger stewardesses that hadn't lasted, and finally the revelation that Vicky too was a victim. Not just of Chuck, but of Claude too.

'Why are you telling me all of this now?' It just didn't add up for Ore, and she found herself wondering if this was some sort of trap set by Chuck himself.

Vicky sighed loudly. 'I've given years of my life to that man, and I thought a lot about what Daniel said to us all, that we've all come to just believe he's invincible, but that's just another one of his lies, the most powerful one of all. It's about time I stop falling for it and tell the truth.'

It took a moment for Vicky's words to sink in. It was Daniel who had turned the tide on board. *Why?* Wasn't he supposed to be doing Chuck's bidding, and killing her story? She thanked Vicky. It occurred to her that the things Chuck seemed to look for in the women he surrounded himself with – tenacity, intelligence and practical thinking – were the very things that had, in the end, turned them against him.

'One last thing, Vicky, do you have Daniel's number?'

She sounded surprised when she said, 'You haven't spoken to him?' but then didn't wait for an answer before reciting the digits down the line.

Now Ore was impatient to speak to him. 'Best of luck, Vicky.' She ended the call and began to dial the number, before she lost her nerve. He answered after two rings.

'Ore,' he breathed, and she felt herself melt at the tenderness of that single syllable.

'So you already have my number then?'

He chuckled at her indignance. 'I've been meaning to call you, for a while.'

'Why didn't you?' Ore asked quietly, shocking herself at how wounded she sounded.

'After the last time I saw you . . . I don't know, I couldn't explain myself. I just shut down and let you believe that it was about working for Chuck, because it was easier than admitting that I was a coward.' Ore held her breath, waiting for more.

'I was scared, shit, I'm still scared of this story coming out, of what it means for my job, and for yours, but mostly I was scared because you were leaving, and I'm only brave when I'm with you, and . . .' Daniel faltered and then took a deep breath.

'And because I love you, Ore, in a way that's terrifying, in a way I've never felt before.'

Ore wanted more than anything to see him, to stroke his face with her fingers, to feel the heat of his breath on her neck as he pulled her into his arms. A hot teardrop rolled down her face and dripped onto the notepad in front of her.

'Are you still there, Ore?' Daniel asked softly, but urgently.

'Yes, sorry, I'm . . .' *Lost for words*. Except for four. 'I love you too.'

She could hear the smile in Daniel's voice. 'I'm sorry for everything, and I'm sorry that you had to be the one to call. I've dialled your number probably about a hundred times in the last week, but then again, as I said, you're the brave one.'

Ore laughed. It was a raspy hiccup of a sound, stifled by the tears now flowing thick and fast. 'Vicky told me what you did, that you spoke to everyone and convinced them to go on the record for me.'

'Vicky? I didn't think she was taken in by my speech at all.'

'Your speech? Captain Wilsons, what has gotten into you?' Ore teased.

'You,' Daniel replied earnestly 'I just thought, "what would Ore say right now?" and it all just came flowing out.'

'And what about Agatha? That was a bit of a shock I have to say.' Ore couldn't help herself with the questions.

'That was nothing to do with me, she left right after you in the morning, but I'm glad she came around. I always hated how Chuck treated her.'

'I'm sorry I didn't say goodbye.' Ore imagined him watching her leaving from the tower of the wheelhouse. The thought made her desperately sad.

'It's OK. It was understandable in the circumstances . . .' There was a moment of silence, as they each sat with what a different version of a goodbye might have looked like.

'Anyway,' Daniel said finally, 'I'll do it. I'll go on the record, if that's what you're calling about.'

'How did you know?' Ore replied with mock-amazement, trying to lighten the mood, although getting him into the

364

article had swiftly fallen to the very bottom of the reasons to make this call. 'My editor will be thrilled.'

'So you've found a publisher?'

'*NY Tribune*.'

'Wow, even a southerner like me knows that's a big deal,' she could hear the pride in his voice.

'Are you with the Hartfords yet?' She didn't want the call to end.

'No, I'm staying with my mom. They've pushed back my start date, something about spending another week in Mozambique because they haven't seen a lion on their safari yet . . .' They both laughed. 'But they're not like Chuck. They're demanding, sure, but without the weird mind games.'

'A blessing,' Ore agreed, and then a worry popped into her head. 'The article is coming out next week by the way. Is that going to be a problem with them? I know discretion is a pretty big deal in your world.' Ore was already working out how to explain to Gail that she hadn't been able to get hold of him, or maybe that he'd just flat-out refused again. 'I could probably do the piece without mentioning you at all.'

'No, I've thought about it, and it would be unfair. I'm the captain and I've got to go down with the ship, if the rest of the crew are going to brave the storm, so am I.' Daniel sounded very sure.

Ore's eyes welled again. He sensed that their time was drawing to a close. It was hard not to wallow in the tragedy of it all. For a while they both just breathed, neither wanting to pull the plug, and then both at once.

'I better go . . .' Ore began as Daniel did too.

'It's getting late . . .' Another shared chuckle, another bout of silence.

'Night, Ore, good luck with everything, sending . . . all my love,' Daniel said quietly, the depth of his voice rumbling right through her. She closed her eyes, wanting to savour the feeling.

'Night, Daniel, sending all my love right back.' Ore hung up before he could hear the sob escape from her throat. She cried until her chest hurt. When she realised the recorder had been running she skipped to that part . . . the part where he said those magic words, and replayed them over and over until she fell asleep. *Because I love you, Ore, because I love you, Ore, because I love you, Ore, because I love you, Ore, because I love you, Ore.*

Chapter 71

Daniel

Fort Bend, Texas

'Chuck Regas: the man, the myth, the legend . . . the crook'

Read the headline on the front page of the *New York Tribune*. Daniel couldn't remember ever having bought a physical newspaper but that morning he had driven into town early and then sat in his mom's car reading the article from start to finish. It was enthralling, damning and beautifully written. The pride that swelled in his chest was almost painful.

On the ride home, he flicked through no less than three different radio stations butchering Ore's name as they speculated about this new 'rising star of journalism' who had emerged seemingly overnight to take down one of the most powerful men in the world. Shares in Pagonis were plummeting; everyone wanted to know why they'd never heard about Claude Van Der Bodem before.

'He comes across as some kind of Disney villain. Honestly, the real question is how was he allowed to operate such a profitable and destructive company for so many years completely from the shadows?' came the indignant voice of the presenter as he pulled into his mom's drive.

He switched the ignition off, tucked the newspaper under his arm and walked up to the door, keys at the ready. But before he could use them, it was opened from the inside.

She was even more beautiful than he'd remembered, her hair a cascade of dark tight coils, her smile radiant.

His mom's voice called from the kitchen, 'I tried to call you, but you left your phone. We have a visitor.'

'I can see that,' he replied softly, and Ore grinned.

'I'm sorry it took me so long to come visit. I had some work to finish up.'

Daniel was in shock and it was all he could do to hold up the paper in his hand dumbly.

'It just felt a little lame to just *send* you my love, when I could just give it to you myself . . .' If Ore had had anything else to say, he would never know, because he couldn't help himself any longer. He placed both hands on her cheeks and pulled her to him, kissing her softly at first, but then more urgently as the depth of his longing for her uncoiled itself. She snaked her arms around his neck and the rest of the world vanished.

'And how do you two know each other then?' His mom's voice was brimming with bemusement. They pulled away from each other in a startle.

'This is Ore, we um . . . we met on the boat a few weeks ago.' It seemed such an unsatisfactory explanation, but they'd need a lot more time to tell the whole story.

Chapter 72

Ore

JFK airport
Six months later

Ore waited at the arrivals gate impatiently, checking her phone periodically even though she knew that Daniel wouldn't dismiss the *no mobile phones allowed* signs like everyone else did.

He'd been on a tour of the French Riviera with the Hartfords, and then they had reunited to spend several weeks together over Christmas at Daniel's mom's house. In the new year the Hartfords summoned him for another trip in the Med and then he'd moved his things into Ore's new apartment while she got into the swing of life at the *NY Tribune*.

Then he'd disappeared for another whole month, covering for a colleague in the Caribbean. It had been hard, but they were making it work. She hadn't seen his lovely face in the flesh since he'd left, and much of the time since she'd spent fantasising about this very moment, which was no mean feat considering the new job and the ongoing court cases she was reporting on.

In theory she had understood that the US legal system took

its time, but she couldn't have imagined that it would take six months to get Chuck Regas in front of a judge. He was up for fraud and embezzlement in the US and then he'd have to face the Australian government too. But he was also being represented by the best lawyers in the business so the prosecution took 'as long as it takes' to build the strongest case they could against him.

He'd already forsaken his old school pal Claude who was safely behind bars in Belgium. Ore had been relieved not to be called as a witness for that trial. Even looking at the pictures of him on TV had sent shivers down her spine. She wouldn't have been able to face those dead grey eyes across a courtroom; she had been awed to hear that both Vicky and Annie had braved them. It turned out that all the NDAs were legally close to worthless, as they couldn't be used to cover up criminality.

The investors had gotten off lightly, which was to be expected, Gail had told her. *White-collar crime, and a decent dose of plausible deniability is a great combo for a defence lawyer.*

But now finally it would be Chuck's turn on the docket. The moment the date was announced Ore had known she couldn't do it without Daniel. And he'd worked it out, explained everything to the Hartfords, who for their part had been both very supportive of Daniel and utterly appalled by the revelations about Chuck.

All to say, Ore had been trying to keep it together. Reciting her affirmations in the mirror every morning to reassure herself that being the youngest, blackest person in the investigations team did not mean she didn't belong there. Now though, her secret weapon was about to walk through those doors . . .

'Daniel, over here.' She waved and as their eyes met, he

broke into a wide grin. All her anxious energy dissipated and her heart swelled, beating slower but harder.

'Hello . . . beautiful . . . how . . . are . . . you?' he asked between the smattering of kisses he peppered over her face. She giggled, dizzy with the closeness of him. And then as one particular kiss made her knees go weak and her insides fizz, she had to remind herself they were in public and pull away.

'Did you hear about Vicky?' Ore asked and Daniel shook his head. 'So at Claude's trial she bumped into Agatha, who offered her a job at Herax, her new company, as chief of staff.'

'I guess those two were always kind of two sides of the same coin, and I have no doubt Vicky will make a formidable corporate boss.'

Ore agreed wholeheartedly. She'd been worried when Daniel told her that Vicky had turned down his offer to help find her another job, saying she wanted to leave yachting behind completely. Carlos had followed Daniel to the Hartfords, who subsequently discovered their love of Lebanese cuisine. Dudley ended up the second in command for Daniel's old mentor, Captain Jack Carter. And the junior crew had scattered across various new jobs thanks to Daniel's other connections.

He was the captain after all and he never shied away from his responsibility to look after people.

'I missed you,' she said, glowing with the thrill of freely expressed affection.

'Not as much as I missed you, I'm sure.' A peck on the forehead and he reached for the bag he'd dropped by his feet. 'Shall we grab dinner and head back to your place?'

She chuckled at the memory, glowing with the deep

satisfaction that they had engineered their make-believe into reality.

'Sure, let's do that.' She took his hand; it was sturdy and warm, and it held hers tightly.

They headed for the exit. By his side, she knew that together, they could take on the world. They basically already had.

Acknowledgements

As ever my undying thanks to Amy, my editor, and all the rest of the team at Avon. Your professionalism speaks for itself, and your parties aren't half bad either.

To Emma and Tilly, thanks for being the first eyes on the manuscript, and giving me an injection of confidence when I needed it most by banishing those 'second album' jitters.

Thanks mum and grandma for respectively hosting my 'writer's retreats'.

Spencer, thanks for being my metaphorical port in a storm and my happy place.

A shout out to Brixton public library for being my wonderfully overheated haven when I was struck by a terrible plague of dodgy Wi-Fi.

And to everyone who read my first book, both strangers and friends, but most especially the ones that said things that made my cheeks burn with giddying pride - you have all my gratitude.